T0120978

VLORs &
VICE

VLORs & VICE
UNITED

SEAN L JOHNSON

VLORS & VICE
UNITED

iUniverse books may be ordered through booksellers or by contacting:

iUniverse
1663 Liberty Drive
Bloomington, IN 47403
www.iuniverse.com
844-349-9409

Because of the dynamic nature of the Internet, any web addresses or links contained in this book may have changed since publication and may no longer be valid. The views expressed in this work are solely those of the author and do not necessarily reflect the views of the publisher, and the publisher hereby disclaims any responsibility for them.

ISBN: 978-1-6632-3025-6 (sc)
ISBN: 978-1-6632-3024-9 (e)

Library of Congress Control Number: 2021920940

Print information available on the last page.

iUniverse rev. date: 10/21/2021

SEASON 5, EPISODE 28

On Sunday, September 17^{*th*} *....*

He awoke at the sound of slapping from the helicopter's blades, still hallucinating from the dose of Benzodiazepines injected in him. Worm could barely see a thing as he recalled the last incident before he passed out. He was on his way to being transferred to a maximum prison to do his time for older cases of drug trafficking and recent child abduction.

Silence engulfed the helicopter as he observed the rotor decelerating, followed by an approaching speed boat. Worm was reluctantly dragged out and handed to the coxswain. The man lifted his blindfold, and he could not believe his eyes. He is in the middle of nowhere, an island. He was trying to make sense of the strangeness when he overheard one of the agents heading back to the helicopter and radioed, *"the prisoner transfer was successful."*

WORM. Prisoner transfer successful! *He repeated.* This is no prison. *He shouts.* Hey! Where am I? What the hell kind of place—

UNNAMED COXSWAIN. *He chuckled.* Welcome to your worst nightmare, Primous Facility.

A super-max prison for high profile criminals, those on death row, is covertly funded by the U.S. Government. It's in the middle of nowhere and is a one-way traffic stop. A criminal goes in and never comes out – Well, besides a few. The Director is currently trying to solve that problem.

The only way criminals get here is by plane, boat, or teleportation. METHPHODOLLOUS island is the second most secured facility. The island has land mines; the fence is wired and rigged with explosives, and any contact goes, **BOOM!** There are 24-hour hi-tech drones with heat and movement sensors programmed to incapacitate targets.

Cordonald Miles, the director of Primous, is a renowned philanthropist and honestly a good Samaritan whose years of volunteer work and business-related skillsets covertly earned him a contract at the facility. He reports to a government official to procure funding. Everything about this place is secret; it is totally off the books, and the budget is done through an offshore account to remove any trace leading back to the Informant.

It has been two whole decades since, and things have been going as planned. Because of the high security, prisoners are secure. As far as he can tell, the Director is gradually making a breakthrough in bringing a more secure system aboard to keep the *interesting* sort of prisoners from escaping – a secret weapon he would not want any peculiar outsiders to know– at least not yet.

Incognito as a Primous guard inside the helicopter with Worm and Snake, decides it is best to wait for an effective opportunity. When they arrived, she needed to sit and wait before acting.

KI. *Gazing out the window, quietly under her breath.* This is it.

The helicopter's invisibility lifts, and it lands. With rifles aiming at the prisoners, she witnessed the prisoner transfer and spotted the coxswain on the ground. He was just the spectacle she was eager to see. Another way off the island – for later. They all walk to the facility.

He is overseeing the work on a newer improved indestructible security system and one that is impossible for criminals to break out. The Director contracted specific individuals who worked for Vale Industries-Corp, a hi-tech security communications company. This person works secretly with the Informant, none of their security systems breached –Why the Informant took an interest in his work.

There must be a system override to install a new security system, which will take about fifteen to thirty minutes to affect the new system.

Little did they know that something was coming fast, and things were about to get out of control.

It has been about fourteen weeks; KI is a sixteen-year-old Japanese girl. She started working undercover for several shipping docks, hoping to find out the exact location of METHPHODOLLOUS Island. She knew she had to find the prison's location. She did not know, but she only had a short window to complete her mission and break out three former Shibarian clan members. She is notable for accomplishing her task, a reputation she is willing to keep.

The ninjas have been on the FBI watch list since arriving in the states years ago. This girl is concealing her identity skillfully. KI is just her code name.

A few months in, she cannot locate the third ninja, one of the people she came to free. She's in the female's changing room, freshening up and going over a plan in her head, at the sound of the next approaching mealtime. KI clasps her breasts and feigns shy as she put her clothes back on with seductive wit. She smiled and remembered what she had done before arriving at this place.

KI injected the coxswain with a chemical that would stimulate the pain receptors in his brain; it won't be physical, but he will feel excruciating pain when she triggers the drug. With this tactic in place, KI secured their ride. The drug gave her details she needed to know from the coxswain – the direction to the prison, the blind spots, the halogen security override, and the timing. From the information she extracted, she would have a significant portion of time to break two prisoners out from one of the most secured facilities on earth. When she would do this, she didn't have a clue yet.

Friday, January 04, 2108
11:54 A.M.

Meanwhile, Kiyla is sitting on a toilet inside the girl's restroom. The stall door is locked, her knees are touching, and she's holding onto her face praying that she stops liquefying.

Jayla enters the girl's restroom.

JAYLA. *She whispers as she's trying to figure out which stall the girl is hiding in.* Kiyla.

KIYLA. *She's whimpering in one of the stalls.* I can't even put on mascara anymore. *She sniffs.* I'm – Scared. *She places her cupped hands under her chin, and her elbows rest on her upper legs.* I don't want to be a freak. *She is not trying to sound offensive.*

JAYLA. *She thinks about mentioning her Xeiar Heritage but changes her mind.* Uh. Well – I think I know how that feels.

4

KIYLA. *She relaxes her arms and looks out in front of her.* Do you, Jayla? I don't think you can fathom the struggles I am going through right now.

JAYLA. I -

KIYLA. How can you help me?

JAYLA. Why are you going down my throat– Do I need to explain myself to my friend?!

KIYLA. I'm your friend now?!

JAYLA. *She exhales and places her right hand on her forehead.* Girl. *She sighs very loud, then lowers her hand and stares at her.* I never stopped being your friend!! You are making up all these fake ideas and believing them! Why?!!

KIYLA. I don't know. *She lowers her eyes to the floor.* Hm. Wait! I do know! Let's ask Valery.

JAYLA. Listen, Kiyla. I'm trying to talk to you! Stop what you're doing and listen to me!!

KIYLA. I'm listening to you! You only wish to hear yourself talk! *She sighs, shakes her head a few times.* I bet you never do that to your BFF Valery. She probably has you here trying to get me to reveal something horrible about myself so she can humiliate me in front of the whole school.

JAYLA. *She's staring blankly.* I'm going to pretend you did not just say that.

KIYLA. Why? Because it's true?!

JAYLA. No one is talking bad about you, girl! You are paranoid!

KIYLA. Paranoid?! I think yo –

JAYLA. No. Listen and shut up!! I am tired of arguing with you, Kiyla! Valery is not telling me to do anything!! I am taking time out of my busy day to explain that I am still your best friend! I have not lied or embarrassed you in any way!! *Exhales.* Kiyla, you can't be serious! Like, what will you get by hiding in there? *She fretted, frowning when all she heard in response were quiet sobs.*

KIYLA. Just go away! *She snapped, sniffing as if she was trying to pretend that she was not crying.* It's not like you care! *She added just out of pure spite.*

It was true, right? Her friend did change and possibly didn't care about her anymore. But– she had something more pressing at hand as well.

KIYLA. Shoot. *She took a deep breath, running a hand through her hair. Still a little shaky, her eyes couldn't help but follow the water spouting from her fingertips, effectively dampening her locks.*

JAYLA. Come on. It's not what you think! *She's starting to lose her patience, but she still stands by the stall, trying to coax the other girl to at least come out. It can't smell nice in there, either.*

Kiyla would have snorted months ago at the terrible joke if she wasn't concentrating on controlling this strange thing happening to her. She could feel this new, crazy power coursing in her veins, and quite frankly, she had no way to control it.

JAYLA. I don't care; I'm going in! *She went to tear the door open, scrunching up her nose as she took a step, only to realize the stall that the girl was hiding in was locked. It was clear that the girl had no intention to leave.* Seriously! You're still my best friend. Why are you getting so worked up? *Her sharp ears picked up the sound of sneakers hitting the dingy floor—her friends standing right in front of her, with only the door separating them.*

KIYLA. How'd you know I was in here?

Still, the pitiful sniffle gave away her real feelings as the girl stared at her hands, eyes fixated on the multitude of water drops clinging to her skin. The moment her breaths evened out a little, they evaporated one by one, causing her to let out a sigh of relief.

JAYLA. I saw your shoes, silly. And– I saw Zada trying to follow you in here. The perv.

The other girl snorted, but it was evident that she was worried.

JAYLA. Why don't you come out? We can talk about this like, uhh– Adults, I guess?

KIYLA. I want to be on my own, please. Just let me be for a minute! *She grumbled out but rubbed at her eyes as fresh tears rolled down her cheeks. She was cranky, scared, and hurt that her best friend would betray her.*

JAYLA. Girl? I know you better than your mom does! All you need is a hug and a massive bar of chocolate. Come on, now.

The truth was that Jayla felt a little odd about acting as if she's committed a grave mistake, but cornering the girl and shouting at her did not seem like the best idea at the moment.

KIYLA. Why? So that you can leave me when you find someone else? *Rage coiling in her heart, her widened eyes fell on the water that gathered around her feet, a small puddle emerging from nowhere.*

JAYLA. Seriously? Are you going to stay there all day, then? *She huffed out, crossing her arms.*

For a moment, she could hear Jayla shifting, and she grew hopeful. Jayla shook her head a little, forgetting that she could not see her. She soon spoke up, head jerking back when something cold fell on her forehead.

JAYLA. No, just until– Huh? *Confused, she raised her gaze to notice the small hole in the ceiling.* Uh– Can you at least leave the stall? Like, where is all this water even coming from? *She exclaimed, noticing that something was off.*

The girl in the stall sniffled once more but stood up. She was growing nervous, feeling it difficult to get a hold of herself.

KIYLA. I'm coming. Just– I want to wash my face and stuff. You have somewhere better to be at, anyway.

Please, leave– That was what she meant, hoping that she would get the hint.

JAYLA. I – I'm sorry. *Her voice rises.* But you are getting ridiculous!! *Her voice returns to normal.* You're not the only one going through problems! *She starts tearing up.* I – I am struggling too! My mother left, and it's been weeks now! Her boyfriend showed me a note she had written months ago! The handwriting on the note is stressing me out because I know my mom's writing! I don't know who wrote that note, but it wasn't my mother!! *She pauses, being extra careful not to tell her too much information. She sniffs.* I am – I am trying to help you. *She wipes away her tears and shouts.* Kiyla!! *She shakes her head and scoffs.* Fine! *Sniffs.* Be that way then! I don't need you! *She swings her body around and storms off.* Who needs anyone at this stupid school!

Delena Bloome and Marie Mikaelson are standing by Delena's locker, watching Jayla storming off down the hall. The janitor is passing by, pushing a broom. They heard some of it, wishing it escalated into a fight. The two girls start laughing.

JANITOR MARVELLO. Do you girls have somewhere to be instead of loitering? *He passes them.*

MARIE MIKAELSON. Ugh. *She scoffs.* Let's go, Delena.

The two girls start walking to class. Jayla is approaching the back exit, and she pushes the door open. She walks through, locating an isolated area to vent.

JAYLA. Why won't she listen?!!! *She stomps her right foot on the concrete as hard as she can, leaning her back against the building.*

12:13 P.M.

A well-prepared KI is legendary for sophisticated tools and weapons. With the information extracted from the coxswain, she set her electromagnetic pulse (EMP) to the exact time of the security override. The launch of the security override coincided with a massive blast by the resulting explosion of the EMP, followed by a dead silence. From her calculations, it will take ten minutes for the backup generator to kick in. KI knew she had less than ten minutes to extract her targets and escape the drones and the CCTV cameras; the electricity was all down, and the electric doors guiding the prisoner's cells were all disabled. All the prisoners are out of their cells – all that avail is chaos and darkness. KI put on her laser glass and dashed inside through the halls to extract her targets. The furious Director has given orders to shoot on sight; the prisoners are beating each other and the guards, all hell has been let loose. The impatient Director is eager to get the backup generator on immediately and barking orders as he's approaching the island via helicopter.

KI has known from her session with the coxswain how to locate the cells. They're on the same floor.

She spotted Cloudis Monroe with her laser light, dragging Worm to a corner as she's about to make her move to break the two ninjas from their cells.

No time to waste as her laser watch showed they have only five minutes to make it out of the prison before the backup generator kicks in.

She makes it to their cells. There's no need to explain her story because she fits the description to the Lord of the Shibarian clan. They follow her to the lower levels as the prison is under siege.

The weakest link to the security chain is the prison latrine connected directly to the ocean. She quickly fused two C-4s and diffused them on the lavatory, which opened the escape route. They made their way one after the other through a secret underground tunnel, making their way to the end as they were followed by gunshots and approaching the footsteps of a few guards. The footsteps are almost upon them and look like they will not make it out in time, but suddenly, something strange is happening to the guards– something with a fast movement was disarming and dropping them one after the other. It was Snake, the cross-human that can shape-shift into a reptile form.

Suddenly, the backup generator kicks on, and they can hear the advancing speed of the drones.

KI. Let's go! *She shouted.*

They all dived into the tunnel's exit, and with the oxygen cylinders KI had planted ahead of time months prior. Just then, the shields of Primous turns on. Snake tried to dive out of the tunnel, but an invisible force stopped him. He was immediately surrounded by new and improved guards arriving, and they subdued him. They're wearing armor like the child agents who sent him to prison.

The ninjas swam for a reasonable distance and made it to the rendezvous point where the boat of the coxswain was waiting.

Meanwhile, prisoners are going mad at Primous Facility. The Japanese Shibarian Ninjas have created raucous upon their exit. The Director arrives via his helicopter, pilot landing on the front lawn. He is the second to step out as he lays his eyes on inmates running amok.

CORDONALD MILES. *He says in a calm voice.* This is insane. Lieutenant Remuldo!! *He yelled.*

LT. REMULDO. Aye, sir! *He stands at attention, awaiting orders.*

CORDONALD MILES. *He turns his head back to the chopper, locating a few V-Guards!* You four lead me inside; all the others secure the perimeter.

LT. REMULDO. All right, men!! You heard your director! *He cocks his weapon and points it in front of him.* Fall out!!

The Lieutenant takes off running with two other competent soldiers, and part of the new security team leads the Director, as ordered, to the main building.

Making their way into the cafeteria, a buffed-up and steroid African American male shows his dominance over the entire room. He's the one in command right now—the Director and his guard's storm inside. The man raises his head, grimacing at Miles, and he immediately orders all his faithful followers to attack.

DOMINIC REWELS. I own this place now, Director! I'm – The – KING!!!!

CORDONALD MILES. *He sighs.* You're still the same old obnoxious little bitch.

DOMINIC REWELS. *He frowns.* Heh-heh. *He pounds on his rock-hard chest using his right hand. He yells.* I own this place! These are my pawns now, you worthless old newbie! My mother beat me while reading fairy tale stories, all while waiting for my younger sister to fall asleep!

Dominic continues, rambling about his upbringing.

CORDONALD MILES. *He sighs.* I've heard this before many times. *He snatches a guard's shotgun, cocks it, and shoots the supposed leader in his chest.*

Dominic's body shoots backward, and he hits the serving counters, toppling to the floor. All the prisoners' stop what they're doing, and silence falls over the entire room. The Directors' new security team gasp, wondering who they're working for exactly.

SECURITY DETAIL: GUNNER. *He's shocked.* You – You killed a prisoner?! Sir? *He's eyeing his boss in a concerned fashion.*

CORDONALD MILES. *He looks at his guard, returning his gun.* You need to go back to the academy if you think that man is dead. *He turns his head, watching for any prisoner to retaliate.* It's a flesh wound to keep him on the floor. *Realizing the rest of the prisoners are shocked, he starts moving to the doors on the other side of the room.* Now – Get me up to the lobby.

SECURITY DETAIL: GUNNER. Yes, sir.

Before they go any further, several new Primous Guards greet the director.

CORDONALD MILES. What's your report?

Several robotic voices yell out, *Area secured!*

SECURITY DETAIL: GUNNER. Money well spent. Bless the stars, mate.

CORDONALD MILES. It appears so. *Sighs.* Your services are no longer required. No memory will you keep to this place. You all will return to your everyday lives. This place belongs to VLORs now – I'll continue to be a liaison. The turnout was a success, replacing all personnel with robotic agents capable of immobilizing an inmate if needed. The teleportation should commence in 3, 2–

SECURITY DETAIL: GUNNER. It has been an honor to serve.

SECURITY DETAIL: DILL MEACHAM. An honor it has.

All human guards disappear. The director walks down the lonely hall, going to his office. Meanwhile, floating on his back in the Atlantic Ocean...

CHIMOUS. *Chuckling.* Told ya' I'd be free. Hahahahaha.

We last left ShaVenger fighting against an angry VICE commander. He has been avoiding the agency– constantly on the move. He teleports near Westick Blvd, the alley next to a convenience store. He runs to the corner, stands on the sidewalk, and checks all his surroundings for any sign of VICE personnel. There's no one looking for him at the moment. He double-backs, leans against a brick building, and slides down so he is now sitting on the hard concrete ground. He's breathing heavily. He decides to rest.

SHAVENGER. How could I be so stupid. *Pounds the concrete to his right.* That damn girl was right; playing two sides did get me caught. *He's starting to gain control over his breathing.* I – I must keep moving. He can trace me if I stay still for an extended period. *Slowing his breathing.* I hope Flurir's okay. *He doesn't hesitate and teleports away.*

11:54 A.M.
College Station, Texas
A local motel...

DALE JR. This is not Armani. *He's adjusting his collar, envisioning his outfit in his head.* –But this will have to do.

The corporate meeting was today; all the significant branches of Stratum Oil Industries would be there, but he wasn't nervous for some reason. Dale knew what he had to do as soon as he took his seat in the courtroom.

It wasn't his office anymore; Mowton had moved in. Why? He didn't know. What he did know was that before he was sent to prison, he had caught a whiff of something that could finally move that bastard out—an affair. It was a bad one at that, and once the media got ahold of it, well, that would be the end.

DALE JR. *He looked in the mirror and tilted his head.* I got this.

He walked with an unusual nervousness, as if not himself, and that's what he had wanted. Dale made his way to his car and drove off to his office with a determination to get this job done right.

12:16 P.M.
Stratum Oil Industries in College Station, Texas
Main Office Location

For months he had been locked away thinking about how displeased his colleagues would be to see him, but a sheer delight would bring him so much joy. Dressed in a beige button-up, collared shirt, and dark grey jeans, he slid his way through the crowds of people in the harshly lit lobby. He managed to get a hold of a keycard off an intern, who had stupidly dropped the card running through the entrance with coffees. Although he and the intern were not alike in any way, the elevator only knew the card, not the person, and everyone was too self-absorbed to notice a new intern anyways. This was sheer luck, but it was much better than a run-in with security.

He made his way to the highest floor; his eyes flickered left and right as the flood of noise and loud keyboards entered the elevator. He stepped out– *No* –was pushed by other interns, employees, managers. Whoever they were, they were too ignorant to recognize their boss. His appearance had not been that different, despite the metal mask covering scars on his face.

He scuffed up his hair and strolled down the hall to the board of directors' office, knowing if any of his colleagues were there, he would instantly be recognized. He was counting on just one man, Mowton.

Slithering his way past crowds of people, he made his way to the frosted glass door, and placed his hand gently on the glass, took a deep breath, and stepped in.

MOWTON JOHNSON. Ah, Mister Falakar. What a pleasure to see you! *He sat intently at his desk, seemingly on edge for Dale's following statement.*

DALE JR. No. The pleasure is all mine. *He smiled grimly.*

MOWTON JOHNSON. Please, sit.

DALE JR. *He sat.* I'm told you're going to buy out the company. *He spoke, with an odd emotion, or excitement, maybe.*

MOWTON JOHNSON. And who told you that– Another intern? *He grinned deceptively and laughed.* Oh! You know as well as I, listening to rumors only causes trouble. You need to stop listening to them– you know that's how Joan ended up with–

DALE JR. With whom? *He glared as he knew the answer.* Is the girl you hired with someone?

MOWTON JOHNSON. *He's taken aback.* No. *He managed to mutter out.*

DALE JR. Don't lie to me. *He got up from his chair, watching it silently hit the brim of Mowton's desk as it slid.* I know what you want. *He began to stride across the room with a majestic pride.* –But it would be a shame if somebody heard–!

16

MOWTON JOHNSON. *He began to heat up.* Well, this is quite unprofessional. *Almost spitting.*

DALE JR. The unprofessionalism is not me this time. *He grinned, turning to him acutely.* This is my legacy, and I've already been to prison. I have nothing to lose but this. Plus, I help people, what do you do? You buy and buy and buy. You never stop, you just take and never give, and someday the media will pick up on your little glass tower. *He said, slowly making his way over to Mowton's desk again.*

MOWTON JOHNSON. *He slid the chair back from the desk and began to sit.* I have my reputation, but do you? What is your legacy? *He said blandly, almost as if he was bored.* Rewriting your father's legacy to make a better name for yourself?

Mr. Johnson was a hothead and an asshole. Everyone knew, and you could see it in his face. His cheeks flared red, and his face wrinkled into dark crevices. He got up from his desk forcefully and looked down at Dale.

DALE JR. It's no wonder you want to buy so much up. With all this money you have, it could almost cure your temper. I wonder if Joan has seen this side of you. *He left the office delighted, practically skipping. He had gotten what he had wanted but was pulled back in by his arm.*

MOWTON JOHNSON. *How fast he got to the door is incredible.* I can't let you leave. *His voice was almost cracking.*

Dale knew he had won, and Mowton did too, but something about the desperate man led the former owner to stay.

DALE JR. This is between us. *He gritted his teeth and snatched his arm back.*

Mowton's face slumped, depressing as if he suffered a loss – He did! Not only was he about to lose his affair but his credibility, reputation, and millions of dollars, taken by the same media that swept him up by his feet. Dale glared into his eyes stubbornly, and as soon as they had greyed, the fire returned to them. Upon seeing this, Dale turned away to the door, grabbed by his collar, and reddened his neck. The pressure of the collar was choking him. He slid his hands on his collar and pulled the opposite way, allowing him to breathe, but he stayed determined. How could he assault someone in his own office? Instantly, Mowton dropped to the floor, the beige collar slipping out of his grip almost gracefully and setting Dale free. The release of dropping was enough to off-put his aggressive hold and made him stumble backward. And there he was, concussed or dead, either way, that was one check on the list, and on top of that, a new suit became readily available.

Opening the door and stepping into the office, the VICE commander focused on the unconscious gentleman on the floor. He closed the door as he entered the room.

XAVIER. I didn't want you to keep me waiting, Falakar. What's this?

DALE JR. *Standing up straight, dusting off his suit.* A regime. Heh-heh.

XAVIER. You're lucky VICE has the resources to create the best cover-up story.

DALE JR. –Like I need one. Ahem. As I promised you, go back to your little organization, and I'll be there shortly.

XAVIER. *Taking a few steps closer to him, looking directly into his eyes.* Don't – Lose your place, Falakar. You've been warned just now. I expect you at the meeting. *He turns, exiting the office.*

DALE JR. What a terrifying leader. *He chuckles, turning and staring at the corpse lying on his floor.*

PLANET VREC
1:07 P.M.

A single hair from a unicorn's tail and the potion was ready. The male wizard poured the potion on a mirror that laid flat on the table. A burst of laughter filled the room. He had sensed a strong power coming from a nearby planet. He spent the entire night trying to track this person's scent. Unfortunately, despite the powerful aura, he was unable to detect the source accurately. Frustrated, he smashes a nearby chalice on the mirror, causing a loud smashing sound as some pieces stick to his hands. The blood flows freely from the injured veins as the room howls with echoing laughter.

ASARIOS. Hehe. I'm becoming mortal. *Sneers and thinks about his target.* Why are you so hard to find?

All of a sudden, he senses a great power to a planet (DEVINA). He mumbles a spell quietly and out loud once.

The green glow of the teleportation spell slowly fades as he finds himself in a barren land. The dry leaves and dead trees gave the impression that it hadn't rained here for at least a few years.

ASARIOS. Whatever and whoever once lived here must be dead by now. *He thinks as he chuckles.*

He tries to sense the power he felt earlier. The teleportation spells are not accurate and aren't reliable in most cases. Thinking he must have been in the wrong place, as he couldn't sense anything, he decides to head back and try again. Just as he was about to teleport, he felt the power coming from the north.

It wasn't the same power, but he could still sense that it was intense. He was chuckling to himself because he doubted the teleportation spell. He walks in the direction, taking in the view of what he thought would have been a land of fresh water and lush green grass.

ASARIOS. Guess their God wasn't merciful enough. *He thought to himself as another laugh escapes his mouth.*

He senses a source of the power getting closer and spots an old witch in the middle of the field. It's as if she had seen enough springs, survived enough winters, and witnessed enough cruel battles.

The witch was in a trance while in mid-air, muttering something. The wizard gets close and notices a circle drawn out of some material. He picks up a bit of material, making sure not to break off the effect of the enchantment. He inspects the material and rubs it between his fingers.

ASARIOS. Salt, crushed garden weed, and ashes of a phoenix? Interesting. I wonder how she came up with these ingredients. *He thinks to himself and laughs.*

He notices the witch, who's still in a trance. He didn't want to wait long, as he rubs his foot on the circle and removed it a bit. The witch falls on the ground and wakes. The wizard chuckles as she hits the ground- Her eyes glow red with anger.

ITISA. What is the meaning of your act? How dare you interrupt me in the middle of the process?

ASARIOS. *Ignoring her completely. He asks while walking.* First, tell me, how did you manage to get the ashes of a phoenix? *He chuckles.*

The witch is furious with his interruption, launching a ball of energy at him. He stops it quite easily with a counterspell.

ASARIOS. You didn't answer the question. It's rude, you know. *He says with a fake sadness in his voice.*

The witch is annoyed but lets out a sigh.

ITISA. I got it from a wizard I worked for as an assistant once– A long time ago.

ASARIOS. And how did you manage to come up with a ridiculous combination?

ITISA. That is none of your concern. Now state the reason why you interrupted me and leave.

He laughs, amused by the slight attitude she's giving off. He walks behind the witch, inspecting the surroundings. She's on high alert about his movements.

ASARIOS. You are indeed a powerful witch; I can sense it. Not just your grey hair is proof, but your experience in the field. What are you doing in this dead place?

ITISA. I have come to seek a restoration order and to save a neighboring planet. One that a dark force had cursed.

ASARIOS. Do you think you're powerful enough to lift the curse that potentially doomed all living things on Vrec right now?

ITISA. I'd consider myself done with this tasking. In a matter of minutes, planet Vrec will returne to normal. If you hadn't interrupted me, this would be done by now.

ASARIOS. *He laughs.* You are an experienced and powerful witch, but I'm afraid you will have to take a trip to Earth. *He says with sympathy in his voice.*

He laughs as he enchants the teleportation spell he had created earlier. The elder woman seems confused as this is one spell she doesn't know. She attacks the wizard, but before she can, a green glow surrounds her. The wizard had created the circle around her as he was walking without her noticing.

ASARIOS. I'll visit later once I find the last wizard God. *He thinks to himself and teleports to another nearby planet he senses the power.*

His nostrils are filled with the smell of fish and bread simultaneously as he finds himself in a busy market. While passing the market, he sees a guy riding a four-legged animal dressed in the armor of a warrior. He gets near him to see his face. The warrior seems familiar, but the wizard is unable to put his finger on it. He let out an annoyed sigh as he rolled his eyes. He thinks about it for a while, then shrugs, letting out a chuckle.

The warrior enters the forest, and he follows him, maintaining his distance a bit. The stranger notices the seemingly crazy wizard.

ZEN. *He turns and asks with an authoritative voice.* Who are you, and why are you following me?

ASARIOS. Well, don't mind me. I was just admiring your four-legged creature.

ZEN. Don't lie to me. You reek of Xeiar origin. Who are you?

ASARIOS. *He rolls his eyes and replies sarcastically.* I'm one of the Great Wizards. *He lied.*

ZEN. *He's annoyed.* I don't have time to waste.

Before he can finish the sentence, the wizard casts an attack spell to test his strength- This catches the warrior off guard, but he manages to dodge the attack using his quick reflexes. Before the warrior could say anything, he attacked him again. The man dodges the attack using a counterspell.

The wizard smirks. The warrior casts another spell, but the wizard creates a shield as the warrior launches one attack after another. He pretends to yawn as he takes a seed from the pocket of his cloak and chants a spell. The iris of his eyes turns white as he throws it close to the warrior. The seed sprouts and grows into a giant beanstalk which attempts to trap the warrior. The man slashes and cuts at the advancing stems. Getting tired, he chants a spell to set the beanstalk on fire. He's breathing heavily, his eyes now glowing with a light shade of blue. He chants a spell at the wizard, setting his sword ablaze. He attacks the wizard head-on but gets frozen.

ASARIOS. You are quite powerful. There is something off about you which I need to figure out.

The warrior attempts to break out of the ice but to no avail.

ASARIOS. What should I do with you in the meantime? *He whips up a transport spell, sending him to another dimension that's easily accessible.*

1:15 P.M.
Venue Avenue, near Cuues Marketplace
An early release from school.

A man notices a young teen girl sitting alone at a bus stop. He recognizes her and makes his approach. She's kicking both of her legs slowly, one after the other, looking at the ground.

XAVIER. *Getting closer and greets her.* Hello there, Miss Johnson. I knew you looked familiar. How's your mother at the orphanage?

ZHARIAH. *She turns her head slightly, looking to her right.* Oh, what's up. She's fine. *She sighs and looks at the ground again.* Come to offer more money and gifts?

XAVIER. I can. I'll be honored to aid. *He sits near the girl as they wait for the bus to arrive. He sighs.* Life can be full of surprises.

ZHARIAH. *Listens and nods.*

XAVIER. You know what fascinates me about life?

ZHARIAH. Not really, but I'm sure you'll tell me.

XAVIER. *Starts looking at the clouds.* It's not its mysteries but its capacity to sustain the effects of sorrow and then later bloom into something beautiful. *He puts on his coat as he looks down.*

ZHARIAH. What are you trying to say– Is sorrow beautiful?

XAVIER. In a way, it is.

ZHARIAH. That is a terrible way to start a conversation.

XAVIER. Maybe, but you're missing the point.

ZHARIAH. Am I?

XAVIER. Ha, okay young lady. Shall I finish?

ZHARIAH. Yes, you can. *Looking interested as she adjusts herself on the hard, metal bench.*

XAVIER. Over time, you'll start to notice things. *Takes a breath of fresh air.* Life has a unique process from its very beginning to the end that it produces beauty only when the suffering has reached its peak.

ZHARIAH. So, you mean that everything beautiful has once been torn apart?

XAVIER. To say the least, yes.

ZHARIAH. That is not beautiful at all.

XAVIER. It takes a lot of struggle and hard work to be able to understand beauty. To be happy, you need to be able to appreciate its worth and importance.

ZHARIAH. *Ponders and stays silent wondering how correct that statement.*

XAVIER. *Noticing the girl in a deep-thinking process. He realizes that he is making progress with her.* This is my chance to get in. *He soliloquizes.* I see you're trying to understand or gathering an idea inside. Just think about it like this— We have all been through worse times but also the best.

ZHARIAH. Yeah... *Looks down the street.* There are all kinds of times we go through.

XAVIER. The fun thing– and this is a secret nobody will tell you. It is that the good and happy times are there. They are around us when we are least aware of them.

ZHARIAH. *Smiles.*

XAVIER. *Laughs slowly and softly.* Look at you! You look beautiful when you smile. You should do so more often.

ZHARIAH. Thank you.

XAVIER. I don't think the bus is going to come anytime soon, is it?

ZHARIAH. Nah. I wasn't catching the bus; I have no money. I needed somewhere to think. *Sighs.* I'll just walk home.

XAVIER. Okay. As you like. It was nice talking to you. *Gets up and walks away as his phone rings.* Hello, Xavier on the line– *He walks as he fades into the fog.*

ZHARIAH. *Watching him go and notices a business card on the bench that seems to have fallen from his coat. Intrigued by his conversation, she picks up the card and sees the writing on it. The card reads, VICE.*

Meanwhile, ShaVenger is standing on the roof of Valousse Convention Center, watching a boy's smile widen. He's hovering in mid-air in front of him. A black cloth covering the dragon-looking blaster on his entire right arm, something he had never seen him use.

The boy who resembles Agent Z smirked.

CURDUR. *Eyes going to the spot where he's being watched.* Come on, Shadow boy! Heh-heh. Aren't you supposed to take me down? *He tilts his head mockingly, making his opponent growl.*

SHAVENGER. OH! Bet? *Tightens his fists.* I'll see to you till your last breath.

A hysterical chuckle sounded from the other side as Curdur continued making fun of him.

CURDUR. I'm looking forward to it, friend.

SHAVENGER. I have no friends!

With that, the shadow cross-human leaps from one shadow clone to another, appearing right behind the agent lookalike who hadn't moved even an inch from his position.

ShaVenger's moment of surprise was halfway when Curdur spooked him from behind. He spun to kick the calm boy standing. His kick hit nothing.

CURDUR. Boo! *He chuckles tauntingly.*

The boy instantly turned to punch him, but his fist was grabbed. Curdur smiled, tightening his hold. ShaVenger spun his leg in mid-air and strikes at his head. The impact sends air gushes around them, but Curdur's position didn't even change one bit. Instead, he sighed and nudged away from the shadow kid's leg as if it were a fly he was shoving away.

ShaVenger freed his hand and bounced back from one clone to another. All he knew was that his opponent was strong, and it would take a lot of strength to beat him. This is not the agent he's used to fighting. He had to use some other way to defeat this chuckling bastard.

The boy teleported behind Curdur. He kicked him, and just as he vanished, ShaVenger didn't waste a second and turned around. Knowing that his opponent would appear behind him, he punched with all force.

Curdur still somehow managed to dodge the attack and gave an even blow right into ShaVenger's guts. The air escaped out from his lungs, and he was sent crashing into one of the buildings behind him.

Alarms sounded in the quiet of daylight, but his ears hardly apprehended anything. He laid between the broken glass, staring while avoiding the sun's harsh rays. The power gap between him and this agent imitation was too much. No matter how hard he tried, the recent exchange of blows between the two had already proven the outcome of the fight; maybe his head wasn't in the game. He was on the run, after all.

The shadow teen huffed slightly; this was not going to break him down. He was still going to fight with everything he got.

While ShaVenger thought, his eyes contacted the silhouette of the other boy coming towards him while splitting the air beside him. The sun's rays behind shone, spreading its light. All ShaVenger could think about was dodging the attack. As Curdur got closer, the cross-human instantly curled into strips of shadows - vanishing from the place. His attack hit the wall, breaking it down and turning every bit of it into ashes.

CURDUR. *He straightened.* Silly, silly! Teleported again! *He chuckled and then cracked his knuckles.* Well– You must know, there's no place you can hide from me. *He said, then he jumped into the sky, vanishing just like that.*

Somewhere in the dark alley, ShaVenger rubbed his sore arm and sighed. Nothing came to his mind as to how he was going to deal with him. Why did he start this fight? He smacked his fist into the wall feeling frustrated.

CURDUR. Awww. That feeling!

His voice startled him, and he whipped around to see a flash right in front of him. Curdur appeared, smirking.

Before he could say another word or move an inch, Curdur spun and kicked him on the side, sending him flying into a car driving from the front of the alley's entrance. The driver couldn't keep the car balanced and drove it crazily on the road, eventually colliding into a pole and was upside down in the next moment. Curdur casually walked through the commotion of people. He looked like a cosplayer to them; they looked and kept walking. He stood in front of the ablaze car with his hands tucked into the pockets of his pants.

CURDUR. Come on out already. *He said as if bored.*

The car wriggled and was suddenly thrown up into the air, falling a few paces behind, and exploded upon hitting the curb. ShaVenger stood in front of him, breathing heavily and bleeding.

For a few seconds, just voices to a few startled people and metal burning remained between them.

The shadow teen thought for a second, taking glances at the nosy people. A device materialized in his palm, and he clicked it. Lights flashed all around. He tilted his head after taking in a few details and then darted towards Curdur, but right at the point of contact, he transported into another shadow clone on top of his head– aiming his kick right for his skull.

The ground beneath his feet cracked, and the impact shattered the glass to nearby buildings and cars. Curdur did not flinch; he stood at his spot, scratching his head.

ShaVenger himself felt this was a cruel joke. His mouth hung low while he stared at him. It looked like he had just woken up and have had a satisfying bath. This couldn't be real. His eyes were wide, and now a tiny spark of fear began to dance from within them.

This strength? ShaVenger didn't think twice as he immediately teleported and reappeared in another corner, but he could feel Curdur behind him.

SHAVENGER. Shit! You know what! Screw this!!!! *He yelled and aimed at the imitation of Agent Z.*

CURDUR. *Continues to chase him thinking it's a bluff.* You're hopeless. Heh-heh.

The cross-human's body flickered, leaving his opponent in a state of shock. This gave him an advantage. He reached out and grabbed him. He was strong, sure, but ShaVenger knew he was faster. They both disappeared. The shadow teen took the imitation for a ride through dark portals, reappearing and disappearing throughout several spots around town.

He was becoming aggravated. Blazing red around Curdur's dark pupils glared now. Shivers went down ShaVenger's spine, but he was not stopping. He was proving that he was stronger.

Every nerve in his body was now unsettled as he appeared at the top of Ciemere Peak, the highest point near the Clifaran Mountains. Immediately, he jumped from it, disappearing into another shadow. ShaVenger hesitated, but for a second only, he left the area through another portal.

The imitation dropped out the dark portal and landed on his feet—a glimpse of the place formed in front of him. A creature was in front of him, slowly turning to see who suddenly appeared.

CURDUR. Heh. The bounty hunter who's after the fused scientist.

TIEMIORIFTHRIFT. *Confused, staring at this imitation of the boy he fought months ago.* You again.

CURDUR. Nahh. Not again. You have me confused with the human boy who has my face. *Chuckles and walks forward.* Let's have a –

Before he took a third step, the alien bounty hunter blasted him. Reality warped all around and finally settling to one point in time.

FLASHBACK! *(TIME REWRITE)*
SATURDAY, MARCH 4TH 2107,
1:00 P.M. *(EARTH TIME)*

Curdur's standing near a cliff, trying to look out beyond the horizon. Part of himself. Part of his being to how he exists feels like it's detached. But how?

CURDUR. Heh-heh. *He shakes his head and stares at the clouds in the sky with a smirk resting on his face.* It would seem I need to take extra precautions for my BIO-Being collection. I lose another one, and that's one more life I won't be able to use to stay alive in this meaningless world. *He laughed.*

Friday, January 04, 2108
1:25 P.M.

Meanwhile, a tomboyish teen girl strolls through the street, lost, confused, trying to find her way. She's on her way to the mall for an errand. She minds her business, looking through a map on her phone to see where the hell she's going, then goes left into a corner: nothing odd but another teen rushing through the urban jungle.

VALERY. *She pocketed her phone.* I'm on the outskirts now.

She looks at a window of a shop in the alleyway she's in, seeing what she's not expecting– Orina. There's no escape. Her spitting image was charging at her, with murder in her eyes. The evil clone launched into the air, growling as she sped towards her twin sister. Without a moment of hesitation, *she thought she could shut her eyes, taking a deep breath– and* **WHAM!** In an instant, she ducked just in time, making her clone break through the window in front of her, covering her skin in splinters.

The girl reached in and pulled her out, dragging her across the pavement by her right heel. She dropped her and went for the lookalikes right hand, pinning her down and climbing on top of her. She grunted as the force of a knee met her stomach. She goes in for a swing and misses. *THUD!* Down she goes to the ground.

VALERY. Is this all you got? *A ragged breath escaped her lungs as she kicked out to her side.* We can talk this out, right. *Does a double take. She grew tenser and tenser.*

The clone hadn't said a word; she just stepped closer, up to her face, and shoved her to the ground, knocking down garbage bins. The human girl had enough. She didn't need this disrespect. I mean – Could the twin demon speak or comprehend what she's saying? All the years in training don't mean she got to be a doormat when she stepped out. The creature opened her mouth, but before she could get a sound out, Valery swiped at her feet and got back up.

VALERY. *With fists raised, she said.* You're gonna pay for attacking my dad! No, I ain't forget. *She smiles.*

The creature lunged at her, bringing both to the ground in the alleyway. She didn't even hear her body go down; she was fast on her feet. Valery tried her best to keep cover, but she's too strong – more robust than most fighters she fought.

They stood. Orina sent blow after blow against her torso. Valery braced herself, kicking her off to the side against the overflowed dumpster. *Clang!* She kicked, and she kicked, as she brought her leg back for another. Before the hit, the clone yanked on her right leg as she tucked and rolled. She flails as she hit the ground against the hot concrete, gashing her cheek. Her head hit against metal. She pushed and kicked off the trash bags. *Now, she looks angry.* She grabbed a bottle, smashing its ends on the floor. The human girl saw and picked up a metal pipe.

VALERY. What do you– *She dodged, but too slow as the makeshift shiv flew past her left arm, cutting through her sleeve and parts of her arm?* Ahh–! *She clutches her arm; it is wet and sticky from the blood. She started gripping harder against the pipe.* I'll aim for that head! *She shouted.*

She struck for the head, but it was blocked with ease by the creature's forearm– not even a flinch. The creature sends a punch to her gut and another to the side of her ribs. Valery staggered backward as Orina inched closer. She grabbed hold of the pipe and took it away. The creature struck at her twin's right knee; she howled in pain, falling onto her side. She looked up and could see her eyes. They were ink-black, no whites in sight and baring her teeth like the common predator.

The creature felt her sharp nails seared onto her scalp as she pulled to see her face to smile– before her head jerked back from the impact of her knee, but not before she lifted her left leg back and at her torso. Valery could hear the slight cracking of her ribs on her knuckles.

She didn't take her eyes off her as she struggled to get up. Her right knee wouldn't budge. Orina grabs hold of her by the neck and pushes her against the wall. She can feel the breath on her face. She kept holding her arms in a firm grip. She tried to kick, but nothing.

VALERY. *Choking out a breath.* What are you trying to do– Kill me? *She staggered forward, on uncertain footing, squaring her shoulders and braces her fists to her twin's face.* Still with that stupid smile. *She fakes a jab for a hook, and her head jerks to the right. She freed herself.*

She got her where she wanted her and kept swinging, hammering on and on—left and right. She was furious, and she was going to show her. With a surge of adrenaline, she could feel a pulse rage against her neck. She begins to falter in her footwork, and she takes this as a sign to subdue her, and tilts her hips, left forward and right across her ear. She leans against the beige wall.

Sweat prickled, the hairs on the back of her neck, and air rose. You'd think this was the end of it.

The smirk on the creature's face, and a come-hither motion of her hands beg to differ.

She swayed as she pushed herself up and did a little jig. She clutched on her fist, popping each knuckle. Valery could feel the exhaustion begin to settle in her body with every breath that escaped her.

Her twin lunged forward, hook after hook, each met with a stiff arm. Sideswiping her back to the ground, she pulled her down with her. She grabbed hold of her arm and pulled it far back. A scream of extremities rose from her throat as it felt like her left shoulder dislocated with a pop. Luckily, that wasn't the case. She rose back up without letting go. She couldn't quite hear. There was only white light of pain in her head; she was on the verge of passing out.

Then she let go, leaving her for a moment with the searing ache of a potential torn muscle.

VALERY. I must get up. Fuck! *She careens to the side, right before what could've only been a small brick replaced where her head was. She glares at her.*

With a grin, she sent another kick across the base of her spine. Valery's vision partially gave out, and she rocked on forward to her knees. She was persisted, clutching her shoulder as she rose to her feet. She shook everything off and took deep breaths.

Everything in the world felt lopsided. Her twin stood tall and proud. But she could see her exhaustion.

VALERY. *Thinking.* We once shared something, didn't we? Heh. *She smiles and sniffs.* Let's see.

She ran towards her with all her might and swung with her right. Just as she expected, she held it above their faces; still, teeth bared in a grin. This time, the human girl gave her twin one back then she slammed her head against hers. Their world spun, and they both fell.

Orina growled and jumped to her feet. She curled her left fist and aimed for Valery, who just got to her feet as well. She's blocking, her twin using continuous jabs against her opponent. The human girl fell in her twin's trap, now held in a rear-naked choke, but a few ground strikes allowed her to escape. The creature soon grabbed her head, fingers holding her by the hair until Valery was dangling by the tip of her toes. Then, she launched a round kick at the girl's abdomen, making her wince in pain. Orina threw continuous overhands.

The two were at each other's throats constantly, at the same time trying to break free and finish the other. Valery pulled away from the clutches of her evil twin and stood up, but still ready to fight.

VALERY. Not this time. *She would repeat in her head.*

But Orina was already crawling back to her, grabbing her ankle, and climbing back up. They looked in each other's eyes and saw nothing but sorrow and rage and knew that there would be no way out. Valery threw her leg up in the air, Orina parrying the blow with her left arm as she tried to hit her opponent. Valery's uppercut caught her by surprise, turning her to the side and exposing her to a southpaw. After that, she punched her twin in her abdomen, knocking her backward, then proceeded to hoist her arm into a lock, trying to immobilize the half-Quinoragoras spawn.

Without hesitation, Orina broke away from the lock, hitting her continuously in the abdomen and then finishing the combo with a hard kick to the thigh, which took away her opponent's balance and forced her on all fours. Orina then pounded her twin with her kicks, but even then, Valery found the strength to grab hold of her foot and get back up once again. Orina climbed the walls of the narrow alleyway and won the high ground over Valery, charging at her once again with her animalistic rage and growls. The human girl quickly followed her trail, climbing the walls behind her, trying to even the odds of the battle. They exchanged blows on their way up, throwing punches and kicks into each other's faces. Finally, Orina stopped and grabbed her twin, reaching the rooftops, propping herself securely, and hanging Valery over the edge.

This was the end; they both knew it, but in a split second, Valery grabbed the ledge and threw her twin over. She fell on the hard rock of the alley, badly hurt from the impact. Before Valery could jump down to continue the fight, Orina already fled, limping in pain.

VALERY. Why'd – Argh. *Groans and holding her left side.* Why'd she run?

She slowly makes her way to a brick wall and leans on it. She pulls out her cellular and speaks a person's name. The person gets a notification. Within a few minutes, Agent Z arrives on his flight board to her location. He swerves near, jumps off, and runs to her.

AGENT Z. What happened to you? *He takes her arm and places it over his shoulder.*

VALERY. Orina happened. *Holding onto him.* Please – Take me home. I don't want my father to know.

He nods, and the two disappear, going to her home. They arrive inside her home, upstairs. He walks her to her bedroom and pushes the door open. Something dives last second into a pile of laundry on the floor.

AGENT Z. *Sees out of the corner of his right eye as he stepped inside.* You got a pet?

VALERY. I wish. *Limps to her bed.* I'm good from here. Thank you, Zada.

AGENT Z. *Smiles.* No problem. Why did she attack you?

VALERY. I wish I knew. I tried to end her, though. I hate being weak. *Scoffs.* Without her inside, I'm more human.

AGENT Z. I'll be on the lookout for her. You get better. See ya'. *He teleports.*

Planet Vexion – Afternoon

Jessica lands on the outskirts of the Volsus Caverns. She immediately hears clashing and sounds of battle. A Voice in her head instructs her to take a look.

Upon arrival, she sees boys and girls around her age surrounded by creatures. The children look tired and in need of saving.

The girl's eyes glow. She teleports right before the creatures are about to attack – dead center in front of the children. She extends her left arm, and a sonic screech blasts the creature's back. They retreat, running into the bushes behind them.

The girl lowers her hand, and her eyes return to normal. What she just did, she was unsure. It felt natural.

She saved our *AOH* heroes from an attack. She immediately turns, locking eyes with the group. Her eyes glow once more, and they are transported somewhere else on the planet.

JESSICA. *Lowering her arm.* That'll buy them some time until I return with help. *She starts fading away as the wind picks up.*

Elsewhere...

JOSEPH. Guys. Did you see her clothes? I do not know, man. But I'd say she's from Earth.

DOMINIX. Like the boy who called himself an agent.

GORIAH. *Scoffs and rolls her eyes*—some friend.

VICE HQ – 3:12 P.M.

Inside the operations room, an older gentleman is visually checking out all the latest hi-tech equipment. There is no personnel to operate. A much younger male in his early thirties approaches him.

XAVIER. It's good you've maintained a close connection with work, Mache.

MACHE. Heh. Well, someone must. After all, without the prime database of its sister command base, the systems would have died years ago. *Looks at his commanding officer.* The gentlemen you hired – Are they exceptional for–

Just then. Two individuals teleport inside the room. An older African American male with an average body frame wearing a metal mask and a much younger Caucasian man with a toned yet slim physique.

XAVIER. Finally. You two have a difficult time working the transportation devices?

DALE JR. *Walking up to the scientist, extending his hand to shake but speaking to the commander.* You have a way with words, my boy. You must be the lead scientist.

MACHE. Indeed I am. *Shakes the man's hand.*

XAVIER. You'll be working closely with him. *Nods in the direction of the other man.* As well as you, Mr. Helms.

DARIUS HELMS. Respectfully, Xavier, I'll appreciate the code-name, Dyro.

XAVIER. Very well. *Sighs.* I'm afraid we're one short.

MACHE. *Eyeing computer surveillance that went active.* Sir... Umm?

XAVIER. *Shakes his head with a smirk.* That'll be him.

The doors to the room open, and a middle-aged African American man walks into the room. He's a bit eager, touching his hands while eyeing the room's décor.

JAYN TALGITX. This is nice!! *Eyeing the others in the room but addresses the commanding officer.* All right, all right. I did not realize you had it like that, boss man. *He walks up to the commander, fist bumps him, and nods at the others.*

DALE JR. Who is this ruffian?

JAYN TALGITX. I'll stop that disrespect right there. It is Jayn. Don't bother looking into me unless you want this hurt, ya' feel me?

XAVIER. And this is where I step in. Let me set one thing straight. You three were brought here due to your skill sets to be part of my new commanding officer team. I will be acting commander with you three under myself. *He thinks for a minute, then points to the eldest in the room.* Dale. You'll be acting commander with Dr. Mache. *Looks at the two younger men.* You two will be field commanders.

JAYN TALGITX. Sounds like a plan. *Chuckles.*

DYRO. *Calm and quiet.* Will you finally tell us the reason you brought us here?

XAVIER. If I wasn't clear in my exclusive message to you three, I am expanding this here facility due to a corrupt and adolescent structure that failed. I am currently working to exterminate the issues permanently.

DALE JR. Sounds messy.

JAYN TALGITX. … or savage. *Laughs.* How can we help with that?

3:45 P.M.
Somewhere near Duurtsville, Missouri…

Edward Morris is making his way to a cul-de-sac and walks up a modern-day home. When he unlocks the door, his head gets smashed in the center of the oak wood right under the door knocker, and he's out. The door was opened due to the blow. A dark figure stands over him and drags him through the threshold.

Meanwhile, later that evening, Valery awoke from a nap, feeling a bit well rested after the fight she had with her demented twin. She is in her bedroom speaking to her friend from planet Vexion.

The two are speaking about random stuff. A conversation about its planet randomly comes up.

QUETSEY. *He hops off the bed and walks over to her clothes bag hanging up on her closet door.* What is this contraption?! *He reaches for it.*

VALERY. Don't touch that!! *She immediately rushes to the closet door, gets in front of the creature, and prevents him from touching her things.*

QUETSEY. *He jerks his tiny arm back quickly.* Well... Someone's a bit embarrassed. *He turns around and starts walking toward her computer.* Oh, my! *His eyes fill with an intrigued sensation.* What are my eyes seeing?!

VALERY. *She rolls both of her eyes.* Oy vey. *She rushes over to her computer.* Stop it, Quetsey! That's not a toy!!

QUETSEY. Fine. *He pouts. He remains quiet for five seconds.* What is there to do for fun around here?

VALERY. Nothing. I go to the arcade or the mall. *She sits down at her computer station, spins around in a full circle, and faces the creature.*

QUETSEY. *He's looking at her strangely.*

VALERY. What?!

QUETSEY. Okay. What is there to do around here that *I CAN* get into without getting caught?

VALERY. Oh!! Heh-heh. Sorry. I wasn't thinking.

QUETSEY. Ya' never do, do ya?

VALERY. *She laughs a little.* Shut up! Heh-heh.

QUETSEY. *He's looking up at her.* I do have a question for you, Miss Valery.

VALERY. *She looks at him.* Yes.

QUETSEY. The top and bottom that you put on when you go fight is too revealing. You do know that, right?

VALERY. *She sighs.* I'm not the best at making outfits, okay!

QUETSEY. I say contact the superhero you are always saving from robots. He sure has style.

VALERY. *A surprised expression appears on her face.* Huh?! How'd you kn – *She shakes her head a few times to forget the topic.* It doesn't matter. I'm pretty sure he realized that I can't have my mind erased.

QUETSEY. Heh-heh. You are full of mysteries! Ha-ha. What he doesn't say, may work to you in your favor. *He smiles at her.*

VALERY. Aw! That's got to be the nicest thing you've ever said since I brought you to my home. *She reaches for him, pulls him closer, and she starts squeezing him tighter.* You are the bestest friend a girl could ever, ever ask for!!

QUETSEY. *He's trying to resist the ultimate Valery hug.* No, no, no, no. Uh, uh. Lemme go!!

VALERY. Okay. It's late, and I have school tomorrow. *She cleans her space and pulls her blanket to the side, allowing her room to get into her bed.*

QUETSEY. Since when do you like school?

VALERY. *She pulls the blanket over her, grabs one of her stuffed animals, and throws it at the creature.*

QUETSEY. Woah!! *He moved to his left, avoiding the stuffed animal.*

VALERY. Good night! *She lays her head down on her pillow.*

QUETSEY. *He walks over to the stuffed animal, picks it up, takes it over to the bed, and places it next to her.* Night. *He crawls onto the bed, gets to the rear, curls into a ball, and goes to sleep.*

The girl opens her left eyelid and smiles.

Meanwhile, at her home of residence…

Jessica Bodega apparated back inside her room. The ordeal isn't too familiar for her body to handle.

JESSICA. I – I don't feel too good.

GUARDIAN (CONSCIOUS). Apologies, human. I forget transporting is highly tiresome to mortals.

JESSICA. *Holding her forehead, smiles and shakes her head.* OMG. I think I'll be fine – I need to sleep. When I wake up, I expect you to tell me who those people were. Some of them looked human. Like, from Earth. *She lays in her bed and closes her eyes.* Good night.

8:54 P.M.
Later that night…

The streets of Veils Dune, Missouri pulse with neon lights, illuminating the asphalt and walkways underneath to guide tourists and residents to their destinations. The high-rise buildings and billboards hide the sky above, and the only semblance of time was the ticking of wristwatches and the occasional yawns from weary pedestrians.

Cael checks his phone and reads ten minutes past eleven in the evening. He slips his phone back in his jacket's inner pocket and zips it, keeping the cold air at bay. The streetlight across signaled him and other bystanders to walk. The pedestrian lanes glow a faint white whenever shoes walk on it and continuously flash red if someone steps out of the route, warning them to stay within the lines while crossing.

Once he was on the other side, he turned left, following the path straight ahead. The crowd of people around him thinned at every block he turned, and the quieter residential areas muffled the loud noise of the clubs and bars. The blinding neon lights melted away into lampposts and trees, and upon arriving at the park, everything went silent except for the humming wind passing through the leaves and branches.

The man settled on one of the benches in the park and rested on the backrest, eyeing the dark sky. The stars hid, ashamed that the lights on the ground finally outshone them. Cael never understood why humans on Earth enjoyed stargazing; stars were dull, and they did nothing for them.

UNKNOWN STRANGERS VOICE. Yo. *Echoes through the man's thoughts.*

Two glowing green eyes covered the sky. Cael stood when he felt the blazing wind all over his face and in his brain– there's magic infiltrating. It seeps through his pores and fights with his thoughts; his hands clambering towards the mysterious eyes and clawing at them as a desperate attempt to escape.

His fingers barely fought to move; then, his body acted against his will. His arms lower themselves, and he clambers back on his feet to face a newcomer.

CAEL. Come out! *Breathes out, regaining control over his senses.* I know you're there, Asarios.

The wizard smirked at his brother's newer disguise. He shifts to an expressionless face.

ASARIOS. You were hard to find. How I had to shuffle through different worlds and realities, warping three others' minds I collected – to see – you. *He chuckles and with a wave of his right hand, two mindless minions stand at full attention, and wait for his instructions.* Get out of that ridiculous human form.

Amras (Cael) knew someone had been following him. The presence of a pursuer was like the terrible aftertaste of bile in his mouth. His senses couldn't pinpoint where, but he felt their eyes hawk at him, stalking him. So, he used the wind to surround him and caused his physical form to disappear. If he shows his face, Asarios will make sure to give him a slow and painful death for locking him away.

The little brother's about to give them their orders when one of his minions skidded on the grass, hitting his head hard and knocking himself unconscious. Asarios glanced at the incapacitated minion, salvaging what little information he could from him.

ASARIOS. Hm. Perhaps I went overboard with the mind control spell. Or not. *With a wave of his right hand, the one stood closer as a shield. From the chopped hair on the other side of his head, he found the general trajectory of the shot. He aimed his right trigger finger at a cluster of trees from where the shot came from and snapped two of his fingers together.*

Amras focused on the sound, amplifying its vibrations and stripping the canopy of leaves, hiding as the wind. The traveling wave of air should be loud enough to stagger his opponent and throw him off his hiding place.

His stalker leaps into the trees, sending a magical shockwave of energy to a two-mile radius, and brings his brother out of hiding. He jumps to the ground and chuckles.

AMRAS. You've gotten stronger in Valdesmon.

ASARIOS. You have no idea. Heh-heh. Enjoy my new friends for a while.

The older brother is in his usual Xeiar Great attire, as his staff appears in his left hand. Winds kick up as he is getting ready for an attack. Asarios sends his minion, and the newly revived one, to charge forward and intercepts his wind charge; their inability to cast spells made up by their muscular bodies to stall. One of them swings their fist towards the Great's head while the other kicks him in his back.

The man did not even bother blocking, his body is invincible, and no human could harm him.

ASARIOS. *He blurts out.* I should tell you; they have been enhanced!

One of their attacks makes it through the wind's shield, but Amras deflected the punch with his forearm and rolled forward with the second kick's momentum. The minions follow, kicking at his body and one grabbing him from behind. The man blocks the kick with both his hands and headbutts the minion and tackles him after he stands up. Guess he'll be getting dirty after all.

The minion reels back and clutches his jaw while the other throws another punch at his head.

Amras weaves under the punch and lands a palm against the minion's chest, sending him back with an explosive blast of air. Asarios weaves another spell with his fingertips, snapping once again and pointing towards his opponent. The air vibrates from his snap, but this time into a focused line, aiming at his brother's head. The magically formed bullet, made of pure wind, whistled through the air and shot through the opponent, missing his heart by a few inches.

The remaining minion tries tackling him at his hips this time and plants his feet on the ground. The man struggles and tries to move forward while his trapper throws a few blind punches to his sides. He cringes at some blows but hammers the sides of his fists on the minion's shoulders and head, causing his grapple to weaken. Asarios fires another shot, this time pointing his finger at the brother's left knee. The opponent shifts his left leg, safely getting out of the bullet's path. The squelch of the bullet hitting his minion's flesh rang in the empty park, his arms now grabbing his knee and screaming from the pain of the wound. His opponent swings his hand at the minion's neck, knocking him out.

With his last minion incapacitated, Asarios assumes his stance and studies him.

Judging from the spells he cast, the two of them were proficient in the same element, having witnessed the opponent use the air in his body movements to amplify his strength.

ASARIOS. Why Magis sent you away to Earth only delayed the inevitable. I killed him, and I'm going to kill you.

AMRAS. You're not my brother anymore. You're not Asari.

ASARIOS. That's two innocent people you injured. *He chuckled.*
Don't you feel any –

AMRAS. *He interrupts.* They will live. *He swiftly punches forward; massive amounts of wind are heading straight at his opponent.*

The little brother sways his head away from a blast of air formed by his brother's punch. His movements are too predictable from a long-range. Asarios laughs as he crouches under another blast from a roundhouse kick. The wind from the man's next punch crunches the lamppost behind him, cutting off its power and darkening a part of the area.

ASARIOS. *He spins and glances at the lamppost bending into itself then faces his opponent again.* Not even a lecture about preserving life? *He snapped his fingers once again, forming the sound vibrations into a solid wall to deflect an incoming blast of wind.*

His opponent hops forward once, using the force of the wind from his step to seal the distance between them, and throws a left fist towards Asarios's jaw, but he slaps it away with the back of his hand and brushes his fingers at his older brother's muscled forearm.

He forced the air around his fingers to amplify the friction between his hand and the older brother's arm, scraping out a few layers of his enemy's skin.

Amras hissed nonchalantly and stepped back, holding his new wound. Asarios takes the scraps of skin on his fingers close to his mouth. The older brother watches him chew on his flesh, as the younger brother barely stifles in his laughter when his opponent cringes at sight. The thin meat slid between his teeth while he chewed, but it went down smoothly when he swallowed.

ASARIOS. *The taste fades away, and he licks his lips.* That was a tasty appetizer. *He remarked, curling his fingers at the brother and beckoning the fight to continue.* I'd like the main course now, please.

AMRAS. What – What have you become, Asari?

ASARIOS. Do not call me that!! *Anger arises from his core at the mention of that name. He takes advantage of the range and snaps thrice to form a triangle of wind blades.*

This disturbs the canopy of leaves underneath them, exploding everywhere when it meets against the Air Greats' wind arcs. At the same time, the winds collide, Asarios sprints around and knee the Great in his traitorous face. He ducks, taking position allowing the last blade to miss.

He stretches his arms and legs and leaps at his brother's waist, taking him down to the ground and assaulting him with fists. The man's fist lands square on Asarios's jaw, sending him back-first to the concrete sidewalk. He grunts from the impact but rolls into a ball, saving himself from a stomp.

His opponent keeps his guard up, shifting whenever Asarios tries to punch the side of his jaw. The mad wizard reels in for another punch but throws off his enemy when he amplifies his kick off the ground using the wind. The two rolled again to find their balance and rose back up.

The two of them circle each other, waiting for the next person to strike. Both he and Amras controlled their breathing, trying not to hiss in pain from the hits they both received. The older brother (Xeiar Great) clenches his hand around his bleeding shoulder and scrapes his arm. He did this and showed no weakness. Asarios can feel his eyes watching and gauging his next movements.

The Xeiar Air Great weaves in once again and jabs at his face, which his brother deflects, only to feel another fist dig into his chest. Asarios steps back and watches his hand movements closer, blocking an incoming right hand into his face. He feels another hand dig into his chest, sapping him of air. Asarios sucks in and breathes, this time letting the jab to his face hit to step outside the range of a body shot.

The older brother steps even closer, applying more speed and pressure to his punches. His right-hand grazes his little brother's cheek, and he barely evades it by leaning the other way. His left hand soundly hit his rib, feeling it crack under the older brother's strength. Asarios steps back again and clicks his tongue, slapping away another punch, and counters with his hook to the jaw. His opponent dipped under the curve, and swung another fist at him, hitting the center of Asarios's stomach and sending him stepping back once again.

His opponent's fists became faster and faster but never grew to the same intensity that pummeled the two minions he brought to this fight. Asarios struggles to keep up with his speed, growling in frustration as he finds himself in a more defensive position than before. His hands are sore from blocking and his body is numbed by the flurry his older brother unleashed.

What annoyed him the most was that his brother was showing no intent to kill. His conscious talking to him in his mind – Why did he not speak up when he was blamed for a crime he did not commit?

Asarios grunts and falls on his back. His arms and legs gave in and were too sore to move. He glares at his brother, forcibly sending signals to his body to get up or cast a spell.

The Air Xeiar Great stands over him.

Asarios spits at his face. It was the best greeting he could give to his elder brother. It also explained why he felt sick when he was watching him in the shadows. Their so-called familial bond was trying to resonate with him, but Asarios honored that bond no more.

AMRAS. You're coming with me.

ASARIOS. To where – Grand Xesus? *He laughed. Good* luck! I destroyed it and sent the last Great away. *He loathed this commanding tone in his brother's voice. He remembered from childhood that he felt he was trying to rub the fact that he was always the superior brother, whether in combat or in making basic decisions.* Heh. You would bring me back as what? *He retaliated.* Your trophy or your proof of loyalty?

AMRAS. *He shook his head.* Neither.

That was a lie. Asarios saw through his little trick. His brother was nothing more than a tool for the council, ready to sacrifice even his own younger brother to figuratively lick the boots of the higher-ups and hog all the fame, all to become a Great Wizard of the planet Xeiar. It was what made them fall apart, which made Asarios the person he was today.

Imprisoned in Valdesmon, he knew his brother chose himself over their brotherly bond. The tool even stayed silent during the trial. He did nothing to protect his younger brother, all because he wanted to prove that he was loyal to the high council and would never betray them. Asarios became his scapegoat and victim. While Amras mute, the past Great Wizards of Xeiar threw Maleena and himself into the deepest depths of Valdesmon to suffer alone for something they did not commit.

Looking at the tool's face made his face cringe and his blood boil. How dare he mock him! He felt his fingers regain their senses through the waves of pain in the rest of his arms. The rest of his body ached from his brother's forceful punches, but they were beginning to respond as well. He eased his muscles and readied himself, taking long breaths through his nose.

ASARIOS. I know you. You always have a hidden agenda whenever you talk to me. *He spat back, leering at his brother from the corners of his eyes.* Did they expect me to die in that horrifying place? Asari was scared!! Where were you?!

AMRAS. *He shakes his head, taking a step closer to his younger brother, looking down on him with those emotionless eyes.* No. I'll say it again – you're coming with me.

Talking to him was pointless. Asarios hated every syllable that came from his mouth and wished he could shove all the words little Asari wanted to say in his mouth. He patted the ground underneath him and used the same technique his older brother used to amplify his speed to lift himself off the concrete. He felt blood rushing all over his body, waking every muscle from the numbness it suffered minutes ago. His legs stiffened themselves and carried his weight once more.

ASARIOS. I'm going back on one condition —your lifeless head in my hands.

AMRAS. *He let a breath escape his lips. His stoic face bore no sign of disappointment or anger, only focus.* You've truly changed. Is this the effect of Valdesmon– all those lost souls entering one lost body?

If only his brother knew. The constant murmurs of the spirits in Valdesmon did not turn him insane. It enlightened him, telling him the depravities he could do to get his revenge on Amras. Their suggestions on how he should exact revenge strengthened his will to return to the surface and do as he wished. When he did escape the dark prison, the whispers followed him wherever he went. They accompanied him, whispering sweet nothings in his ear, bubbling the desire to kill his brother even further. Up to the point where the Quinoragoras Redileon killed Maleena, he gained more insight and additional power.

He also knew that his brother would easily overpower him if he appeared before him as soon as he emerged out of prison. He needed time to prepare for the fight, honing his skills and finding new ways to implement the secrets whispered by the prisoner's souls. It was then he discovered how to influence minds by using the winds and his hatred on others. He could hear their whispers fueling his magic. Therefore, he controlled the cross-human, Christen, and the creature who fused with Dante Skalizer.

He assumed his stance again, easing his fingers. Amras readied himself, ready for another clash. He rushed forward and ducked under his older brother's defenses. His fist traveled quickly, clocking Amras's chest before he could react. The older brother steps back and answers with a fist square at Asarios's face. The punch scrapes his cheek, and the latter uses the friction on their skins to peel more of his elder brother's skin off his arm.

The Air Xeiar Great grits his teeth and catches a spinning kick aimed at his face. He hooked Asarios's foot with his own, sending the other to the ground. The younger brother fell on his back again and kicked upwards toward Amras's chest, the force sending him staggering backward. He jumps back up and slices the air in front of him. Its winds zoomed past his brother, who stepped to the side and created his arc.

The air shield collapsed when it met his brother's air blades. He snapped thrice while he ran out of the park, sending more blades to Amras, who sped past them with his enhanced speed. He's about to tackle Asarios when he suddenly spins and claws his cheek, his face stinging when the doubled friction cuts deep wounds on him. Amras stepped to the left and kicked his little brother in his chest, sending him a few feet back. Asarios skids on his feet then snap his fingers, sending an air wall at his brother. The Air God slashed the air only to find another one immediately behind it and cut again. The younger brother walked forward while releasing his barrage, watching as his brother had spent most of his energy to create a gap in the winds to save himself.

Amras leaned forward and slashed two more times before stepping forward and fighting against the strong blasts of wind with his speed. He takes three steps to close the distance between the two of them. He raises his arms, expecting another hit to his head or body. He winces when he feels deep cuts in his arms. His fists loosened while his exposed tendons screamed in pain. His elbows locked themselves in place, and his nerves burned, no longer responding to his will to drop or move them out of the way. Asarios grins at the sight of his brother's useless arms. He admires his brother's effort to remain to stand and resist screaming. Amras dropped to the ground when his little brother booted his chest and stood over him. The sight of his brother underneath him and helpless drew a sinister smile on his face. His heart races, and a giddy feeling in his chest bubbled. He stomps on him once, eliciting a pained groan from him. He stomps again. And again. And again. He could not control his laughter anymore. He was enjoying the assaults he made on his older brother.

He finally knew what it felt like to dominate his brother. It was beautiful, watching him squirm silently on his back. He hears his loud cackling echo all over the park, sweetening the sight even more. Gone are the days when he overshadowed him behind his emotionless eyes. Gone was the day when he betrayed him. But it would be more fun watching his brother struggle while he takes his head off. Asarios did not plan on giving him a painless death. He needed him to feel the same pains he felt that day and after being tossed in Valdesmon.

ASARIOS. *He reaches down and claws his brother's hair, forcing him to look into his eyes.* Brother! *He chuckles, slamming his head on the pavement.* Aren't you going to beg for mercy? Very uncharacteristic of you.

AMRAS. Listen to me! *His hands held onto the arm clutching him and tried to resist his brother's second slam.*

The enraged younger brother sped the slam with the winds around him.

AMRAS. The council had –

Asarios groans, displeased. He slammed his head on the concrete sidewalk again and glared when he strengthened his grip on him. The younger brother reels his arm back, readying to break his head on the park grounds.

AMRAS. Th – They – They made a mistake, brother. *He coughed.* They would've pardoned you.

ASARIOS. Pardoned?

He must be hearing things. Boigos, Anielias, and the younger Magis would never pardon him. Why would they? Amras was their shining beacon, the favorite apprentice to the Air Great Boigos. Why would the new Greats take him back in the fold? To humiliate him further– To rub his brother's status on him– To remind him that his brother was better. It was nonsense.

AMRAS. The real murderer to the residents on planet Xirxion was never revealed. *Breathing heavily.* I – I was going to – get you out.

His older brother was spitting nonsense. It was making him angrier and angrier. He wanted his brother to beg for mercy, not spout more useless rambling about the council. He was more robust now. He was better. He murdered a council Great and destroyed their home – Grand Xesus on his own as he heard the mumbling voices of Valdesmon inside his head, encouraging him to pursue the thought.

ASARIOS. Shut it. *He spat, letting go of his brother. He leaned back up and stepped on him, glaring into his brother's stoic eyes.*

His brows arched when he noticed the first emotion in his brother in years. It was not pain, or anger, or pity. He was not disgusted by his actions, either. Asarios racked his brain, trying to find the word for it. He was so distracted in looking for the word his foot barely had any pressure on him.

No, this would be the last time he saw this emotion in his brother's eyes. After his parents died of natural illnesses, Amras never praised him. And now the look haunted him right now, even if the fight battered Amras. Did that mean he was telling the truth? No. No, he was not. Why would he let his brother fool him now? Why should he listen to him when he can end him here and now with his own hands? He just learned how to falsify emotions as time passed to manipulate him. Besides, the council has never gone back on their prior decisions, even on the smallest ones. Amras must be driving him, appealing to this brotherly connection to try and beg for his life.

Amras let out a low growl and gently pulled his brother down to his level, their eyes meeting for a moment. Asarios face eased into a smile, and he relaxed his shoulders. He is studying his gaze. His blood rushed in excitement. Perhaps it was time for his brother to have a taste of Valdesmon.

He snapped his fingers, manipulating the sound vibrations in the wind to his command. Its sharp sound reverberated over the park, transforming its shortness into a long drone resembling a voice. Amras eyed around in confusion before looking back at his brother. Before a word could escape his lips, the single voice turned into two, then three, then all voices melting together in a swirl of chaos. The older brother covered his ears to muffle the screams, but the look of terror on his face showed that there was no escape. The winds close in on him, surrounding him in a canopy of leaves and dark voices. Asarios savored the sight of his brother fighting for control. He flailed around in his prison, trying to cut a swathe in the voices, only for them to meld back and fill his senses with darkness and screams. They appealed to perverse thoughts and desires he stowed away in the back of his mind, probing him for even the slightest hint of evil.

The voices must have tugged on something that caused him to scream, making Asarios wonder what evil his brother had in mind. He watched his face twist in horror as he fought his temptations within him. Amras tried reaching his hand to his brother and saying something, but the winds drowned him out. The swirl of voices tightened its grip, its force enough to paralyze their current prisoner. He struggled to move his pinned arms, even with the strength of his winds, only for Valdesmon to fight back. His bones crunched and splintered at its overwhelming power, forcing voiceless screams out of his body. His limp arms squeezed further into his body, and pieces of his ribs flew out of his chest. With one loud crunch, Amras became an unrecognizable mess of flesh and bones on the ground.

Asarios's chest and shoulders eased while he stood tall and gazed down at his brother's form. He had accomplished his task.

He walked out of the park as the winds and clouds cleared the darkened skies. Amras's protective barrier had been lifted after his death.

Asarios's heart was filled with satisfaction he had never felt in years. What was there to do now? His glowing eyes wandered to the sky, and there was no breeze to whisper what to do next.

10:13 P.M.
Moncealton's Shopping District in Peloppelas, Ohio

The shadow boy appears near a local shopping district and chooses to rest in the backroom of a furniture outlet.

SHAVENGER. *Sighs.* This looks quiet for a few hours of sleep.

The teenager lays his eyes upon three returned mattresses sitting on a wooden pallet in a corner and walks over while removing blankets out of the packaging. He lays them down evenly, yawns, and stretches as he lays down.

SEASON 5, EPISODE 29

6:16 A.M.
Wednesday, January 23, 2108

The sun rose with the glorious wings of a peach unbound by its sides and embracing the morning skylines, but after, grey clouds engulfed the waking sky's ethereal glow.

Jessica groaned and shut her screaming alarm. She was still walking the lines of her dream world. Her head felt heavy as she tried to change her side.

JESSICA. I wonder if I slept too much. *She thought, turning over, so her gaze fell on the window.*

The murky sky and soft winds rustled through the leaves of the trees guarding her window, then a wave of calm swept over her, and she nearly slept again when a sudden tingle pricked her brain. She grunted under her breath and rose in her bed lazily.

JESSICA. Maybe I should take a shower to get my head back on track. *She yawned, sliding the blanket away, and descending her bed, putting on her pink bunny slippers.*

As she lazily strolled to her window, rubbing her eyes, which still overflowed with drowsiness, her head buzzed once again, and she merely lost her balance.

The enthralling dark golden brown of her eyes narrowed at her reflection in the mirror.

JESSICA. *She swore at another tingle.* It hurts! What the hell is happening with me? *She scrubbed through her messy curly hair, wondering the cause for this annoying migraine, and walked towards the washroom. Her eyes stung when she rinsed her face. For a while, she kept blinking then touched her forehead.* Maybe I am running a fever, or was it the weather?

The weather yesterday had been as lively as her, and today the sky flowed with her feelings. Dreary! She brushed her teeth while thinking about all she had done the day before.

JESSICA. It was quite fun, but I was tired. *She spat out the lather of the toothpaste and stared at her pale face in the mirror.* Man, I've had a charming amount of sleep, yet I feel like a corpse! *She cleaned her face with her towel and came out of the washroom.*

After searching through her closet, she changed into dark blue jeans and a draping white shirt. She felt feverish, so she slid on a dark brown coat.

With a huff, she tied up her hair in a loose bun. Beauty reflected through her from every angle and lazy step; she was as elegant as a swan spreading its wings in a glassy-moonlit lake.

It didn't fade even when she disgracefully swore after stumbling on the top stair but immediately crouched down, holding her head in her hand. The pain gnawed on her brain like a wild beast.

She whimpered, pressing hard on the sides of her head. After minutes she was able to stand again. She hurried to the kitchen, preparing herself a glass of salted water in case her head was hurting because of low blood pressure.

While she was taking her breakfast to the table, the pain returned, but it was much more severe this time. It hit her head as if a hammer had crashed on top of it. So still! Darkness clouded her eyes instantly, and vision left them, but she was standing.

The food dropped from her hand, and the glass plate fell on her feet, but she stood there numb and silent. The colors of the deep sea left her eyes and became as pale as a vampire's skin.

Sirens blew through her mind. Sharp and evenly hoarse whispers were hitting her head. Her brain was partially under her control. The darkness in her eyes shifted like electrified liquid.

Her brain did allow her to recall encountering similar summons last night.

As the voices started to shriek against her cerebrum, pain coursed through – not just her head but her whole body and she began to scream out of pain and realization that something had infused itself with her mind and consciousness. Did it control her?

Hot tears streamed down her face. Whatever it was, she didn't like the feeling. The thing was now as much owner of her brain as she.

Visions of unforeseen events crossed her mind. She thought if there was some unworldly medium in her house, but she realized that the thing, whatever it was... It was using her mind for its existence.

JESSICA. *In a whisper.* Does this intruder have a voice? *She waits.*

GUARDIAN *(CONSCIOUS).* I do.

JESSICA. Wow. *She's a little spooked, checking to see if anyone is around. Suddenly remembering.* I have a little time for you to tell me your story. *Starts walking up to her room.*

GUARDIAN *(CONSCIOUS)*. What did we just put into our bodies?

JESSICA. You mean, my body. The one which you're inhabiting right now. *Smiles.* And it was Cinnamon Oatmeal. Very nutritious meal to start the day. *Makes it to the top floor, enters her room, and locks the door.*

GUARDIAN *(CONSCIOUS)*. The word –

JESSICA. – Delicious –is what I think you are looking for? But yeah. Where did you come from?

GUARDIAN *(CONSCIOUS)*. A planet far from Earth, in another dimension. Namorant.

JESSICA. This, Namorant – It's what exactly?

GUARDIAN *(CONSCIOUS)*. Quite different from what humans are used to.

JESSICA. What made you come here?

GUARDIAN *(CONSCIOUS)*. *Sighs.* A wizard visited the planet where I stand to watch over Namorant. Planet Junio's moon.

JESSICA. Okay. Is it a moon or a planet?

GUARDIAN *(CONSCIOUS)*. If this helps – It's like Pluto. A twin of it but lies in a mirror dimension.

JESSICA. So, Junio's moon and Pluto are the same?

GUARDIAN *(CONSCIOUS)*. In terms, yes! I reign over two dimensions as protector. That is until a Xeiar wizard's spell caused powerful rifts to send me hurtling through time and space.

JESSICA. – And sent you here?

GUARDIAN *(CONSCIOUS)*. That wasn't his intention, I believe. Just wanted to remove me from the throne. I feel that was his downfall. As the clash of our attacks hit each other, his lifeforce was extinguished. His physical form was no more.

JESSICA. So, you beat the evil wizard? That's good!

GUARDIAN *(CONSCIOUS)*. Yes, but I am unable to return to Junio. Due to myself being sent away from my post, I've lost a percentage of power. Other than that, I am what you may call a God–type. This is all I am afraid I must talk about myself.

JESSICA. It sounds like you need a battery to recharge to your full capacity—a person to inhabit for you to get up to speed.

GUARDIAN *(CONSCIOUS)*. That's right.

JESSICA. I just guessed because we're in that predicament right now. *Smiles.* No worries. I'll do what I can to help you. So, um… Those humans I saw fighting those creatures.

GUARDIAN *(CONSCIOUS)*. They were fighting on the Vexion planet; it's in Namorant as well. A creature was affected with dark power and transformed. He's taking over the world as his own.

JESSICA. We can stop it, right?

GUARDIAN *(CONSCIOUS)*. Not yet. There's training we must do mentally and physically before we go back there. I do not wish to see harm come to you.

JESSICA. Heh. I appreciate that.

11:23 A.M.
Centransdale High School.

Zadarion has gotten a call to meet at VLORs for a scheduled meeting. He ran to the boys' restroom, teleported from there, arriving in the Geared'NReady Room, and started making his way to the operations room. Upon his arrival, stepping through the sliding doors, he sees all agents present.

AGENT Z. Hi everyone.

AGENT RIT. Sup.

AGENT REV. What good, Z. *Walks closer to him and smiles with his eyes closed for a few seconds.*

COMMANDER ADDAMS. Ahem.

Everyone present in the room looks to the commander as he speaks.

COMMANDER ADDAMS. A fellow agent requested this meeting for all of us to speed on what we are dealing with now. Agent Caj, you may take the lead.

AGENT CAJ. Thank you, sir. *Looking at the agents.* Due to the battle at Primous, a few prisoners have escaped. Some old, some new.

AGENT Z. When– How come I wasn't aware?

AGENT CQUA. None of us were.

AGENT RIT. I believe Director Miles wanted to keep this top secret because of his troop transfer.

AGENT REV. New troop?

AGENT CAJ. Yes. Primous Facility has gone away with human bodyguards. There are robotic agents now. Their armor is like our own.

AGENT CQUA. So, who escaped?

AGENT CAJ. The wizard Z put away and a few ninjas my teacher locked away years ago. I've talked to the director, and he informed me a stowaway was on the helicopter that brought the criminal Worm to the facility. It's unknown who, but the coxswain believes it to be a female.

AGENT Z. How does he know the person's gender?

AGENT CAJ. He told me after shaking away the effects of a drug; he remembers a female guard. There were no female troops stationed there at the time.

AGENT RIT. Were there any others that escaped?

COMMANDER ADDAMS. No others. The facility was placed under much heavier security. A few inmates are getting stunned for long periods if they act up. The whole building has been upgraded to prevent escape. After Max Gerald, Techy Andy, and a few others kept escaping. Director Miles had enough and went through external resources to prevent future escapes.

AGENT RIT. That's great news.

AGENT CQUA. Are the assignments ready to be passed on to us?

AGENT CAJ. Glad you brought that up. The two ninjas were captured long ago by the very first VLORs agent. Whoever freed them must be of equal strength. You guys do not know the ninja abilities these guys possess. I am proposing different missions to track these guys down.

AGENT JEIFII. What about the Xeiar wizard Agent Z captured?

AGENT CQUA. *Chuckles.* She does speak.

AGENT CAJ. He'll pop up. And when he does, all hands-on deck will be in effect. Agent Rev, you can sit that one out if you want.

AGENT REV. No! I'll be fine.

AGENT CAJ. *Smiles.* That's what I like to hear.

AGENT RIT. So! The last time I was here, there were two others with you that aren't here anymore. That was irrelevant, but I heard a similar rant from Commander Addams saying Primous was secure. I'm back, and now I hear it is not as safe. Are we positive the facility is secure this time? Explain?

COMMANDER ADDAMS. Yes, Rit. There were complications with villains during your absence. It has been corrected thanks to Primous's director.

AGENT RIT. Let's hope so.

AGENT CAJ. Ahem. There's something else – A much more important matter. *Nods his head at Agent Z.* This affects you, little dude. *He activates his V-Link, and a light shoots out of it, forming into a widescreen.* Pay attention to the video.

The recorded footage starts playing…
FADE IN

INT. LAB. The laboratory has voltmeters, oscilloscopes, spectrometers, radiographers, various kinds of knives, three different chisels, and computers of all brands. They're all placed around the room evenly. The laboratory is fully illuminated, such that you cannot see who is behind the glass of the observation room. In the middle of the room is a table with six chairs. Two of the scientists are sitting and talking. The other three are currently doing work in the room.

COBEY TOBIAS ADDAMS. I don't understand how this metal works. I have gone through radiography and everything. As we know it, the metal is for sure not like the ones we have ever encountered before. It's too hard to cut through. Perhaps our weapons have made this bizarre metal immune, thereby causing a radioactive transformation that made it evolve. *Sighs.* What is this? *He continues as he shouts in shock of what may be their greatest nightmare.*

MURIEL JANE-ADDAMS. *Hands clasped.* I am honestly confused. I was expecting this to be just a massive chunk of carbon or metalloid. I can't decide what this thing is! I hope this is one prehistoric alien that is now faded into oblivion – with the sands of time! Our research and previous data have no tangible result on this alien metal we've discovered.

WAYNE ADLER. *Lights a cigarette and looks up at the ceiling.* Can't we abandon this project? What if our equipment is not powerful enough? We let the engineers work on it while we work on other projects. It would seem we're just not capable scientists after all. Perhaps archeologists could give it a go. *Sighs.* Or work hopelessly while I smoke this expensive cigar and live life.

MURIEL JANE-ADDAMS. Do you even know what you're talking about! *She slams both of her fists on the table.* Do you even know how much this equipment cost?! The company that sold us this equipment is restricted from performing all its research for objects unknown to Earth. I admit this object is not from Earth. Of course, it fell from the sky! But look at it! We can detect what it is. All we need is time, not your skepticism!

The other scientists, Jedediah Jones and Cyphur McDonald work on their computers on the other side of the room.

WAYNE ADLER. Look, take it easy. You don't have to drag all this into a situation. Maybe, you're right. Me being skeptical isn't helping matters. It's beyond my imagination to think that this state-of-the-art equipment is not able to fossick its structure. *Pauses briefly.* What are we going to do?

INT. The voltmeter deflects from 220V to 600V and above. The oscilloscope probes are attached to the box where the unknown metal is placed. The screen of the oscilloscope shows a sine wave. The wave deflects into a sine wave and then diminishes later. Samuel Marshall enters the room.

SAMUEL MARSHALL. What's going on?

CYPHUR MCDONALD. These here boys– *Clears his throat, looking at Muriel.* Excuse me. –*Moves his eyes from her to Samuel.* –are trying to solve the mystery of the spooky element. *Chuckles.*

JEDEDIAH JONES. Cut it out! At least they're engaging in something productive!

CYPHUR MCDONALD. *Scoffs.* Speak for yourself! This thing stumped me hours ago. We ain't got not a thing done since we got here. At least playing cards ain't so bad to kill some time.

SAMUEL MARSHALL. Alright, then. *Moves closer to Cobey Tobias.* How are you doing right now? Any luck?

COBEY TOBIAS ADDAMS. Just the spiked voltage surge, the usual, you know. *Shrugs.*

SAMUEL MARSHALL. *Eyeing Jedediah.* Okay. Guess we'll have to see about this now.

MURIEL JANE-ADDAMS. You want some coffee? How's the little one holding up?

SAMUEL MARSHALL. He's alright. Been missing home. I haven't figured out how I should break the news to him.

MURIEL JANE-ADDAMS. You're gonna have to tell him sooner or later about the project and home.

SAMUEL MARSHALL. Yeah, I know. I just can't compose myself and tell him the facts. It's not easy for me. Just the other week, I was not expecting to have my son with me in this secret facility. I was hoping we'd be through with this project, but here we are.

MURIEL JANE-ADDAMS. Yeah. We'll make progress. *Walks out of the room, heading to the cafeteria for six coffees.*

CYPHUR MCDONALD. *Sighs.* Yoo-hoo! What's the current voltage reading?

COBEY TOBIAS ADDAMS. *Aggravated, he slams both hands on the table, turning around to face Cyphur but speaking to the lot.* It would behoove everyone to shut up!! *Turns back around.* I can't work with such negative vibes.

CYPHUR MCDONALD. Oh 'kay. *Turns back to his work.*

WAYNE ADLER. *Sighs.* Everyone's starting to lose focus.

COBEY TOBIAS ADDAMS. *Speaks while eyeing blueprints from his computer.* I don't know why he's still here.

JEDEDIAH JONES. *Pats his little brother on the back and says in a whisper.* It's still better than working alone.

WAYNE ADLER. *Lights another cigarette and eyes the notes on the dry erase board again.* We've got to be missing a major component.

SAMUEL MARSHALL. *Walks closer to Adler, eyeing the board.* What do you think it might be that we're missing?

Muriel returns with six freshly made caffeinated beverages. She walks to each scientist, and they grab their containers. She makes her way to Cobey Tobias last.

MURIEL JANE ADDAMS. *Whispers in his left ear, handing him a coffee.* Remember Cobey! We'll make a breakthrough and show our findings to the world. *Kisses his left cheek.*

COBEY TOBIAS ADDAMS. *Smiles, looking into his wife's eyes.* Thanks! *Turns his head back to his computer.*

Muriel starts working at her station, right next to her husband. She places her coffee next to her.

INT. LAB INTERIOR.

The scientists all keep working and talking. Samuel is not looking connected to the discussion, but then something happens. Flashes emanate from the metal, going off in a sequential pattern.

SAMUEL MARSHALL. *He raises his head and stares at the metal.* Hey guys!! Something is happening here! *He's bidding them look at the metal as he points at it with surprise formed with a wrinkle on his face.*

JEDEDIAH JONES. The metal is flashing lights in sequences. I have seen it make two flashes in three seconds four times in the last minute.

MURIEL JANE ADDAMS. You've got to be kidding me?! *Typing on her keyboard, checking diagnostics.* We have checked and checked it, but it gave no result. All data has… *Her computer screen cracks. She jumps back in shock, only to be caught by her husband.* Th– Thanks.

SAMUEL MARSHALL. *Eyes never leave the metal on the table.* Look now! *He bellowed.* The metal is making flashes just like signals the Military personnel when they communicate during a mission.

CYPHUR MCDONALD. This looks bad.

WAYNE ADLER. What do we do?!!

INT. Lab lights start flickering, and power surges begin happening with electronic equipment blowing up.

COBEY TOBIAS ADDAMS. Oh no! *Takes his hands off his wife.* Looks like we've made a mistake. *Exaggerating an unimaginable theory.* This is a signal to their mother ship. *Pointing to the metal with a pencil, he directs their eyes to a black but transparent vapor under a gray metal surface.* That is the signal. I better do something.

CYPHUR MCDONALD. Hallucinating idiot.

Immediately! Everything in the entire room starts shaking. Glass breaks, and things start falling to the floor. A few seconds pass, a loud thud strikes the ceiling.

JEDEDIAH JONES. That was pure energy from the metal. I'm positive.

SAMUEL MARSHALL. Pure WHAT?!! *Looks away from his brother to his colleagues.* Everyone!! We must evacuate! Save what you ca— *A computer falls at his feet, and he jumps back, avoiding the shattered glass.*

The building is falling apart. Invisible energy waves leave the strange metal and strike the walls. Cobey, Muriel, and Wayne smash into computer equipment. Samuel is trying to send all files worked on to a private location before his computer powers down.

SAMUEL MARSHALL. Shit!! *Slams both fists on his computer desk.*

In a sharp vision, Samuel's son runs through his mind, and he takes his leave. He rushes to the children's playroom. Wayne and Jedediah are passing the lavatories, and pieces of overhead lighting fall on them.

WAYNE ADLER. Every man for himself. *Dashes off down the hallway, leaving Jedediah.*

Mr. Jones can hear voices not far behind.

Screams consisting of **HELP, HELP, HELP!!** It was all he could hear until his hearing left him and smoke from the lab swept through the halls.

Everyone took their own time to clear the main room, escaping as they all feared that they had made a grave mistake by not being thorough with their research.

The scene cuts to black.

Lights fill the area around the destroyed laboratory.

Ten minutes later, waiting outside in a field...

Wayne Adler sees a shadow walking towards him from the destroyed laboratory. Samuel is seen carrying his young son in a fluffy but torn blanket and calling out to them from the facility.

CYPHUR MCDONALD. *Shouting to the smoke figures.* Where's Cobey and Muriel?!!!!

Samuel places his sleeping son on the ground and gazes up at Wayne and Cyphur. He launches at both. He strikes Wayne across his face with all his might, and Cyphur pulls him away.

JEDEDIAH JONES. *Limping closer to Samuel, and shouts.* Brother!!

Samuel's eyes start watering, seeing his brother's wounds. Cyphur releases him, and Sam runs to his older brother.

SAMUEL MARSHALL. *Gets closer to Jedediah, bending down to his level.* You– You going to be, okay? Can you walk?!

Jedediah winces after being touched because of the burns on his body.

WAYNE ADLER. *Speaks strongly.* AH! He's– *Interrupted.*

SAMUEL MARSHALL. *Turns around angrily and shouts.* You SHUT your mouth!!!!

JEDEDIAH JONES. They didn't– *Coughs harsh.* They didn't make it.

SAMUEL MARSHALL. No. *Starts shaking his head.* I must go back–

WAYNE ADLER. And do what? Die a hero?! There's nothing left. There's smoke and no more fire!! The building is gone, Mr. Marshall!

CYPHUR MCDONALD. *Looking directly at the destroyed lab and shaking his head.* A tragedy.

The four remaining scientists mourn the sudden death of two brilliant scientists they have known for years.

A few minutes later, Cyphur starts speaking...

CYPHUR MCDONALD. We must keep this to ourselves. If this gets out–

WAYNE ADLER. This whole operation isn't US Military. How will it get out?

CYPHUR MCDONALD. What?!! *Shocked.* Oh!!!

SAMUEL MARSHALL. We make a pact to keep this between ourselves.

JEDEDIAH JONES. Going our separate ways would be best.

WAYNE ADLER. There's no need to stay together. The alien metal fled.

SAMUEL MARSHALL. Fled? *Looking at Adler in disbelief.*

CYPHUR MCDONALD. What Mr. Adler means is… After emitting strange energy out of its metal structure, it shot through the roof.

SAMUEL MARSHALL. So, we have no verification and no actual coordinates, which may lead us to its whereabouts?

WAYNE ADLER. We will find it again if it remains on Earth.

CYPHUR MCDONALD. You guys are crazy. After all of that!! You guys are daring to try this whole mess again?! Pfft. *Rolls his eyes, turns around, and walks off.* Do not bother me again.

WAYNE ADLER. *Shouts.* You speak to any–

JEDEDIAH JONES. Shush! Let him leave with some dignity.

WAYNE ADLER. Yeah. We will drop it for now.

Samuel walks over to his son, still asleep, lying on the ground wrapped in a blanket. He picks him up and holds him tight in his arms.

WAYNE ADLER. I will be heading back home. You two– *Pointing at both brothers.* –leave this be. *Drops his arm.*

JEDEDIAH JONES. *Coughs harsh three times.* Just go, Adler.

FADE OUT!

The recording finished, and the light shot back into Caj's V-Link. Commander Addams has a calm expression on his face with his right arm raised and playing with his chin.

AGENT RIT. Uh… That was –

AGENT JEIFII. Bizarre.

AGENT CAJ. You okay, sir? *Watching the commanding officer closely.*

CO. ADDAMS. Never better. *Lowering his arm, eyes still stuck on the spot where the recording played.*

AGENT Z. I'm confused about what they were doing.

AGENT CQUA. Looks like they were trying to extract information from it, but due to limited resources were unable.

AGENT Z. They didn't calculate the risk.

AGENT CAJ. Those are great conclusions. I might add, this happened on Oirailie Island. Due to various missions there, I've concluded it's where the event took place. *Sighs.* There's, unfortunately, no real evidence but the recorder I found with that recording.

CO. ADDAMS. What this means – Agent Z. You're in more danger than any of us. The agency, VLORs & VICE were not active as much until after you found that device. This is what you know already. The side missions you've been on aren't far from this in any way.

AGENT CAJ. What he's trying to say, we're keeping a close watch on you. VICE will be stepping up and will possibly seek you out more.

AGENT JEIFII. Why haven't they singled him out yet?

AGENT RIT. Yeah?

CO. ADDAMS. Before Z found the alien metal, its signature was hard to track. It cloaked itself. Attaching itself on the boy's arm reversed that. He was able to be tracked. The V-Links themselves have cloaking mechanisms and not being transformed helps to hide your identity – like when you're at school or home.

AGENT RIT. So, you have been monitoring the alien's signature like VICE?

CO. ADDAMS. To answer your question – VICE broke from VLORs, but the systems are very much the same. Our designs are similar. The recording you all saw had the founding members working on that alien metal years ago, before VLORICE.

AGENT JEIFII. That – Makes sense.

AGENT Z. It does.

AGENT RIT. About those people in the room, including the little boy.

AGENT CAJ. Two of them were killed in the explosion. As for the others, we all know Mr. Wayne Adler is the Informant. He will be hard to touch. Cyphur McDonald became a ghost after that day. No one knows what happened to him.

AGENT CQUA. What about the other two men?

AGENT Z. *Looks at the floor guiltily.* I think my grandfather knew something.

AGENT CAJ. It's a possibility, but we have no information on that yet. We've sent scouts to search, and nothing has come back. Those other two men, including the young boy in the video, are all that's left. We must discover their identities.

AGENT RIT. That's like finding a ghost. They've vanished without a trace.

The eldest agent catches the commanding officer looking elsewhere for a while.

AGENT CAJ. You good, sir? Anything you wish to add?

CO. ADDAMS. I'll continue having you run this operation and have Agents CQua and Rit assist.

AGENT CQUA. We'll help with this case.

AGENT Z. I think I should be on it, sir.

CO. ADDAMS. Negative. You know why. You'll be assigned at a later time. Agent Caj. Anything else you'd wish to share with the group?

AGENT CAJ. *Shaking his head, thinking.* Nothing I can th– Oh, yeah! *Sighs.* I'd hate to bring up my enemies. Rit knows him.

AGENT RIT. I know what?

AGENT CAJ. One of my old friends returned. He threatened you all.

AGENT RIT. Oh. You mean one of your homeboys that you joined with?

AGENT CAJ. Yup. *Looks at all the younger agents.* If you see any young man around my age. Call for backup. He's up there with me, trained to a higher degree. You all have gotten stronger, but I don't know where he's been for the past few years. He's picked up new skills.

CO. ADDAMS. You all got the latest up to date information and be careful of a former agent. We'll worry about these villains one at a time – or at least try to. The ninjas will be our priority. We will contact you all soon when a plan is in place. You're all dismissed now.

Meanwhile... At VICE HQ...

RAHZ. *Leaning near a wall at the training center. She looks depressed and is looking down, facing the ground.*

XAVIER. *Enters the room, looking to his left.* Hey there.

RAHZ. *Speaks low and murmurs.* Hey.

XAVIER. What's the matter? You seem a little down.

RAHZ. I am okay.

XAVIER. Is it one of those days that not-so-trustworthy folks cloud your life?

RAHZ. No.

XAVIER. What's the matter then?

RAHZ. *Cries.* Nothing is the matter!

XAVIER. Okay.

A few moments of silence.

XAVIER. Training to improve what you're already capable of achieving?

RAHZ. Yeah.

Another few seconds of silence.

RAHZ. You know, you can't make everyone happy in your life. You have to be that person who fully understands who the right people are and who are not. It's just so difficult to sort out the right and wrong ones.

XAVIER. That is true, but I would like to amend that by adding a few words. You don't have to please someone or to upset someone to make yourself satisfied.

RAHZ. What should be done then? Suffer until one of the sides is happy?

XAVIER. That, I clearly did not say. I think you should convince them first. Use all your logic and rationale to make them understand your point. It usually works and, trust me– *He smiles in a kind manner.* –that is the best and straightforward option for their sake.

RAHZ. What if it does not work?

XAVIER. You crush them.

RAHZ. Sounds fair.

XAVIER. It is. *He says with a smile.* You know there was a time in my life when I was sad, depressed, and angry with life?

RAHZ. You don't say! You seem like a happy-go-lucky person.

XAVIER. We all have our happy and sad times. I recently recalled a memory. I just found out recently I lost a fiancé before waking up from a 14-year coma.

RAHZ. Huh? *Curious.* That is sad.

XAVIER. Thank you. You are kind. But I am okay now. I got help, and I am better at things in life now.

RAHZ. Really? Where? How?

XAVIER. It is... *He stares at his wristwatch.* Oh no! Is this the time? I must get going. Goodbye.

RAHZ. *Watches him leave.*

After he is gone, she continues with her intense training.

Thursday, January 24, 2108
2:15 P.M.

An early release from school calls for vibin' at Teen Realm. Zada and friends are sitting at a booth.

ZADARION. There are no wings when I transform into the mechanical, metallic monster.

VALERY. Are you afraid of flying too close to the sun? *She said with a smirk on her face.*

ZADARION. What, No! *He shakes his head once.* Why would I do that?

JAYLA. He obviously never read the story about a boy who flew too close to the sun.

ZADARION. Oh! Him! Pfft. I forgot the book we read in our Literature 301 course freshman year. *He's quiet for a few seconds.* He was hard-headed and stubborn. Wasn't he?

JAYLA. Yup! That describes you to a T, Zada.

VALERY. Yes! It describes you perfectly! *She says with a joyful spirit.*

ZADARION. *He puckers his lips in a sour way.* I'd punch both of you.

VALERY. *She doesn't hesitate and gets all up in his face.* What?! Run that mouth! Let's see what you got!

JAYLA. *She's watching her two friends acting like immature children.* Shit.

ZADARION. *He respectfully grabs her shoulders calmly.* Chill, dude. I am only joking.

VALERY. *She takes two steps back.* What I thought, kid. *She lowers her head, exhales, and raises her head with a smile on her face.* It's cool! *She's smiling with her eyes closed.*

JAYLA. *She shakes her head twice.* I know the only female who can turn off her serious switch and turn on her chill switch so effortlessly.

VALERY. *She opens her eyes, looking at Jayla. She heard what she said and smiled.* Heh-heh! *She closes her eyes again and has an innocent smile on her face.*

They all enjoy a laugh and eat their food for a while. After several minutes, one of the girls has an idea of handling one of Zada's enemies.

JAYLA. This alien – I can stop him! I can erase his memory of your friend.

VALERY. Your– Your spells?

JAYLA. It's more like powerful–

VALERY. *With a smile.* –Like magic and spells.

JAYLA. *Shakes her head and smiles back.* Yes.

ZADARION. What will you do?

JAYLA. If I can get close enough and touch him, I can channel the thoughts around in his mind, thus expelling every memory he has of your secret identities.

ZADARION. I– *Shakes his head.* Unlike the commander, he doesn't like being discreet and out in the open. I can help draw him out of hiding.

VALERY. I'll help too! *Smiles with both eyes closed and opens then seconds later.*

ZADARION. Your skills have gotten– slower. Even without your Quinoragoras half? Heh. Eh, just a tad bit.

VALERY. *Scoffs.* More like 75%. *Looks away.*

JAYLA. So– You can die out there now? *Shakes her head.* Absolutely not, Valery! I'm with him. You should stay here.

VALERY. *Rolls her eyes.* Yeah, we'll see.

Someone enters the place and sees the group laughing, having a good time. The boy makes his way to their table after recognizing one of the girls.

JOEL. Hey. Can we talk for a minute?

ZADARION. Guys, I'll be back. I need to use the little boy's room. Excuse me. *He nods at the boy and makes his way to the restroom.*

JOEL. Alone, please. Could you excuse us for a minute? Just one minute.

JAYLA. Umm, sure. *She gets out of the booth and walks over to the video game area.*

VALERY. *Unconsciously considering removing the Silent Dyber left under the table.* Uh, what is this about now?

JOEL. You were right, okay. I shouldn't have played two sides. I can handle myself perfectly fine, but Morgan cannot.

VALERY. Umm, what are you saying about her?

JOEL. I'm saying – You have to talk to him. You know who. I have a plan to save her from DiLusion's dimension.

Zadarion exits the boy's restroom at this time and sees his friend is still talking to the boy from school he never once spoke to before. He looks around, and Jayla waves at him. As he's walking over, his V-Link vibrates, and he halts. Jayla sees the expression on his face and nods at him. He takes one look at Valery sitting down and turns the other way, exiting the premises.

2:36 P.M.
Dowers City near DQ's Deluxe Grocery Store

Sparks fly down around two teenage boys as they stare up at him. All they see is a villain living in the shell of the boy one of them knows.

Shocker crumbles one building after the next with his electrical powers, sending showers of sparks soon to form fires on the ground around him. He is falling in and out of consciousness, hearing a deep laugh knowing that it was his own. Inside his consciousness, he cannot figure out why he can't stop destroying. His deep-centered thought process right now is to destroy everything.

Slowly, he drifts to the ground upon spotting a couple of boys on the pavement, aware that a fight will soon be underway, building up excitement within.

Suddenly, both boys break out in a full sprint. Shocker, playing a bit of a game, gives chase. He turns and runs from the boys.

Their footsteps grow louder, and he felt his right knee buckle as one of the boys behind it kicked his leg in. Tumbling to the ground, he quickly rolls to the right as Agent Z brings down a fist in the spot he had been a moment before. Quickly he brushes himself off and rises to fight. Catching Agent Rit out of the corner of his eye, he grabs his leg as the dancer was mid-spin to kick him in the head, quickly punching him in the chest before he can regain his stability. Shocker hears a satisfying crack and Rit shakes his head.

Agent Z, trying to back the dancer, bolts at the electric boy to take him down. Both boys begin forcefully punching at each other, both trying to get a hit. Z goes over Shocker and locks onto his waist. Now, repetitively kneeing him in the waist, Rit starts cheering, thinking that he has succeeded.

The boy begins channeling electricity around him, locks onto Z, and electrocutes him to get out of the death grip. Stumbling back, Z scolds him and shakes off the tingling that coursed through his body.

Rit comes up behind and drives the side of his hand near the boy's neck. Unstable, Shocker trips over himself and blinks away black dots. Panicking, the boy channels his electricity around him, creating a shock wall, blasting them ten feet away. Flying back, the boys moan after the counterattack. Shocker takes this moment to try to run but turns around to see where they are. Suddenly, he runs straight into a cold hard surface that sends him crashing to the ground.

Feeling hands on his shoulders, one of the agents forcefully tries to slap V-Cuffs on his wrists. Sparks came from his fingertips, and the device disappeared. The agent stepped back.

He found himself surrounded. Two trained agents are staring at him as he stands back up against a brick wall. He couldn't imagine a world in which he would win this fight, but his determination had not yet failed him. Looking up, he stares into the cold eyes of his enemies as they walk ever closer to him. He vowed never to allow his fear to show. The streetlights around them go dark, and the boy's body begins glowing as he musters all his strength to harness the power around him.

He could feel the electricity in his veins, running through every limb in his body. Tingling rage, he channeled all his power and forced it into the bodies of the agents in front of him. They fly back, knocking into street railings behind.

Out of exhaustion, the electric boy slowly drifts to the ground as his glow fades. A broken melody cries to be heard behind him as the fifteen-year-old moves toward him. Gracefully, he appears to float on air. Before the young boy could register what was happening, the dancer had reached him and landed his grand leap dead into the center of his chest.

The younger agent is watching from the sidelines with a worried expression on his face, challenging his superpowered friend to get up. Resilient, the boy slowly rises off the concrete and once again begins channeling the power around him. He decides to focus on defense this time, looking for a way to escape the situation. He's accepting that he is at a loss in this battle. Caught off guard, he ends up staring the thirteen-year-old dead in the face.

He feels a blow to his stomach and retaliates with a punch to the agent's jaw. While he is reeling from that, he sends another punch to the boy's nose. A satisfying crunch rings through the air, and blood trails down the thirteen-year-olds face as he howls in pain. He electrocutes the thirteen-year-old, hoping that the pain will keep him from interfering in his escape again.

SHOCKER. One Down. *He murmurs as he searches for the dancer.*

He spots him stumbling forward and clutching his stomach from the attack. He convinces himself to stand up straight, moaning he does just that.

Strength failing him, the dancer laughs, mocking himself almost, like fighting him is a waste of his time.

The boy refuses to remind the dancer of his weakness and throws electricity at him in damaging rays, glowing like a neon sign. To no avail, his power drains, and the snarky dancer still stares at him like his power was a joke. Then he lunges at him, turning midair and connecting his heel with the boy's jaw, blood instantly poured out of his mouth. The dancer lands behind him and again rises. He elbows the boy in the back of the head, knocking him to the ground.

Trying not to give up, he tried to count on his powers once more, but all he could manage in his weakened state were gentle sparks out of his fingertips. He picks himself up off the ground and leans to punch the dancer. The dancer spun before the punch could land, and the boy once again landed on the ground. The dancer picks up the boy by his shirt collar and stands him upright, a sense of mockery playing on his smile, knowing he is too weak to defend himself.

He releases him and takes a few steps back, and the dancer then sprints full force. A massive jump sends the dancer flying. Twirling midair, the electric-powered boy stares in awe, knowing that there is nothing left he can do. But then he thought!

He closes his eyes, and instead of counting the seconds of silence, knowing that brutal pain is near, he uses his electric powers to move faster. He reversed the dancer's attack, and the dancer felt the force of two hundred pounds land on his ribcage. An ear-splitting crack rings in the ear, and suddenly Rit felt as if he could no longer breathe.

AGENT RIT. *Spits out a small amount of blood.* Clever. *A small trail of blood leaks from the corner of his mouth as he lay staring at the stars in the sky.*

A single tear finds its way from the corner of his eye, sliding to his ear and dripping onto the cold concrete below him. Shocker leans over him, smiles a satisfied smile, and walks away, making a rhythmic noise from the shoes below him. Then the world around him went silent.

After an anguishing eternity, the boy's consciousness begins to fade, choosing comfort over fear and trying to melt into the concrete. Footsteps approached him, and towering above him was his enemy, standing in a mechanized army suit. A grown man with a tablet attached to his wrist forms a smile on his face.

Agent Z didn't waste time. He got up and materialized his blaster and shot at the tablet; the man screamed and looked at his minion.

Shocker was summoning the electricity throughout his body and looked at the man with a smile. The control chip was no more, and he was free at last.

SHOCKER. *Electricity built up in one hand, he yelled.* TAZER PUNCH!

Techy Andy's laid out on the concrete, and his tablet computer is damaged beyond repair.

AGENT Z. *Laughing as he's walking beside the other agent toward Shocker.* That plan worked! *He smiles.*

AGENT RIT. I didn't buy it at first. *Smiling.* That was brilliant.

SHOCKER. Thanks. How'd you know?

AGENT Z. Well, for one. I know you wouldn't be destroying anything. You had to be controlled. It took me a minute to figure out who, but I eventually had an idea.

AGENT RIT. I'll be seeing you, Z. Make sure he gets to you know where. Later. *He teleports.*

SHOCKER. Your newest mentor?

AGENT Z. Nope. Just another agent. *He presses a few buttons on his V-Link, and the enemy is sent to Primous.* He's done for good. *He looks up at his friend.* You have nothing to worry about anymore.

SHOCKER. I owe you a million. Please! Call me whenever you need help. *He throws up the peace sign, channels his electricity, and flies off into electrical wires.*

The agent throws out an Invisi-Dome; it works its magic and disappears. He makes his way back to Teen Realm Media Center.

As he enters the building, his friends are not in sight. He checked everywhere and decided to make a call. Valery picked up, explaining they went to the local ice cream shop. She tells him they will head home for the day, and he decides to go home.

4:45 P.M.

The boy is making his way down Tarainound Street. Unaware, an older homeless man is watching him from afar. Zadarion crosses the street, and the man chooses to push his cart in the other direction.

Zada is eating cereal at the table while his mother is watching the news next to the kitchen counter, drinking her cup of coffee. The boy receives a text message from a friend asking him to come outside. The boy nearly choked, trying to finish his food. He stands up, grabs the bowl, makes his way to the sink, pours excess milk into the drain, and then sets the bowl with the rest of the dirty dishes. His mother turns and stares at him. He has a mouth full of food as he's making his way to the door.

HAILIE. Zadarion Jones. Swallow your food, please.

ZADARION. Sorry, mom. *Chews faster and swallows twice. He opens his mouth and sticks his tongue out.* Ahh!! *Closing his mouth.* All done. May I go out?

HAILIE. *Shaking her head.* Teens. Have fun, boy.

He opens the door and sees Valery standing outside on the lawn, waiting for him with her phone in hand. Zada closes the door and the two start walking.

Elsewhere, near HighTech City…

UNNAMED MAN 1. This city is trash, you hear me. Garbage!! *He shouted.*

An older adult is visibly drunk to his drinking companion outside a crummy bar. It's lit up by the poor illumination of neon lights in the streets, which the rain had already damaged.

UNNAMED MAN 2. I came here twenty years ago looking for the dream that only the city can give you. HA! All I got were ulcers, kidney damage, and damn lumbago.

UNNAMED MAN 1. Let's not exaggerate. I've done well. *He replied as he held the bottle of rum in his hands to his mouth.*

The previous angry gentleman, as if resigned, started staring at a puddle of water with a lost look. By the time he realized what was happening, it was too late. Some black whips came quickly out of the puddle and rolled around his neck and limbs, devouring him. Everything happened so fast that his partner barely had time to scream and pee himself. When the shock went away, and he came to, he ran as far away from that place as he could, screaming with fear. And suddenly, silence claimed the site, and the rain came down again.

Three agents, hiding in plain sight, saw what took place. They're in shock, on a mission to investigate an abandoned subway station on the outskirts of the city.

CQUA. What – What in the world was that? Doc Krarns back?

JEIFII. Judging by those tentacles, I think not. It's possible a new cross-human or a genetic experiment gone wrong.

RIT. Scary. Are cross-humans capable of doing that to people?

CQUA. Who knows what we're getting ourselves into.

JEIFII. Don't lose focus on the mission. Some ghost organization is out there capturing people with abilities. We have to locate the ex-military members Z fought.

CQUA. Yeah. We'll find them.

JEIFII. Good, you're back and not a complete zombie. Now advance – and this time, please don't fall.

The young man looked at his partner with a punchy face.

CQUA. Well, if you give me a good impulse this time, I assure you that I will not. You need more strength in those little arms. *He responded in a burlesque tone as he put his foot back into his partner's hands.*

His companions told the boy that he was distracted while seeing a man being eaten alive.

RIT. This mountain is excellent at this height, you can see the whole city, and the sky is clear today and... *A blow to the head interrupted him. He said, realizing. He turned slowly and angrily.*

JEIFII. I – *Shakes her head.* Will you two be quiet and pay attention? Don't keep wasting time, or I'll put on my suit and throw a much heavier one.

Rit was left wanting to answer his partner, but he knew he was right. He got up and went to the ledge and stretched out his hand so his fellow agents could pull him up.

CQUA. Well, it looks like I found an entrance. *He said as he lifted the grate, he found hidden in the middle of rocks. He looks to the female agent.* Jei, just as we planned, you're staying here to see that no onlookers find us. Rit... You are coming with me. *He jokes.* Don't be thinking of any nonsense while we go in, or we're dead men. We don't know what's down here. Remember to maintain additional power to the invisibility. Wouldn't want our presence known just yet. This is just a recon assignment. No combat.

JEIFII. *She sneered, answering thoughtfully.* If he wasn't capable enough, he wouldn't be here in the first place.

The two boys jumped through the grate and fell many feet below. The girl readied her eyes to the surroundings for any intruders then heard a splash behind her. She turned slightly in disgust. A few seconds later, a voice came from the background.

JEIFII. All clear? *She shouted.*

CQUA. Affirmative. It's almost five meters, but there's more up ahead. I'll radio you. Continue keeping watch. Come on, Rit.

She could hear the slapping of water as the boys walked, advancing further. The last thing she could hear then silence.

Meanwhile…
New Waii Island …
On the beach…

Young Rivi's glassy eyes scanned the blue surface, which stretched as far as one's gaze traveled. The soothing winds which swept over the ocean now carried a strange foreboding smell. It hit his face giving him the exact caution he needed.

It was time to duck as a massive ball of water plunged out of the ocean, ripping the waves apart from where it emerged. He stumbled, hip-planting into the sand as he stared up at the ball hovering in midair. Due to the blazing sun behind it, his eyes squinted, making nothing clear, but he sure saw the water crazily dancing itself into the shape of an orb.

As unbelievable as it already was, a voice echoed from within the water orb. *LAND!*

In an instant, Rivi knew he commanded more than what a man could dream. He dove aside just moments before the orb came crashing down where he had been a while ago. When he whipped his head around in uncertainty, things became even harder to grasp upon finding a man; a young man with a light beard and eyes of the devil now standing where the ball had landed.

CHIMOUS. Hello, little one. *The man chirped.* From the aura you are giving off, I'd say we meet again.

He didn't stand too far away from him, yet the boy was still in a state of surprise when the wizard informed him of the reason for his sudden arrival.

CHIMOUS. I, Chimous, have come to take your life. Runner.

Not understanding more than just 'Hello,' the boy tilted his head. Not that the man needed the small, frail boy to answer back. He was just fulfilling the formality before he could officially begin with the task he just announced.

Chimous straightened his arm, having his palm face the ground as he began to whisper some unfamiliar words.

The ground starts to shift beneath them. Rivi scrambles to his feet, staring at the sand, which had suddenly started to fly around the man. His shocked expressions made it hard for him to stop staring and start running.

The amount of sand thrashing against the man was crazy. Everything started to become muddy, and suddenly, Chimous whispered the final command.

The sand collided against itself and formed into large black spears was enough to throw the boy off balance. He had not even had a proper look or straightened up when, with a flick of Chimous's wrist, one of the spears came flying like a bullet towards him. His eyes widened, and between the shock, he rolled away. The moment the black spear dug itself into the ground, it deformed back, mixing with the sand.

Then two more of them came, and Rivi dodged them successfully. He did not try to counter the attacks because he wasn't sure how it would turn out for him since it was magic, and he was not familiar with the art.

CHIMOUS. Cocky little brat, aren't you? *He clicked his tongue and raised both his hands by his side.*

His face was towards the sky, which suddenly grew darker, and the waters were as if being tortured. The waves climb upon themselves, daring to drown humanity.

Watching the man lifting from the ground as he released enormous amounts of energy, two things Rivi was sure of. The man commanded magic, and so, he was a wizard here to kill him... He was the magic-user from before. The one Z helped send to Primous. But how did he escape?

While in his thoughts, he missed out on the rest of the spell only to hear the final call.

CHIMOUS. CONQUER!!

And suddenly, lightning struck the ocean, bringing the water to life. The water, filled with twitching lightning, was advancing. It crawled upon the shore, taking the form of a beast.

No matter how fast Rivi ran, it was at his heels, and then it roared. The amplitude of the voice made the boy drop down to his knees and quiver under his skin. While the sky and the ocean faced a storm, the boy turned his head around only to be horrified by a water monster with lightning twitching in its eyes and fluid-like claws.

When it opened its mouth, there was a void – a black hole fixed in its throat. It rumbled like thunder, ready to suck everything in and reduce it to pieces.

Rivi's eyes were still wide in the face of death, but he wasn't afraid when –

The monster busted suddenly, reducing to nothing but some stains of water on the beach's sand.

The clouds twisted into themselves, leaving a clear blue sky behind, and the ocean's cries died down like a wailing baby put to sleep.

With a quick turn of their heads, both the boy and man faced another who had a galaxy-like portal closing behind him. His fingers were still in the position of a snap.

And now the boy wondered. The monster, the storms, all that magic had faced – its end to that was one snap of a finger?

He found this chance a golden one and immediately scrambled to his feet. Though his legs shook due to the magic pressure, he still managed a good pace.

Right after feeling an offensive magic power Chimous once again summoned a weapon. The new guy lands on the ground. The wrapped water around his arms formed into crystal-like chains with sharp-headed kunai. He jumped and swung in the air to provide the necessary force to the chains, and the kunai clashed with the other man's blade.

The magic fight turned into a battle of skills. Chimous was pushing this new guy back to the water's edge. He jumped and slammed his dual blades, but before he could slice the man up, the man deformed the chains into a spear, and it tore through his arms. He took it out and stabbed it again through his ribs. The wizard did not back off and made a cross attack that scratched through his shoulder.

This new guy jumped back and took back steps on rushing water waves. He had a surge of magma rising from deep within the ocean and circling his suspended, cloaked body. The wizard had cast a shield around himself.

UNNAMED WIZARD. Fiery Envelop! *He spoke the spell quite indifferently, and the strings of magma excitedly wrapped around Chimous's shield.*

His urge to resist wasn't enough. The magma shattered the shield into tiny pieces, like glass eventually tightening around a frantic, screaming Chimous. Wherever they touched, his body turned into melted wax, but the strings never stopped, not even after reaching his inner organs.

The new wizard watched him with an indifferent expression plastered over his face. When the anguish-filled screams died down, he sluggishly turned on his heels in midair only to disappear into the portal, leaving no remains of Chimous behind.

LENE. *Her heart sank, having watched the whole thing.* Why were you so stupid, brother? Please, don't let it be true. *She mumbled amidst tears, sensing his life force fading away, and had come to inspect, but she was late to the scene.*

The woman watched helplessly. She let out a guttural wail. With a deeply hurt heart, she glanced up at the man leaving the scene – Asarios, a wizard she never encountered before.

LENE. You'll pay for this. *She stated, as her voice conveyed pain.*

Landing in a different area, somewhere near Eximpplest Town, South Carolina.

ASARIOS. *He took a few steps away from his manifested portal, looking out at the surroundings before looking back at the portal with a smirk seeing a woman exiting.* Really? *Facing her completely.* Then, make me. *He challenged as he took several paces backward.*

LENE. *A single thought dominated her being – vengeance.* **Conjuregris Horrenuds aeris**. *She chanted angrily.*

Two air blades flew at the young man, one aimed at his neck and the other at his midriff. He was ready. He jumped and rolled between the blades.

Blinded by anger, Lene began to run forward in a sprint to finish him off. She did not hear him utter a counterspell. And she did see him fall flat on the ground. The last thing the female wizard heard was a whooshing sound as the air blades rushed back at her to slice through parts of her body and part of her head off by the mouth. Silence filled the air.

ASARIOS. *He stood and stared down proudly at the spectacle before him.* Hmm, I thought she would be a challenge. *He chuckled.*

There was someone else nearby; Asarios picked up the scent just now. He inhaled and sighed, closing his eyes with a smile.

Rage was visible in Rodgist's eyes as he glanced at the smirking figure before him. Asarios stood slender but muscular. With the gentle, bemused expression plastered on his face, one couldn't have guessed he had just murdered a wizard in cold blood. He used instant teleportation to appear thirty paces away from this murderer.

RODGIST. *His blood boiled with overwhelming anger, shaking his body lightly.* You'll pay. *He muttered in-between clenched teeth, pointing at Asarios to drive his point home.*

ASARIOS. *Shrugs nonchalantly.* Make me.

As soon as the words left his mouth, Rodgist jumped in the air, muttering a spell under his breath, and sped hurriedly towards his opponent, throwing a few kicks at him from midair. Asarios sidestepped the first kick and grabbed his second leg, throwing him onto the ground. Dust rose high.

The fall was hard, but Rodgist couldn't bear to dwell on the pain as he jumped back up again, rushing at Asarios aggressively as if he had not just been slammed onto the ground. Asarios parried each of the heavy punches with ease, dodging and sidestepping several others. He launched a counterattack, punching Rodgist in the chest where his rib cages diverged. Rodgist flew backward several yards but landed on his feet and hands this time. From under his eyes, he glared up at the chuckling wizard stranger.

ASARIOS. Your attacks are feeble. You want to hurt me? You'll have to do better than this. *He teased.*

RODGIST. *Provoked beyond reasoning.* **Augumentes Geodis.** *He incanted. With his arms outspread, he raised the stones around them, sharpening them into blade-edged rocks. The objects floated in the air for a couple of seconds before he hurled them at his enemy.*

ASARIOS. *With a quick reaction, he slams his foot against the ground and shouts.* **Protecto!**

Instantly, a transparent protecting dome covered him, repelling the sharp projectiles. However, one of the stones infiltrated the space and lodged itself in his arm. He winced in pain, but he made sure not to bring down his dome until the last of the projectiles had bounced off it.

When he knew he was momentarily safe, he brought down the dome and inspected his arm. He was lucky; the blade stone had hit the edge of his shoulder. The cut was substantial, but it would not prevent him from using his arm.

ASARIOS. *He pulled out the stone with a groan and gripped it in his right palm. Absurdly, he took it to his mouth and licked the stone's edge.* Hmm. Sharp, and the juice on it – delicious. *He darted out his tongue to show the blood on his lip and swallowed down hard, maintaining eye contact.*

Rodgist was taken aback by the oddity his adversary was displaying. He took a defensive pose in anticipation of whatever may be thrown at him. He would not be distracted into letting down his guard.

ASARIOS. *After completing his self-gratifying theatricals, he lifted his chin, pointed the blade stone at his opponent, and calmly stated.* Should I gut you with your blade?

RODGIST. You'll try. *He retorted.*

It was evident in his gait that he could not cover at the sight of a threat adversary. Asarios chuckled heartily, but his expression turned ice cold in a flash, and he charged at his opponent.

If Rodgist had not been quick on his feet, he would have lost his life. Asarios had cast a spell to increase his running pace, and he had tried to slice his throat with the stone blade. The towering man jumped backward in the nick of time and saw the edge pass right before his eyes. His reflexes were as good as his mind's processing speed as he had leaned back all the way. He touched the ground with his palm to brace himself while his legs flew up. One kicked the stone out of Asarios's hand and the other connected with his neck. Asarios tumbled sideways and went down.

RODGIST. *Not cutting him any slacks.* **Restraino Geiodis!** *He barked, and parts of the ground protruded to form cuffs around Asarios's limbs.*

Like an animal in a hunter's trap, Asarios struggled to pry himself free, but the stone cuffs didn't budge an inch. Rodgist wasted no time; he went for the kill. He jumped up, intending to land his foot on this murderer's neck to crush his throat. Asarios saw impending death come at him, and he knew even if he could break the cuffs, he wouldn't be able to roll away quickly enough. An idea, though far-fetched, crossed his mind, and he decided to act on it as the delay was a luxury he and his dear throat couldn't afford.

ASARIOS. *He called out.* **Windus Exvicteum!**

Just as Rodgist was about to land on his throat and end his life, a whirlwind shot out from the ground beside them and hit him in the chest, throwing him away. He traveled a long distance in the air before using a counterspell to balance himself and land gently. By then, Asarios had found a way out of his restraint; he had cast a spell to absorb soil, and he slid a few meters into the ground before coming back up, with the cuffs having fallen apart. He stood up, shaking sand out of his hair as he cast another spell.

Rodgist's eyes widened in a mix of shock, amazement, and trepidation when he saw rocks begin to cling to his enemy's body like a magnet. They covered every part of his cloaked body except his eyes, ears, nose, and mouth. He struggled to comprehend what his eyes were seeing as it seemed like he was staring at a boulder-shaped man. His confusion turned into fear when the boulder-shaped man began to charge at him. Rodgist hurled winds to deter him, but they were parted with counterspells. Asarios balled up his fists, and they glowed red as he muttered spells after spells to maximize his abilities in this form.

When the gap between them had been reduced to only a few meters, Rodgist admitted that the wind fights were futile. The two adversaries stared at each other in the eye, trying to read the expressions in them to anticipate their next moves. Rodgist considered saying something, but being a man of few words, he was short of any. He would instead let his fist do the talking. He created air gloves to cushion his hands and threw a left hook at Asarios's head. The punch landed with a dull ***thunk;*** Asarios felt his head ring, the blow compounded by the stone suit. He hadn't thought that move through. Still, he didn't get any second to think as his opponent threw a left uppercut at his jaw. This time, Asarios's quick reflexes came to his rescue. He leaned sideways, the blow missing him by inches, and counterattacked by grabbing Rodgist by the wrist.

RODGIST. Ahhh. *He cried out as searing pain wracked his body, emanating from his fiery wrist.*

In his moment of distraction, the air gloves disappeared from his hands, but he wasn't aware of this just yet. Realization dawned on him when he threw another punch at Asarios's head with his free hand, and he heard a crunching sound. He couldn't tell which came first – the sound or compounding pain.

ASARIOS. *He capitalized on this by grabbing his second hand.* Gotcha. *He said, smiling behind his stone mask as he gripped his wrists tighter.*

The sound of sizzling flesh filled the air, shortly followed by his opponent's screams. Asarios grinned widely, subtly mad that his enemy couldn't see his face. He threw his head back as far as he could, and like a swinging wrecking ball, he slammed it against Rodgist's forehead with all his might. The man cried out as his face contorted in pain. When he hit his stone head against him a second time, Rodgist believed that his skull was starting to crack. His senses were jarred, his eyes were blurry, and the only thing in focus was the splitting headache that seemed to scream at him every second. The pain was so much that he even momentarily forgot that his wrists were being fried. A few seconds later, the scent like that of roasting mutton was a subtle reminder of his predicament. Rodgist knew a spell or two that could help him in this situation, but his head was being slammed so hard that his brain couldn't sit in his skull peacefully enough to conjure a coherent thought. Asarios loved adversity; he was competitive.

After pounding Rodgist's head a few more times, he realized he had incapacitated his opponent. This thrill was starting to drain from his body. He craved to fight, to taste blood in his mouth once more before finishing off this opponent who had put up so much struggle. He hadn't battled a wizard this powerful in a long time, and he wouldn't want that fun to end just yet. Asarios let go of his hands, grinning as he watched his opponent keel over with his head hung low, his arms flailing about lifelessly like paper in a storm, and blood dripping from his bloodied face. His mouth and nose were like canals for the crimson liquid.

Asarios felt close to fulfillment. At superhuman speed, he delivered quick punches into Rodgist's stomach with his hot, stony hands.

Rodgist leaned further forward with each blow until his legs betrayed him; they could no longer support his muscular frame anymore, so they parted, and he came crumbling to the ground. Like a fallen gladiator in an arena, there was a sense of inevitability to this noble wizard's fall. Rodgist lay still, face down in the sand. Every single nerve in his body reminded him of how much suffering he had gone through. His pain was absolute.

ASARIOS. Here lies the great wizard, Rodgist. He fell to the might of Asarios, the brave hero of Xeiar. *He said with arms wide, as he looked around at the barren land with pride in his eyes as if he was being cheered on by thousands of invisible spectators.*

As he spoke, the rocks on his body began to fall away, revealing a champion underneath. There was no need for the protection of the stones anymore; his enemy had been pounded into the ground. What remained was the finishing kill. He thought of beautiful, sinister ways to send the wizard before him into the abyss.

At the grim reaper's doorway, Rodgist's shroud of pain was infiltrated by memories. There were places, people, times, and emotions. However, of the lot, what stuck to his mind the most were thoughts of his comrades. From a void, he heard himself whisper, *"I should've killed her."*

At that moment, Rodgist felt like he had been transported into Nirvana – a complete state of peace. He felt no pain, worry, or sorrow. Never in his life had he ever had such clarity. He knew what to do.

RODGIST. *While lying flat on the dusty ground, he croaked.* **Memento restorarmus.**

At first, nothing happened. A few seconds later, his injuries began to heal. The scars on his hands slowly dissipated, so did the ache in several parts of his body. His head still hurt. The spell couldn't fully heal him, but it restored a quarter of his health. It was enough to give him more of a fighting chance.

ASARIOS. *He's surprised to see his opponent move as the man feeble attempts to stand up.* Ha. You've got some tenacity. I feared I had lost you. It would've been a real letdown to lose a plaything. *He stated with a mischievous glint in his eyes.*

The towering man was able to stand on his feet. He turned to his opponent with murderous intent in his eyes. Asarios was spooked, but he tried to play it down with a nervous chuckle and playful quip. Rodgist was out for a pound of flesh, and he would get it even if he had to rip it off his enemy's body.

RODGIST. **Malevendus.** *He uttered.*

An adrenaline pump spell had a downing effect when it wore off in an hour or less after casting it. Rodgist did not mind the side effects. Deep inside, he knew he would finish him off within the next five minutes, way before it wore off. Asarios was nearing the end of his game. There was no more pleasure left in this battle; he was ready to finish off the wizard. He began to conjure a mighty whirlwind. With his new energy surge, Rodgist charged at him with a renewed spirit. The whirlwind was rushing towards him at an incredible pace, but he did not relent.

RODGIST. *About two yards away from the angry ball of air, he incanted.* **Levitaotum Geoidis.**

The rocks that had fallen to Asarios's side suddenly jumped up and enclosed him. Rather than just protect him, they crushed him into a pulp before he could even blink. Instantly, the whirlwind died down. The weary wizard didn't stop running until he got to Asarios position. He looked down wearily at the pool of viscera and limbs before him.

RODGIST. *He watched in satisfaction for a minute before spitting at what was left of him.* Pathetic. *He muttered as he sat beside the pile of rocks, weary.*

ASARIOS. Pathetic, indeed. *Reappearing ten paces from where the dummy was crushed as he's dusting himself off.*

RODGIST. H – How? *He's dumbfounded.*

ASARIOS. An artificial copy I manifested. Think back. *He laughs.* I'm sure you'll remember when I cast it.

RODGIST. *Feeling the effects of his boost wearing off. He's breathing heavily.*

ASARIOS. You know. You are one evil wizard. *He taps the right side of his forehead.* Xeiar Hunter, eh? Going after your kind with three others, including a boy's mother here on this planet.

RODGIST. *Struggling with the effects of his spell.* They – They are traitors.

ASARIOS. And what are you to your people? *He chuckles.* Xeiars are terrible. *Laughs.* Too bad the Greats aren't around anymore to pass judgment. I'll reward you.

RODGIST. Do not mock me. *He channels an aura around his body and speeds at the wizard mocking him with one last effort.*

Asarios doesn't hesitate. He snaps his fingers. Daggers made of stone shoot out of the ground and impale him, stopping him from advancing. Fire engulfs the man's body and incinerates him to ashes in a matter of minutes.

ASARIOS. Long live the last Xeiar hunter. Hahahaha.

Elsewhere, an older woman is released from magical light-based restraints. She disappears into light and appears at her home in Florida, passed out on the kitchen floor.

Meanwhile, somewhere in the vicinity of HighTech City…

A mechanical door was blocking the long, narrow road full of wires and with very little visibility.

RIT. *He advanced further.* First obstacle– *He said, analyzing the door.* Any idea to open it? *He continued longer, watching the door.*

CQUA. *Grabs Rit's right arm firmly and whispers.* We have our answers. After three places, this one is giving me strange vibes.

RIT. Well, what is it? One we search for. *He is pulled back and pulls his arm out of the agent's grip. He steps back without saying anything.*

CQUA. See the lines below. Notice the off-changing aroma in the air. Behind that door isn't registering with our V-Links.

RIT. *Nods.* Yea.

CQUA. It was opened not too long ago. We're not the first ones to come through here. Let's return to HQ.

Rit's walking behind CQua, still thinking about what lies behind that door.

CQUA. Don't let the invisibility lose power; we're almost close to Jei's location. We'll teleport out together. From here, we must be much more careful.

The Asian-American teen boy nodded his head, and the two continued down the tunnel.

10:47 A.M.
A mile away from Drekal Park District...

ZADARION. That plan sounds a bit far-fetched. You got this from Shadow boy? We can't trust him!

VALERY. Listen, Z. He's messed up in the head, but I think he's trying to atone for what he caused. He wants us to rescue Morgan from that alien monster.

ZADARION. Or somehow get this device off my arm. No, we are not doing that.

VALERY. Pfft. *She rolls her eyes.* What plan do you have for getting her back? I would love to hear it. He has the most logical planning.

ZADARION. So, you can go out in the field and have VLORs and VICE target you. No, thanks.

VALERY. I don't need you protecting me.

At this time, his V-Link goes off.

ZADARION. Oh, great. There's trouble near Laroouse. *He looks at his friend.* Please, Veri. Trust me. I have a plan to get her back. Later. *He takes off running to a safe place to transform and teleport.*

VALERY. Hm. *Smiling. She turns and walks off in the other direction.*

11:09 A.M.
Meanwhile, at Anqua Industries...
Laroouse City, Illinois

The terrible news is making rounds this morning as a villain wreaks havoc in the city. He's invincible, destroying everything that crosses his path and putting down anyone that's trying to stop him. He is dangerous and ruthless. No ordinary bullets can penetrate his armor. As he's continuing his assault, there appear to be some flashes of familiar color.

A hero is headed straight towards him at indescribable speed. Soon, they both collide and crash. The impact is felt throughout the building. The collision caused a massive eruption, shattering a few windows, bending support beams, and damaging the water pipes gushing water from different parts of the building.

The villain starts shooting fire at the hero, but the agent kid is making a run for it– crouching, ducking, and jumping from one rooftop to the next, trying to escape from the direct heat of the villain's assault.

The hero dived inside a nearby swimming pool to escape the intense fire. Omnifari followed suit, chuckling. He squats as he places his left palm on the edge of the pool. At a split second, the pool begins to freeze until the entire surface is covered with ice. The villain looks for the sign of the hero and thinks he has frozen to death.

Skepticism would not allow him to leave as he peered down into the pool, searching for a corpse.

Suddenly, the hero leaps out of the pool in minutes like a projectile rocket tearing the surface of the pool and landing a devastating blow center mass. The villain staggers back a little at the second, avoiding a potentially fatal blow. He managed to grab the hand of the hero. With the boy in shock, he reaches for his other hand, spiraling him around before he releases him. He's sent crashing to another part of the pool with a frozen surface.

The hero's back is hurting, and he is breathing heavily on the ice surface. The villain takes a leap and tries to land on his stomach, but the hero quickly shifts from the position, and the villain cracks the ice open and sinks in.

For a while, everywhere was quiet, with no movement beneath the ice. Agent Z heaves a sigh of relief. By the time he makes a fifth step, the villain pulls himself out with force like an erupting volcano, shattering the ice as he emerges. It appears he triggered a seismic quake from his boots. The vibration from this eruption struck the hero hard, and he fell—the boy groans.

The angry villain comes all-out, gun blazing, firing incessantly toward the boy's line of sight. Few attacks strike near, and explosions go off. The boy stands and speeds forward, zigzagging to avoid being hit. In his attempt to maneuver around them, he lands in an awkward position on his back and sprains his left leg.

The villain smiles and tries to take advantage of this outcome. The agent manages to stand up, though his leg is hurting. It's not as bad; he'll be careful not to put any extreme pressure on it.

He sprints forward in a hurry, grabbing a piece of steel off the floor of the rooftop and strikes the man's armor. It's futile. The villain's armor is too strong. Omnifari grabs the hero by his throat and slams him on the floor. He releases him and attempts to stomp him, but the hero swiftly finds his feet and countered. He gave the villain a sidekick to his jaw using his uninjured leg. The villain staggers. The hero throws himself at him, launching a series of punch combos, straight punches, low jabs, two spinning back fists, and an uppercut.

This assault has angered him. He yanks the hero's left arm as he attempts a left hook and deals him a jab to the face. The agent falls, exhausted and gasping for air. The villain lifted a heavy piece of nearby concrete weighing approximately five hundred pounds to decimate the hero. Still, he caught his breath and performed a swift twisting maneuver before it landed on top of him. He throws a small object at the villain to distract him and sends a punch straight at the villain's left cheek. The villain is standing firm, half his body twisted to the right. It's like the attacks from the hero are not hurting him.

Omnifari runs straight at the hero with a spear-shaped metal. The boy ducked and countered with a materialized blade. He swings valiantly at the villain, and he's struck across his body. He recovers quickly and sends a bicycle kick to the advancing hero.

The agent lowers himself, trying to send a blow to a kneecap, but the villain quickly maneuvers by delivering a swerving strike with his right leg to bring the hero down. He grabs his legs, spirals him around for a second time, and shoves him over the ledge of the roof and to the street light stand on the ground below. He fell quite a few stories.

The man jumped off the building and landed a few feet away from the boy. He did not wait at all and charged. He grabs the hero again as quickly as he can and pulls more strenuous on his head.

He transitions to the Up Knee, using the knee strike to hit the hero right in the face.

The boy staggers; he could have a concussion.

It looks like he's scampering for breath using a recovering advantage, but the villain won't let him have it. He uses the extended knee and moves forward with his strike; he aims for the soft parts of the abdomen to exert some damage.

The hero is in so much pain now, and the villain is about to finish him off, but as he approaches the boy, he feels a sudden loss of strength. The armband on the hero's upper right arm starts glowing. It seems like the armband is reacting to something.

As Omnifari is losing his strength, the hero's power is growing, and the glowing brightens through the white sleeve of his shirt, emitting a gold-like glitter. The radiant extends to his entire body. The light gets so bright that the villain must cover his face, shielding himself with his left arm.

There was a superposition effect with the lights; it shines so bright and explodes like an EMP. The hero is suddenly transformed, wearing a glowing suit of armor and helmet. He's like a shiny cybernetic dragon, and charges emanate from the armor.

The hero's filled with overwhelming energy now. Within seconds, it sends him into a frenzy.

The villain becomes scared and unsettled after experiencing the mysterious transformation. He decides to throw everything he has all at once. He launched fire and ice strikes, but this proves powerless against the invigorated superhero. The attacks are obliterated before they even get near him.

The hero charges at him.

The villain tries to launch a final devastating flaming-ice spear attack combo, but the armored hero manages to get a grip on the villain's head under his left arm and launches elbow strikes repeatedly to the back of the neck. He grabs his right arm, twists it a bit, and slams the man over his shoulder; it almost felt like the hero ripped his arm out of its socket. The villain is on the ground, wailing in pain on top of the cracked concrete. The villain's right arm is incapacitated. He has only his left arm and legs to fight with, but it doesn't look like the superhero will take any chances.

The man is unsteadily starting to stand.

The hero starts sending some punches to the defenseless villain's body, turning his body into a punching bag. He nearly cracks a few ribs and finishes up with an uppercut that throws the villain off his feet. He lands hard on a parked bus. The superhero launches his fully armored right foot and stomps his stomach— blood gushes out of the villain's mouth and nose. He steps off his heels, speeds away, and aims at him. He lands near and sends a straight punch right at the man's chest, destroying the mecha-suit in the process. The meteorite inside shattered into several pieces. Lights expelled out of it and into the hero.

Omnifari has been defeated, but another fight starts— internally. The suit is so powerful that it's fighting him on the inside, wanting to take over for control. He throws both arms out to the side. He's yelling at high decibels. Lights are shooting out of him; they're not harmful. He tries to pull the suit off, but it's not happening. Although the suit helped defeat the villain, he cannot fathom the strangeness he feels now. He struggles with his new identity and destroys things around him to subdue the new power he has acquired from his new suit. It's different from the transformation at Boosechaimou, in the

MieLiMeiLi Desert – *The place resembles a giant desert, but it's just a vast crater-sized hole in the ground.*

Whatever the case, Zadarion is inside trying his most challenging to find the sheer will to resume control over his body.

Meanwhile, the recent activity resulting from the transformation has triggered interest in headquarters. The operators at VLORs HQ have been monitoring the activity closely since the beginning. Strange alien elemental properties are coming from the boy's new suit of armor, along with health warnings.

CO. ADDAMS. *He's watching the operators at work, looking at the monitors. He's concerned for the poor kid.* Whatever that is, it doesn't look good. *Tightening his fists.* We don't have a choice. I don't want to do this, but – *He raises his voice.* Send another agent down there to contain him. Do it now!!

They send another to Agent Z's coordinates to investigate the new development and put things under control.

Downtown Laroouse City, right outside of Anqua Industries...

Agent Rit arrives. He sees a man lurking near and acting suspiciously. The man is posted near the side of the building. The agent tosses a rock at the man who is not paying attention, then he turns his head and finds that Z is still struggling with his new power. He did want to attack, but this wasn't the time to show a test of who's stronger. He ran closer to the massive spikes of energy. The boy is constantly yelling, expelling white lights everywhere. Rit noticed there's no Invisi-Dome, so he activated one. Upon materialization of the dome, the creature turns to the new person. There's no yelling anymore, just low growls. He looks like he wants to attack Agent Rit, but then something manages to get a hold over his senses.

AGENT Z. Rit!! *Breathing harshly.* What are you doing here?! I could hurt you! Please– I can't control it. It's– It's too powerful! Aahhh. Please go! *He exclaimed.*

AGENT RIT. Z! You could've hurt me if you wanted to, but you didn't. You stopped!! I know you are still in there. You're the one in control! Don't let that armband take possession of you! Do you hear me?! Hang in there, buddy. You got this!!

AGENT Z. Ahh!! *He's struggling internally, but the pressure's starting to diminish.* Listen, I can't. *Breathing erratically.* It's too powerful; I can't shut it off. *He winces.*

Suddenly, he fires back. No yelling. No screaming. He tightened his core and controlled his breathing.

AGENT RIT. *Realizing the calm, internal battle his comrade is having inside of him.* There you go, buddy! Yes, you can. You are in control, man. Never forget! Now – Take over!!!! *He is closer now, placing his left hand gently on Z's right shoulder.* Fight it. Take control.

The white lights disappear, and his entire body glows again. He's returned to his agent attire in seconds.

AGENT Z. *His blood has stopped racing; his heartbeat is normal, and the suit is under control. He looks up at the other agent.* Thank you. *Breathing heavily.* You're good with words, ya' know.

AGENT RIT. Hehe. Yeah, whatever. By the way, I found Cameron Casey lurking. The two must've teamed up after escaping prison last year. I threw a rock and clocked him in the head. He's at Primous now. You're welcome. *He helps his comrade stand.*

AGENT Z. *Confused stare.* What the –?

The two teleport to HQ.

Meanwhile...
Somewhere near Newoluir's Lake

SHAVENGER. You can't defeat me by yourself! You're hiding in the form of a human!!

DILUSION. *He stops and relaxes his body. He has his eyes closed. After five seconds of breathing in and out slowly, he reopens his eyes. Lilori speaks.* I wanted this. He has no control over me. *DiLuAH speaks.* Do you see? *He chuckles.* I thought you knew, Joel?

SHAVENGER. Don't you call me by my real name!!! *He pounds his fist into his other hand.*

DILUSION. Heh. How did you think this would go? You are the one who has been deceiving me and VICE HQ. I cannot have my ascension ruined. You know that.

SHAVENGER. *He tightens his fists and slowly stands, grimacing at his former mentor.* I'll have to kill you.

DILUSION. Say what now? *He positions his left ear closer to him.* Seriously. I do not think I heard you correctly. *He turns his head, facing him.*

SHAVENGER. *He exhales.*

DILUSION. Well – Make a move any day now. You already know I can track you wherever you teleport. *He shakes his head.* No friends – At all. Who would– Could! –Save you from me?

Joel knew the odds were stacked against him but fight; he must. The evil, alien-human had to be subdued. He's in his shadowy form and glaring at the man across from him. With the bright illumination of the place, he knew it was only a matter of time before he was spotted. At that moment, the middle-aged man glanced up and saw the solo shadow cast against a wall without a body.

DILUSION. *A smile crossed his face.* Your parlor tricks are amusing. Come out of the shadows and face me like a grown-up.

The teenager knew his cover was blown. He clenched his fists in his shadowy form before appearing in his human body.

SHAVENGER. Let's do th– *He's interrupted with a heavy punch in the guts. He slid several paces backward.*

The man had eliminated the distance between them by teleporting, and the boy wasn't in any way prepared for it.

DILUSION. Way ahead of you. *He said with a mischievous cock of his eyebrows.*

The boy's eyes lit up in anger, and he teleported behind the man to land a blow on his head, but the moment he reappeared, the man had predicted his move and grabbed him by the throat. Joel gasped for air as he tried to pry his hands away from his neck while kicking frantically. His struggles seemed to fuel DiLusion's determination as he lifted him off the ground and slammed his back against a white concrete wall.

Joel tried to grab at the man's face with the hope of sticking his fingers into his eyes or pushing him away, but the attempt was futile. The man saw the hand come at him, and he slapped it away. Throwing his head back to gather momentum, he head-butted Joel in three rapid successions. Tiny whimpers escaped his restricted lungs, and his eyes bulged in response to the doubled-up assault.

The younger man's nose broke, standing askew to one side as blood trickled down his nostrils.

With the intense, emotionless look in the man's eyes, Joel knew he was hell-bent on ending his life. DiLusion was currently close to achieving that as Joel began to get dizzy. His brain seemed to embark on a strike due to a lack of oxygen. He had to act fast if he wanted to stay alive.

He decided to teleport down the hallway, but the man had anticipated that move as well, and he teleported with him. When Joel reappeared, it was right in front of the grinning, crazy-looking man.

DILUSION. Gotcha. *He said as he made to grab his former apprentice's throat again.*

Joel would instead jump into a volcano than allow the evil man to grip his throat once more. Before the towering man could react, the boy fell on one knee and came back up, pumping his fist like a protesting rebel—his knuckles connected with the enemy's lower jaw and the sounds of bones breaking rented the air. The uppercut lifted the man clear off the ground, sending him flying several meters backward. He immaterialized, turning into a shadow.

The man hit the reflective floor with a loud thud. An average human would've been knocked unconscious by that kind of punch, but this was no ordinary human; a good part of him was alien.

Joel could see him trying to get his bearings and pick himself back up from the floor. He knew it was only a matter of time before he lunged at him again, but Joel was grateful for every second he had to catch his breath.

While he sucked vast amounts of air down his lungs, his brain began to wake from hibernation, and his mind raced wildly in search of the following best possible course of action.

At that moment, the man interrupted Joel's thoughts by getting back up on his feet with a martial arts acrobatic move. He spat onto the floor, not minding staining the pristineness with his crimson bodily fluid. He flexed his jaw, and it was evident that the bones were rearranging themselves from the noises it made.

SHAVENGER. Damn you. *He muttered under his breath.*

To maximize the field of attack, he placed his back against a wall to prevent the man from appearing behind him.

DILUSION. You've done more than just break the hornet's nest; you dipped your hands into the mouth of a viper. Now, you meet a brutal end. *He stated confidently, wiping off the bloodstains at the corner of his mouth with the back of his hand.*

Like a viper, his eyes thinned. They focused on his former master like a mouse about to be struck down and devoured.

SHAVENGER. Bring it on. *He encouraged, even though there was trepidation in his heart. He took a defensive stance, bracing himself for whatever havoc the man was about to wreak on him.*

Elsewhere, in a dark, deserted place…

Valery's eyes roved around panicky like an eagle would over an open hunting range. With her best friend, Jayla, beside her, they quietly navigated the dark lair.

JAYLA. He was right about the transportation spot near the arcade. My magic was able to absorb radiation into a portal that brought us here. You certainly have trust in him.

VALERY. I believe when it comes to a friend. I don't know Morgan, but she seems nice. You and Zada always talk about her.

JAYLA. She made something that affected Shocker's powers and got my friend sick and me after a party. She ran away, but it wasn't her fault.

VALERY. Hopefully, she's here, and you all will get to apologize.

JAYLA. Even though he said no, thanks for coming to get me.

VALERY. Yup. And I did need you. Friends have each other's backs.

They were in a deserted place, and this dimension was unfamiliar. It was one more reason for them to tread with care.

They continued walking, neither speaking a word to the other. The only sound that emancipated from the girls was their gentle, shallow breaths. Not even their footsteps were audible. Although Valery was only thirteen years of age and without her other dual persona, she was well-skilled in the art of stealth.

As they made a turn, a short distance ahead of the girls was a door with a red bulb casting a hollow glow down on it. They glanced at each other and gave knowing nods. Behind that door stood the reason they had come to this dark, desolate place. Jayla could feel danger lurking in the shadows, and she was pressed to be done with the mission as soon as possible.

Valery raised two fingers, and she sliced the air using her right arm as a makeshift blade. The sign held a single meaning: Advance. They crept quietly and only let out short sighs of relief when they got to the door without an encounter. The girl retrieved a couple of pins from her pocket and went to work on the locks. A few minutes later, a single click sound was heard, and the door slowly eased open. She pushed it all the way in, the two girls quickly entered, ensuring to leave the door empty. The room was dimly lit, but she could make out the shape of a girl standing calmly at a corner of the room near a lab table.

VALERY. *Whispering.* Is that her? *She asked her friend quizzically, an unconvinced look in her eyes because of the metal helmet.*

JAYLA. It has to be. Unless it's one of the alien's tricks. *She replied as she started advancing to the girl. She crouched before her and took a moment to conduct observation.*

The girl had her head bowed, and her short, dark brunette hair covered her face as her helmet digitally disappeared.

When she sensed someone being close, she raised her head, parted the hair covering her face, and glared at the intruders.

VALERY. Are you *the* student or an illusion? *She asked, studying her newly exposed face as if they held the answers.*

FLURIR. Perhaps you forgot about me kicking your butt the day you saved Dani. Remember me now?

VALERY. I remember kicking *your* butt!

JAYLA. Shhh. *Grabbing her friend's right arm.* Stop starting drama.

VALERY. I guess I am. *She replied in a calm, gentle voice and laughed.*

The girl immediately recognized Jayla and her mouth went dry. For someone in seeming captivity, Jayla thought that she seemed somewhat unperturbed.

FLURIR. Who are you and what do you want? *She asked.*

VALERY. *She's slightly taken aback by the direct question.* Am I not supposed to be making the inquiries? *She thought.* My name is Valery, and this is my best friend, Jayla. We're here to rescue you.

FLURIR. *Scoffs.* Rescue, huh?

VALERY. Yes, what's wrong?

JAYLA. Can you walk? *She asked with genuine concern in her eyes.*

FLURIR. *She chuckled heartily.* Of course, I can walk. Nothing is wrong with me. I'm just amused by your heroic idea to *rescue* me. *Stares at Jayla.* Is this a trap – The police are waiting at my parent's home to arrest me for what I did to you and Kiyla, right?

JAYLA. Uhh, no. No one even knows about what you spiked the punch with, Morgan. Seriously! Surely, you've seen the wanted posters going out on missions for this mad man.

FLURIR. A clever strategy to get me. It won't *work!*

VALERY. Oh... *She muttered with confusion etched on her face.*

Seeing the expression she wore, the girl stood up, pulling V up as well with her gaze.

FLURIR. I am not a prisoner; I do not want to be rescued.

VALERY. That's bull – You're scared. ShaVenger told me the way you act around him.

FLURIR. He – He what? *If she had looked confused before, she was stupefied now.* Wha— What do you mean? *She said, raising her voice a little.* Why would he send you two to –

JAYLA. Shhh... *She cautioned from the lookout position she had taken earlier.*

They could not risk drawing attention to themselves.

VALERY. It's unbelievable. The evil scientist must've done something to you. I'd say brainwashing. *She said in a lower voice.*

FLURIR. *She walks to the center of the room, drawing attention from the two intruders.* Listen. I was not brainwashed, intimidated, nor cajoled. I was also not kidnapped; I am here of my own volition. I offered myself to the scientist willingly.

JAYLA. Why?

VALERY. That's both absurd and insane. *She retorted.* Who would want to join that mad man willingly, and why would you do that?

FLURIR. *She said with a shrug.* ... It has its perks.

VALERY. What kind of perks is that? *She queried, conveying enough sternness in her voice while still ensuring that she did not raise the tempo of her voice.* Look around you? This is nothing but a desolate land, and you and I know that whatever things you are gaining from the scientist, he will turn on you in the end. Nobody wins when it comes to that madman. Look at ShaVenger! He's on the run from him. Don't you see that?

FLURIR. He – He's trying to get him back.

JAYLA. Totally oblivious.

The girl seemed to consider this for a while.

FLURIR. You might be right. He hasn't delivered on several promises he made to me. Hearing your words, I'm starting to think he might just be playing at my weaknesses like a fiddle.

VALERY. Yes, you know we're right. *She stated. With hope in her voice, she added.* We went through many risks to get here just for your sake; you should come with us.

JAYLA. And I think you should hurry. Someone's fighting that man right now just for us to get you out of here safe. I mean, I have no issues knocking you out cold with a spell and dragging your ass outta here, Morgan. Just saying.

VALERY. Damn.

FLURIR. Okay. I will! God. *She responded.* You know the way out?

VALERY. Don't worry, that's why she's here.

JAYLA. Yeah. I got it. *She reassured.* Let's move!

The three girls filed out of the room and noiselessly made their way for the exit, where Jayla created a magical gateway that would take them out of this godforsaken dimension.

Meanwhile...
Somewhere near Newoluir's Lake

ShaVenger dodged left, right, and left again, creating enough pockets of space to slam the back of his foot against his opponent's neck. He could feel the muscles turn momentarily denser on impact.

The man staggers backward, engaged in combat with his former apprentice for a while, and he has proven to be a better fighter than he thought.

Joel cracked his knuckles and hit his chest a few times to psyche himself up. Never had he been engaged in such an intense fight, especially one that seemed to be turning in his favor. Although he had taken a few hits more than he would've liked, he had been able to land counter-attacking blows on him. Regardless of the man's status, he could tell that DiLusion was starting to wear himself out.

ShaVenger decided to deliver a finishing blow by teleporting to the man's side, prop a foot high against a wall and land it right in the middle of his skull. The idea seemed ingenious in his head, but he realized it was a colossal mistake when he implemented it.

As soon as the man saw him descending, he grabbed his approaching foot and kicked the other one off the floor. Joel lost his balance and crashed onto the floor with his foot still in the man's hand.

Without hesitation, the man twisted the foot to an angle of about ninety. The teenager cried out, kicking the man away with his second leg. He quickly dragged himself up and began to hobble away, groaning in pain with each step.

At that moment, he got a signal from Valery that they had rescued the girl. The three girls appeared at the scene; their mission was accomplished, and he had no more reason to be engaging in combat with this maniac who just doesn't stop. Joel had to end this, or they all had to escape.

DILUSION. Heh. I figured this was your diabolical plan, ShaVenger. A tip off the old block. Distract me, eh?

A crazy thought crossed his mind. Ignoring his hurting foot, he jumped up, grabbed a gas pipe, and yanked it free. A hissing noise began to emancipate from the leak.

DILUSION. What are you doing? *He asked, bewildered.*

SHAVENGER. Watch and burn!

He had timed this perfectly. Mid-Sentence, he had teleported to the end of the hall where the gas hadn't gotten to yet. By the time he uttered the last word, a lighter was in his hand.

DILUSION. NO!!! *He yelled, extending his right arm out.*

It was too late. ShaVenger hurled the lighter forward. He waited for a second to watch the gas catch fire before he teleported to the meeting point where the girls awaited him. In a split second, the alien disappeared from where he stood and appeared right where the lighter would land and caught it.

VALERY. NO!!

DILUSION. Ah, but yes. *Crushing the lighter in his palm.* What are you to do now, young protégé?

SHAVENGER. *He's laughing.* Oh, you loser. Got Ya. *He snaps his fingers, and a portal opens above the alien's head.*

DILUSION. Whaaattt!!!

A woman falls out, lands on top of the man's shoulders, and grabs both sides of his head. She starts chanting unfamiliar words repeatedly.

JAYLA. Mom?

Colorful waves of all sorts flood around the two as if they're dancing. DiLusion screams are loud and he's in pain. He manages to grab the woman by her wrists, and throw her off. She rolls in the air gracefully and lands like a cat on all fours while looking at the enemy squirm.

DILUSION. YAAAAAAAAHHHHHHHHHHH!!!!

After a few minutes, he goes quiet. His arms drop at his sides, and his body falls on the ground motionless. Before anyone moves, his body is enveloped in purple smoke and disappears.

JAYLA. Momm!!! *She's running to her mother.*

Miryova meets her daughter halfway and hugs her tight.

JAYLA. Don't ever leave me again, you hear me? *Squeezing her mom tighter as if she never intends to let her go.*

Eventually, they stop hugging. ShaVenger manages to stand despite the blows from the alien he took. Flurir (Morgan Wiles) is standing very close to Valery.

VALERY. Umm. What happened to him?

SHAVENGER. She erased his mind. Heh-heh. A plan I had on the side. We would not have been entirely free.

VALERY. Clever.

JAYLA. I don't know you, but thanks for reuniting me with my mom.

VALERY I would ask, but I know you knew where DiLusion must've been hiding her.

MIRYOVA. The alien will be suffering internally for a while. Let's say he's in the form of a coma. *She turns to the children.* Thank you. You kids are quite strong and adventurous. *She looks at her daughter.* Let's go home. *She looks at the others.* All of you, I'll make this easier. No need to head home by yourselves. *She closes her eyes for a second and opens them. With one word, she spoke.* **Translotimore.**

Everyone vanished to their respective homes.

11:21 A.M.
VLORs HQ …

Zadarion has recovered from his wounds. He is exiting the Infirmary Center and making his way to the Geared'NReady Room. He sees fellow agents exit. Rit and CQua nod at him as they leave. Caj greets him.

CAJ. What's up, Z man?

AGENT Z. Hi. Uh… What was that about?

CAJ. Little debriefing about the missing cross-humans. They believe they've found a hidden location near HighTech City. JeiFii says they found a mechanical door blocking a long, narrow road full of wires and very little visibility.

AGENT Z. Oh.

CAJ. Hm. Something bothering you? You don't appear to be excited.

AGENT Z. It's nothing. I'm fine. *Shakes his head.* I just – I don't know what this thing wants from me. Why did I have to find it?

CAJ. I see. Just look on the bright side. The transformation is one step closer to uncovering the truth. You hang in there. Be safe. *He walks off, exiting the room.*

Z decides to head home for the day and possibly take a nap. He teleports.

2:42 P.M.

Zadarion's searching through his closet, looking for his pajamas, when he heard the scream. His ears perked up, and he dropped the clothes racing downstairs. His eyes landed on his mother, perched in the corner of the living room, holding onto his baby sister. Blood flowed in rivulets down her cheek, and tears filled her eyes. Nano Guy was staring at him in the form of his grandfather.

ZADARION. MOM!!

The sight made him not think twice as he leaped onto the tall man and locked his arms around his neck. The man growled, unimpressed, flipped the boy over, and banged him right on the floor as if he was a toy.

HAILIE. ZADA!!! *She screamed.*

The woman's motherly instincts kicked in as she rushed towards her boy. His baby sister wailed, scooping deeper into the corner.

HAILIE. Please! Stop!

The man gripped her neck, depriving her of oxygen before she even got close to her child.

ZADARION. Let go of my mother! *He bared his teeth and dug them right into the man's calf, making him release her with a wince.* Mom! LEAVE!! *He screamed, not loosening his bite.*

The man reached down, clutching at his hair as he shoved him away. The boy groaned, but before he could retaliate. The man sent a punch right across his face. The impact of the blow was so strong that he was sent reeling back into the corner of a table. The intruder leisurely walked towards the small boy, delivering another punch into his stomach, and then by his neck, he shoved him into the table, breaking it in two. The strength he used was insane. Another punch came and landed into his abdomen. The air escaped his lungs.

ZADARION. This— Is crazy! *He let out a huff feeling as the man walked away towards his family.*

His mother picked up her little daughter and started to run upstairs. The man watched her futile attempts of escape with a comical smile as he strolled after her.

This was not going to work. The boy stood up, wiping the blood away from his face. No one was touching his family as long as he was alive.

ZADARION. Hey! Pick someone your size. YOU BASTARD! *He ran towards the man who raised his fist for another punch, but that wasn't getting him again.*

Right when he shifted his hand to hit him, the boy sidestepped and jumped, shoving his elbow right into the nape of the big guy's neck. With a surety that the hit would cause the man to faint, Zada's heart stopped beating when he turned his dark eyes towards him as if he was never hit. The boy vigilantly stepped back, getting rid of the surprise with a shake of his head, and aimed his kick into the man's side, which was grabbed even before it made contact. Their eyes met for just a second where the guy raised a brow making the boy sick to his stomach.

The man didn't give him time to force his leg back and sent him flying into one of the kitchen windows. The glass shattered, scratching Zada's body in several places.

He fell to the floor with a grunt.

He lifted himself to the elbows but just then, a heavy boot over his chest forced him back on the floor. A squeak escaped his lips as the man reached down and clutched his neck, blocking out the air from his windpipes. Zada struggled under the hold. His hands desperately tried to rip the man's grip off his throat, but the hold was so strong. He wondered if anything else could hurt this guy and his hands fondled around for a glass piece which was too far.

NANO-GUY. You... think you can beat me. You are such a weakling and therefore should die here. *He sneered and tightened his hold.* You got lucky the first time, boy.

Zada felt his eyes roll back into his head as he squirmed against the hold. With all his might, he shifted himself at a proper angle and jabbed his knee right between the man's legs. Instantly, the guy swore and released his grip.

The boy gasped, taking in quick breaths as he reached out for the sharp piece of glass and pierced it through his shoulder. The intruder groaned in agony as he twisted it deeper into the guy's flesh. The man grasped his wrist and threw him away. Zada landed against the kitchen's counter, but without waiting for another breath, he ran to grab the knife. The man was already walking towards him with the murderous glare that could waver any man's will but not Zada. He was a boy who had dealt with men double his size, but the most important thing was that he couldn't let his mother find out about his identity, so he had to fight this one differently.

He could see that the man's footing was unsteady due to the attack below, so this was a good chance.

Zada slipped over the counter, dodging the punch, and pushed the knife between the guy's ribs. If his strength wasn't enough to defeat this man, he needed to use other ways to deal with him. The guy let out a deep groan reaching out to grab the boy, but he was already flustered, and his small height gave him an advantage. He grabbed the saucepan from the shelf and slipped from under the man's arm, reaching behind him. With all his might, Zada aimed the saucepan across the man's face after he turned around. It didn't hurt him much, and he immediately straightened up, banging his head right into the boys'.

For a moment, he couldn't hear anything as he stumbled back against the oven. His world spun in front of his eyes as if he could feel the rotation of the Earth. The man held the same knife into his hand and reached out to slit the boy's throat. With shaking hands, Zada reached for the oven behind him. He might not be as strong as the guy in front of him, but he sure wasn't so weak either, and he was not going to die here like this.

NANO-GUY. It's over for you, boy.

ZADARION. Not yet! *He summoned all his strength, pulled the oven above his head, and landed it right on top of the man's head.*

The knife dropped along with the dude. Zada forced in heavy inhales and quietly reached out for a hammer. He held his bleeding head as he tried to crawl out of the kitchen and flee, but Zada was already on top of him.

ZADARION. You wanna run? *He slipped his foot forcing out the man's arm, who face-planted into the tiled floor with a hiss. He stepped over his stretched-out arm, which twitched under his feet to be free.* I won't let you or anyone hurt my family.

Zada raised the hammer and boxed it down, right at the man's elbow joint breaking his arm. The man let out a scream and writhed on the floor, holding his arm. Zada reached out to break some more parts, but the dude grabbed his foot, forcing him on the tiles, and started to punch him hard. Once, thrice, fifth time until he felt his strength wavering, and the need to escape became worse. Zada was slowly losing his vision. He was numb on the kitchen floor, with a stream of blood almost flowing out of his entire body. The man crawled from top of the groaning boy and, with unsteady steps, started to walk away. Zada shifted his body. One of his eyes was swollen and purple because of heavy hits. He slowly regained his vision but couldn't see the man anywhere in the house. He twitched, reaching for the hammer and dragging it along, started to follow the man's bleeding footprints. The pulses in his head worsened with every step but letting that man flee was the last thing he was going to do.

Realizing the boy would chase him, the guy tried to speed up, but too much of his blood had flown, and now he couldn't see anything straight anymore.

3:27 P.M.
Westick BLVD. Hidendale Springs

The man hid in some bushes. He could hear the boy's footsteps getting closer, and then he was right behind him. With all the murderous intentions, Zada was looking for who destroyed the peace of his family in mere moments. The man also knew that he wouldn't let him escape no matter what. This was their second time meeting after the disappearance of his grandfather. The last single sparring was all it needed for both.

The blood strains were not chase-able because of tall grass. The man restored his breath and stood in the tall grass from a distance to the boy. He looked behind himself with a death stare.

ZADARION. So, you decided to show up, old man? All you have is Repliara Crystatite strength and nothing else ... with my agent form, I can match your power. You are a big muscular brainless shrimp to attack my family. *He growled at him.* Here, I can put him to rest because there will not be anyone to witness my true self. *He thought to himself.*

Both Zada and the man ran towards each other with a hammer and a heavy blood lubricated fist. Zada slipped himself through his fist, and before he turned around, He threw a deadly hammered blow between his jaw and neck. The man screeched in agony; he could not move an inch now. The final decisive blow was the one that Zada won. He supported himself against the tree, and the reflection from the streetlamp showed the hammer raised above his head. Zada smacked his shoulder, making him drop. He strode forward, standing in front of him. His body was supported by the hammer, which he slowly lifted again, and the man's eyes followed the motion. As more blood flowed from his head, his consciousness began to fade away.

DANIEL WILLIAMS. See you in the afterlife.

Zada raised the hammer to his head with all his might as his form changed into his agent persona. The man screamed. A sharp pain arose from the side of his head, and then all Z could hear was only his heavy breath. The boy heard a noise behind him and was looking that way. He never dealt a final blow.

A familiar face. Rahz was standing there with two grown adult men in business attire.

JAYN. The violence in a child. Is this what VLORs have become?

DYRO. Pfft. Step away from Daniel Williams, agent.

AGENT Z. *Sidestepping to his right, turning to face them and locking eyes with a former friend.* R – Rahz.

RAHZ. You heard them. Step away from him.

AGENT Z. What do you want with him?

JAYN. None of your concern, agent.

AGENT Z. He's going to Primous after I get answers from him. But if ya' want him, try going through me. *Dropping the hammer and blade appearing into his hand.* Try me.

The teenage girl takes a few steps forward.

Agent Z and Agent Rahz get into the position. Z makes the first move towards the girl by throwing a punch to the side of her head. She blocks the attack by slipping her arm under his incoming punch and evading the attack. She then puts pressure on his neck and locks his elbow by moving his arm downwards to prevent cross attacks. He uses his upper body strength to duck before she can close the elbow and pushes himself back while hitting his head below her chin to get free from her grip. Stumbling back a bit, she reacts quickly by punching him, aiming for the solar plexus; he dodges the attack by moving to his right side. He uses his legs to deliver a roundhouse kick. She weaves, then delivers an upper kick, which strikes him on the head. She aims again for the head, but he ducks to avoid the attack, and she uses this opportunity to put him in the headlock and throw a punch from below. He slips his hand behind her knee and swipes her off her feet.

She quickly stands, as not to show any weakness in front of her opponent. Turning the hips a few degrees downward allows her foot enough room to move towards his ribs. She successfully delivers a power-angle kick. Stunned by the sudden impact, he finds himself on the ground. She attempts to deliver a kick to his abdomen, but just as it is about to have an impact with the face, he grabs her foot and twists it to a certain angle. This causes her to move in a specific direction to prevent dislocation. Seeing her defense down, he pushes her to the ground. She uses her palms to cushion the effect of the fall.

Wasting no time, she gets up and aims for his face, but he uses his forearm to block the punch. Seeing her close enough, he uses as much strength as he can muster to his elbow and aims it towards the opponent's head to deliver an elbow strike. Seeing the incoming strike, she ducks and quickly delivers a punch to the solar plexus. The impact throws him a few steps away. He jumps up and concentrates his body force onto the knee. He lands a knee strike on the head.

Unable to block the attack due to it being fast. The impact throws her a few feet away on the ground.

She gets up and dusts her clothes off. Feeling a bit frustrated, she runs towards to build momentum and attempts to punch him square in the face. The attack is blocked as he grabs her arm and holds it down. He tries to counter strike, but she acts quickly and uses her other hand to stop the attack, then she frees her other hand from his grip by twisting it upwards and using her finger to jab a nerve on his wrist. The impact causes the grip to loosen, and she delivers a punch to the face, aiming for the nose. This makes him lose balance, and she uses the opportunity to deliver a knee strike by moving her knee up while using her other leg to maintain equilibrium. She grabs him by his shoulder and strikes his head onto the knee that acts as a solid surface for an impactful strike. The impact causes his head to move backward as he tries to regain his focus.

On the side-lines...

JAYN. Whoa. Those two are badasses.

Agent Z gets back in the position and delivers a roundhouse strike on her side, aiming towards the ribs. She tries to block it by moving to the side, but the strike hits her abdomen. She tries to catch her breath and delivers a punch to the side of his body. This causes the breath to be knocked out of him as he loses his balance.

Both stand up, panting, and she puts up a mocking smile and encourages him to use his speed abilities. He refuses initially but agrees, transforming into Vex Z. He uses this speed boost to run behind her. He delivers a blow on the back of her head, throwing her off guard. She quickly gets up, but Z strikes her down again by running as fast as possible to build enough momentum. Using this to his advantage, he punches her hard enough to send her flying to a tree. He gets close enough to deliver another blow, but she blocks it quickly and pulls it downwards with enough force to make him move as well. He tries to use his other hand to punch her down, but she grabs him by the neck quick enough for him to be unable to react. She forcefully puts his head against the tree and kicks him in the abdomen. He regains focus just in time as she is about to aim once again towards the solar plexus. He blocks the leg using his free hand and using his leg to send her flying towards the ground.

He speeds at her, thinking he will be able to finish the fight. She gets on her feet, and just as he is about to land a fatal kick, she blocks it and counters. He is surprised at her new ability to block his speed abilities. He aims to punch her again, but she uses her forearm to stop the attack and counterstrike. He then aims towards her thigh, and as if she can read his thoughts, she prevents the attack by quickly using her foot to hit it behind his knees, making him lose balance. The boy's form returns to his agent attire.

RAHZ. Due to your tiredness, I knew you couldn't manage the Vex Armor for so long.

AGENT Z. You what?

RAHZ. You should've thought ahead. *Shakes her head.* You never think! Battling that man has you exhausted.

AGENT Z. We're still evenly matched.

RAHZ. And you're dense. I was obviously throwing my punches to allow those two to take that man over there.

The teenage boy turns his head and sees Jayn and Dyro holding Daniel Williams and they're at a far enough distance. All three teleport away.

AGENT Z. *Turns his head to look at Rahz.* A distraction? Why – Why do you want him?

RAHZ. I don't. Someone does. We'll fight again. Next time, be prepared. *She teleports away.*

AGENT Z. I'll get you back to our side and get answers about Nano Guy. *He sighs and teleports home.*

He throws an Invisi-Dome out of his home; this wipes his mother's and his baby sister's memory.

Somewhere down south Ohio, five miles from the nearest bus station...

After Asarios sent Nathan away, he's been trailing around angry since his grandmother was killed in front of him. Xanpo appears before him with two younger pre-teens. He walks closer to the teenager and tries to grab him.

NATE. *He turns around and pulls away from the man.* Man! Don't touch me!!

XANPO. Okay, okay. *He's calm*—No need to act like a kid.

NATE. Dude, what?!

XANPO. Your race is being hunted by a powerful–

NATE. What?! *Shakes his head*—My dude. You best get outta here with all that.

Xavier cuts him off from pleading. He has been making tons of excuses since he arrived. Xavier grabs his left arm and throws him to a steel wall.

NANO-GUY. *Groaning, on his hands and knees.* Please. Spare me. *Panting.* What would Talgitx do?

At the sound of that name, Xavier uses an energy attack, and he kills him in the blink of an eye. Jayn had to look twice because it was so fast.

COMPUTER AUTOMATED VOICE. Daniel Williams – The Nano Guy. A forty-two-year-old test subject for the Repliara Crystatite. He uses nanobots to become another person—the creator, unknown. A repliara crystatite is a rare crystal that copies a person's identity. If the imposter's appearance cracks, it could mean two things. White lights expelled out of the person, returning to their usual self, or another person struck them (using the unique crystal) by fist, causing the crystal to may or may not heal.

A flashback to when he accepted being the host for the first crystal is displayed on-screen inside the office.

DYRO. This man felt humanity was hopeless. Religions were a joke. Everyone's trying to find a false "God" to idolize.

JAYN. It doesn't matter what moral or righteous values a leader has or what a capable leader has done for society. They'll go unappreciated.

DYRO. He was done.

XAVIER. He felt the world was done. He wanted to bring the idea that people on the planet aren't capable of change.

JAYN. He was foolish.

SEASON 5, EPISODE 30

After the events in …
VLORs & VICE: THE ZERO SERIES

4:10 P.M.
Thursday, January 31, 2108
Varilin Capitol, New York
Tipalerdale Manor

Deep inside the walls and vents, there's a small space – not big enough to be considered a comfortable room. There's a small opening, only a crack big enough for Samuel Kerry to fit. He's sitting on the floor.

SAM. *He's breathing relatively faster than usual.* He– He turned all the recruits into slaves while I was gone! *Exhausted, trying to control his breathing.* S– Someone must stop him!

Wednesday, February 06, 2108
Tipalerdale Manor

A week passed, and his supplies were running low. Sam only leaves the small space for nourishment. Any ninja personnel who finds him get knocked unconscious and have their memories wiped with T-04 Zero Memory Gas Spray.

Meanwhile…
Hidendale Springs…

ZADARION. *Staring at his grandfather's home.* I'm going to get you back.

Suddenly, his V-Link turns on. He answers the call.

UNKNOWN CALLER. Agent Z. Your presence is needed! Report to Varilion Capitol, New York. Coordinates are being sent to you now.

The call ended.

ZADARION. Was that a woman? Who – *He scrolls through new messages and finds the address.* Guess I'll find out later.

The boy reads through the files and information for this mission. He double taps on the link. There's a voice message included.

COMPUTER AUTOMATED VOICE. Hello, Agent Z. This mission will take you to New York City. There's not much to tell. The only information I've found is on Primous's escaped prisoners. I'll say them now. Ada Kobayashi – She's twenty-nine years old. Quiet type. Her skills dictate her family's ruthless nature. Njara Ikeda – A thirty-nine-year-old skilled ninja. Quiet type. He uses a mace as his weapon of choice. He's dangerous for brute force, killing armies of men in battle. Dexter Ikeda – He's twenty-seven-year-old. The younger brother of Njara Ikeda. He uses twin blades and is incredibly speedy. The Ikeda family shouldn't be taken lightly; they were intelligent and rivaled the Shibarian leader before their empire crumbled. The one who freed the three is unknown, but it's likely it's a young woman.

AGENT Z. Whoa. This is a mission for Caj. *He shakes his head, exhaling. He immediately transforms and disappears in a flash.*

He arrived at the exact coordinates. He's in a forest. Agent Z reacts quickly when he sees a flying leg of the hooded ninja coming towards him. The incoming leg is blocked. He jabs the ninja in the back of his knee joint, which causes him to loosen his stance. The time is enough for the agent to slip under and pick him up. He tries to carry him and slam him against a tree, but the ninja puts his hand on the ground as he forces himself to spin within the boy's grip and lands a precise blow to his head.

Shocked and uneven, Z drops the ninja and falls.

Getting back in the position, he makes the first move and charges to the ninja. Z fakes a right hook, which the ninja tries to block. The boy reacts quickly by putting his body to the ground and swinging his feet to make his enemy lose balance. Z stands and punches him straight to the ground. The punches miss their target as the ninja moves his head away and uses his legs to lock the boy's head in place, forcing him to the ground.

Z uses his hand and upper body strength to free himself and stands. He jumps up and turns around to use a spin kick to strike the ninja. The hooded man blocked, but Z managed to throw him back a bit.

The ninja is quick to his feet – without even hesitating, he dashes to the agent. His arms are behind his back as he jumps into the air and kicks Z across the face. The boy uses his left arm to block the attack and grabs his leg to bring him to the ground. The ninja uses his hands to balance while on the ground, wrapping his legs tightly around Z. The kid agent frees himself. The ninja runs to build momentum as he throws multiple shurikens his way. Z reacts as fast as he can when he hears the flying shuriken cutting through the air. He is quick to move and dodge to his right. The ninja pulls out a Tanto, a small knife, and charges at him. With the knife now involved, all Z can do is dodge until he can find an opening to strike back. The hooded man is constantly slashing at him, hoping for the perfect strike.

Agent Z has an idea, and as the Tanto blade comes closer to him, instead of dodging it, he grabs it. He feels the sharp sting of the blade as it cuts his hand, but it gives him enough time to land a solid uppercut and send him flying back without the knife. Z grabs the knife and throws it at the ninja, who ends up catching it with two fingers; the boy charges simultaneously. With his right fist in the air, he throws a right hook. It's blocked and responded to by a punch to the face. The agent grabs both the ninjas' arms and uses his right knee to strike him in the stomach. He releases him, and the ninja rolls back and reveals a dagger from his left sleeve. He throws it at Agent Z. The boy manages to dodge the precise aim of the throw narrowly. The man spins in the air while throwing sharp thin needles his way.

The needles, made for paralyzing an opponent, impale him on his left knee.

Z's unable to move his left leg. The ninja comes forward as he grabs the boy's left arm, pulling him down, kicks him in the face, and roundhouses him to the ground. The boy immediately gets to his feet and tackles the ninja to the ground. He rolls to his right as quickly as possible, taking a knee.

He painfully removes the needles from his leg. Just as he is getting the feeling back, a man twice the size of the other ninja comes out of nowhere and tackles him to the ground. He reacts by punching the giant ninja in the face repeatedly, using his fists and elbowing him, but nothing seems to make a severe impact.

The hooded, smaller ninja now has a knife in his hand, and the giant-sized ninja brings out his mace. Both are ready to attack.

The giant ninja charges. Z stands there waiting for the right moment. The man swings his weapon, and the agent moves to the right just as it is about to hit. This causes the spikes of the mace to be stuck in a tree that was just behind the agent.

The giant ninja struggles to get the mace out. The more petite guy uses his blade to strike the boy. He switches to use his hands and flips backward, getting a reasonable distance away. The roar of the enormous ninja alarms him as he ducks to avoid the mace being swung over his head. Agent Z spins around and kicks the hilt of the mace hard enough for it to fall on the ground and out of the man's hand. The agent runs to build momentum to help him climb up the giant ninja. He tries to hit him in the back of the neck, looking for weak spots.

The giant man became angry, planning to crush the pesky kid.

Z moves out of the way to avoid the onslaught of attacks by the hooded ninja. He returns to the big guy approaching, materializes his Vactra Boppers, swings in, then kicks the man in his left cheek, causing the ninja to fly a few feet and crash into a tree.

Z realizes he won't win this fight, so he thinks about one of his gadgets. He swifts into his Vex Armor, with boppers, still manifested and speeds to him in the blink of an eye.

VEX Z. V-Tracer!! *He shouted and sent a flying punch into the man's abdomen.*

The V-Tracer latched onto his Vactra bopper. The moment his punch made contact, it attached itself to his body. Vex Z smiles and throws out multiple Q6 explosives flying his way. The hooded man avoids one, and it explodes just inches away. Another is headed for him, and he backs away. He notices they're circling him.

HOODED NINJA. What trickery are you doing? *Avoiding flying explosives.*

VEX Z. They hit you; you're dead.

The hooded man leaped to a tree and left the area. The Q6 explosives pursue him.

A taller woman strikes the agent in his back, and he goes flying into a tree. His form changes into his agent attire.

The boy hears another noise and looks behind him as the big guy comes gliding down from the tree above. He carries the large mace, laughing insanely.

The boy felt something grab him and move him a few feet away. He looks up and sees a middle-aged African American lady; she looks from one villain to the other. She takes out her ninja katanas from her leg strap.

UNKNOWN WOMAN. *Eyeing the enemy ninjas.* Let's fight!

AGENT Z. *He stands up.* Who – Uhh? Are you the one that called me?

UNKNOWN WOMAN. My name's Lisa Miller. I'm sorry we must meet in these circumstances. I have been on a mission; that's why you've never seen me at HQ.

AGENT Z. You must be one of the VLORs trainers Caj told me about.

LISA MILLER. *She smiled hearing that name.* Glad my reputation is holding with the organization. *Sighs.* There is no time to talk. You continue, Z. Up ahead is Tipalerdale Manor. Go, NOW!!

AGENT Z. Aye, aye. *He speeds to his left on foot.*

Ada and Njara run to cut him off, but Lisa gets in their way. Ada thrusts her left dagger to Lisa's right hip. She swerves and blocks the dagger with a swipe and then turns as Ada pushes to her left hip with her right dagger. Njara runs at her swinging the mace around in the air wildly.

Lisa kicks Ada in the stomach with such force that she flies back and impacts into a bush. Njara runs at Lisa violently. The woman runs to him and drops to the grassy ground, sending a sweeping leg kick to his knees. Njara buckles slightly but does not fall and looks at the woman laughing insanely. He swings the mace around his head, getting a faster spin, and crashes it down on the ground. Lisa rolls out of the way. She sees Ada getting up again and throwing darts out of her armor. Njara misses Lisa, and his mace crashes into the ground. He tries to pull it out, but it is stuck. In this instant, Lisa kicks him in the face. As he falls, she jumps to her feet. Ada starts throwing ninja stars at her. She dexterously avoids them, making swirling motions with her hands, with three fingers outstretched in each one—rings of a light blue circle around her hands, and aimed at Ada. The light hits, and she falls back. Lisa advances with purpose. Ada takes out her daggers and attacks, slashing wildly toward her face. Lisa dodges repeatedly. Ada, now angry, thrusts towards the woman's stomach. Lisa blocks the dagger with her katana.

Ada slashes at her face with the other dagger. Lisa flips backward. Njara pulls the mace out of the ground and runs at Lisa angrily with ambition. His mace was glowing with fire, and he ran faster. Lisa flips backward to face him. He smashes the mace down; the entire area vibrates with earthquake-level shockwaves. Lisa jumps in the air. Njara looks up and realizes he is in trouble.

Lisa sends a high-flying kick to his face, and he is sent crashing to the ground. The VLORs Ninja teacher turns to Ada, now gliding down from the trees by a metallic-looking rope. She takes two nasty daggers out, charging threateningly. Lisa blocked the incoming attack with her katanas as they were thrust to her stomach again.

Lisa sends a roundhouse kick around Ada's profile, sending her to the ground. She stares at them.

LISA. Surrender.

Njara shakes his head with furious frustration. Ada is getting to her feet.

NJARA. I ain't going back to prison.

ADA. Neither am I.

They get to their feet and run to her. The woman sighs, confused why they are so heavily motivated. There must be a reason why Shibarian ninjas are here.

Njara swings his mace wildly in the air. Lisa lets him come close; then, she drops to her knees and slices at his stomach with the katanas at the last second. He falls to the ground. Simultaneously, she spins to avoid Ada's oncoming assault. Lisa sent a raising cut up from her left stomach area to her right shoulder.

As Ada falls, the woman stands up victorious, but this is short-lived as a new guy landed ten steps away from her position. He is in full garments with a hood covering his identity.

The hooded man is furious to see his comrades defeated.

He unsheathes his twin blades and attacks her, running violently and going for a decapitation move. She blocks his attack. The hooded ninja tries to slice her shoulder, but she stops it. He immediately tried the other shoulder, but she blocked it again. He goes for her left leg and then the other.

This is happening fast. She kicks him in his stomach, and she sends a rising upwards cut to him. He blocks and thrusts her weapon out of the way so that her back is now to him. He quickly tries to slash her back, but she spins and blocks, shunting the blades up in the air and slashing at his face. He backs away at the last second. She sees her chance and runs to him with another upwards cut from her left side to his right shoulder. He does a flip to his right. Lisa goes for a head-on attack, but it's avoided, and she hits a thick tree. The man runs with his blades. Not stopping, he advances to her, raising them for a strike. Lisa pulls her katanas out of the tree's trunk. He desperately swipes at her face. She blocks and dodges with such force that his blades go flying in the air. She brings a low cut on him, slashing at his chest, and his top is cut open. There's a cut on his chest. He winces in pain. The woman steps forward, and he steps back. She raises her katanas, ready. The hooded man seizes the opportunity and runs away, disappearing by a smoke bomb.

Meanwhile, on New Waii Island...

Rivi is in his usual spot on a beach, looking out past the water's horizon; Kamalei is present, sitting beside him. The two speak in Portuguese.

KAMALEI. Você diz, um homem veio do mar e quase te matou?! (You say, a man came from the sea and almost killed you?!)

RIVI. *Nods his head.* Sim! Ele é um mago ou algo assim. (Yes! He like a wizard or something.)

KAMALEI. Eu costumava acreditar em magia também. (I used to believe in magic too.)

RIVI. Sério, mana. Eu nao minto. (Seriously, sis. I not lie.)

KAMALEI. *Leans closer and hugs him.* Estou contente por você estar seguro. (I'm glad you're safe.)

RIVI. Obrigada. (Thanks.)

KAMALEI. Vamos para a cidade tomar sorvete. (Let's go into town for ice cream.)

Vantlonon City, Florida
The noticeable separation from the heart of the city to Ever Wanderah…

During a training session, Sally accidentally shot a dangerous spell at Xanpo and injured him.

SALLY. *Gasps and clasps her hands over her mouth.* I'm sorry! I'm sorry! I'm sorry! *Removes both hands away from her mouth, placing them at her sides.*

The man spirals in the air, descending to the ground, and hits twenty feet away from two tiny teens. He's out of breath.

SALLY. Oh my god! Are you okay, Xanpo?

XANPO. It's– *Exhales painfully. Rubs his forearm and shakes away the pain.* –fine.

NATHAN. *He's a few feet away, leaning on a tree stump with arms crossed.* Aren't you supposed to be some big hero or something?

DONNY. Think fast!! *Throws a football at the teenager.*

NATHAN. *He leans back, avoiding the ball, and shakes his head.* Amateur. *Uncrosses his arms and makes his way into the house.*

DONNY. *Runs to his ball.* No game today?

NATHAN. Nah, little man.

DONNY. Don't call me little!

XANPO. Stop arguing. *Continuously rubbing his wound.*

SALLY. I – I can heal now!

XANPO. *Blurts out.* No!! *Calm manner.* It's fine, Sally. It's nothing more than a flesh wound. *Laughs to try to fake how much pain he's in right now.* At least I can tell the training is paying off. *Smiles and laughs a little, trying to catch his breath.* If we're going up against Xeiars, we must be ready.

DONNY. How do you know they are Xeiars?

XANPO. A few, calling themselves Xeiar hunters, are here on Earth. You haven't felt their presence, but I have. They've killed a few already. The atmosphere seems to have been relieved, though.

SALLY. Like, they're gone.

XANPO. A significant drop of magic.

DONNY. But, how? Nothing can stop our kind.

XANPO. A Quinoragoras could.

DONNY. But they're all dead.

XANPO. *Laughs.* Something's out there.

SALLY. Who would've known that Quinoragoras's experiment on you worked that well!

XANPO. *Unblinkingly.* Huh. How'd you know about that?

SALLY. Jorgo told me! *Smiling with her eyes closed for seconds.* In Darkeil.

XANPO. Wow. You sure have seen some things, I'll bet.

SALLY. *Shivers with both eyes closed, making a discomforting face.* Don't remind me.

XANPO. *Laughs.* Say less. Heh-heh. Your parents would be proud of you.

SALLY. Aww. *Walks up to him and hugs him tight.* You mean – YOU are proud of us!

XANPO. *He's smiling, looks to the sky, and says in his mind.* They must be ready.

Varilin Capitol, New York
Tipalerdale Manor

Meanwhile, Agent Z stood inside the vast mansion, staring at the massive space with expensive furniture inside. After looking around, he gaped at the man in front of him. The big guy looked furious yet calm. One glare while fixing his tie, and the agent knew he was a big deal.

His gaze darted to the other slimmer hooded guy behind the boss, who seemed desperate to lash out at the agent. He didn't feel as dangerous, but he was something; otherwise, there was no reason for him to be here. Their earlier exchange of fists had proven that.

The agent tilts his head slightly as he gets ready to land some blows on the two guys standing in front of him. He is a bit tired, but he's not going to give up on the mission.

CINAH. Don't expect us to go easy on you, agent. *He scowled proudly while running a hand through his hair.*

AGENT Z. *Responding as casually as he could.* It would be a mistake if you did.

They exchanged a few hostile comments, smirks, and grunts before leaping at each other. Agent Z was quick on his feet to dodge the boss's attack. He had learned a few ways to deal with ninjas; strength and speed were significant factors. He had to find the best chance to attack. He swiftly ducked and let the kick hit space above his head.

The boss straightened, and in that tiny second, the agent tried to kick off his head, but he had to instantly back up before the shadow clone from the masked ninja appeared between them.

AGENT Z. This... *He groaned as the clone lurched at him in mid-air.*

He began to land punches and kicks at the agent wildly. The speed was so much that if an average person witnessed the fight, they wouldn't tell the movements or even see them correctly. Some of the hits, the agent blocked, and others he dodged, but some got him.

The clone vanished, reappearing behind the agent, and kicked him. The agent was sent flying forward, where the boss landed a heavy punch. He crashed, and the whole floor shook, cracking at the impact. Little pieces rose around him. He grunted, feeling his face heat up due to the blow.

He scrambled back on his feet, stepping away. The masked ninja leaped forward in mid-air and swapped his hands and fingers quickly, chopping "static" through his mouth and making the agent stuck in one place.

AGENT Z. What the hell? Why can't I move a limb? *He felt a pang throughout his body.*

The boss smirked at him and threw an up-thrusting punch to his face. The agent took a heavy impact as he collapsed with the wall in just one punch. He rested himself on the wall, another groan excluded from his throat.

This was getting nowhere. The boss jumped out, preparing to land over him. The agent rolled on his back, straightening up, and braced himself as the boss tried to punch him again. The punch landed on his forearm; he twisted his arm around the boss's and flipped him over, pinning him. He aimed his blow for the boss's neck and hit with all his might; this did not affect the boss. He took his hand over his head, grabbed the agent from the collar, and rolled him over. He slammed him on the tiled floor.

CINAH. Do you see the difference between our abilities, son? No matter what you do... You still are a fourteen, fifteen-year-old puny nuisance! *He called him out.*

The Boss engraved his bare fingers into the wall, scratching it. The boy's crawling away until he finds a safe place to stand. The other ninja was not attacking right now. The agent became suspicious.

AGENT Z. *In his mind.* Is he waiting for his turn to beat the shit outta me? *He got up, cleaning his mouth with his shirt.*

The boss started to move. He curved himself, opening his tie and shirt button by button. The masked ninja moved away from where he was standing.

CINAH. I only use raw strength. But in strength, no one can surpass me.

He was almost fierce, losing consciousness and overwhelmed with murderous intentions. He rushed at the agent. It feels like he punched through his stomach with great speed that the agent could not follow with his senses. The boy could see stars before his eyes as all pressure rushed to certain parts of his body. His backbone felt the impact of that punch. Luckily, his suit protects and heals him to a certain extent.

The boss grabbed his neck, threw him at a wall with all his might, and quickly followed by several punches. Those punches were strong enough to penetrate solid metal armor. With every hit, the walls of the building crumbled, and the cement broke out like dry bread crushed between hands.

He gave his body a complete spin and kicked the agent at the side of his head, sending him soaring through the air and crashing back into the ceramic-tiled, glistening kitchen. The walls were broken, and there were holes in places. If this continued, he was not sure if the building would be left at all. He raised himself.

The masked ninja was up to something. He had blue flames rising from his skin and twirling around his arm.

AGENT Z. These so-called magicians. *He coughs and spits blood on the floor.*

CINAH. Magicians? *He laughed.*

The boy was good at martial arts and combat, but ninja art was not his thing at all. He helplessly watched the ninja's eyes glisten in a shade of blue. The intentions of murder overflowed them.

The agent stood up. His legs wobbled due to the beating he had received; exhaustion bathed his body, sweat, and bruises. He forced in a few heavy breaths, ready for the blows.

This masked ninja was tough to deal with, but he could not handle anything if he used the Vex Armor. He had to do something about this enraged boss.

The masked ninja jumped to a wall, running over it, and leaped to Z. His movements were rapid as he tried to land a fatal blow. They were chasing and pinning each other down, using brutal kicks and heavy impacts. Some of them were received by the masked ninja as well, but most landed on Z.

MASKED NINJA. *Aiónia krísi.*

CINAH. Heh. Eternal judgment. *Crosses his arms, smiling while watching.*

The masked ninja muttered again—the very next moment, the agent was grabbed and pulled into heavy chains.

CINAH. Using an ancient illusion technique. Heh-heh. Nice job, guy.

The masked man develops a specific movement pattern. The boy thought that mainly the masked ninja was the support, and the boss was all strength. He figured the tricks were illusion-based, but it was too late to react. The boss had already grabbed him by his ankle. He raised him and, with full might, slammed him once on the floor. If he weren't in his agent suit, he would be broken like vegetables.

CINAH. Why in the world did that exclusive organization send you? *His tone was laced with mockery.*

Getting this ninja off his tail sounded much more critical to Agent Z now.

He shifted to Vex Z. He zoomed past the boss, attacking the silent masked ninja giving him a severe blow across the face. The ninja stumbled backward, losing his balance, and fell. Z didn't wait for another second and leaped mid-air for another blow, but the boss was already above him. He kicked him in the back and, before he could hit the floor, shifted below him, punching him in the guts and sent him breaking through the roof.

AGENT Z. *He smashes on the floor in seconds, groaning and holding his abdomen. He crawled on his elbows ready to stand up again, but someone stepped in front of him. He shifted out of the Vex Armor to his agent form.*

UNKNOWN SMOKEY FIGURE. Need some help, Z?! *Smoke bombs are disappearing.*

CINAH. *Looks over at the hooded ninja and back at the small figure.* He was here this entire time. Ha-ha.

The agent barely looked up. He recognized the voice all too well, yet he needed to have a glimpse of the face. All he saw was a mask and the same suit the masked ninja wore. He didn't know what to do. He's shocked.

A young boy, almost his height and size stood there stretching out his hand. Agent Z smirked. He reached out, and the boy pulled him up with no effort.

UNKNOWN SMOKEY FIGURE. It's rare to find you in so much trouble. *He mocked.*

Z punched him in the stomach lightly. While the two of them goofed around and laughed, the boss and the masked ninja were already standing a few feet behind them, wanting to land a few more blows on the agent.

The hooded ninja dispersed a few talismans. They activated and glowed.

AGENT Z. Careful! *He jumped backward.*

The other boy leaped to the right, rolling on the floor, and then straightened up. To his shock, Z dodged the explosions, but they were coming from everywhere – even on the floor.

AGENT Z. *He thought.* I have an idea. *He lightly touched the floor with the tip of his shoes before jumping to another position and avoided some explosions. But the last one got him, burning him slightly from the side of his arm.*

SAMUEL KERRY. That's Nuaiatsu. A simple Shibarian Ren tuh Chu technique.

AGENT Z. I must learn the skill.

The two boys managed to get out of the talisman trap with help from a counter move.

The boss was waiting for them and ready to deliver justice to the traitor who hid away skillfully.

They exchanged glances before the boss lurched at the masked boy and landed a heavy blow, but agility was the boy's skill. He slipped from between the boss's legs and stood upright behind him. Then before he could turn and reel away, the boy jumped, landing a hard boot at the side of his head. This was the first hard blow the boss had received during the day or even the first one in a long time.

SAMUEL KERRY. Training others to use such skills will be your end.

The boss immediately went for the agent, but his attack was evaded.

AGENT Z. I'm extra cautious now. *The boy tilted his head and smiled in a taunting way.*

CINAH. Guess I'll have to step up my teachings. *He finished his sentence and smirked.* You'll know it soon yourself.

Saying this, they all lashed out at one another. They were exchanging blows, kicks, and fists. Not even one landed on the other one. The attacks were flawless from either side but so was the defense.

The agent whipped around, knowing the boss would appear behind him, but as he turned around to look, the boss was already in his face. He gave a few numbers of quick heavy fists to the boy's chest, stealing the air from his lungs.

Samuel Kerry and the hooded ninja finally clashed their blades. The silent man never failed to get the upper hand in armed battles in his past, but now it felt different. Every hit blocked, and one of the blades would always come for his head. He backed away a few feet performing triple backflips. The ninja's high speed now started to get troublesome.

AGENT Z. *Landing on his back after avoiding the boss's roundhouse kick.* Ahh! What a pain! *He groaned out loudly.*

Just then, a smoke bomb exploded, another and another. Now a real issue. Within this smoke, the agent was sure he would lose his head somewhere.

Samuel vigilantly stood with his blade ready because an attack could come from any direction at any time. Through the mist, he could feel something approaching. It happened quickly—the twin blades technique; there was nothing in the world this guy hadn't mastered. The ninja boy used his blade to counter the attack. The masked ninja spun and attacked again and then from above.

Agent Z continued blocking from the boss's assault; he wasn't getting any chance for an attack. The ninja appeared from behind. Now the agent knew, at this rate, things were going to get ugly. Samuel landed right next to his buddy. They both drew some distance between them and caught their breath. A few heavy inhales and exhales.

AGENT Z. I see what you are doing there! *He growled at the enemy in a lower tone.*

The agent looked behind through the giant hole in the wall; the boy and hooded ninja disappeared inside. He rose with a smirk on his face. Before you know it, the hooded ninja crashed into a window and smashed into the fireplace behind the boss. Samuel jumped through the same window.

SAMUEL KERRY. *Getting beside his best friend.* And that's how it's done.

AGENT Z. Showing me something amazing?

SAMUEL KERRY. *Laughing.* I gotta show what I've been up to since the last we saw each other.

CINAH. ENOUGH!!! *Turns to the hooded man.* Get up! NOW!!!!!

AGENT Z. *Materializing blade.* Someone's mad they're losing.

The ninja got to his feet and stepped back as he saw the agent mysteriously moving his giant blade. Agent Z, in a flash, advanced his weapon at the ninja. The ninja's pupils contracted as he was not anticipating a heavy strike. He blocked the agent with both blades. He jumped back and tossed a few daggers at the boy.

SAMUEL KERRY. *He ran up and grabbed them with his hands.* So slow.

The hooded man sheathed his blades, dropped his arms at his sides, and exhaled.

HOODED NINJA. *He closed his eyes, lowering his head.* **eXpaa Dosper.** *He murmured.*

CINAH. *He does a double-take, eyeing his battle partner suspiciously.* He speaks at last.

Black markings appear, a circle around Z. He quickly dug his blade in the floor, stepped on it, and jumped out.

The agent thought about using a new feature to one of his weapons, Vactra Bopper Claws. He materialized the giant claws, wearing them on his hands, and leaped at the ninja.

Now the stats were different. The boy being exceptional at martial arts was brisk enough. Just by switching his weapon from boxing gloves to deadly sturdy, sharp claws – he was now on another level of defense and attack.

He kept on his rapid attacks because he was now used to his tactics. He believes he's found a weakness. He makes an extraordinary move, then attacks him, and between one particular attack, there is some duration when he cannot cast another trick.

The ninja was astonished that he somehow figured out the weakness in his ninja art. Also, he came to know that all the beatings that the agent received were just to read their movements and techniques. The agent's training must outclass ninjas with might, agility, and foreseeing.

Both fighters kept on surging their weapons on each other.

The ninja slashed his weapon forward, nearly piercing through his heart, but the agent backflipped and stepped on the wall, using it as support to jump behind him. The teen boy saw an opportunity now. He avoided the blade with one claw and twisted his hand to unarm the ninja. He then shattered his claw through his flesh and cut through ligaments in his right leg.

HOODED NINJA. Now jump. *Pulling off his mask and spitting blood on the floor.* Show me some circus tricks, you shitty monkey.

He could do nothing but plop around all dozy and injured. He could not move normally. Samuel rushed close and threw a punch to the man's left cheek, and he laid out on the floor. The teen agent stood triumphant. He spat on the floor in a fit of his victory.

CINAH. Let's see how you fare with my students. *He stated and clapped twice.*

In a split second, about twenty to thirty ninjas came flying with their ropes. Some leave sand behind and raised dust. Samuel narrowed his eyes and huffed.

He was about to pray silently for his best friend when he heard the whooshing sound of metals flying as Agent Z flew, striking at a few absentminded ninjas.

The agent flashed a half-smile at his buddy as he did a quick nod. They both cried out and rushed for the ninjas. Sam decided to do a furious wind style as he ran with the brisk wind, harnessing its power and delivering fast and powerful blows to about five to six ninjas that approached him till they fell flat.

The ninjas were not deterred as they kept rushing at both.

SAMUEL KERRY. They're increasing in number! *He cried out to his friend before deciding to utilize the flowing water style. He easily deflected the powerful blows with direction, turning the blows against his opponents, dodging, and weaving.*

He was as slippery and ever-changing as water, and his blows, though few, carried the force of a tidal wave slamming on the shore. With each punch the ninjas threw to him, Z knew what was next and quickly maneuvered, landing substantial blows to their guts and ending with a slamming kick to their chest that sent them flying backward in the air and landing with a big thud.

AGENT Z. Come get some!!!! *He shouted at the ninjas.*

The agent yelled to Sam, and Sam nodded even though Agent Z did not see it. Sam was about to say something to him but did not. A ninja rushed up to him and landed a heavy kick to his ribs. Sam's eyes were dazed, but he shook himself out of the trance quickly. He grabs his attacker by the right leg when he attempts a second kick. He punched his face with the bottom of his palm, making his head wobble around.

SAMUEL KERRY. Pretty hard to do with three to four ninjas on your back! *He yelled back at Agent Z.*

AGENT Z. Behind you! *He informed his partner, an alarmed expression on his face.*

Sam had heard the movements coming at him, and without an idea of what it was, he instinctively brought out his sword and placed it over his head at a 45-degree angle, blocking the shuriken from getting to him. He grinds his teeth angrily. Placing his hands in his pocket, Sam brought out as many shuriken his hands could carry and ran a safe distance away from his opponents. He threw the ninja throwing stars strategically to the floor as about six ninjas rushed at him. He smiled within as they ran towards him unsuspectingly. They had already stepped on the shurikens before they could turn back.

Sam watched them cry out in pain, their boots unable to fend off the inflicting pain the shuriken's poison gave. Topping things up, he threw a shuriken at each affected ninja's chest before they could attack, forcing them into a deep state of unconsciousness.

Becoming light on his feet, he rushed out of the scene and went to help his friend, who he feared was overwhelmed. Finding a hidden spot, he crouched down and began shooting darts expertly at the ninjas who were closing on the agent.

Agent Z stared in disbelief, admiring his friend's versatile skills. On his end, things weren't going so well. It was hard warding off the ninjas as they were annoying, fast, and light on their feet. They had no weapons on them for unknown reasons, and he presumed Cinah had sent them specifically to him for a fair fight. Allowing for crepitus to occur in his shoulder, he ran to a safe corner and took a firm pose before three ninjas were before him.

The first ninja rushed at him and attacked with three unsuccessful kicks as Agent Z quickly sidestepped and shot a quick blow to his back without a single thought. The two others leaped forward, and the fight began. Z avoided several punches from three ninjas, focusing solely on one as he quickly hurled three punches and slaps at his opponent, sending him unconscious with a heavy kick to the gut. He narrowed his eyes. Doing a quick run, he managed to grab one of the ninjas and did a quick somersault with him. He was unable to continue as another ninja kicked him hard in the tum, momentarily destabilizing him. He groaned. Setting his sights on the ninja, he calculated his actions and subtly avoided each throw.

As the ninja was about to send a front kick to his throat, he held his right leg and did a sidekick to the ninja's left knee and then his stomach. Letting go of the ninja's leg, he sent him plummeting several feet afar with a wheel kick, spinning his body along with his right leg till it hit the other ninja square in the chest.

Z did not wait for the ninja to recover; he brought out his blade and let it sit firmly in the ninja's chest. He did flying leg kicks at several ninjas that approached him, daggering them in vital places.

AGENT Z. They're not relenting! Sam! *He called out to him, who was becoming overwhelmed on his end.*

His best friend heard the call and decided to use a Jutsu move he learned at this place. Z watched from the corner of his eyes as he did some weird hand movements. Sam was fast with the hand movements, and Z could not risk watching him, as he had ninjas constantly on his neck.

SAMUEL KERRY. Lighting style; Lightning Release Wall! *He yelled and instantaneously, the sky rumbled angrily, and a wall of lightning bolts appeared, repelling those ninjas who touched it or even bumped into it in their haste.*

The ninja boy could not dispel many ninjas as an arrow in his glenohumeral joint struck him. He sprawled to the floor in pain, and the wall disappeared instantly. On the other hand, Z couldn't keep up with the number and let his guard down. The two were surrounded by the overwhelming army, which loomed over their heads and closer to their tired eyes.

SAMUEL. Even if it takes the last drop of my blood, I won't stand back till your backs are under my sole! *He looked up at the looming figures, rubbed the back of his left fist against his lips, and at the sight of his blood, he declared.*

The statement was followed by a blow to his jaw, with blood escaping from his mouth.

JACOB. Let's see how your soon-to-be lifeless body stands up tall to place your inexperienced soles on our backs.

One of the ninjas he knew all too well mocked and shared a brief chuck at the dark humor.

As the ninjas closed in on them, the two partners' heads shot up instantly as their eyes beheld the ninjas falling flat to the floor.

They smiled in relief as they saw Agent Caj rush to the venue with shuriken's flying after him and hitting the ninjas in their vitals.

AGENT CAJ. I've brought someone to help us out. *He shouts.* Now get on your feet; we've got business to finish! *He called, leaving them. Sounds of metals began to clash.*

Lisa Miller helped the boys up and went to fight alongside Caj. Sam and Z fight side by side, immobilizing ninjas near them and moving on to the next opponent.

Cinah was watching everything, puffed in anger. His army had worn out. In his state of rage, he screamed. He threw a shuriken at Caj. The agent avoided it seamlessly, but the boss was too fast.

Before he could move a fist, Cinah had descended on him, kicking him in the chest with both feet and throwing a jab at Caj's right eye. He had extended his hand to throw another punch when Lisa attacked from behind, kicking him hard in the back of his right knee and then his kneecaps.

Cinah was poorly hurt, but he absorbed the pain and decided to execute a style of Kung Fu known as the drunken fist. He gave Caj a blow that was sure to knock him out and then staggered over to Lisa. Breathing furiously, he watched the woman become confused. She pondered on attacking him immediately or waiting. Cinah fell to the floor with a further act, crouched, and pushed on, trying to get up.

The woman went in for a close kill and kicked Cinah multiple times in his gut severally; the last kick was her undoing as Cinah rolled over with the speed of light, brought out his shuriken, and struck her feet in time. Lisa let go of everything she held and furiously tried to stop the bleeding as she bit down hard on her lip, suppressing the pain.

CINAH. Who's next? *He said menacingly, looking up at the two friends who were left.*

Agent Z screamed furiously and rushed at the boss. Rage blinded his sense of reasoning that he didn't realize when Cinah started doing the weird hand movements he had seen Sam do. Cinah's middle finger and pinky formed an angular arch while his ring finger and index fingers intersected with the thumbs touching tips.

CINAH. Wind Style: Falling Petal Dance! *He hollered, and instantly, a worm-like vortex of wind sent Agent Z flying immediately. He came at close range with him.*

Sam narrowed his eyes; he brought out his sword and struck a ninja pose. Sizing each other up, Sam hit first. They could predict each other's moves. Cinah decided to try something else.

CINAH. You know, for a teen, you fight well. *He began, subtly blocking a strike from Sam with his blade before releasing it.* But you're no match for me. *He finished with poison in his words as he spun around and struck Sam in his left arm.*

Sam winced before striking again, still unable to draw blood from Cinah. The boss blocked his weapon and pushed him back with it. The effect was minimal as the boy moved only a few feet apart and maintained poise. With each advancement Cinah made with his blade, Sam either blocked or jumped over it. The last jump he did allow him ample time to strike Cinah in the arm. He groaned and continued without relenting, throwing flying kicks at Sam, of which he dodged easily. The boy was momentarily distracted by Caj's coughing when Cinah circled in on him and punched him severally in the knee and gut before sending him flying to the floor with a hard flying kick.

CINAH. Surrender! *He yelled and released heavy punches at Sam, the latter blocking them all even as he was on the ground.*

The boss was about to strike Sam when Sam breathed, and with every ounce of energy left in him, he rolled over swiftly and jumped to his feet.

SAMUEL. *He yells.* Never!!!! *He placed the tip of his weapon to the man's laryngeal protuberance, but Agent Z grabbed his hand before he had a chance to do something he'd regret.*

Suddenly, a smoke bomb goes off in the middle of the destroyed guest sitting room. A teenage girl appears and is standing, looking extremely disgruntled. Lisa helps Caj stand.

AGENT CAJ. Who are you?

UNKNOWN TEENAGE GIRL. The name's Caitlyn Wasaki, and don't you forget it!

SAMUEL KERRY. Well, we beat the Shibarians leader and Dexter Ikeda, who was the hooded ninja. You're next.

LISA MILLER. Miss princess here freed the two ninjas from Primous and sent them here.

CAITLYN. *Angrily.* Yes, I did! They weren't supposed to be beaten so easily! I only wanted Mr. Eroiisaki dead. *Starts talking to herself loudly.* What do I do? What do I do?

AGENT Z. Run, now. *Smirks.*

CAITLYN. Oh! I'm not through yet. My plan's only getting started. *She immediately tosses a few smoke bombs and vanishes.*

LISA MILLER. She's alone now; we'll get her. *Turns to face the two teen boys.* Thank you. Mission Accomplished, Agent Z and friend.

SAMUEL KERRY. *Turns to look at Z while speaking.* That's my best friend to you. *He holds his right hand high toward his friend.*

Agent Z quickly grabs his hand and pulls him into a tight hug. The two are glued to each other for some time.

Eventually, the agents teleport to HQ to give their report and head home. Samuel returns to his home in New York. He used a memory charm on his mother, so she didn't remember how long he's been gone.

Some time passes on New Waii Island, Rivi is walking inside his home.

A middle-aged man dressed in a fancy business suit is standing over the body of Krojos. Rivi walks in and stops just in front of him; he looks down at his father-figure lying on the floor.

RIVI. *Eyes tearing up.* K – Krojo?

XAVIER. Didn't expect children to visit.

The little boy seems bewildered and stands there, glued to the spot, unable to take his eyes away from the corpse of his caretaker, who he loves very much. He opens his mouth, but no more words come out. He looks at the man and tries to say something, but he cannot. Xavier stares back at him. The boy looks back at the dead body. He takes a step back and shakes his head, muttering, *no,* under his breath.

He mutters repeatedly and stares at the body; his entire body is shaking and twitching.

Rivi does not quite know how to process what he is seeing. He looks at the body again and begins to cry. His tears soon turn to anger, and he screams at the unknown man. He runs and attacks him, throwing some wild punches to his face. Xavier bends his back and arches his body to intensely difficult angles, avoiding punches. Rivi punches towards his left side, but Xavier arches out of the way. The boy tries to kick his lower right leg, but the man effortlessly blocks it with his left leg. He goes in to punch the right side of Xavier's head, but he steps out of the way, kicking Rivi in his ankle, thus making him unbalanced, and simultaneously blocks Rivi's punch with an open hand block. He slides along his wrist and then twists. As he does so, he changes the angle of his body, taps the boy's right ankle with his left ankle, and crashes down hard on his foot. His other hand connects with the hand he blocked on the elbow. He has his wrist locked and pushes his elbow, dangerously close to breaking it.

The boy screams in pain. Xavier uses his fist to punch him in the chest three times. He steps back, kicks the boy on the back with a kick, and lets go of his wrist and elbow. Standing around, he watches him fall forward.

Rivi spins around, somewhat disorientated; he turns to face him. Xavier is in a power stance, fists raised and stance strong, ready to fight. The boy moves forward. Xavier smiles. Rivi screams with anger and runs at him, wildly throwing a barrage of punches. He tries to punch him in the face from the left-hand side, but Xavier sidesteps to the right. Rivi throws a punch to his right side, Xavier agilely and effortlessly dodges to the left. The boy sends an uppercut up to the man's chin, but Xavier sends an open palm block downwards and connects with his fist. Then, he uses an open hand strike on his wrist followed by a bent knee kick to his elbow and moves his right hand towards his neck, which connects, while his leg interlocks the boy's ankle. He pushes his chin back with his open hand, locks his ankle around his ankle, lifts his leg. Rivi is totally out of balance, and Xavier flings him to the ground. Rivi gets up again, even angrier.

He runs at his opponent. The man steps out of the way and positions himself behind the boy. Rivi looks confused. Xavier sends a high-flying kick at the back of his head. He falls to the ground again.

Rivi gets up; he is furious and sobbing, and emotional. He screams and transforms, revealing his agent form. He runs at Xavier, jumps in the air, and fires a high-flying kick at his face. Xavier dodges the kick and punches him in the ankle hard, spinning him around in a direction away from him. He lands on his feet but limps painfully for a second before regaining his fighting stance. He runs at the man again. He is relentless.

Xavier sidesteps and looks behind the boy. Soldiers come swarming into the room. One of them strikes the boy from behind. Agent Rev turns around and kicks the soldier in the stomach, sending him flying back. Two soldiers grab Xavier by his shoulders. The man spins toward one and grabs his arm, which he uses to punch the other one with. Simultaneously he arches his body and jumps up in the air so that he is upside down and wraps his legs around one soldier's neck and pushes him to the ground. He lets go of the other soldier who moves in closer, then he spins, arches his back again, and sends a kick from the floor up to the soldier's jaw, which knocks him back. Xavier quickly jumps to his feet.

Rev blocks a punch from a soldier with his wrist and then sends an open palm to his chest, sending him flying back. He turns just as three soldiers run at him from three angles. He kicks one in the stomach, but two others grab him from behind as he does so. He tries to wiggle free, but they are too strong for him. The soldier he kicked regains his strength, gets up, and punches him in the stomach and then the face. He grabs the unconscious Rev by the legs, and the three soldiers carry him off. The other two have him by the arms.

Xavier looks around as two brainwashed cross-humans approach him summoning firepower. The man tightens his fists, and dark energy spheres appear around his hands. He fires an attack, and so do the two strange men.

As the blasts rise, Xavier drops to his feet and dives on the floor past them. He shoots the blasts forward and crawls into a nearby hiding place, undetected, where he teleports out.

Hidendale Springs, Illinois...

Kiyla is at her home, sitting in her room. She's keeping her head low as memories of her deceased grandfather flooded her mind. She sniffled hard, struggling to restrain the tears that were ready to burst out of the dam in her eyes. Her heart weighed heavy like a sinking ship.

Her grandfather had been a significant factor in shaping her life, and it was unfathomable – there's no comprehending the thought of proceeding without his stern but loving guidance.

Her eyes fell on the *shinais* at the corner of the living room, and she couldn't hold back the waters anymore. She burst out a loud cry, weeping.

The *shinais* are beside a pair of *bogu*. The bamboo swords and helmet set sent the teen down memory lane, back when she was learning Kendo.

Kiyla was eight years old when her grandfather started to train her in Kenjutsu martial arts – Kendo. She was at first confused, guarded, and unsure, but he guided her well. The older man was a great teacher, finding the right balance between discipline, compassion, and guidance. She remembered the first time she had done Kendo. Her grandfather had laid the equipment before her and ordered her to put them on. She had stared at the strange equipment and back at him, dumbfounded. She had no idea which item went where, and she voiced her concern, but her grandfather had implored her to try them on whichever way she saw fit.

A brief smile crossed her sad face as she recalled how she had stepped gingerly towards the equipment, unsure of which to pick up first. She settled on the helmet; it seemed like the least complicated item of the lot. She grabbed it and placed it on her head, her eyes visible from the slits in the mask. The helmet was somewhat big for her stature, but the pad rested on her shoulders well.

He urged her to pick up another item to wear, and her hand rested on the *kote*. She slipped the gloves over her hands and flexed her fingers.

She now wept. She could vividly recall the approving look on her grandfather's face when she had attempted to wear the fibre Dō – the chest protector. She couldn't on her own, and grandfather had helped her fasten the ties from behind. When he attached the *tare* as well to protect her legs, he had taken a step back to access the young girl before him. He grabbed a shinai by the hilt and handed it to his granddaughter.

As if time had reversed itself, she could feel the weight of the bamboo sword again, just like the first time she had held it. Waves and waves of sadness washed over her as she wished she wielded power to turn back time. She would do anything to bring her grandfather back to life.

How could she forget the smile grandpa had worn on his face when they were done with the first lesson at the yard that fateful evening?

GRANDPA GERALD. You have the heart of a warrior. You fight like one already. *He had commended with a pat on the shoulder and a smile.*

Her face had broken into a wide grin. Even now, reminiscing, she beamed happily at the thought of her old man. Pages after pages of memories drifted through her mind as she lingered on particular sparring lessons at the town's stream. They had spent hours after hours casting training while her grandfather regaled her with sage words. They had retired to the house full of bruises and smiles.

KIYLA. *She wiped the tears that trailed down her cheeks with the back of her hand.* Goodbye, grandpa. *She muttered as she allowed herself to wallow further in grief.*

*It's evening...*The hue of the environment was unusual. It's dark, but not dark enough to be considered night.

The mall was a few meters from class. A girl hopped along, her hands in the pocket of the purple hoodie and one earbud fixed to her right ear. The flowers arranged in different forms lined the path to the mall.

A blooming purple hibiscus caught her eye. She loved purple, and the purple flower just a few paces from the mall felt like a good omen.

Or was it?

She took the final left turn when she heard strange sounds. She looked around her; every other person was walking like nothing was amiss.

Was she hallucinating? Were there sounds, or was it just her head?

She continued walking, then paused mid-step. She could hear voices.

UNKNOWN MAN'S VOICE 1. You should learn to stop poking your nose in things that are none of your business. *Someone said in a deep angry* voice.

The girl removed the earpiece from her ear.

UNKNOWN GIRL'S VOICE. Everything that concerns the people is our business. You're going to regret that decision, trust me. *A second voice that sounded not so adult as the first said.*

UNKNOWN MAN'S VOICE 2. This is the second time; don't you think you should back off? After one of you defeated Mageario. He was ours to finish off!

The girl heard the landing of a punch.

UNKNOWN GIRL'S VOICE. We don't think alike.

VALERY. Where are the sounds coming from? *She looked around, but nothing. She blinked her eyes twice like she usually did whenever she wanted to see more accurately.* Why is it harder to find those invisible domes suddenly?

She started looking all around. She focused her mind, and she could finally see past the invisible dome's protective barriers. Inside are two knights, a yellow and blue knight, who are fighting with a third person. It was none other than one of those superhero agents standing at the back.

The ground (yellow) knight jumps and aims a kick straight into the agent's chest. She stumbles back and is caught by the other knight, who strikes her hard in the back. The agent falls to the ground, using her hands to prevent herself from falling face down.

The girl outside the invisible dome hesitates for a moment. Every other person around was still walking like a bloody fight wasn't happening right beside them.

VALERY. *She wonders what sorcery this secret agency can create.* I still do not understand how no average person can see inside these invisibility domes. I can't be that far from ordinary.

She finds a tall metal box on the corner. She jogs to it, stands on her toes, and places her backpack on top.

VALERY. *She starts singing to herself.* Don't look suspicious, don't look suspicious. *Too late!*

The girl raises her hood and runs through the barrier, heading straight for the ground Knight. She raises her fist and strikes him on his back to distract him from the agent; then, she utilizes his confusion to roundhouse kick him right on the diaphragm.

The water knight quickly comes for her. He grabs and drags her by the hair, pulling her backward.

VALERY. *She gritted her teeth.* When someone pulls your hair, you can always use it to your advantage. *She thought, remembering the words from one of her past martial arts teachers at HighTech Academy.*

The girl spins with his hands still pulling her hair, then grabs the part of her hair in his possession with both arms. She turns to face him and aims a hammer fist on the most prominent muscle on his forearm, penetrating deep. He covers his hands, grits his teeth, and squeezes his eyes shut. She's free of him.

She made a follow-up attack and struck him with her right palm hard on the bridge of his nose. He felt it even with the helmet. He collapses to his knees and sits on the pavement.

WATER KNIGHT - NAVAS. Who the fuck are you?! *He asked in a painful but annoyed tone.*

The agent was on her feet again; she glared at the two knights, fury in her eyes. The irritation crawled on her skin like the webs of a spider. She dilated her pupils and cracked her knuckles, her back still aching from the impact.

She approaches the ground knight, oblivious to every other thing– especially the man whose hands were chained that she wanted to rescue in the first place.

The girl gives him a swift punch to where his kidney is located.

EARTH KNIGHT – GOBON. Ah! You motherf– *He yelled, covering the left part of his stomach.*

Valery's in a head-on battle with the water knight; they're circling each other, hands ready to attack. Sweat drips from both their faces. The teen girl is focused unblinkingly while her opponent breaks the circle and rushes full speed at her. She chuckles inwardly, despite anxiety in her chest. She counts one to five waiting at the spot, then runs to him at full speed a few seconds before he could land.

They crashed into each other, the water knight landing flat on his back– the impact on the back of his head causing blood to flow.

Valery calculatedly landed on her knees.

The agent takes a final strike at the tired water knight, right to his jaw. He falls. The hooded girl punches the ground knight seven times. Four times to the right side of his chest and three times to the left of his ribs. He fell, the painful sensation spreading all over his body. The battle feels over, at least for now. Sure, it seemed more manageable than the last time.

The agent materialized V-Cuffs– the silvery metallic device with a cursive imprint of the agency's name on one side. She flings them in the air.

AGENT JEIFII. I told you we don't think alike. *She said to both with a smirk.*

The two knights avoid the cuffs and stand as they land on the ground and disappear.

NAVAS. You won't be putting me in cuffs. *He said.*

AGENT JEIFII. *Closely watching both knights.* Watch me.

The ground knight's busy with something in his fingers. The agent nods to the hooded girl with a look of curiosity. She shrugs and watches her move to put them in the cuffs; then, she hears an eerie sound as the dome is starting to get thinner and thinner.

The agent lowers her arms, exchanging a sideways glance with Purple V, and tries to reinforce the dome barrier with her V-Link.

She's unable to no avail. The dome canceled out, and both knights regained their momentum. They stood. The ground knight throws a punch at the agent. He barely missed as the agent leaped out of the way. Navas throws a few smoke grenades.

GOBON. *He shouts.* Let's go!! We're done here, Navas.

They both ran. Purple V places her hands in the pocket of her hoodie. The smoke cleared, and she bit her bottom lip.

PURPLE V. Why did the knights escape?

AGENT JEIFII. *She's releasing tension in her fists and turns to the girl.* How does she get to see inside the dome? She has no V-link! *She thought.*

A thick fog soon encloses the area where the agent stands, obstructing her vision. She closes her eyes, blinking twice, and opens them. She tries to cancel it out using her V-Link, but the fog remains thick.

Valery hears galloping steps. But there are no horses—no animal sounds.

People are approaching, and they mean business. She takes a deep breath and presses her hands to her sides, bracing herself. The girl's hands became cold, her chest pounding and legs shaking. Her adrenaline was in full swing. A tiny creature with a Christmas tree-like hat comes running to the girl. It's her little friend.

PURPLE V. No! Quetsey, you're supposed to be asleep in my backpack. Why did you come here?

QUETSEY. *He stops and looks her way.* You're not in trouble?

Just then, two unfamiliar soldiers in helmets forcibly grab the girl and the tiny creature. They drag her by her elbow, and another throws a chain at them. She tries using one of her elbows to hit them. One of the soldiers elbows her from behind. A wave of pain rushed through her. They're wearing armor that hurts like Hell.

She swerves and tries to kick the second soldier. The first one catches her leg and holds it mid-air, causing her to fall to the ground and landing on her upper back with a great thud.

The first soldier extends his hands to her. She irks and pushes herself up. The soldier casts the chain around her and looks at her with a stern expression. She steals a final glance where she last saw Agent JeiFii, unable to see her because of the thick fog. She's somewhere close, trying to attack nearby enemies which she can't see.

She felt a glimmer of hope for a second, although she knew she couldn't save her.

Suddenly, the agent catches her eye and tries to use her speed power from her V-Link to catch up to the people trying to take her. She's running towards the soldiers at full speed; the anger of having them cart away Purple V propels her forward even more. She lands a blow to the ribcage of the one closest to her. The soldier swiftly turns and bends down. The piercing pain was defying his training as a military man to absorb punches. A flicker of panic shows on the second soldier's face. Agent JeiFii comes for him too. The man in armor turns to his colleague, who nods at him. The agent tries to stun her enemies, but it backfires, and she's blasted away. This provides her adversaries the perfect escape as one of them quickly makes a hand gesture, and they disappear with the girl and the tiny creature.

AGENT JEIFII. No!!! *She returned as the fog was no more.* Where – Where did you go? *She immediately turns her V-Link on, but she can't locate her signal anywhere.* No – Nooo!!

Angrily, the girl turns to the man in special cuffs and walks to him.

AGENT JEIFII. *Reaches the man and pushes him.* Tell me?! Why were they after you?!

SAMUEL MARSHALL. Easy, child. I don't know who those soldiers were, but you managed to save me from those treacherous knights.

AGENT JEIFII. Oh s'il te plait. (Oh, please.) I'm not your kin. *Shakes her head.* I'm taking you to meet the boss.

As the girl turns, the man smirks. JeiFii activates her V-Link and calls HQ. An agent answers the call.

AGENT RIT. You've reached the exclusive but most–

AGENT JEIFII. C'est assez. (That's enough.) A group of mystery soldiers took someone. After battling the knights, they ran. However, I saved this older man, and I'm bringing him to HQ for answers. It's weird they just left him like that. Plus, he's giving me strange vibes.

AGENT RIT. Uh. Well, there's something else too. I'll notify the commander. See ya soon.

AGENT JEIFII. *Hanging up the line and turning to the man. She raises her V-Link, and the man passes out.* Let's get some answers.

The agent grabs him and teleports to headquarters. The Invisi-Dome cleanses the area and disappears.

VLORs HQ…

JeiFii appears at the interrogation center and locks Samuel Marshall inside the room. She immediately makes her way to the operations room. Agent Caj peeked his head out of the GearedNReady room as she was walking, ushering her to come inside.

AGENT JEIFII. Why are you all here?

AGENT CAJ. We're about to leave for the day. *Laughs.*

AGENT JEIFII. Right. *Turns and sees Z near his locker.* Um, there's something you should know.

AGENT Z. If it's those two knights, I don't wanna know.

AGENT JEIFII. The girl wearing a purple hoodie. Unknown soldiers took her.

AGENT Z. WHAT?!!!!

AGENT JEIFII. There was a thick fog and –

AGENT RIT. Rev has gone missing too. His signal was lost on New Waii hours ago. Do you guys think –

AGENT Z. Oh, I know. They have them.

AGENT CAJ. Hold on, Z. Instead of rushing in blind, we need to –

AGENT Z. NO!!! They have my friends!

AGENT RIT. One of your friends who shouldn't be going out in the field. A friend whose mind you should have erased a long time ago.

AGENT Z. Why don't you shut up!

AGENT CAJ. Okay, both of you shut it. *Sighs.* We'll start fresh tomorrow. We might, again, we might know who's behind this kidnapping, but don't jump to conclusions. You've all experienced what running into battle blind and angry does to you. Am I understood on the plan?

AGENT RIT. Aye.

AGENT JEIFII. Aye.

AGENT CAJ. *Stares at Z, who's not making eye contact with anyone.* Am I understood?

AGENT Z. Aye, Caj. *Exhales.*

Z teleports out of the room, and JeiFii does the same.

AGENT RIT. *Walks closer to Caj and whispers.* Any reason why you wanted everyone in here and not the operations room?

AGENT CAJ. I have my reasons. Go get some rest.

Meanwhile, at an undisclosed location, Valery felt a strange feeling in her stomach. Her head's spinning, and she thought she would throw up.

Unknown guards ordered her to put her hands in front of her friend and attached a silver band to them. As soon as she wore it, she felt dizziness in her head that was stronger than anything she'd ever felt.

The place looks weird, weirder than she thought the new city she and her dad relocated to the first time she came to Hidendale from HighTech City. At least she had felt intrigued, but here she only felt wary in a mysterious way. No one needed to tell her it was dangerous or something was wrong.

The two guards led her to a small room and left.

The room was too bright, brighter than the outside. She held Quetsey tighter, unable to put him down because of the device around her upper arms.

VALERY. Isn't this weird? *She whispered.*

The creature could barely wag its tail and whimpered.

A new guard entered, and she walked down a long corridor, not as bright as the first one. A total of eight guards wearing face masks and special armor, revealing no part of their bodies, were lined on the walls.

This one guard led her to a special cell where they separated her and the creature. She shouts, but they don't care. They shoved them into their respective rooms, and the doors were shut.

It's the darkest room, and it's tranquil. She cannot even hear the breathing of the other people on the other side of the door. Probably also captured.

One of the guards clicked something on his wrist, and a small five-centimeter radii illuminator brought a dim light to the room. She can see how the space is composed. There were others – separated by thick glass walls—people who are now in different compartments.

VALERY. Wait a minute. *Taking a closer look.* These are kids around my age. *She's shocked and surprised.* Why – Why are we here? *She felt the cold around them sweep her skin to the point of shivers. She concludes they had been asleep for a long time in their individual, cold compartments.* What did they do?

At another part of the room are people whose cages have a person's outstretched hands chained to a board. It's obvious, like the others, he'd also been in the position for long enough to eradicate motion to any sort out of his body. She looked around and noticed a few other prisoners were in their cells alone and pacing.

A guard outside the individual prison rooms paused right in the middle of the hall.

A tall, dark man enters. He nods at the soldier, and he continues his duties elsewhere.

Valery's pacing around, checking every corner of the tiny cubicle space, when she hears a beep. There's an intercom system in the room. A man speaks to her. She curls both her fists into a ball, ignoring her martial arts lessons of not letting fear show in front of your captors or enemies.

His bald head reflected all the little light in the corridor as he looked inside her cell. He looked at her closely. His small eyes are not blinking. He cracked his throat and spoke in a voice that sounded like the squeezing of papers. His square jaw articulated every word he said.

DUNAN. You may call me Captain Dunan. One thing that distinguishes me from other people you see is that I get it when I see something with potential. I waste no time in utilizing it. I know you have abilities way more than just being able to run very fast.

VALERY. Wrong. I'm not fast. *She swallowed, understanding his message, and spoke to herself inaudibly.* Don't try to escape.

DUNAN. I've been at this game for a while now. I know that look. Do realize, we have different things we can do to you if you try to escape. *He stands tall.* I'll be honest with you since you're curious. I won't mince words. I have a hatred for mixed breeds, and I know the truth. You have an attachment to that strange animal from another place, not from Earth. I won't dispose of you– Not yet.

VALERY. Pfft. Or you can't because you're not the one in charge. The baddie never reveals himself so earlier in the game.

Quetsey let out a loud screeching sound. The older man turned and eyed the creature with mild amusement, then turned back to her.

DUNAN. Welcome to your cross-human Hell.

VALERY. *She blinks once, then twice. She couldn't see a face, only could hear a voice. She takes a deep breath, speaking inaudibly again.* I need to get out as soon as possible.

The huge man caught a reflection of himself staring at her, a flicker in his eyes and something like fire.

VALERY. *Looking all around her environment, speaking inaudibly once more.* Oh. This battle is going to be a tough one. *Sighs.* I hope Agent Z gets here – soon.

SEASON 5, EPISODE 31

10:10 A.M.
Friday, February 01, 2108
Border of HighTech City, north of Techy Mountains...

Everything was quiet until they both stopped suddenly.

CQUA. Do you smell that too, Rit?

RIT. Yes. That strange, stank magic feel in the air when I fought that woman.

CQUA. I – I don't know what you mean by that, but thanks to our V-Links we can detect it.

RIT. Due to constant battles with them, the devices recorded their signature abilities.

The road continued quietly, and the strong smell of magic became stronger.

CQUA. It will be a great help, although I will have to ask some questions dealing with cross-humans and Xeiars.

RIT. What's to ask? They're humans with superpowers, and the Xeiars are wizards who look like ordinary humans. I hear they're from another dimension.

They didn't walk very far until they heard a roar and ran towards the noise. When they reached the source of it, they were both stunned by the scene. A brown-headed, caramel-skinned, brown-eyed girl beat up some guards, but not with her fists. Using her hands, she was moving boxes, shelves and throwing them to the guards. She was moving very fast, almost like someone with special powers or suits, and when she touched a guard, the weapons on him exploded. This sent him straight into a wall.

When the girl hindered the last guard, and she noticed the presence of the agents, Rit immediately moved behind her; the speed that his suit gave him was incredible, like a flash. The girl could not react.

RIT. Who are you, and what are you doing here? *He said with contempt.*

JAYLA. That doesn't concern you. *She said as she placed her hands into her pockets.* It's been a while since I've seen my friend. Now, kindly tell your colleague to let me go, or the only thing left of him will be a pool of blood. *She said with bulging eyes and a smile that wasn't normal at all.*

AGENT CAJ. Rit, let her go. This has to be a friend to Agent Z. She's on our side.

JAYLA. Huh. What did you say?

AGENT CAJ. Your friend doesn't like to erase his bestie's memories after meeting one of us or whatever we're facing. *Shaking his head with a smile.*

AGENT CQUA. That sounds about right.

Rit makes a bad gesture, but he doesn't take his eyes off her because of what she can do.

JAYLA. I've been told about you guys. You all work for a secret agency. I'm here because my friend is here somewhere. I can offer my help. I know this is an activity that requires discretion. *She rolls her eyes.* Secret agency stuff.

AGENT RIT. Okay, let's leave the explanations for later. I think something bad is coming.

A monster with a titanic shape just arrived. Despite its size, it moved very fast, and Jayla created a lightning barrier to protect herself.

AGENT CQUA. Don't worry. *He walks forward as the others are looking at him.* With these suits, this thing will not be able to make us n– *The creature's breath sends him into the air.*

The monster overlooked Jayla's lightning barrier. Agent Caj jumped considerably, taking the impulse from Jayla's shoulders. Once face to face with the creature's face, he connected around twenty punches and forceful kicks that made the target fall, only to be received by a high voltage blunt shock from attacks that she provided as support.

AGENT RIT. Very resilient.

The creature started getting to its feet and glowing.

AGENT CQUA. *Speeds to the area on foot, close to the others.* Is that thing healing?

The creature appears to have adapted to her magical attack.

AGENT CAJ. Rit. Assistance, please? *He screamed as he continued to evade being knocked on his rear.*

A cold breeze blew against his face as he climbed down the side of a dusty ladder, nearing the bottom. As he moved closer, it felt cold. The icy sensation would've been stinging if not for the layers of protective clothing that covered his body from the neck down to the toes. His eyes and scalp were shielded with a mask as well, and so far, the facility had dark areas, so this person blended in perfectly with his black attire.

He climbed down quickly without a noise. He glanced at his unique wrist device on getting to a window, and the dim red LED lights indicated that he was in the correct spot.

He reached the bottom and surveyed the room. He sees a window that looks like it leads to another area. Nothing was in this room. With one of his gloved hands, he let go of the rope momentarily to dip a hand into his pocket to pull out a cutter. He sliced a sizable hole in the glass, big enough to fit his body. Once done, he placed the glass down gingerly and slipped into the building through the hole.

The masked person glanced at his watch again. He was sure of how to navigate the heavily guarded facility and where exactly to go. He pushed the metal door open and stepped into a brightly lit hallway. The walls were spotlessly white, and every surface of it was reflective. He had no time to appreciate the décor, as he had a mission to accomplish.

He drew his weapon and began to trot gently down the hallway. He came upon guards garbed in protective gear and face masks, but he did not confront them. Instead, he hid while they patrolled, and once they were out of sight, he resumed his walk towards the holding cells.

His covert assignment was to free a group of super-powered people held captive in this facility.

He looked up and saw a split path ahead. At the intersection was a sign that read **Section 4** and **Section 0**. One had an arrow pointing to the right and the other left. He took a quick guess and made his decision. He began heading towards **Section 0**. As he got farther along, he made a turn and came face to face with two soldiers armed with blasters. He moved quickly. Before the soldiers could react, he shot them squarely in the chest, neutralizing and eliminating the threat. He let out a deep breath, thanking his stars for getting through such a close shave.

He noticed the soldiers were guarding a door. The masked person pushed a button on the door's panel, and it opened with a hiss. What he saw inside confirmed his mission – there were indeed super-powered people in the place.

Before him was an upright glass pod, and from where he stood, he could see a girl in it. He moved closer and read the inscription:

> *Subject 9*
> *Name: Floral*
> *Age: 12*
> *Ability: Chlorokinesis*

MASKED PERSON. This is it. *He muttered to himself as his eyes scanned the buttons on the pod. He saw one inscribed, **Open Pod**. Without hesitation, he pushed it.*

Just then, a small screen displayed a status bar that was slowly filling up, followed by the words, **INITIALIZING RELEASE.**

MASKED PERSON. *He let out a sigh of relief.* She's a fighter. She'll be fine on her own.

His mission wasn't done; he had others to free. As the status bar was getting to the final percentile, he left the room to proceed with the second phase of his mission.

Border of HighTech City, north of Techy Mountains...

Suddenly, a slash appeared on the creature's chest. Rit was behind it with his right hand full of blood.

AGENT RIT. I'm going to hit you back 100-fold! *He yelled as he began cutting the monster simultaneously with Caj and Jayla's help.*

After a minute or so, it was over. The creature succumbed to the attacks, and its form changed into a human.

AGENT CQUA. I think our work here is done. We should withdraw and report what happened to the agency. The infiltration mission will have to stop for now. This monster was not in our plans, and if there are more like him, we'll need more agents.

JAYLA. You're leaving? *Scoffs.* Fine! I'm staying to help my friend.

AGENT CAJ. I've already made up my mind last night. *Turns and walks closer to the girl, making eye contact.* We're going to save your friend, Purple V, together.

AGENT RIT. That's – an interesting codename. What? The Glistening Midget wasn't available?

The girl quickly turned towards him, fists clenched, about to punch him, but Caj pulled her back.

JAYLA. I don't like people talking about my besties. *Jerks her arm out of Caj's grip.*

AGENT CQUA. Douchebag, bro. *Walking past Caj and the girl, shaking his head.* Let's continue. We won't return until this mission is done.

AGENT CAJ. We could use your help, just not the mouth. Can you watch yours?

AGENT RIT. No chill at all. *Shaking his head.* I'm in. Let's see what these soldiers want.

When they were about to leave, they heard some boxes fall. One woman had survived. She didn't look like a guard but a scientist. She stayed hidden behind some boxes and was scared to death; she couldn't even speak.

AGENT RIT. Looks like we almost missed someone. *He said, sighing and approaching the scientist.* Ma'am. We won't hurt you, don't worry. Look, see this? *He pulls out a kind of small, square device with a crystal in the middle.*

UNKNOWN FEMALE SCIENTIST. *She looks at it and is in a trance.* Listen, there's been a mistake. There were dangerous chemicals in one of the boxes, and the guards dropped it, making everything explode.

AGENT RIT. Didn't want to hear that nonsense.

JAYLA. Oy vey. *Rolling her eyes as she approaches the hypnotic woman.* Can you tell us if we're at the exact location where they're keeping these so-called humans with extraordinary abilities?

The scientist nods her head.

AGENT RIT. *He leans toward Caj and whispers to him.* She might make a good agent.

The agents continue walking victorious, not knowing that they've made a serious mistake. There was another person who saw everything and stayed hidden.

Elsewhere...

Lieutenant Ogdo sits in his quarters, polishing his weapon.

A usual group of special soldiers, commanded by this military man, were sent to capture creatures and humans with superpowers worldwide. The primary weapons were powerful sleeping pills compressed into small sphere bullets of a weak material that put the targets to sleep on the spot and a high-tech bottle-shaped molecule reducer where the Lieutenant and his team could capture maximum bodies. The latter was the creation that took the longest to perfect for the skilled group of scientists. It cost a lot of time and money.

OGDO. *Mockingly.* I'll need as many test subjects as I can get. Do not allow yourself to be followed. Ha! *He laughs and remembers something.*

A week ago...

Dunan's ambition blinded him; he gave orders, and Ogdo obeyed. That day, the confrontation was imminent. An espionage agency was monitoring them. These spies did not know where these guys came from – they're too meticulous. Ogdo and troops found a group of spies, where they exchanged blows.

OGDO. *Exhaling, exhausted.* Who are you, and why have I caught you spying? *He asked.*

The spies looked at one another and would not say a word.

OGDO. Well, if you do not speak, I will make you! *He exclaimed, advancing rapidly towards one spy. He started punching the man in the stomach a few times viciously. Afterward, he shoved him to the floor.*

When the man bent over in pain, the Lieutenant took his skull between his hands and turned it the other way with force, immediately breaking his neck. He continued circling the head three times until it hung lower.

The two other spies stood, perplexed. Then they threw down small spheres that deployed a cloud of intense smoke. This strategy immediately blinded the Lieutenant and his team; the spy grabbed one of the soldiers by their neck. The Lieutenant regained his vision and was furious. Someone had one of his men.

The spy took the captured soldier to their agency and questioned him inquisitively. After three hours of continuous interrogation, the soldier finally uttered a few words.

UNKNOWN SOLDIER. You will not oppose Captain Dunan.

He made a sudden and precise movement where he threw his forehead against the sharp edge of the interrogation room's desk. He must have applied a lot of force because he fell dead to the floor, with his eyes open and bleeding considerably from his forehead.

Ogdo and the rest of his team stormed the place and killed everyone in the room. He wouldn't allow his brother's secret to get out.

Floral coughed heavily as the air suddenly filled her lungs. She jolted awake as if she had been in slumber for eternity. Her head was dizzy, and her mind was foggy.

She climbed out of the pod and glanced around, seeing an expanse of space. Undoubtedly, it was a high-tech facility. As she travailed her mind, her eyes suddenly bulged when she remembered the last thing that occurred to her – armed men were capturing them.

Regardless of how serene her current environment seemed to be, she knew she wasn't safe. As she paid more attention to her surroundings, she realized that she was in a prison cell, a pristine one at that. Whoever these guys were, they were not messing around.

The girl walked to the door, and the motion detector noticed her approach and eased the door open. Outside, she saw two soldier's unconscious on the floor; their weapons destroyed. She wondered what had happened to them. She didn't want to stall around to find out; she had to locate her friends.

She ran down the hall, but she came to a halt a short distance later when a pair of soldiers spotted her.

UNKNOWN SOLDIER. Hey! Stop there! *One of them ordered in a guttural voice. His hands and his partners went to their blasters.*

The threat was well-communicated.

The girl stood there for a moment, contemplating what to do. There was no plant around for her to manipulate to her defense. It was a tricky situation. She had two options – give herself up to be returned to the cell or fight. The moment the thought crossed her mind, she knew deep down that she would never give herself up for captivity without a struggle. She made her decision.

She gauged the distance between herself and the guards as an ambitious thought crossed her mind. There were only six meters between them. Her muscles became taut as she gritted her teeth and braced herself.

MULTIPLE SOLDIERS. *They could note the determination in her eyes, and they raised their weapons.* Don't move! *They chorused.*

Their words fell on deaf ears as the girl was already in motion. She dropped onto the floor and rolled forward twice, hearing the blasters hitting the floor inches away from her body.

Now in front of the soldiers, she kicked one of them in the knee, and as he leaned forward. She grabbed his blaster and pulled him over her while the other soldier fired into his partner's back without remorse. His goal was to hit her, even if it meant killing a fellow soldier.

The girl had capitalized on that, and once she heard the blaster go off, she kicked the standing soldier hard at the ankle, knocking him off his feet. As he landed with a thud, she whirled her legs over her head and got up acrobatically. Before the soldier on the floor could raise his weapon, she shot him with the blaster she had acquired.

Once she was sure that they were eliminated, she pushed the button to the guarded door. Inside, there are many glass pods, and one of them housed her friend. She rushed over to release them. She pressed a few buttons, and the calibration had begun.

A painful memory...

The seven-year-old Lin and her pure Chinese mother are running away from Guerilla Warfare troops in a foreign land. They've run through trenches and hilltops. Lin makes it to a hill and looks down, searching for her mother. Just as her mother is close, she's impaled by a sharp object and falls to her death.

Lin's eyes widened, watching the entire event. She backs away, drops to her knees, positions herself, so she's sitting on her rear, and pulls her knees close to her, crying her eyes out.

Rogue Guerilla troops are approaching, shouting in a different language the girl doesn't know. One of them grabs a loose rock and chucks it forward. It clocks another guy in the head. He falls to his death.

The men unintentionally fall into traps, and explosions go off around the sobbing girl. The men are buried in the rubble.

A few hours pass, Lin is walking alone in a strange, deserted area. She's sweaty, hungry, exhausted, and heartbroken. She finally falls to her knees, dehydrated and tired. She lowers her eyes to the ground. She wants to give up and let external forces take her to a better place. There's no way she can survive in this heat. She hasn't eaten in days.

Suddenly, she hears galloping horses. She stares out in front of her. There are three men on horses. One of them is pulling a carriage. They halt when they reach the young girl.

A man steps out of the carriage. He smiles at her.

JOE SVAL. *Heh.* Today must be my lucky day! *He's smiling.*

Lin and her mother have been on the run since she was six years old. They were running for their lives because her mother stole food to feed her daughter. A man purchased her mother at the age of fifteen from an underground slave auction.

A hunter – Joe Sval – finds Lin and pretends to be her friend. He was on assignment to find new humans to sell. He had Lin placed on a boat and carried far away from her place of birth. The girl arrived on dry land and found herself standing on a stage. She heard strange voices past the stage shouting things out in a not-to-familiar language. They were shouting about amounts of money, trying to buy young girls.

A rough-looking man bought her, taking her back to his place. The girl worked as a slave, forced to cook and clean. Every night she cried herself to sleep, praying to a God to send someone to save her. Days passed, and no one came. One night her owner placed candles in every room in his house and played soothing music that made Lin feel uncomfortable. The eight-year-old girl was cornered as the man got closer. He leaned in and sniffed her neck. She closed her eyes, tears falling down her cheeks. The man placed his stubby hand to her face. She slowly opened her eyes, wishing it was all a dream.

The man whispered, *"Everything is fine. It will feel beautiful."* Lin stared past him, looking to the other room. She thought she saw a figure, but who knows. There was no one there to save her, she thought.

The man dragged her up the stairs to his bedroom and threw her on his bed. He left the room.

Lin immediately heard a noise. It sounded like a head being smashed into a wall. The man was thrown into the room she was in. He was now lying on the floor in front of her. Another man entered and stared at her. Lin looked into his eyes, terrified. She fainted and woke up the next day in another place. The girl remembered last night, and she started bawling her eyes out. This man heard crying, and he ran into the room to check on her.

It took a while for Lin to adjust to the man who saved her life. She was nine years old when she started to trust him. She found out the man was a special hunter. She found weapons and armor in secret places around his home, even a secret compartment inside the sofa.

One day the man left her home alone, but instead of staying there, she secretly followed. She was almost struck with an arrow if the man did not see her in time. This man trained the girl. She gained a little confidence in herself.

At twelve years old, she was a novice hunter. She learned to gather food and how to kill a few animals for consumption. She learned to fire guns. She learned how to handle sharp weapons. She eventually learned the English language, including two others fluently.

That afternoon, the man did not return home. Lin went looking and discovered clues that he had been taken. She found her teacher chained up by lowlifes inside of a barn. The men were looking for the girl. The man that bought her put a bounty on her.

She defeated them, and the man who bought her came out of hiding. He approached. All those memories of being a slave came back, even the thought of her almost being raped. She choked and froze. The man raised his hand to her, and Lin surprisingly caught his hand. She grabbed the blade at her side and sliced his chest open, blood-spattered onto her body. He was killed right there; the other hunters got up and charged at her. She killed every one of them out of rage.

The girl went inside the barn where her teacher was tied up and freed him. He smiled at her, impressed. They returned home, and she laid him on the floor. He suffered from the brutal beatings; he was bleeding out. Lin cried and watched him die. There was nothing she could do. She eventually strapped up and left that house after watching it burn to the ground.

At fourteen years old, she found a hunter hauling an animal inside a net toward his truck. She approached and killed him. Lin cut the ropes, and a strange creature looked at her. Lin met Kysis for the first time.

In the present...

Floral waited around until the calibration had completed and the glasses slid open.

LIN YIU GUSTOV. *She screams out.* No!!!! *Sweating and panting, she blurts out in Vietnamese.* Tôi đang ở đâu? (Where am I?) Where – *Looking at her surroundings.* Oh, great. It was a dream. *Wiping tears from her eyes.*

FLORAL. You were crying while asleep. What did you dream about?

LIN YIU GUSTOV. Nothing good. *Hops down from the pod, noticing the small creature isn't beside her.* Where's Kysis?

FLORAL. Probably in one of these. *She helped each of the captives out in turns. She gave them a quick rundown of their current predicament, emphasizing the need to find an escape route.*

After Lin released Kysis, Floral freed the young knight and an overweight teenage girl, Calebra, who had the power to transfer kinetic energy into objects and make them explode, threw her arms around her.

CALEBRA. Oh, thank you, thank you!! I'm so glad to see you're here! *She confessed.*

FLORAL. Uhm... Me too. *She replied, patting her back pacifyingly.*

A younger boy, Jaylin, looked on with worry and impatience in his eyes. Floral could relate; there wasn't time to waste on a reunion.

FLORAL. We've gotta go! *She muttered into his ears.*

CALEBRA. Alright. *She said as she broke away from the embrace.*

The girl with plant abilities unlocks the last pod, and something speeds out. They all turn their heads and see a teenage boy standing by the door. He looks about fourteen years old.

JACOB LANDSLOT. Call me, Jacob. Thanks, ladies. *He smiles, showing pearly whites.*

The five of them rushed out of the room.

Elsewhere...

Captain Dunan cussed as his eyes glared at the monitor before him. The screen showed a group of kids running through the facility's halls, eliminating his soldiers as they went along. They were supposed to be in cells. He's infuriated and has to release his secret weapon – a super-powered man who's under mind control. However, when he attempted to push the button to release him, the captain's eyes roved to the screen that showed his holding cell. What he saw made his eyes bulging wildly.

DUNAN. Goddammit! *He exclaimed.*

On the screen was a masked person in all black fighting the cross-human he was planning to unleash. The masked man knocked the man out cold,

DUNAN. *Banged his hands against his table.* I'll be damned!!!

Instantly, he picked up his phone and called his brother, Lieutenant Ogdo, the soldiers' head that guarded the facility, to inform him of the prisoners' escape. On hearing this, the Lieutenant triggered an alarm that rang throughout the facility. He gathered a unit of soldiers, and they rushed into the hallway to hunt down the escapees.

Meanwhile, Floral's eyes reflexively shot up when she heard the sound of an alarm ringing. It had been expected. She knew sooner or later; they would discover their escape. Glancing behind her, she felt hopeful with the small force she had garnered. With Calebra and Jacob included, she had freed eight people, each with extraordinary power – excluding Lin.

The group of teens ran down the halls, headed by Floral and a super-powered girl her age whose ability was geothermal sensitivity. She could tell the location of different room chambers with her feet and mind, and in essence, the exit door.

ANAWEL. We're close. It's only a few turns away. *She stated.*

FLORAL. Good. Keep moving, guys. *She encouraged.*

At that moment, a loud booming voice yelled from behind them, **"Stop, or I'll kill you all!"**

LIEUTENANT OGDO. Stop! *He repeated, holding up two fingers to signal this as the final warning.*

FLORAL. Guys, stop. Let's hold on. *She called out to her companions.*

They all obliged, turning to face their enemies.

The girl's heart did a double skip. She stopped in her tracks and glanced back to see the Lieutenant, a mind-controlled Darkstras, and a herd of guards behind him. They had their blasters pointed forward. Floral whirled around to the direction they were running to and realized that the next turning was still far ahead, and with the narrowness of the hall, they would be right in open range and shot down.

LIEUTENANT OGDO. *He smiled lewdly. His eyes focused on each of them in turn as he added.* It's best you listened. Now, come here and turn yourself over—all of you.

CALEBRA. Not a chance. *She replied.*

LIN. I agree. I'm not going back to being a guinea pig for whatever evil plan you have for us! *She declared, taking a defensive stance.*

FLORAL. That's right; we can't let them take us. *She stated.*

LIEUTENANT OGDO. How cute. You don't want to defy me. Then you'll die. *He said with a cold stare in his eyes.*

FLORAL. *As harsh as the threat seemed, she wasn't ready to cave in.* Anyone with powers that can help us here? *She said to the people around her in a low voice.*

CALEBRA. There's nothing around me I can transfer my energy to as a projectile. *She said as she turned around in futility.*

FLORAL. Darn. *Grits her teeth.* Who else? *She asked.*

JACOB LANDSLOT. I can run at super speed, but it's only for a second before I snap back to my initial position. *He stated.*

FLORAL. That'll come in handy.

A girl from the group, Tarina, stepped forward.

TARINA. I can absorb elements around me and their properties.

FLORAL. *A smile crossed her face.* That's great. I'd like you to—

LIEUTENANT OGDO. Enough talk. Stun them! *He ordered.*

Prompted, the soldiers began to fire at the escapees.

TARINA. *She stepped forward, kneeled, and touched the concrete floor. Her body began to morph into stone.* Get behind me!!! *She yelled, spreading her hands to protect everyone.*

Floral and the other super teens filed behind her, making sure they were well-positioned behind her frame.

FLORAL. Get us out of here! *She barked at Jacob.*

JACOB LANDSLOT. On it! *He replied with a nod. Within a couple of seconds, he grabbed two of the teens and took them to the end of the hall, to safety. When he snapped back to his position he asked.* Who's next?

FLORAL. Calebra. Now, go!! *She ordered.*

Jacob grabbed her by the arm and pulled her along as he ran. When Calebra blinked, she found herself already at the end of the hall.

LIEUTENANT OGDO. Don't let them get away!! Bring them down! *He flared.*

The soldiers began to approach the young super-powered kids on his command while they fired their blasters incessantly, with the shots bounced off Tarina's body.

TARINA. They are closing in; we need to get out of here soon! *She stated while she remained a human shield for her companions.*

JACOB LANDSLOT. *He glanced at Floral.* I'll take you and Tarina out of here now.

FLORAL. But that'll leave you behind. How'll you get away? *She asked with concern etched on her face.*

JACOB LANDSLOT. *He smiled weakly and replied.* I won't.

FLORAL. No—

She had started to say when Jacob grabbed her and transported her to where their super-powered peers were before he came back and did the same with Tarina.

When Floral regained her composure, she saw that Jacob was far away, standing defiantly against the soldier's advances, who were very close to him now.

FLORAL. Run!!! *She cried out, but she knew it was futile.*

With no shield to guard him against the blasters, he won't be able to get away before he is shot down.

JACOB LANDSLOT. *It seemed as if he was aware of this, too, as he did not attempt to run. Instead, he turned to Floral and shouted from across the hall.* Get out of here; save yourselves!

The soldiers aimed their weapons on him as he spoke, and they fired upon him with no remorse. The girl whimpered as they watched his body hit the floor.

LIEUTENANT OGDO. Give yourself up, or that'll be your fate as well.

LIN. Let's get out of here!! *She pleaded as she tugged at Floral's shoulders.*

Just then, the soldiers began to run towards them at top speed, reducing the head start they had.

CALEBRA. Let's go!!! *She repeated.*

FLORAL. *Running beside Lin.* We can't get far. They'll catch up to us. *She replied.*

CALEBRA. You're right; we need to stop them. I have an idea. *She stated as her brain worked on overdrive.*

FLORAL. Don't you dare stop and do the same thing!

There was no object around for her to utilize as a weapon, so she made use of the only thing she possessed – her clothes. She quickly pulled off her shirt and rolled it into a ball in her palms. She focused kinetic energy on it, and a second later, the cloth had turned into a glowing red ball.

CALEBRA. ADVANCE FASTER!!!! *She yelled at her companions, who ducked while running on hearing that. She took a few steps forward and hurled the projectile ahead.*

She had aimed for the ceiling above the soldiers, and when the ball contacted it, an explosion occurred, raining down glass and stones. The men beneath didn't stand a chance, as they were crushed to death by the falling debris. The Lieutenant and all the soldiers included.

Without waiting for the dust to settle, the super-powered younglings headed to an exit.

The navigator led them into a dimly lit tunnel with a moldy scent. They kept running but were halted in their tracks when they made a turn and saw someone standing in their path, waiting for them. Behind him were about thirty soldiers in full combat gear.

DUNAN. *As soon as his eyes locked with Floral's, he wasted no time before barking orders.* Bring them down, dead or alive!

With the narrowness of the tunnel, the soldiers couldn't risk shooting as not to bring down the rest of the building.

They had to get close to attack with their weapons. They walked around the captain to close the gap between themselves and the kids.

FLORAL. *She glanced sideways at her companions, with rage and bitterness in her eyes. She states.* Let's rain down hell on them. Give it all you've got!

DUNAN. You guys take care of this mess! I have to check on something. *He walks off, going the other way in a hurry.*

With that, they charged at the soldiers, armed with their special powers and willpower to survive.

Outside Neirolo Cavern...

The group hid a short distance from the entrance without losing sight of it. They were patient and managed to see how a group of men armed with guns entered.

Shocker shot down in his lightning form and changed to his flesh form; Agent JeiFii appeared next to Caj. This wasn't planned; they happened to arrive together.

SHOCKER. Agent Z thought y'all could use my help.

AGENT RIT. He's not even here! *Laughs.*

AGENT JEIFII. *Eyeing the cross-human suspiciously, and exhales.* He was right. *Turns to look at Caj.* What are we doing?

AGENT CAJ. Waiting for the right time. Any minute now.

AGENT CQUA. Caj, don't tell me you were okay letting him go in there by himself?

AGENT CAJ. *Smiles.* You know Z's nature. He wouldn't have listened anyway.

XANPO. As any teen doesn't.

Five people appear in a cloud of smoke.

SALLY. I'm sorry, I'm sorry. Still working on proper teleportation. *Smiles innocently.*

AGENT CAJ. *Slightly turns his head and fully stands, laying eyes on the grown man dressed oddly.* Who are you?

XANPO. I'm from Earth, don't worry. A few of my students were taken and sent here. I had Sally – *He pointed at her.* – bring us here.

AGENT JEIFII. The more, the merrier. *Sees one of the newcomers and grimaces at him.*

CHRISTEN. Ready for round 3? Heh-heh. *Looks at the girl agent.*

XANPO. Christen, what did I tell you about acting that way? *As he takes a knee, looking at the cavern's entrance.*

CHRISTEN. Yeah, I'm not your student. *Shifts into his beast form.* But thanks for teaching me self-control over my transformation. *Getting into position.*

AGENT CQUA. *Watching the group of newcomers.* This is weird on a whole 'nother level.

SHOCKER. Tell me about it.

XANPO. So, you're the leader of the agents, I'm assuming. What do we got?

AGENT CAJ. Staking out the entrance until the time comes.

Meanwhile, inside the facility, the masked individual guided a group of captives to a secure room. They're all being quiet as the person lifts his mask.

ZANARI. You're just a boy.

AGENT Z. A secret agent that saved you. You're welcome. *Peeks into the room, eyeing a few individuals.*

Someone's running to the room, quickly. The agent cloaks the group using one of his gadgets. The room's door slides open, Dunan jogs into the room, and the doors close behind him.

SABER. *Tightens her fist.* The traitor.

AGENT Z. Huh.

ZOEY. He used to be one of us at HighTech Police Force.

MAX. That man sure hates our kind.

AGENT Z. *Stares at Max for a bit before looking into the window again.* Cross-humans, I'm assuming.

Inside the room, there are a few people inside. Dunan approaches a man wearing a lab coat.

AGENT Z. *Gasps.* What –

NIARA. What do you see?!

ZANARI. What's stopping us from leaving this prison?

AGENT Z. A terrible man we thought was dead. Kelort. That's him, alright. *He moves his eyes around the room. At first, he sees nothing out of the ordinary, and then he notices two of his closest friends.* Rev! Valery!

MAX. We can't see! Mind telling us what's going on?

AGENT Z. They're getting ready to do something wicked.

Inside the room, Dunan speaks to the man who Z recognized.

KELORT RITZORI. Are the intruders silenced?

DUNAN. Everything's going as planned. They won't make it here in time.

KELORT RITZORI. Good. *Hands interlocked behind his back as he stares at the tubes to the right.* These two are cross-humans from the other dimension, correct?

DUNAN. Their biology, according to scientists, picked up unusual properties in their DNA. They were brought here to see if we can pull whatever it is out of them.

KELORT RITZORI. Finally, to have two specimens survive a mutation process without changing physical appearances.

DUNAN. *Looks at him, concerned.* You have the other one.

KELORT RITZORI. Pedro is nothing more than a lap dog. Carry on with the infusion.

DUNAN. *Speaking to scientists in the room.* You've h –

Just then, Agent Z crashed through the two-way window. He has his blaster materialized and starts shooting at all the equipment.

AGENT Z. This place isn't so crash!!

NIARA. *Jumps through the window with a barrier surrounding her body. She aims her right hand at the scientists.* **Ventis!** *She aims her left at the tubes station.* **Nozespro Cuulazostras!**

The cloud of paralyzing poison hit all the scientists. Kelort eased himself into a corner without being seen. Dunan runs to another room as fast as he can. The two teens aimed their attacks at the cylinder prison tubes simultaneously, and the glass cracked. Shards are falling to the floor. In beast form, Zanari sprints inside jumps and grabs Valery, and Rev. He exits the room without stopping. Z and Niara are now back-to-back, watching the clouds in the room. Both are ready to attack anything that decides to sprint at them. They start backing out of the room.

Downstairs, Floral and her group neutralized the soldiers and are headed down the long corridor towards the exit. They soon run into Agent Z's group.

The masked Z ditches his garments and is now in his agent attire, ushering everyone toward the exit. As the last one passes him, he stares down the hall and sees an elevator starting to close. Kelort smiles at him, and the doors completely close.

AGENT Z. Oh, you'll get yours. *He shakes his head, turns around, and takes off running to the exit.*

The wait continued; the agents and Jayla were getting impatient. The group outside decided to enter. It was time to act.

The agents activated their special suits, and Jayla's eyes are shining with unquestionable intensity. JeiFii, with incredible skill, sprinted to the entrance as she saw a group exiting. She attacked a soldier chasing after the group, knocking him unconscious with a blow to his temple and another to his throat. Rit joined forces with the well-positioned CQua, who helped him push his hands to jump high. Rit let himself fall; appearing close enough, he gave a quick series of blows to another soldier's stomach. He braced himself as he fell to the ground. While this was happening, Z was quietly punching another soldier in the nose. He was at the back of the group leaving the cavern. That man smacked the back of his head on a boulder.

The two groups are now out of the cavern, Floral's group following behind.

Just then, something crashes down in front of the cavern and creates a small crater. Everyone avoids the dust by holding their arms up or turning their backs.

As the smoke starts clearing, magical blue lights emanate from a figure. It's a man standing inside the crater.

He's stepping out, taking a few steps forward as he's eyeing all the people in front of the cavern's entrance.

ASARIOS. *With a smirk, he introduces himself.* I am Asarios, from planet Xeiar.

XANPO. *Stepping forward as if protecting the younger heroes while keeping his eyes on the wizard.* Are you one of those on Earth killing your kind?

ZANARI. *Shouts.* They'll be none of that today!! *He lets out a beastly growl.*

ASARIOS. Oh! Was that a Damonarian? *Points at them both.* Nah, you two – You're both from planet Vrec. *Lowers his arm. Shaking his head and stares at Xanpo.* Something about you feels… human. By the way, you've got me all wrong. Uh uh. But you won't have to worry about those three anymore. *He says while smiling.*

SALLY. Xanpo. Do you know this man?

ASARIOS. Ah! The young Xeiar. That aura feels quite like a lost companion of mine.

XANPO. What are you talking about?

ASARIOS. Oh! Short story – For you all!! Ha-ha. *Clears his throat jokingly.* As a young lad on my planet, I had... fun! The kind to get you into trouble. Harmless fun, though. Know what I'm saying, kids? Anyway, a flash in the sky. *POP!* A young Quinoragoras I met... Hm, what was his name? Ah-ha! Kweezan. He disappeared. Next thing I know, the Greats had both myself and my dear friend on trial for an incident we had nothing to do with. Fast forward! They're dead. The new ones as well. Uh, besides the new female. I sent her elsewhere so she wouldn't interfere with my fight with the Great wizard, Magis.

SABER. Sounds like you were falsely accused.

ASARIOS. Exactly! Your name is?

SABER. Saber Lenosha.

ASARIOS. Thank you, young human. *Smiling.* So, we were both cast to Valdesmon. It's pretty much a dark hell. No sounds. None of this. *Waves his arms at trees and the sky.* Nope. Just darkness. We were stripped of our magic. But! Here's the good part. Being – *He does air quotes with both hands.* – a hell, others from different places have been sent there. As a boy, I learned to harness energy. We eventually discovered a way to escape but only projected our thoughts into others on the outside.

CHRISTEN. *Tightening both his fists and gritting his teeth.* You mind controlled me.

ASARIOS. Yes! That was easy. *Laughs.* You were in a funk. You're okay now.

XANPO. Enough. You killed the ones who did you wrong. So, why are you here?

ASARIOS. Those two standing right next to you. The two Xeiars. We were going to absorb them to restore our powers. Every fifty years, give or take, two special Xeiars are born with enough potential to lead our world. They eventually become more powerful than Greats.

AGENT RIT. What the hell is a Great?

ASARIOS. Three trained wizards pass selective tests and are chosen by the royal family to protect all of planet Xeiar. Like I said, they're dead now —all but one.

NIARA. You murderer.

ASARIOS. I'd prefer to call it getting even.

ZANARI. More like revenge.

ASARIOS. Hush, puppy prince. *Laughs.* No one told you to speak.

The prince growls.

XANPO. Nice story. But you're not getting them.

DONNY. Yeah! There's only one of you and more of us.

SHOCKER. *Sparkles are emitting from his fingertips.* I'd suggest you go away.

ASARIOS. A Jolt'tweiller. Interesting. Did you know you're technically one of us wizards?

SHOCKER. Huh?

ASARIOS. This was before my time. I'm not much of a reader, but there are stories passed down from different Xeiar families. One day, a wizard traveled to the Isolated Dimension on Earth and established a colony on a cloud. A spell here and there, a potion, and you got yourself a few lightning-based humans. Yup.

AGENT CAJ. Okay, enough story. We're a bit busy here. I'm afraid we're to take a raincheck on your attempt at trying to take those two kids today.

ASARIOS. I fail to understand why you say try.

Captain Dunan, with the help of his brother Ogdo, and a handful of scientists whom he subjected to his command using his influence as an Ex-Lieutenant, established a secret prison where he operates covertly. This underground facility had all kinds of traps and defenses against monsters and superhumans. This prison had wide corridors and rooms protected by various traps meticulously designed to reduce and disable the most common movements; there was a cryogenic scenario for those fire users, rooms with high temperatures, to weaken those skilled in handling ice. The purpose of this prison was to retain these species, to study them. Dunan would achieve, through his scientists, to genetically reprogram them and control their powers. He is a strong character who was impressed with the hero's escape and very angry about what his eyes witnessed. Monsters, gifted humans, magicians... The world just doesn't make sense within the past year. This man, who had once been the chief of a fire department in HighTech City, was influential, strong, and determined, and he was not going to sit back and watch what he had just seen.

The man approaches the end of the cavern with a few soldiers at his side, peeking out at the freed cross-humans and the heroes who rescued them looking at an unknown person wearing unusual clothing.

He removes a handgun from the holster on his lower right leg and takes it off safety. He looks around at all the people and finally sees the one resembling the boy in the mask.

CAPTAIN DUNAN. *He shouts.* All right, men, charge!!!!

His team ran out of the cavern, aiming their blasters at the group. JeiFii materializes her Shibarian Swiggers. The laser whips wrap around their legs, and they fall to the ground. As they're starting to get up, CQua speeds at them, throwing punches and roundhouse kicks.

Jayla's hands start glowing purple. Asarios cocks his head, surprised to see another while watching the random outburst. She throws out a spell blast, but Dunan falls and rolls on the ground to evade it. Saber runs to him, jumps, and kicks forward at his head. The man raises both arms to block. The girl bounces off, doing a backflip before he has a chance to grab her legs.

Dunan sees Agent Z and immediately fires his gun out of pure anger for the trouble he caused. Valery comes out of nowhere and shoves the agent to the ground, taking the hit. She's struck in her lower back, barely avoiding paralysis. She sees flashes before her eyes as her vision worsens; she's falling slow.

Z's too slow, and Valery falls forward. He froze up. JeiFii and Sally run to the girl's side.

At that moment, Asarios freezes too. Everything around him reverted to home when he was the teen boy, Asari. The teen smiles innocently at him with both his eyes closed. Reality warps back to the present day. A moment returned within Asarios, remembering a time as little Asari after Valery is gunned down.

ASARIOS. *Staring at the military man, shifting to an angry mood.* You – You hurt innocent, unarmed children. You have no compassion for people who are different.

The wizard's eyes begin to glow. As he tightens his right fist, the man drops his weapon and immediately grabs his chest, feeling a heart attack coming.

ASARIOS. Time you seek justice. *He tightens his right fist tight, and Dunan silently drops to the ground.*

AGENT CQUA. What – What just happened? *Shocked expression.*

AGENT RIT. He just killed him.

The Damonarian prince growled menacingly and charged at the wizard.

XANPO. Zanari, don't do it!! *He shouted.*

The wizard raised his right hand slowly, and the prince was pulled into a portal and disappeared. He lowered his arm calmly.

NIARA. No!!

DONNY. Where'd you send him?!

ASARIOS. Far, far away. He'll be happy I returned him to his home.

Valery groans on the ground. Agent Z looks from the wizard to his friend then at Shocker; the two make eye contact.

AGENT Z. Buddy. Get her to a hospital.

FLORAL. Take them too!!

Anawel, Calebra, Jaylin, Quetsey, and Tarina are standing right behind Floral.

JAYLIN. I staying. *Pouts with his fists clenched.*

The lightning teen doesn't hesitate as he channels electricity throughout his body. He turns into pure energy and whisks the four teens and the one Vexion creature away from the area.

AGENT CAJ. *Stares at the exhausted foreign agent.* You able to do battle, Rev?

RIVI. *Transforms into his agent attire.* I'll revvvv it up!

XANPO. Everyone, new friends, and all, be careful with this one. With all of us, we'll win.

ASARIOS. Heh. Nice short pep talk. I'll get what I came for and have some fun.

The two cross-humans, Akiru and Max, shift into their beast forms.

BEAST-CHRISTEN. Fighting on the same side for once. *Cracks a smile.*

BEAST-AKIRU. Let's get this — *Something fast speeds toward him and he's taken away from the area in a flash.*

BEAST-MAX. Aki!!!!! *He shouts and stares at the wizard.* What did you do?!

XANPO. He did nothing. *Maintains eye contact with the evil wizard.* Akiru has his demons to face. We'll see him soon.

SALLY. His doppelganger.

Our heroes move towards the wizard, some raising their weapons. Asarios stands unthreatened. He calms and starts muttering in a not-so-familiar language. The agent heroes scan the perimeters, slowly moving around in defensive poses. They are all standing, slowly moving around, watching the area, and glancing from left to right at each other to make sure none of them have seen something that they haven't. Suddenly, versions of Asarios appear out of thin air.

AGENT CAJ. Get ready, agents!! *He shouted, leaping a few feet off the ground.*

A few clones aim at Caj. He uses a Nuaiatsu – Ren tah Chu hand technique, and all clones around him disappear in a puff of smoke.

The other agents sprinted in opposite directions, leading a few clones away from the cross-human and Xeiar heroes.

Little Jaylin moves forward to attack a clone, raising his sword to smash down on it. Another clone appears, and Saber steps forward to attack it. Two more clones appear, and Kase and Zoey move in the direction of the two to attack. Four clones appear in four different areas; Niara, Crebeon, Pichuel, and Floral move towards them. Another appears to the right of the cavern and three more to the far left. Lin signals Kysis to take out the one on its own. The creature goes towards the clone, ready to do battle.

Lin moves towards the three, her arm blades ready as she stands in front of them. There is a puff of smoke, and six more clones appear in a circle around her. She gulps, realizing she may be in trouble. All hell breaks loose as the fight commences.

Jaylin crashes his sword down on a clone. As he smashes him, it disappears into a puff of smoke. The boy turns around in surprise. He is shocked when two more appear behind him. He raises his sword as they advance, sparks coming out of their fingertips.

Very near, Zoey punches her clone but misses. The clone dodges her and spins around, hitting her in the back. Winded, she stumbles.

The clone lunges at her. She kicks it in the face, but the clone dodges. The girl readies herself to attack again.

Kase runs at her clone, jumps in the air, and bangs her two fists down on its head, sending it crashing to the ground. She feels a presence behind her and turns to see three more. Two lunges at her – one from the left, the other from the right, both try to punch her. She steps back, avoiding both. The third runs at her, and she drops to the ground so she can throw a stomach kick, sending it falling back. She turns just as the first clone is up on its feet again and running to her. She does a backflip, throws herself in the air, spins around, and kicks the clone in the face with a roundhouse. The clone disappears into a puff of smoke. She looks at the three other clones who are walking towards her. She looks behind her and sees three more. She readies herself.

Saber punches at her Asarios clone. It ducks and swerves, sending sparks flying from its open hand at her. The sparks hit, sending her flying to the ground a few feet back. With mixed feelings of embarrassment and anger, she quickly jumps to her feet and runs at the clone, which fires more sparks at her. She dodges each one, her body swerving to left and right. She jumps in the air and aims a kick at the clone's face when she is close enough. It grabs her foot and sends her crashing to the ground.

Saber, groaning, gasps for air and grabs her stomach as she winces. The clone moves forward, and she gets up again. It goes for a punch, but she dodges slightly, grabs it by its wrist and slides her foot between his ankles, and flings it to the ground. As it falls, she punches the clone hard in the face.

Niara is battling a clone near, so is Jayla, who seems to be struggling in combat. Niara dodges some sparks that it is firing and moves forward with hands raised. The clone runs at her, but she sidesteps and smashes a hand down on the clone's face sending it to the ground. She turns to see two more clones running forward and immediately goes into a defensive position, ready to defend from any angle. She turns around, seeing Jayla knocked on her rear.

NIARA. *Extends her right hand, shouts.* **Blitargo!**

The clones approaching Jayla are immediately pushed away by a gust of wind. Niara lowers her arm, nodding her head at the girl.

JAYLA. *She stands, dusting herself off, and makes eye contact with Niara.* Thank you.

They prepare themselves for the clones that are getting closer to them.

Crebeon stands in the center of five clones, facing each one frantically and making defiant sounds. Each time a clone steps forward to attack, the creature sends a blast from its mouth at one – enough to stun it and send it falling back. He's conserving energy and waiting for a moment. One nearby clone runs at him. Another blast flies from its mouth to the clone, making it erupt in sparks. Crebeon turns to see another clone one step away and claws at it with an open hand, sending it falling to the ground. The creature turns to see three more running forward. He sends a massive blast from the mouth that impacts the clones and sends them flying with a tremendous roar. He turns to witness six new clones appear, moving forward, and he gets ready for a more intense battle.

Three wizard clones surround Pichuel, and they fire energy attacks at the yellow creature. He grabs his tiny hands and mold balls of green lighting mid-air. He fires them at the clones one after the other, stunning them immediately. With no time to waste, he creates more lightning and fires them. All the clones fall. He laughs, but this is short-lived. The clones stand up, and as they do so, six more appear behind them. He creates thunderbolts using his hands, ready and determined to be victorious.

Tired but persistent, Floral gets punched by a clone and goes flying to the ground. Three surround her, but she smiles and raises both her hands. The clones look around. Roots shoot out of the land and twist around the clones. They are struggling to break free, not making any sound. They are pulled below, swallowed up whole. Floral turns to see the carnage of the entire battle.

Nearby, Pichuel is surrounded and ready to do battle. The cross-human girl moves forward, but she is grabbed from behind and sent spinning almost to the ground. She caught herself last minute. She advances, grabs the clone by the throat, and knees it in the stomach. The clone buckles back, and she pushes it to the ground. She looks up just in time to see three more come closer.

Lin is swiping at a clone with her right arm blade; the clone dodges her and sends an uppercut to her face. She falls back. Another lunges at her. She slashes at it with her blade, but it escapes. She immediately sends a kick to its chin; it's sent falling back. She sees two more running towards her and jumps in the air sending a roundhouse kick down on one clone's head. She smashes against another's head as her foot follows through. Both clones fall. She lands just in time to see another clone firing a firebolt at her. She dodges. The clone fires another blast. She ducks and moves forward slowly.

Jaylin dodges several clones and smashes his sword into another one. It disappears upon impact. He turns around to see five more running at him.

ZOEY. *Punched in the face by a clone and stumbles backward.* Ow!
Grabs her head, patting her hair into place. I'm gonna beat your–
She sprints forward.

The clone moves forward. Angry, the girl kicks it in the face wildly,
sending it stumbling back. She follows through with a spinning kick,
which sends it crashing to the ground. Another fires a lightning
bolt from behind at her. She doubles up in pain and turns to face
her attacker, who fires another bolt at her. She spins to dodge, rolls
on the ground to the clones' feet, and kicks it in the legs, sending it
falling. She immediately punches it in the face. She hears a sound
and rolls away, narrowly avoiding a ball of sparks sent flying in her
direction. She runs at it, screaming. She jumps and knees it in the
face. Four more runs toward her from different directions.

Crebeon grabs one clone and throws it to the ground, sending a
blast from the mouth to its face. Two more runs at the creature, who
lets out a huge roar and sends a massive blast their way, obliterating
them. He turns to see five more rushing to his location. He gets in
a defensive stance, ready for action.

Floral is pushed to the ground by three clones. She screams, and
suddenly massive roots wrap themselves around the clones and pull
them away from her. She watches as the enemies are drawn into the
ground.

Lin punches a clone – **BANG** – in the center of the face. It disappears.
She is startled to see five more appear. One punches her, which she
blocks; another is running to her. She grabs the one she punched by
the wrist and waist, then flings it at the clone, sending them both
crashing to the ground.

Kysis runs at five clones. They fire sparks; the small plant creature
is enraged and unphased. It smashes on the ground and then grabs

a second, flinging it in the direction of a third. Two grab Kysis from behind. It is struggling. They pull the creature to the ground, but eventually, it wiggles free, smashes one in the face, and then strangles the other.

Saber punches a clone in the jaw. The clone moves forward, sending another spark flying. Another sends a spark flying at Saber, which stuns her slightly. The girl dodges this and runs at the clone, fists swiping wildly.

Lin slashes at three clones with one deep stroke. One falls, but the other two merely stumble back. She moves forward. A bolt hits her from behind, and she spins to see a clone firing another. She ducks. Another clone rushes at her. She turns and trips it with her feet. The clone that fired at her sends another, but it misses and hits the clone she tripped, making it erupt in flames.

Jaylin dodges one clone as it rushes at him and slashes the stomach of another. A fireball flies overhead. The boy spins to see two more and swipes at them with his weapon.

Zoey is punched in the back of the head. She spins to face her enemy and blocks another punch. Niara hits a clone in the face, turns to face, and kicks another, which crashes. Another swipes at her, but she ducks. Lin dodges a blast from a clone and turns to see another clone running to her. She drops to her knees and slashes its stomach with her arm blades, spinning round all in one motion to face the next coming towards her.

Meanwhile…
Planet Vrec – Crayos Forest

The Prince stumbled back. His footing was uneven on the forest floor. Breathing unevenly, he plastered his back against a thick trunk of a tree to take in a few heavy inhales.

The monstrous creature was not too far from him, crawling around in semi-circles, so he made sure to keep a vigilant grip on his claymore.

ZANARI. *Looking around and back to the creature in front of him.* He sent me back to Vrec and somehow pulled out my beast form.

Anytime now, the beast would leap at him with the sole purpose of separating his flesh and bones.

The Prince was quite impressed with himself that he's holding on for this long. Perhaps Damonarians do not need their inner beasts to survive.

Its body is covered with umber hair, which glistened under the moonlight. Scars from many battles embellished the face but not a single wound from his twin blades he'd swung in the struggles they've shared in the past.

He spared a sharp glance around him. Everything was stationary –almost lifeless– The forest seemed spelled under the moon. Even the clouds seemed to have been frozen in time as if scared.

He sighed, separating his back from the tree trunk, and tightened his grip on the claymore. The monster slowed his pacing at a small distance, focusing on the man who was to be his meal.

He let out a series of low growls as the prince raised the tip of his blade, pointing it at the monster's face. The time to be surprised had long passed. He stared right into the creator's fierce eyes filling him with rage from head to toe.

The beast screamed and sprinted in his direction. The prince didn't change his position. He wanted the beast to leap at him. His big body wouldn't let him reposition, and stabilize instantly and that might give him a chance to land a blow.

But that didn't happen.

The moment he avoided being taken away by the large claws which moved above his head - it was only for a moment that he saw a huge tail land right in his guts and sent him breaking through a tree and landing against another one. His vision blurred, but the considerable body running towards him brought all his senses back.

It was a battle of seconds. A moment's delay could cost him his life.

He rolled away, making the monster's claw rip through another one of the tree trunks. He launched himself at the beast with a determined scream. The beast whipped his head to see the man's blade going straight for his eyes, but when the prince swung to land an injury, he was slashing through empty air.

While his blade was halfway through where the monster's body was supposed to be, it appeared behind him. The growl involuntarily made him plant the tip of his sword into the ground and aid him in drawing distance between him and the foe.

The wild predator missed him by an inch only, and he slipped through the vegetation after jumping away from the beast. The demon roared out of rage and annoyance. The guy seemed acquainted with his moves and attacks after a few minutes.

The beast snarled at him—strings of saliva connecting his fangs and raining down his mouth.

The Prince panted and stood up again. There was no going anywhere without beating this thing, and luck wouldn't be aiding him every time. His movements sure were agile, but that wasn't enough to beat the monster.

They lurched towards each other at almost the same time, with the same purpose. The forest echoed with the clattering sound of the blade's metal and the monster's claws once again; sparks emitted their every-second interaction—the movements swift, the determination unfaltering. None of the two are ready to surrender.

It wasn't after a few more severe attacks that the blade ripped right through the beast's left eye. In a fit of agony, it wildly kicked the prince away into a rock and then began to scream around. The entire forest convulsed at the loudness of the roar. The trees were shrinking into themselves at the agony-filled cries.

It rubbed its face into the grass before standing its ground with lower growls, but now the prey wasn't in sight.

The prince held his leg with shivering hands. Blood flowed in rivulets down the corners of his mouth and injuries he received during their exchange of blows, but none of them were as bad as the wound on his leg. He bit down on his lower lip, shutting his eyes, and rested his head against the rigid structure of the rock.

If he wouldn't have used his blade to divert the direction of the monster's claws while it was going mad, then maybe he wouldn't have had his right leg anymore.

Sweat was rolling down his face, and his breathing was heavy, but he made sure not to let out a sound yet; a low, raspy breath right next to him made all his senses stand on edge. His eyes widened at the shadow of the claw raised above his head and instantly neglecting the pain throbbing above his leg as he rolled away right before the foot came down, breaking the vast boulder into bits.

The prince hissed, stumbling to his feet as he held out his blade, watching the beast appearing through the smoke. The huge tail waggled behind it. His vast, clawed paws ground the bits into powder as he slowly walked out with a feral eye while the other bled crimson -almost black in the dark- drops on the ground.

The prince was grateful to the moon; otherwise, he might be like the boulder under the monster's paws, but he had no idea what to do next. His leg was bleeding relentlessly and aching. He could hardly stand, but he still held out the blade, and somewhat he wasn't scared at all. Earlier, he had thought of running away, but now his nerves felt satisfied, as if he had a master plan that couldn't fail when he didn't even know how he was going to tackle the next blow.

ZANARI. Bring it on!! *The words escaped his lips on their own, and even if he did move, he wasn't sure how.*

While the beast was still in midair, ready to crush the man below him, the prince side-stepped, making sure not to put much weight on the leg that had half of the organs within visible, and swiftly let his blade slide through the monster's thick skin. It was as if there was suddenly a surge of power in him. As if the contact with the beast had given him some beastly strength or confidence. He stumbled towards the monster, who, after madly running into trees and turning the grass bloody with his blood, had finally settled down to gasping on the ground. His left eye was slightly open, and his body rose and fell unevenly.

The prince stood right next to his massive face and brought his blade to rest at the beast's neck.

ZANARI. *Breathing heavily.* You – Me – We're one. I can't call myself a true warrior of my race if I cannot learn. *Exhales.* The wizard's spell separated us both. This – could be a gift. *His breathing is becoming regular.* Obey me or... *He straightened the claymore to let the monster feel the sharpness that even its thick skin wasn't so thick against.* Die!

Niechest Town, outside of Neirolo Cavern...

Xanpo uses energy blasts to incinerate the Asarios clones closest to him; rescuing his wards was the first part of his current challenge. The other was battling the Xeiar wizard that had attempted to drain their powers.

ASARIOS. Ha, I knew you'd be unphased by the weaker versions of myself. *He teased, slightly irritated by the unwelcome interruption.*

The remark struck a chord in the Damonarian's head, and he charged at the wizard. He threw a left-handed hook at his head, but Asarios parried it with his arm and attempted a counterattack. Xanpo dodged, and the punch sailed wide of his head. With his arms drawn up to his face, Xanpo threw three quick jabs, but the wizard blocked them.

The close combat was intense, and their strength seemed equally matched. They threw ferocious punches while blocking, dodging, and counter-attacking at the suitable openings.

Asarios timed a kick perfectly, and it connected squarely with Xanpo's chest.

The Damonarian's eyes turned a deep hue of red, and he began to transform. His bones grew longer and denser, and his limbs extended, with sharp claws replacing his fingernails. His height nearly doubled in size. Thick fur covered what his skin was, and he let out a howl as he completed his metamorphosis.

ASARIOS. Your parlor tricks amuse me. *He stated, watching with a smirk at the corner of his mouth.*

Xanpo felt a strong surge in his beast form, and he lunged at the wizard. His claws swiped the air, aiming for his neck. If the attack had been successful, the wizard's head would've been taken clean off his body, but he was too quick to be caught unguarded. He had jumped backward and kicked Xanpo in the solar plexus. Unbalanced, he staggered back, his thick fur absorbing most of the force. He shook his head vigorously as if to get his mind right and then huffed, his nostrils twitching hard. With heavy thuds, he marched towards his opponent.

ASARIOS. *His opponent got a few yards away, and he chanted.* **Ignis Palme!** *Instantly, his hands began to glow as the heat emanating from them. He channeled the heat into a fireball.* Burn! *He yelled with a wicked grin as he launched the fireball at his enemy.*

Beast-Xanpo was moving too quickly to stop or dodge. In a flash, he felt excruciating pain as the fireball hit him in the chest, throwing him off his feet. He landed with a heavy thud that shook the ground like a mini earthquake. A cloud of dust ascended, engulfing all within a twenty-meter radius. Accompanying this was a scent of burning fur as his skin sizzled. The hit was sufficient to end an average being, but he transcended that. His superhuman agility and healing power helped him minimize the damage.

Under cover of a dust cloud, he began to walk towards where he had last spotted the wizard.

Asarios kept his eyes open, scanning the environment rapidly with each movement he sensed or heard. His nerves were on end, and he remained alert. Little did he know that his opponent had already circled him and was now approaching him from behind. What cued him of the impending attack was the sudden thicker concentration of the smell of burning fur. He whirled around and saw the Damonarian's huge figure looming tall above him. Instantly, he cast a spell to clear the dust cloud. Xanpo had anticipated this, and before the clouds dissipated, he jumped at his enemy, claws out, and teeth bared, ready for blood. Asarios was in luck that Xanpo had missed a few inches as his sharp teeth sank into his shoulders rather than the initial aim, which was his jugular. Asarios grimaced. Sensing an opportunity to do greater damage, Xanpo turned his bloodshot eyes to the wizard's face and tried to bite it off.

The close quarters gave the wizard very little room to navigate, but when he saw the long, sharp teeth coming at his face, he threw up his hands and gripped his jaws, just as the mandibles got close to snapping his nose off.

Xanpo tried to bite so that he could cut off Asarios's fingers, but the wizard restrained his jaws with all his might. Asarios was much stronger than his slender stature let on, and the fiery battle was a testament to it.

With the wizard preoccupied with keeping his hands from being munched, his focus was solely in one place, and it gave his opponent ample opportunity to launch a stealth attack. Xanpo threw his furry left paw at Asarios's face, scratching his cheek with his claws. He growled in excitement; he lusted for more. He envisioned slashing his adversary all over until he was nothing but a pile of viscera. The sinister thoughts boosted his energy, and he tried to recreate the former attack with his right hand.

Asarios saw the paw come at his face two seconds before it would've sliced him open. He quickly let go of the Damonarian's jaw and fell freely backward like a log of wood, with his arms to his sides. He heard a whooshing sound, and time seemed to slow down as the dark claws passed before his eyes by a hair.

ASARIOS. Damn! *He muttered.*

Moments before, his back would've touched the ground; he extended his hands and landed on his palms.

ASARIOS. *He chanted.* **Augumentes Geodis Peribitis.**

As soon as the last word left his mouth, rocks levitated to cling to his right leg, which he threw up angrily, hitting his furry opponent's lower jaw.

The clattering sound Xanpo's teeth made when he was struck was very audible to everyone around. He flew high and remained midair for about a second as if suspended, his heavy arms flailing around aimlessly, before he crashed into dust, several feet away.

The sound that rented the air was akin to one of a collapsing planet, or a falling titan. Even with his super strength and agility, there was no way Xanpo could get back on his feet instantly after such a hard crash.

From the corner of his eyes, Xanpo could see his enemy getting back on his feet already with barely a scratch. He knew the wizard would be heading towards him, and he didn't want to be on the ground when he got to where he was. It could be fatal.

Summoning all the remaining strength in his body, he put his fist to the ground and got up on one knee, his head hurriedly brainstorming ideas that could get him out of this predicament.

Thinking of something quickly, the Damonarian pushed himself to the fullest and whirled around in a circle, amassing up a huge cloud of dust – more than enough to temporarily impair the wizard's sight. Rather than strutting, this time he decided to move quickly as he charged at Asarios with his claws fully out and teeth bared. The Xeiar wizard could predict what it was he would do. He saw the ball of dust rising. He would not be caught off guard this time.

ASARIOS. *Summons a see-through barrier.* **Nieeth!** *He yelled, screaming through the dust, and narrowing his eyes to prevent dust particles from blinding him.*

Xanpo could hear clearly, and knew it was a protection spell. He huffed and puffed as he kept charging, pushing his limbs forward with all the strength in him. A new surge of adrenaline rushed through every nerve in him as he threw his right paw at the wizard's annoying calm face, only to be rebounded a few meters away by a strong force.

His face reddened with rage and his body shook terribly as he realized Asarios had put up a transparent protective dome. He let his body tumble a few times before fixing his paws on the ground and holding still. The Xeiar wizard wasn't quick enough in putting the dome up as he uttered a yelp in pain.

The pain began to register. Xanpo had struck him on a temporal bone, almost ripping his ear from his head by a hair's breadth, just before the spell he chanted became effective. He groaned further when he examined the gash and felt the hotness of his blood as it trickled down.

ASARIOS. Impressive. *He clapped, a boyish smile attacking his lips like a virus as he felt his cheeks where he had earlier been scratched, and then examining his temporal bone.*

Xanpo watched on from a defensive position, allowing his body enough time to heal.

ASARIOS. My turn. *He said blithely and allowed the joints in his neck to experience crepitus before shooting a wicked glare at his opponent.* **Impetus Aves.** *He intoned and in a split second, an unkindness came rushing at his opponent from all sides.*

Xanpo chuckled within him at the small snag the wizard had thought to throw at him. In an instant, he let his claws do a wiper in full force going first, in a clockwise direction, and again in an anticlockwise motion. The hit he gave was strong enough to send them flying to the ground in all directions. He growl-barked sonorously to silent their persistent cooing as he focused on getting them off him.

From the corner of his eyes, he watched the wizard keenly, observing his every move. He could see his lips moving silently and realized the spell needed uninterrupted attention for it to be effective.

Xanpo let out a loud howl before fully standing upright and counter-attacking the creatures with both his head and claws.

ASARIOS. *He's getting bored with the show of persistence his opponent had put on and decides to switch things up a bit.* **Impugnatione cessare, et in ruina.** *He chanted continuously.*

Xanpo noticed that all the sizeable all-black passerine birds fell lifelessly to the floor. He looked confusedly at the wizard as he took his time chanting the spell.

ASARIOS. *His eyes closed as he kept repeating the words.* **Ruinam gelu super eum et protecto.**

Xanpo decided to close in on him, and without closing his nictitating membrane, he charged again. He had not looked up at the sky when it was gathering; all he wanted was to get the flesh out of the wizard and then detach his head from the occipital bone.

The sky rumbled angrily upon being interfered with, and with a sharp growl, it released ice blocks on Xanpo instantly, sending him tumbling to the wizard's feet.

The Damonarian struggled to run to shelter as the ice blocks pierced through his fur, leaving deep cuts. The ground was slippery, and he respired heavily, getting his claws out fully to walk better. Asarios had made sure to protect himself this time, and he grinned satisfied at Xanpo.

ASARIOS. You could do better, beast! *He charged, conjuring a spell to make the ice blocks fall faster. He laughed heartily as each block drew blood from his opponent's skin before falling to the floor.*

Xanpo could feel his strength failing him. The grim reaper would waste no time coming to claim him if he fell to the floor because he would transform back to his vulnerable state, his human side. He struggled to keep his eyes open as Asarios approached.

Back to the others, who are dealing with Asarios clones, Sally and Donny teamed up and obliterated the clones attacking them. They had been watching and trying to get away from them to help their mentor. It's horror watching from a far distance.

Asarios' spell was too strong, but somehow Xanpo's beast form survives.

DONNY. He's too strong. *He shouted to her through all the noise.*

SALLY. We have to save him. *She whimpered.* We can do this. *She breathed with renewed zeal.*

DONNY. *He's determined.* We'll stand a chance against him, together. *He hammered on the last word, bringing solace to his partner.*

Three more clones materialized near and attacked the two youngsters.

The wizard had gotten to where Xanpo laid, soaked in blood and weary. He laughed and snapped his fingers, causing a cease to the ice blocks that had been falling tempestuously. His protection spell dissolved too, and he dropped his arms proudly.

ASARIOS. It would be a shame to end this fight so soon. *He stated, hovering over the warrior.*

The Damonarian's breathing was greatly ragged, and his eyes were heavy.

ASARIOS. **Geminum videri.** *He implored, and with a whirlwind, a clone of the warrior appeared with bloodshot eyes.* Found this guy wandering around a planet in Namorant.

Xanpo swallowed and prayed for strength.

ASARIOS. I knew you looked familiar. This guy had been dying to meet you. *Sella videretur. He enchanted and sat down regally.* I'll leave you to fight with yourself, Xen. Do try to amuse me. *He said, and instantly as if on cue, the clone pounced at his counterpart.*

Xanpo was at a loss whether to transform back to his human form or not. He was thankful that his healing abilities were top-grade, for he had regained a little strength. He noticed as his clone began to murmur incantations to fortify his hand, and he decided it was safer to be in his beastly form. He narrowed his eyes and huffed as he waited.

XEN. Burn! *Yelled the clone who had thrown his fiery hands at his twin.*

Xanpo had calculated this trick and quickly held his hands. He stared his clone down and twisted his wrists sideways, making sure he got a whimper from him before breaking his wrist bones. He huffed again. Xen let his wrist joints pop and waited a minute for it to heal back before conjuring up rocks and hauling them at his opponent. Xanpo avoided them at full tilt and made a lunge for Xen's wrists again. This time, Xen was quick to invoke a spell that would make his wrists fiery, and Xanpo, unsuspectingly, grabbed them. He released his wrists instantly, letting out a yelp. He let his hands flail helplessly in the air for a split second. Without being given a chance to recover from the pain his burning paws had to endure, three mighty kicks were thrown, and he staggered back with a groan.

Sighing exhaustively from the long fight of the day, he channeled his frustration and anger into energy and rushed at Xen again. The counterpart was prepared. With each strike Xanpo gave, a counterattack weakened him thrice as much as Asarios' magic would do. It was as though Asarios was channeling power from somewhere into his body, making him twice as strong.

The wizard stayed still, concentrating on channeling some of his strength to Xanpo's look-alike while the fight continued. He could not afford to be distracted, else the warrior would instantly rip the clone's head off, for, without a power source, he was nothing. Xanpo could feel his strength failing much faster than it would, but he continued.

XEN. You're much too weak to be me. *He taunted, striking him a blow in his lower jaw and drawing blood.*

Everything in him wanted more of it; the pain Xanpo was feeling, the blood that was released. He wanted to see more.

XEN. I'll kill you. Then there'll be one of us. That'll be much better. *He continued, kicking Xanpo on his furry body till he was too weak to maintain his beastly form.*

The warrior fell flatly to the floor and switched inexorably.

Meanwhile, Xanpo's students had succeeded in freeing themselves from the Xeiar wizard's clones. Sally rushed furiously to the scene, Donny solidly behind her as she yelled out his name.

SALLY AND DONNY. Leave Xanpo alone! *They yelled in unison, switchblades in their eyes.*

Asarios rolled his eyes annoyingly to the rude interruption but chuckled nonchalantly before choosing to focus on the students. Xanpo, who gradually lost his grip on life, gasped immediately as the wizard stopped his chants.

ASARIOS. You know, for students of this Damonarian, you two are witless. *He sighed and moved his lips sideways.* Took you long enough to set yourselves free of my minions. *He added with a mocking smile, hearing the young girl scream in anger.*

SALLY. *Ignitiatious. She yelled, and stones around them quickly rose and shot themselves at the villain.*

The skilled wizard subtly dodged them all. He chuckled, then narrowed his eyes.

ASARIOS. **Ignitiatious Vlornoc.** *He repeated, and the stones returned to life, this time, to attack the girl.*

Donny quickly muttered a protection spell, and the stones bounced off against the transparent dome before falling lifelessly to the ground. He stood as he looked at the wizard.

ASARIOS. Aha. Much better.

SALLY. Darker magic.

ASARIOS. You're right. From Valdesmon. *He grinned before turning around to face Xanpo, who was still lying weak on the ground.*

Xen had moved and was now closer to the students than Xanpo. He was ready for a kill.

ASARIOS. Meet your opponent. *He bowed slightly before them, stretching his hands dramatically to the counterpart, and manifested a chair to sit.*

Xen looked formidably before deciding to combat them.

The two students inhaled profoundly and walked hurriedly towards their opponent. Donny threw a few kicks at him from midair while Sally punched from below. Xen sidestepped the first and second kick and grabbed the boy's first leg, throwing him to the ground while he butt-headed the girl, sending her flying backward and landing hard on her butt. Asarios applauded. Sally was in great pain to get up immediately, but Donny was already up on his feet and rushing back at Xen, throwing heavy punches with Xen sidestepping all. He was super skilled, just like his mentor, and Donny could not but remember all the times he was training them. In his moment of temporary distraction, Xen did a reverse sidekick, and his right leg landed on the boy's jaw. He cried in excruciating pain as he held his jaw. Sally laid low and mumbled a spell that made the ground beneath Xen quake. The man, daunted for a moment in time for Donny to cast a spell.

DONNY. **Temtres turbo celessisius.** *He cried, and a whirlwind came at Xen for a minute.*

Dust particles shot at his eyes, further destabilizing him. He was about to say a spell when Xanpo, now in his human form, got up quickly and did a jump spin hook kick at the doppelganger, drawing blood from him and moving swiftly again. He circled his legs around Xen's neck, and without a thought, he snapped the life out of his evil clone.

XANPO. Enough… *Exhausted, on one knee panting.* No time for these games.

SALLY. Agree. **Fileepio.**

The remains of Xen burn to ash.

DONNY. *Leaps high and shouts.* **Cofrea camoses Tarar**!!

A mixture of colorful lights streams down into a barrage of attacks.

ASARIOS. Huh. *Shakes his head, smiling.* Don't make me laugh. **Lutrids Spponallo Zracnqium.**

The boy becomes bound by an unseen force. It's like he's struggling in invisible ropes.

XANPO. *Raises off the ground a little.* Donny!! *Falls back down, too exhausted to stand.*

SALLY. *Shouts.* **Rieeisco** –

ASARIOS. *Interrupts the girl's spell.* **Parulliysis Sustotalus.** *He shouted.*

Immediately, the two teens are frozen. They're paralyzed, just not in stone. Xanpo tightened his fists, channeling enough strength to jump high and catch the paralyzed Donny before he hit the ground. He lands with the boy safe in his arms, placing him beside the paralyzed girl.

ASARIOS. Heh. You are quite peculiar, Xanpo.

HighTech City, Georgia
Techy Mountains

An unknown entity continued pushing Akiru mid-air, passing a tarred road with the boy whimpering in pain. He's in his human form; he could feel his strength failing him as this unseen force continued kneeing him randomly in the gut.

He got tired and pulled himself closer to his attacker into a tight bear hug. He tightens his grip, sinking his claws into the person's backside.

UNKNOWN VOICE. *Yelps, then giggles.* There's the Akiru I remember.

The person had taken him out of sight, to a dark side of the mountains. Akiru shifted into his beast form, gained the upper hand, and threw him off. They both landed on rocky terrain, staring at each other.

MIROKU. How could you forget me? *Grinning.*

Beast-Akiru blew fire from his mouth, striking the other person. He stopped his attack, narrowed his eyes, and became light on his feet. He runs toward his clone, breathing fire as he fully transforms into a hybrid dog creature. He howled before rushing at the clone, who easily avoided his blow.

Miroku held his left paw with one of his hands and gave him a quick jab to his jaw. Beast-Akiru spat fire again at him, but his reflexes were sharp as he rolled over, getting away with barely a scratch. The clone stuck out a tongue at Akiru and utilized both his upper and lower body to produce punches and kicks, which were linear and forceful.

He glanced at Akiru in disdain as he spat and hurled another blow at the boy's jaw. Miroku resorted to taking strides with his hands at his back around Akiru, who lay wasted and incapacitated on the ground.

He accompanied the strides with two-handed punches, hurling quick blows and thrusting his feet to launch a sidekick at Akiru. The clone's foot slowly landed on his lips, drawing blood. Akiru grinds his teeth as he writhes in pain.

Akiru gave his paws time to heat up, breathing ragged as fire shot out of his paws toward the clone. This time, the clone did not evade it; he ran through it as quickly as a hare, running through the hybrid and taking a back long stance known as kókutsu-dachi.

The clone positioned his rear leg, bending it at the knee and straightening his front leg. In a flash, he turned ninety degrees away, keeping his head to the front as he got ready for the attack.

Akiru's head was pounding, and he was not thinking. He dived at the clone in anger, but the clone was skilled. He slid under him, then got up and swung two solid kicks to his back, sending the hybrid flying meters away. The boy's languid figure lay exhausted on the ground as his clone walked out of the dark corner out into the open. Akiru could see the clone punching his fist and signaling him to get up from where he lay. He enjoyed every bit of this, and he made sure Akiru realized this from his smirks and body movements.

The boy, who was now human, spat blood and rubbed his left fist against his lips. He closed his eyes and summoned the strength to lie on his back. He groaned in agony with his face contorted in pain as he made to take his desired position. His nose was dripping blood intensely, and he could not muster the strength to keep his head erect. He moved a few meters to a wall and laid there writhing in anguish. With dazed eyes, he caught a glimpse of his clone walking with so much agility towards him. He saw his life flash before him momentarily, and at that moment, he had to decide to either accept to die a painful death or fight for his life with all the strength he could muster.

As the clone advanced nearer, his eyes widened at the sight of a very impressive backflip the clone did, shooting Akiru a leg kick as he landed. The hero groaned from the hit and began to move back quickly with the help of his hands, dragging his body until he stopped abruptly when his back had hit another wall.

The clone increased his speed and soon broke into a run, screaming as he approached. He raised his left hand, hurling swift blows. In a split moment, there was an adrenaline rush in Akiru. He successfully eluded the blows with an instantaneous move to the right, and his clone's fist struck the wall. Without allowing himself time to recover from the pain, the clone threw a jab again, but this time Akiru was only fast enough to hold the clone's arm to prevent the hit. There was a brief struggle as the clone bore down on him, with Akiru trying all he could to hold off the one blow.

The boy held his stance, but his feet were beginning to quiver when the clone spotted it. He got a good hold of him and lifted his arm, catching the hybrid's leg and going in for a knee strike. After the knee strike, he took a good grip around Akiru's neck and swept him off balance.

A sudden wave of strength overwhelmed Akiru, and he sprung to his feet with the speed of lightning. He assumed the Kabi Dachi, which had him positioned as one riding a horse; the clone assumed the Neko Dachi with one foot behind and another foot on its toes placed in front. The fight was brief but fierce. The clone launched a kekomi, a long strike followed by foot at the boy's neck and jab punches aimed at his upper body. Akiru was fast enough to ward off many of the jabs even after the first kick inflicted on his neck. He quickly served the clone's flying kicks to his lower body. They both advanced, with his clone doing more of the attacking and Akiru the defense.

Akiru had the upper hand as he was able to let the clone's back kiss the floor in a swift throw. He immediately transformed into his beastly form and got atop the clone. He held him down, growling and gnashing his teeth at his face.

Too surprised to think, the clone struggled to come off the firm hold until he sighted a vital spot he could hit. Quickly, he did a side punch to the back of the dog's head, just as the dog was about to rip him apart.

It howled in pain, and its grip on the clone loosened. The clone, too tired to get up from the ground, lay beneath the dying creature with an irregular breathing pattern.

Unable to hold it, Akiru shifted back into his human form, his head bleeding. He took a deep breath and breathed out whatever strength was left in him, and fierce bouts of flames landed right on the clone's face.

The fire was so fierce that it caught up so fast, with every inch of both human forms lying next to each other: one lifeless, the other unmoving.

Meanwhile, Neirolo Cavern...

Beast-Christen circles around Asarios, sizing him up and down. Beast-Max circles around the other side of him. The wizard watches the two teens, also noticing Agent Z is slowly moving towards him. Beast-Max lets out a few sparks that emanate from his body, almost like a warning of what's to come.

Christen lunges, but the wizard effortlessly sidesteps out of the way and places his feet in a stance where he knows he has the upper hand.

Max turns to face the wizard.

Asarios sends a flying kick to Christen. As he does so, his body spins in the air all around the boy. He knocks him hard in the face with his right foot along his jawline. The boy stumbles backward, completely off-balance. The wizard lands forward and moves in on him.

He sends multiple hand-rolled, open palms to the pressure points on the cross-human's neck. He uses a technique with two fingers outstretched and makes a stabbing motion. Each one of these attacks winds the boy. Max runs in and throws a blind punch; Asarios grabs his right wrist and sidesteps. As he does so, he locks Max's left elbow with his other hand and squeezes hard. Max winces in pain and starts kicking at the man's left knee until he releases him. The wizard is pushed back slightly. Christen gets to his feet and runs at the enemy with his claws outstretched and swipes at him wildly. Agent Z comes cartwheeling and sends a kick at Asarios, who promptly dodges. Christen slashes at him; Asarios dodges and evades the claw strikes. The wizard smashes his open palm on the right side of his face, then his other open palm on the left. He does this ten times at such fast speeds that his movements are a blur. Agent Z returns and kicks the wizard in his stomach; he falls back a few steps.

The agent jumps in the air and aims for his head. His elbow blocks this, but the agent places his other foot on his chest and then uses that to spring himself up higher in the air and kicks the man under the jaw with a rising kick which sends him flying backward. The boy backflips and lands on his feet, looking down at his opponent starting to fall. Asarios stumbled back only a few feet, catching himself from falling. He wipes his chin, chuckling.

Christen releases a massive energy blast at him. Agent Z smiles and slowly walks forward. Asarios uses quick movement and sends a spell blast flying at the agent and repels the massive blast from Christen. His clothing gets torn by the excess energy.

The attack is heading toward Agent Z. He cowers and raises his right arm, foolishly thinking it'll be deflected. He's not thinking straight right now.

BEAST-CHRISTEN. *Turns and looks over at Agent Z.* DUCK!!!!!!!!!!!!!! *He shouted.*

The attack struck, but there was a pause. It's decreasing in size. Agent Z looks over his right arm in shock as he's standing. The attack is absorbed.

Asarios notices the glow on his right arm as the energy attack is no more. Seeing an opportunity, Christen runs at the man, claws out. Asarios does a twirl, sidestepping to the right. The boy throws a punch to his face, but the man grabs his fist in mid-air and twists his arm. The boy's body buckles under the strain, and he drops to his knees. The wizard jumps in the air and kicks him on the left side of his face, sending him smashing to the ground. Max runs at the enemy with furious anger and slashes at his face. The man calmly side steps, spins and smashes his right fist into his back. Max loses balance, and Asarios sends a roundhouse kick flying at his head and then several rabbit punches at high speed to his chest and stomach. The lightning boy falls to the ground.

Agent Z is sprinting at lightning speed; his two fists clenched tight as he's gaining speed and momentum. He sends one hand forward, open palm, with two long fingers outstretched and jabs Asarios in the throat. He's immediately winded. This surprisingly hit, and the man got a huge awakening. He's utterly shocked. He glides his hand upward, opens his fingers, and puts his hand under Asarios's chin. He pushes his head back. The man jerks away, freeing himself. The agent teleports a short distance before the terrifying wizard can get a grip on him.

ASARIOS. I don't know how you managed to get that close.

AGENT Z. Skills!!! *He shouted.*

ASARIOS. A human harming a Xeiar? Almost laughable.

AGENT Z. You'll see.

The wizard uses immense speed and reaches the agent in no time. He brought his knee up, hoping to strike him out, but a glowing aura covered his entire body, and his attack was stopped.

The wizard leaped a few feet away, observing him.

Agent Z bends his leg forward, shifting into his Vex form. He starts sprinting and sends his foot crashing down on the enemy from above. The wizard raised both arms to block. There's a crunching sound, and he groaned. He shakes away the pain as his bones start their healing process. He jumps on the balls of his toes and thrusts his body to Vex Z. He sends multiple rolled punches to both sides of his face, sending him falling backward. Vex Z jumps in the air, spins around, and flattens his foot straight into the man's chest. He grabs him by his ankle and holds him in the air. He spins him around three times, squeezing tight on his ankle. Z's arms are flying around, trying to find something to grab. The wizard throws him in the air in such a way that he flips backward. Asarios sends his open hands flying, smacking him on his back, and then sends a high-flying kick to his face. Simultaneously, all in one move, the wizard holds his two hands together and smacks down on Z's stomach. The boy crashes to the ground, landing in a pile of rubble. He's now in his agent form.

The wizard's body turns into light particles, and he speeds to the ground. Now in tangible form, he reaches his target and sends several kicks to the boy's body. Agent Z moans and tries to think of a plan.

ASARIOS. *Landing a few feet from the boy's location.* Don't tell me your human body is giving up already. *Laughs.* Looks like that twinkle on your right arm isn't doing much of anything anymore.

AGENT Z. You talk too much, goof-butt. *His right arm shines a pale blue color for a few seconds, then stops.*

ASARIOS. *He notices but doesn't think about it much. He's walking forward.* Physical attacks do more damage. You're unaffected by any spells I cast. *He stops walking and points for a second at the kid's upper right arm.* What's under your sleeve? It appeared when you absorbed my earlier attack. What are you hiding under that suit?

AGENT Z. Huh?

BEAST-CHRISTEN. *He yells while aiming a flying kick at the enemy.* SHADOW KICK!!!!

BEAST-MAX. *Speeding at mach ten to the enemy, right fist ready to be thrown as it's charging with electricity behind him.* LIGHTNING JABBER!!!!

ASARIOS. *Raises his pointer and middle finger on each hand in the air.*

Both boys are frozen in mid-air.

AGENT Z. No! *Struggles as a searing pain starts coursing through his right arm.*

Asarios's small but muscular frame hovered over the weakened agent. He's studying him carefully. He stands beside him only for a minute before the other agents come rushing.

A laser whip chain lashed through the air, with Agent JeiFii running lightly on her feet and aiming at the wizard's neck.

The agents, and Jayla, realized the wizard could do much damage with his magical powers, so they devised a means to rid him of his magical powers, even if it was for a short period. After much brainstorming, Jayla materialized a power neutralizing orb, which started to contort a small mass of air and had the ball engulfed in it. With everything she had in her, she released it. The orb strikes him hard in his chest. There was a very brief surge of intense light and electrocution all over his body. He fell and was unconscious for a few seconds before he was able to move his body slightly while lying on the floor, groaning.

AGENT CAJ. Let's see how you fare now. *He spoke through gritted teeth.*

ASARIOS. *He stood.* You call this even? *A menacing look accompanied his reply. With his arms behind him and a smirk plastered on his face, he spoke forth.* **Areæ sit lubrico!**

JeiFii launched at the wizard, full speed. Immediately, the ground became slippery; The girl's eyes widened in shock. She lost balance and came crashing at his feet. Asarios looked down at her with a half-smile, and in split seconds, he did a backflip.

ASARIOS. *In mid-air, he uttered.* **Et venti sonum hoc DEFLECTO!**

What looked like a rushing wind surged from behind and went ahead of him to intercept the blade blaster released by Agent CQua.

The intercepting mass of air came with a powerful force, and a considerable amount of energy was returned to where it came from. As the others take cover, Jayla punches and kicks an Asarios clone away from her. She raised both her hands, moving them in a circular motion repeatedly. She created a mass of whirling winds which helped to deflect the energy blast coming back at them.

Asarios still stood, surprised and unfazed, until Caj let out a scream and rushed to engage in combat with him. He swung out his arm blades and went first for the wizard's head, which was carefully dodged as he lowered his upper body with the edge flashing above his face. Caj made to strike more in calculated moves, but they are avoided. He grabs one of the arm blades and casts a spell on it, causing both blades to be shriveled. Caj couldn't make any other moves. The wizard landed a power kick to his stomach, causing his body to lift off the ground and moving a considerable distance away. The agent would not give up. He caught Asarios off guard as he thrust a blade, hidden in his armor, at the man's thighs. He groaned. Before he could regain his composure, another strike came from behind and knocked him over. It was JeiFii who circled the wizard's legs with her laser whip chain and pulled it, causing him to fall.

Agent Rit took center stage and cut short the man's show of mischief with a blow to his jaw while Rev made it to Agent Z.

The next blow from Rit was held by Asarios, who had him off the ground the next second, with a power sweep from his leg. The boy stood up immediately and struck a dancing pose. This had the wizard bursting into laughter.

ASARIOS. You can't even...

Jumping lightly on his feet in a bid to steady himself, Rit threw a straight punch of which the latter avoided easily.

ASARIOS. Let's see how hard you can try to hit me. *He teased further.* Get it on! *He was mistaken.*

Rit let his right leg lead the other in a bout of fuelled-up anger, moving subtly toward Asarios again and striking a double-hand punch first at his gut, then an elbow jab to his back.

The others wasted no time joining the attack as the wizard tried everything he could to ward them off. He was skilled, but he was like honey before a colony of ants, continuously attracting them as soon as he warded them away. It was a bit difficult, but not too hard without his magic.

The agents threw calculated punches at him, and at one point, he felt some of his flesh being ripped off by the whip chain. Suppressing his groans, he jabbed at them from all corners, but a punch to the eye from Caj had him staggering backward. Rit pushed him forward with a hopping sidekick till he fell flat.

The agents were not done, and he knew that. He was about to get up to continue the fight when he felt a sudden surge of energy through him. He sensed the power neutralizing orb weakening. His magic was too strong. The surge was so powerful that the gents rushing toward him now were pushed a reasonable distance away. They were all surrounded by thick darkness for a few seconds.

ASARIOS. *Chanting.* **Revertere ad defaltam.**

All the agents except JeiFii found themselves incapacitated and lying helplessly on the dirt ground as light restored. Asarios had his power back. Agent Z regained some strength after fighting the armband's searing pain.

ASARIOS. What do you say we go again? *He asked with a glint of dark, malevolent eyes. He laughed boisterously.*

The warrior Xanpo tried to sneak up on him from behind, right arm charging power.

Asarios immediately speeds closer and slams his palm on Xanpo's chest, fingers spread using his peripheral vision. His right-hand lights up, and the warrior is pushed back; he strikes the left side of the cavern's walls and falls to the ground. He yelled out in excruciating pain.

ASARIOS. What's dead should stay dead. *He backs away from the warrior.*

Xanpo grew silent. He can feel his inner beast in severe pain. The wizard turned to the agent boy, sensing mysterious energy coming to the surface. He chants a spell and fires it his way.

Rev appears and blocks a spell blast, repelling it easily as a glow surrounds his entire body for seconds. Everyone's shocked. Asarios smiles as he finds a new Xeiar.

ASARIOS. A hidden Xe -

AGENT Z. *Screams out.* Noooooo!!!!!!!!!!!! *His arms out to the side, fists tightened.* No - No more!!!!

Agent Z is now covered in new armor; he gets up. The wizard looks at him, surprised. Z sprints forward. He jumps in the air and smashes his face with a double roundhouse kick. Asarios stumbles back. Z opens his hand-like claw and grabs his face, twisting and pinching with his fingers. Steam is rising from his opponent's face. Z lifts him by his face, swings him like a rag doll, and throws him to the ground. Asarios is now completely frustrated and runs to the boy. He uses an open fist technique with three open fingers. He fires it at super-speed; three to the throat, two in the chest, and one in the stomach; all in one seamless movement. Z takes the pain and raises his two clasped hands, and smashes down on the top of the man's skull. Asarios stumbles back, dazed. Z jumps in the air and kicks him super-fast in the face five times; they are like rabbit punches but with feet. He grabs the teen by his right ankle on the last kick. Z stretches his leg to have more power and then kicks him in the face with his other foot. He slides down so that his legs are wrapped around the man's neck, and he pushes him to the ground. Asarios tries to escape, but he cannot as his armored opponent is too powerful and heavy. He's resisting. The armored boy screams and clasps his hands tightly together. He crashes them down on the wizard's face with pure power. Electric sparks are everywhere. The man slumps entirely on the ground.

Z narrowed his eyes, shooting a death glare at the wizard, who had a grim look on his face. The boy huffed and puffed before drawing out his fists and becoming light on his feet. He sprints at Asarios. The wizard smirks, deciding to indulge him this time. He holds out his fists for a moment before taking a ready stance, the Renoji dachi. His hands were on his hips, and both legs took an L shape.

It was only until the armored Z made a punch to his jaw that the wizard moved, easily avoiding it by taking a few steps to his left.

ASARIOS. My turn. *He said, and with the speed of light, he made to strike the glowing agent at his lateral side.*

The armored boy saw this in time but let him have it. Asarios's fist beamed red from coming in contact with Z's armor. He swung his fist repeatedly and in a discreet manner to numb the pain. The agent watched with a smirk.

ASARIOS. *Ventorum impetum.* *He groaned, and for a moment, the wind came harshly at his opponent, hurling sharp sand at his armor, but the armored hero was unfazed.* **Impetum ignis!** *He yelled in anger, seeing the first spell did not work. He held out his fiery hands, but the agent's armor took it in without an effect.* **Saxa spiritum suum!** *He chanted furiously before gritting his teeth to see his magic was ineffective against the armor.*

The armored boy was momentarily distracted and unable to avoid it. With a loud groan, he swung a straight punch at the boy's head. His head rang from the impact. Before he could regain himself, Asarios sent him flying backward with a front kick by lifting his knee straight forward and striking his lower abdomen.

Z wasted no time on the ground, doing the kick-up technique and flying to his feet instantly. He deflected incoming strikes from the wizards with angular movements. The boy returned with sharp and hard punches that registered pain on the man's body.

Quickly grabbing Asarios's head, he brought his right knee to it and made a forceful hit, drawing blood. The man spat and took calculated steps, moving to his right side. He struck an elbow jab at the boy. The impact was mild due to the armor, so he struck again at an open area.

ASARIOS. *He kept a steady arm. He raised his other hand, aiming straight for his upper abdomen, and chanted.* **Brachium inspiratione.**

The armored boy crouched over in pain and enabled Asarios to turn his back to him. As soon as he had his back facing him, he extended his right leg back to throw a deathly kick in his chest. The boy recovered quickly! He had fast reflexes, even quicker than his opponent. He dodged, the kick missing him by inches.

At that moment, Z realized he had to pull in his full strength as his enemy was out to kill by the look on his face. He aimed his right arm and fired the blaster. A yellow beam shot out of it in his direction. The wizard quickly cast a spell and shot a blast back; a bright white beam hit his opponent's yellow one right in the middle. When the rays touched, a buzzing sound rented the air as the lights began to glow brighter. Asarios gritted his teeth as he leaned forward, pushing his beam towards the boy. The white beam grew more luminous, with stars dancing in his wide, maniacal eyes. The white beam gained more ground and pushed the boys backward. The heat was getting closer and closer to him, and he could feel his arm shaking. He steadied it with his other arm, gripping himself by the wrist. The enemy is unrelenting. He wouldn't rest until he had taken his life. He glanced ahead and saw the vile passion in the wizard's eyes. A thought crossed his mind, something that might give him an edge.

Z eased down on the power of his blast, and the wizard began to edge closer and closer. Asarios thought his enemy's strength was waning out as the beam got near him. He glared intently, wanting to catch the moment the white heat would lick his face.

When the beam was inches away from him, Z took a deep breath, planted his feet in a firmer stance, and shut his eyes. Suddenly, he ramped the power of his blaster up to the highest. In an instant, the yellow beam got blindingly bright as it shot forward fast, consuming the white beam and striking Asarios in the chest before he could blink. The force was so much that the wizard disintegrated right on the spot.

The area was cleared of debris and smoke. Z opened his eyes and saw his adversary nowhere in sight, he let out a long breath as the armor started glowing, and he returned to his agent attire.

Just then, white lights surrounded all over. Z steps back and looks around. The clones of Asarios become streams of light and aim to a single area where the wizard last stood. They're returning to the original.

A figure emerges from the angelic lights. The ghostly form of Asarios started to materialize as well.

It's cold and dark here. All he can see are splotches of red and blue light evading his eyes, frantically covering any view of the place he might have had. His head buzzed with tension, but it was not anger- his body was leaving him. Unaware of his surroundings, of sound, of sight, he bowed his head to the ground below him, which was unnaturally warm, as if the sun was beaming on it- but not on him. His hands shook, and he collapsed, now laid on his side on the warm ground, with little to no sight.

ASARIOS. Is this where I will stay forever? *He thought and began to up himself.* Is this what I deserve?

The thought upon all else would've seemed irrational, but he found comfort in this idea, given the perfect situation.

Then the heat faded. He could see the barren wasteland he had fallen to, and he was alone. A calm wind swept across his back. The wind was slowly flowing through his fragile hair. He knew who this was, and when he turned his head. He saw her.

Her body was a beam of light... A human figure.

She looked as if rays of the sun shielded her through her skin or protruded through her core. There was no way to figure out what part of her the light source came from, but it covered her and the area she stood on entirely.

He glinted and blinked his eyes, shielding himself from the sudden brightness with his bruised and bloody palms as she walked towards him.

The man looks up as it's approaching him. When he looked up, she towered over him and handed him a single blade of grass that looked oddly familiar. He wanted to ask where she had been, how she took on this new form, what to do now? But he couldn't muster the courage to speak.

When he took a breath, she nodded her head and smiled. She already knew.

MALEE. Come on, Asari. *Her ghostly form smiled at him with eyes closed.*

He hesitated for a second, confused. Then, he went for her hand.

Hand in hand, she lifted him, gently pulling him towards her in an embrace and almost as a hug.

When he was expecting to touch her, he passed through her body and became a part of her light. He wasn't alarmed or scared; he accepted it. He embraced it.

This was it.

So, on that battlefield in front of Neirolo Cavern, there lay a single blade of grass.

Some of the heroes who were frozen return to their original state. They inhale deeply and breathes out peacefully.

SALLY. *She's the first one to look around for her mentor and spots him lying in front of the cavern.* XANPO!!!! *She runs to him.*

Niara heard her shout and ran to him too. The rest follow.

Max and Christen make their way to him last and shift back into the human forms. They nod to each other, turning to look at the agents.

MAX TELGUASO. Thanks so much.

AGENT RIT. Any time, mate.

CHRISTEN. Some magical suits you guys are wearing. You all went up against a powerful adversary. You have my respect for ordinary humans.

AGENT CQUA. It's the healing factor. *Smiling, while hiding that he's completely exhausted and his suit is working overtime to keep him standing.*

AGENT CAJ. *Gazing down at the injured warrior.* Apologies for what happened to your mentor.

NIARA. *Sniffs.* It's fine.

SALLY. Yeah. He hasn't completely faded. His soul is intact.

DONNY. He lost his Damonarian power.

JAYLA. Hold on. I'm sorry. His– what?

PICHUEL. Damonarian's are a race of humans with the power to morph into beasts. This one is a human who gained the ability to transform.

CREBEON. *Growls due to his injures.* I wonder how, though.

NIARA. It was when he was a teenager, traveling to strange worlds in Namorant. He told me he met a weird Quinoragoras scientist that extracted a beast from a deceased warrior and spliced it into his DNA.

AGENT CAJ. Quinoragoras. *He turns to looks at his fellow agent counterparts.* That's a name we heard before.

The warrior starts breathing somewhat normally.

JAYLA. I have to go soon.

AGENT CAJ. We all should. *Sighs.* The battle took a toll on us all.

The Adventure of Heroes gang steps closer to Xanpo, then someone lands twenty feet away, and another appears by a lightning strike.

SHOCKER. *Sparks disappearing from his form as he approaches the agents.* They are all returned to their homes. Not NikoLee, though. He kept whimpering, so I took him to see Valery. I had to wait there. Soon as he fell asleep, I returned him to her house. *He looks around, seeing Agent Z in the arms of Rev and JeiFii.* Will– Will he be all right?

AGENT CAJ. He wore himself out... transforming into that armored form.

ZOEY. It was amazing!

KASE. Yeah! The glowy light show at the end. Boom!!

SABER. Okay, chill, guys. *She wraps her arms around their necks, smiling, and looks at the other boy.* What about you– were you able to beat your other half?

AKIRU. *Staring at the cave's entrance for a while before replying.* Yeah. *He exhales and smiles, looking at everyone he fought with today.* I feel great.

MAX TELGUASO. *Playfully punches Akiru and hugs him.* You better!! Haha.

CHRISTEN. Yeah. *Looking at the two boys with his arms in his pockets.*

AGENT CQUA. All right, all right. Time for me to get going. Later. *He teleports away.*

AGENT CAJ. *He laughs.* Like he said.

All the agents nod their heads at everyone they fought with and teleport away.

JAYLA. *She prepares a transport spell to leave the area.*

FLORAL. Um, Miss Wizard.

JAYLA. *She turns and looks at the girl with vines coming out of her head.* Yeah?

FLORAL. You mind taking the four of us to our homes?

Jayla smiles and prepares to take Floral, Lin, Jaylin, and Kysis far away from this area and safely home. When they disappear, Sally and Niara touch their hands and close their eyes. Together they do the same spell as Jayla. They take Xanpo, Donny, Max, Christen, Akiru, Zoey, Kase, Crebeon, and Pichuel to their mentor's home. From there, the others will be sent to their homes.

Shocker starts running, snaps his fingers, changes into electricity, and zooms away.

Meanwhile, inside the training center at VICE HQ...

Rahz stops an incoming punch from the commander, countering using both fists. As she's blocking, she gazes into his eyes. Her body starts glowing in the same color as his fists.

XAVIER. Very peculiar.

RAHZ. *She lowers her hands, staring at them, confused.* I – I'm not sure how I'm doing it.

XAVIER. You're okay. Concentrate on reducing the energies cycling through you and breathe.

The girl does what he says, and the dark-colored energy disappears.

XAVIER. This reminds me of the boy's first transformation in that desert after the space adventure. You came in contact and were exposed to the armband's radiation, didn't you?

RAHZ. I don't know, sir. Commander Addams or Caj never briefed any of us on that. I felt normal after the fight. I think we all did.

XAVIER. I see. *Exhales.* That comet was a failure, but that transformation was astounding. I need you to get Z to do that thing he did again.

RAHZ. I don't think that I can, sir.

XAVIER. You remember our deal? You best think of a way to make him. I see there's a unique bond between the two of you. I cannot wrap my finger around it just yet.

RAHZ. Sir! I'm loyal to VICE… forever.

XAVIER. Mhm. *He's just staring at her before exiting the room.*

After the doors closed, she turned and started walking to her gym bag.

RAHZ. *She says in a whisper.* I'm starting to think coming here was a mistake.

SEASON 5, EPISODE 32

10:45 A.M.
Aions Hospital
Wednesday, February 21, 2108

Two well-dressed young men walk down the hallway; a young girl recently had her blood drawn and tested. There's an unexplained anomaly in the molecules. After running multiple tests, a doctor couldn't find a match on the unusual sample. A billionaire got the word and had his agency send two of their best to extract this patient.

Meanwhile, Jayla meets with Floral and friends at Drekal Park District. They're inside the rest area.

JAYLA. You guys, be careful.

FLORAL. We'll be in and out before you can blink.

LIN. We better. You know the place, after all.

FLORAL. Thanks for assisting us. *She smiles.*

JAYLA. Remember! Jaylin is Xeiar too. He can tap into a portal's radiation for the ride back home even if he doesn't know how to use spells yet.

The cross-human girl plans to sneak inside VICE HQ to locate an office to acquire information about her father. Jayla proceeds to open a portal, and the three teens walk inside.

Meanwhile, at Centransdale High School...

Zada and Veri are walking down the hallway. Zari passes them both. The boy turns his head in confusion – he thinks he recognizes this girl, but he isn't sure. He turns his head back around and continues walking. Valery turns her head, looking at him.

VALERY. Something wrong?

ZADARION. Umm, not sure. That girl we just passed…

VALERY. What about her?

ZADARION. She's dressing a lot differently than how she usually dresses.

VALERY. Oh! You mean Mhariah?

ZADARION. I think that's her name. I thought it started with a 'Z.' Like, Zhariah?

VALERY. Yeah. That's like her nickname. People don't know her birth name. *She agrees with herself by nodding a few times up and down.* And yeah, I agree with what you said before. She is dressing differently. *She pauses for a few seconds.* She's a loner, just like you! *She smirks at him.*

ZADARION. *He laughs.* Bite me.

VALERY. Haha… All right now. You had better watch your mouth before I seismic punch you!

ZADARION. Seismic – What?!

VALERY. *She is laughing.* It's new. *She winks her left eye.* You might see it veeeery soon!

ZADARION. Uh, yeah. We'll see about that. *He shakes his head while smiling.*

A few seconds later he flicks her right shoulder, and takes off running down the hallway.

VALERY. *She shouts and chases after him.* Oh! You are so dead!! *She screams out.* Get back here, Zada!

VICE HQ...
An unoccupied laboratory...

Floral jumps out of a vent and lands on the clean, tiled floor; she sees Rahz standing by the entrance, staring at her, confused.

FLORAL. Uhh. Hee-hee. Hi, Ra –

RAHZ. *Shakes her head.* Don't involve me. *She rolls her eyes to the ceiling and exits the room.*

FLORAL. *She whispers to the vent above.* Guys, the coast is clear. You can come down now.

Jaylin, Kysis, and Lin jump out of the ceiling vent.

FLORAL. Jay. *She places her right hand on his shoulders for a second.* Don't forget the portal spell.

JAYLIN. Mhm. *He nods.*

FLORAL. There's no time to waste. Let's move.

At an undisclosed location… ShaVenger is resting. He starts thinking about his mother and the moment he became what he is today.

FLASHBACK!
Medayo Drive…
Gyrasion Providence, Illinois…

A younger Joel Rodriguez is walking to the basement at his mother's home. She is currently at work. She called the house two minutes ago, asking her son to deliver a message to her husband.

A few minutes later…

JOEL. *He glances at the half-closed door, smelling foul chemicals.* Yuck! Disgusting!! Blech. *Holds his breath, pinches his nose, and he proceeds to the door and opens it.*

Wayne Adler is working on a science project, standing next to a dual-screen computer and his left a table full of vials all storing different chemicals and lying in the center of the table is a rare artifact – A tattered stone shaped like a dagger.

He is checking pressure levels on his computer using a unique program. The boy walks up to his stepfather.

JOEL. Uh, Mr. Adler?

ADLER. *Doesn't turn his head, continues to keep his focus on his work.* What can I assist you with, Joel?

JOEL. Mom called and said she'd be leaving work late. She wants you to get dinner started.

ADLER. *Sighs.* Okay. Run along now. This isn't a place for children.

JOEL. Pfft. *Turns and walks away. Says in a low tone of voice.* And what about grownups? *Shakes his head twice.* Nasty smellin' chemistry set. *Walks out the door and quietly pulls it shut, catching fresh air into his lungs from the air conditioning system near the stairs.*

The older gentleman notices unusual pressure levels from the vials are starting to react oddly. He picks one up just as it changes colors.

ADLER. Phenomenal. *Eyeing the vial up close.*

The portable chemical alert, placed over the door, goes off. The man gets spooked and drops the vial, spilling the contents everywhere.

The chemicals inside the now broken vial splashed onto the dagger-shaped rock. The rock starts moving, causing the table to vibrate. All the other chemicals burst out of their vials, flying across the room and landing in different spots.

JOEL. *He's peeking his head from the side of a coat rack and some chemicals splash on him.* Yuck! *Quickly cups his mouth, lowering his body behind the only two lab coats.*

The man hadn't heard him. He's too busy trying to clean up his valuable treasure, and the object is constantly vibrating on the table.

He's pushed back a few feet by an invisible shock, and his right forearm is severed from his upper arm by sudden purple electric currents that came out of the dagger-shaped rock. He screams, clutching his arm, trying to stop the blood from gushing out. He reaches for a towel next to the table and wraps his arm in it. He gazed at the rock after he finished wrapping his arm.

The rock illuminates in an array of spectral lights, then it rises off the table and rips apart. It's now in two pieces.

There's a hole in thin air over the table. Darkness spills out of it, and the room goes dark, pitch black. The entire world, as it seemed, went mute.

JOEL. *Opens his eyes, waking up seeing nothing but pitch-black darkness surrounding him. He stands.* Mr. A– *Stutters.* Mr. A– Adler?! *In his mind, he feels himself looking around for a spec of light, but there's only darkness.* M– Mom? *Gulps.* Wh– Where are you? *He's scared.* Mom? *Lower lip trembling with fear.* Mommy!!!!!!!! *Voice trails off in an endless echo.*

The teen is beyond frightened. Where is he? Why can't he see or feel anything past his face? It's like it's just him and nothing else.

JOEL. Mom!!!! *Feeling his body moving from one place to the next and so on, but it's like his feet aren't moving.* Wh– What happened to me? *Sniffs.* I want my m– mommy. *Sobbing, tearing up.* I want to go home. *Sniffs.*

It seems like hours have passed. He's scared. He assumes Adler's experiment wiped out every living thing in the entire world, and he's the last living soul.

How was he the fortunate one to survive? Or – Did he guess wrong?

JOEL. Please. *Sobs.* I want my mom. *Cries.*

The wind sweeps through the black darkness, and he can suddenly feel again; one of his primary senses has returned.

He exhales as light uncloaks the darkness around him and he notices he is still inside the basement turned laboratory by his stepfather.

He's hyperventilating on the floor underneath the coat rack. He's confused and in shock. The heat in the room is unbearable, causing him to sweat.

Adler rushes into the room, carrying a fire extinguisher under his right armpit and holding the long hose connection in his left hand.

He puts out the small fire and notices his stepson is lying in the corner.

The man carefully places the extinguisher on the table and makes his way to him. His lower right arm concealed underneath his torn lab coat.

ADLER. Son! Wake up!!

JOEL. Mr– Adler? *Blinking his eyes repeatedly five-to-six times.*

The boy leans forward, and Adler helps him stand.

JOEL. I– I went to the–

ADLER. Hush. *Whispers into his left ear.* Your mother has arrived. This lab doesn't exist. Remember that.

Joel's mind is empty now. He didn't hear anything but... *"Your mother arrived."*

Scene cuts to black.

Present day. *VICE HQ...*

Floral and her friends enter a living space, and someone is taking a nap on the bed.

DREAM FLASHBACK!

Six-year-old Marie Johansson is on the run from the Xeiar wizard Rodgist. They manage to lose him, and her father bumps into a local drunk man exiting a bar. He's so angry that he was just shoved on the ground. He gets to his feet, pulls out a gun, and orders them to give him their valuables. The father steps in front of his wife and daughter and politely tries to talk some sense to him. The drunken man tries to pistol-whip him, but his wrist is grabbed. The drunk attempts to force his hand out of his grip, and the gun goes off. The bullet strikes the wife in her chest. Her grip loosens around her daughter, and she starts to fall. The man becomes furious and starts fighting the drunk. He's violently beating him. Young Mackle is so scared, seeing her father react in this manner. She runs into the bar and into the bathroom. Rodgist showed up moments later. He murders the drunken man, impaling him with a sharp object made of magical light. Mackle's father looked at his injured wife then glanced at him, clenching his fists. He charged, and the two fought for a while.

3:00 in the morning...

The bartender's closing his shop early. He found the young girl asleep in the restroom after witnessing what might've been a gang-related massacre at the front entrance. He contacted Child Protective Services, and the young girl was placed in the foster care system, located in Los Angeles, California, now Qudruewley Island.

She was there until her eleventh birthday. When she was ten years old, Arnold McManon took an interest in one of her inventions at a charity event. Mackle was helping to create a weapon at a warehouse, amplifying a piece of technology and turn it into the ultimate WMD (Weapon of Mass Destruction).

Scene cuts to black.

The girl wakes up, seeing three figures standing over her.

MACKLE. *Rubbing her eyes, yawning.* Floral. *Lowering her arms and eyes fully open.* It is YOU! Florrie, Oh my God! *She rises out of her bed and into the girl's arms, burying her face in the girl's chest.* I missed you.

FLORAL. *She's smiling, and she pats her back a few times.* I missed you too.

MACKLE. *She releases her grip and backs away, smiling at the other three in the room.* Hi! *Waving at them, then sees a creature.* Who's this?

FLORAL. We don't have much time; this is Lin, Jaylin, and Kysis. We gotta get going.

MACKLE. Is ShaVenger here too?

FLORAL. Stop! We– We're going, Mackle.

The girl is speechless. She doesn't know how to process this information. After a second to process it, she holds one finger in the air.

MACKLE. Hold on. *She runs over to her laptop, sitting on the desk. She's doing something on the computer while talking.* I thought you were killed! Mache and Mulon went searching for you near VeVideer Forest. I heard them talking when they came back. They said you were nowhere to be found.

FLORAL. *She thinks.* Why would Mache search for m— *She shakes her head and speaks to the busy girl.* I would've been if it wasn't for her. *She points at Lin.*

MACKLE. What happened?! Oh, never mind. We'll talk. Aha!! I found it! *She pulls out a thumb drive and closes the laptop.*

FLORAL. Uhh… What's that for?

MACKLE. Did you forget already? Your father's whereabouts, silly!

FLORAL. My father's— *She forgot that quick why she was initially there.*

MACKLE. Heh-heh. Yes! He's not dead. I heard Xavier and Mache talking in the lounge. The day the Informant came to visit, I had a device scan information from his mind.

FLORAL. You're a lifesaver!

MACKLE. I know! *Smiling.*

LIN. Uh, guys. I think we should get going. Like, now.

JAYLIN. *Kneeling over by the door.* I hear walking.

LIN. Yeah. *She looks over to Floral.*

JAYLIN. *He's staring at the door, fists balled up.* We fight.

LIN. No. *She places her right hand on the boy's left shoulder.* Not today, young knight. Floral. We must go, now!

FLORAL. Jaylin!!

JAYLIN. *Nods at her.*

The young wizard concentrates, and he's able to open a portal.

MACKLE. Whoaaa! That's new.

They all enter the portal. They exit at the exact location where Jayla opened a portal for them.

FLORAL. Glad that worked in our favor.

LIN. You're lucky the girl didn't start a fight.

FLORAL. Who– Oh, Rahz! *Giggles.*

MACKLE. I should've told ya'll what happened. She's totally on her own mission right now.

FLORAL. Whatever that means. Anyway, we have what we need to find my father. *She turns to look at the young scientist.* Will you come with us?

MACKLE. Like I have a choice!

The three young vigilantes, along with Mackle, go on their own journey to find Floral's lost father, Matthew Delpro've.

The lower level at VICE HQ...

A vigilante girl is chained up; her body resembles an 'X' on a steel wall. She keeps taking glances at her boots for some reason.

Rahz enters the room and sees a huge, wide television screens everywhere. She turns and sees a circular cryostasis machine. She walks over to it, noticing purple energy coming from her hands the closer she gets to it. She reaches for the machine, and it sparks. The girl jumps back. The glow from her hands disappear.

VALERY. *Sees the girl and shouts.* Hey, you!! Break the chains around my ankles.

RAHZ. What?! You do know—

VALERY. Oh, shut up! *Rolls her eyes.* Just... Do it. *Her restraints are cut, and she starts throwing her legs in the air in front of her. She does these three to four times.* Almost... *She struggles. She starts kicking both of her legs forward, continuing this until her feet make it to her hands that are above her head.* There we go! Gotcha! *She grabs something out of her right boot.*

RAHZ. *She's astounded by this girl's acrobatics.* Wow.

VALERY. *She uncuffs herself and jumps to the floor.* Hiya! *She smiles.* So. Where to next?

RAHZ. I'm going to pretend you didn't know I was here to rescue you. *Shakes her head and turns around. She uses her V-Link to teleport the two of them out of VICE HQ*—This way. Hurry!

A few minutes later...

She strode with every ounce of energy while holding the girl's hand. She's trying to get as far as possible. Just when she breathed in relief, thinking they were free, the metal armored Michel landed in front of them, shaking the ground as he stood strong and invincible with the killer instinct dancing maliciously in his glowing eyes.

The girl glanced at Valery, and both nodded at each other. They ran, closing the distance between them and the enemy, and jumped... landing a whirling double kick at Michel.

Returning to the ground, they secured their positions across each other, at either side of the armored enemy. They had no option but to fight the android; they ran to him with their lifted fists.

Valery swoops down to tackle the android's legs, finishing the distance between them, and Rahz approaches with a straight punch. Michel dodged both attacks and grasped their heads, clapping them together.

He throws Rahz at a far distance as if she were a toy and he was a kid. Sick of it, he held up Valery by the neck, blocking her supply of oxygen, and smacked her in the ribs with his right knee. Her eyes rolled back into her head, and her mouth opened, but no scream escaped.

Rahz sprinted in the direction of her limp partner, screaming curses, and jumped above the enemy, sending a kick right at the nape of his neck. The android was ground-borne in an instant. Its lustrous metallic armor and the force of the girl's kick caused the ground to crack beneath him. Disregarding him for a second or two, she ran up to Valery, whose head was bleeding; she tried not to blur her senses. She breathed in relief.

The fight resumed with continuous attacks and dodges. Valery approached from behind and from the front. One ready to kick him away and the other preparing a punch for his head.

The android rolled away, and Valery did not have enough time to retreat from her attack. Her kick went straight in the small of Rahz's back.

VALERY. S– Sorry!

RAHZ. That's okay. *She endured the strike with a groan and helped Valery to her feet.*

Both faced the enemy with determined faces but a vague idea of how they would finish the fight. Rahz knew she couldn't kill Michel; she didn't want to lose him twice. Destroying the android would trigger the auto elimination of his programming. She somehow had to disentangle the android's link from his mind.

The girl leaped towards the android with Valery behind her. The moment she was about to punch, she slipped– hitting her feet at the android's right leg. Valery, from behind, swooshed to pour strength in her kick and smashed his face. He lost his balance, and a piece of metal from the side of his face broke.

The android started to act bizarrely and was giving off weird mechanical noises. He was struggling to get up. Before he could properly get up, Rahz and Valery instantly leaped at him, punching him in his left side and starting to whack his chest to break the armor and reach the core to disarm.

The android punched Valery and sent her tossing and turning. He grabbed Rahz's hair, swung her, and threw a series of punches at her face. He then picked her up to smash her to the ground, but she fastened herself to his right arm and locked his neck with her legs, and gave a half-inch punch at his head. The metal teenager's staggering but managed to get her off before she could hit him more.

VALERY. I think we won... The wireless module is in its head, through which it's being controlled. If we destroy the nape or head, maybe we can stop it and keep the man alive.

Rahz had figured out the android's weak point. They got some hope to fight it off.

Valery ran in circles around him to distract him and then struck from the front so Rahz could attack its rear. The android mercilessly charged at Valery. She punched him, but he grabbed her hand, twisted it, and crushed it into his palm. She screamed in agony, but he held her mouth. Before he could break her jaw, Rahz crashed herself into him and freed her. Valery's now out of it! She's shrieking, holding her broken hand that's bleeding hastily.

The android seemed to be out of control. He was attacking without considering. Rahz rushed at him. He swung, but she took a step back. She lowers herself and punches under his jaw. He shuddered, but she held it and kicked under his arms. He swung his other arm, but she rolled around him at his back and kicked at his thighs.

The androids' on the ground kneeling, and Rahz runs, steps on his shoulder to jump, and crashes her knees at his nape. He fell. His glowing mechanical eyes turned off, but the light from his chest was lit.

It was just as she had anticipated. The neural link was broken without turning off the machine. Rahz fell; she's exhausted. Every joint in her was hurting, striking steel. She drags herself to Valery, who's semi-conscious, and holds her in her arms.

RAHZ. You good to continue back to your place?

VALERY. Appreciate the concern but–

A familiar face crashes in front of the two girls.

VALERY. Mr. Monaldo?! *She yelled.*

The man is holding onto his head, screaming.

RAHZ. Step back. *She runs forward, jumps, and punches the man across his face.*

VALERY. Are you crazy–

RAHZ. *She stands, backing away from the man while maintaining visual.* Look closely.

An object detaches itself from Ren Monaldo's body and falls to the ground. Before it can take shape, a female land on top of the relic and crushes it under her boots. It raises its head and growls, threatening.

VALERY. This is my fight.

RAHZ. You sure? The gun wound...

VALERY. Healed enough. Hee-hee! Just stand by in case I might need backup. *She takes a few steps closer, pounding her right fist into her other hand.*

The girl stops and looks at her reflection in a store's window then at her Quinoragoras twin. She blinks and wonders if she is hallucinating. She does a double-take to see her evil twin. Orina is walking towards her full of evil purpose. She holds two fists clenched, classic boxer style, and turns to face her Quinoragoras half. The teen sees several objects to use as potential weapons, but they are all too far. She readies herself, adopting a classic defensive pose, fists raised, ready to block.

Orina's now running at her, sharp claws raised. Valery waits for her opponent to meet her. The Quinoragoras twin smashes her right fist towards her human side's face. Valery sidesteps and goes to grab one of her hands. The evil twin moves her body so she is not in the wrong position and simultaneously swipes at Valery's head with her left open palm, karate style. Valery ducks and moves backward, having seen something at the corner of her eye. Orina kicks and punches at her opponent with fantastic skill. Each time Valery steps back until she is close to a wall. Orina attacks again, full of evil purpose. Valery ducks and grabs a nearby trashcan lid, which she throws at her. The dustbin hits her in the stomach, and she staggers back, slightly winded. The girl rushes at the clone, grabbing the dustbin lid from the ground and now using it as a projectile shield which she smashes down on the creature's right shoulder. The clone loses her balance slightly. The girl goes to hit her with the lid again, but the evil clone has now composed herself, and she swerves and ducks while simultaneously punching at the girl's stomach many times.

She is winded but manages to get out of the way just before a strike to her head. The evil twin misses and falls out of reach, smashing her fist into a nearby brick wall and throwing her off balance. The human girl now has the upper hand and kicks her in the back. Orina is even more out of balance and lunges at her human twin wildly with her fists. The girl turns and punches her in the arm and then delivers multiple rabbit punches in the stomach, followed by an uppercut and then a right-handed swing to her jaw, showing her incredible fighting prowess.

Furiously, the clone strikes her with her fist again, but she is so angry that her coordination is gone. Valery kicks her left wrist, and Orina scrambles to get the trash lid from the ground. The girl runs and kicks it out of the way.

The creature turns as she kicks her in the face, but the clone ducked at the last second, putting the girl's stride out of range, and her back is now exposed. The evil twin punches the girl in her back. Valery winces in pain, and she turns just as her evil twin throws a punch to her face. Valery blocks another punch the clone sends, but she stops this and responds by outstretching her hand and sending an open palm fist to her face. Orina sidesteps and grabs the girl's wrist and twists; the human girl is trapped as the clone twists harder. Valery kicks her in the left leg, which sends her balance off, giving Valery enough time to grab the clone's wrist and free herself. All in one move, she punches Orina in the face, sending her back. She hits her again, sending her to the ground. The human teen stands over her and pauses. In this instant, the evil twin sends a kick from the ground up, which sends Valery flying. Orina jumps up and runs after her, grabbing the trashcan lid from the ground and throwing it at her enemy. The object skims through the air, and Valery manages to dodge from its impact just in the nick of time, kicking it aside mid-flight. Furious, Orina runs at her. Valery runs at Orina.

They clash in the center, grabbing each other by the throat. Orina pushes Valery to the ground, choking her. Valery has her hands on her twin's forearms and is struggling for breath. They wrestle around on the ground, their grips tightening, neither gaining the upper hand. Valery digs her nails into the twin's arms. She yells, and with one tremendous effort, she stands up, lifting Orina off the ground with her and slams her against a concrete building's wall with colossal force. Orina does not let go and instead headbutts her. Her twin's grip loosens, and the human can breathe again.

Valery still holds on tight, drags her further down the wall, and then rams her against the window, squeezing tighter. Orina squeezes tighter and screams silently. Valery screams.

At that moment, Jessica lands in front of Rahz. She immediately raises one arm, and white lights shoot out at the two fighting.

Their reflection in the window; their two bodies seem to be joining as one. Valery screams even louder.

Suddenly, she realizes her hands are empty, and Orina has disappeared. She looks at her reflection in the window and see's the last part of the evil twin's image merging with hers.

RAHZ. *In awe.* Uh –

JESSICA. *She smiles as the lights are slowly fading away.* That's the end of her and King Gorvin's reign.

VALERY. *Walking closer to the two girls.* Are you sure – There are lots of relics out there with a part of Gorvin's soul attached to them?

JESSICA. I'm sure. The Guardian said this'll work. One relic analyzed and the rest ... *Pew! She smiles.*

RAHZ. Um, that's all good and all, but – We did just escaped VICE.

JESSICA. I don't know much about them but let me offer you two a ride home.

The girl focuses on her guardian powers, and the three girls disappear from the city just as the white lights clear, leaving the skies normal. The metallic body of Michel vanished along with them.

12:15 P.M.
VLORs HQ

Agents Caj, Z, and Jeifii are in the operations room while the ship's operators are out on a lunch break. They are having a discussion, whether their commanding officer could be a traitor.

AGENT Z. I hear what you're implying, Caj, but Eron was the traitor! He sold Intel to VICE.

AGENT CAJ. All made up. Lies.

AGENT Z. What about when he attacked Rev and me?

AGENT CAJ. Z. You told me about that encounter. In your reports, you both said he didn't physically attack. He was just easily evading all your moves, am I right?

AGENT Z. Yes. But he was spying on us!!

AGENT CAJ. My point exactly. He was playing around like he always does. *He looks at the floor and sighs. He raises his head back up seconds later.* That's his way of making sure you guys were strong enough to be VLORs agents. I think I know my best friend.

AGENT JEIFII. *She blurts out.* What about his memories?! He's not supposed to know about VLORs or VICE anymore. How'd he get those memories back? Last time I checked, VLORs technology isn't hackable.

AGENT Z. *He turns his head to the left side of the room, looks at Jeifii for a second then looks back at Caj.* Yeah!

AGENT JEIFII. That– *He scratches his head and stares at the tiled floor.* I guess you do have a point there.

AGENT Z. If we can't trust a VLORs commanding officer... then who can we trust?!

AGENT JEIFII. You guys! *She can hear footsteps outside of the operations room.*

A few seconds later...

The doors to the operations room open, and the commander walks inside.

He stops walking and stares at the three agents looking at him with blank expressions, each of them secretly trying to find out who they may be working for exactly.

He gets an uneasy feeling. He looks away, clearly trying to ignore whatever they could be doing right now.

CO. ADDAMS. *He sighs.* Is there something either one of you wish to address? *He turns his head, looking at all three of his agents.*

AGENT CAJ. *He says very sternly.* Sir. I've been biding my time – waiting. Now is the time you tell me what exactly happened to Agent Eron.

CO. ADDAMS. *He raises his left eyebrow just a little bit, staring at him questionably with a little smirk on his face.* Okay. *He looks away from him and the other two agents. He looks at the operators' stations.* Explain yourselves.

The three agents are all quiet. They do not answer because, in their minds, they imagine that he is a traitor and what he might do to them if they out him. The three agents stare at one another. Caj raises his head, making eye contact with the commander.

AGENT CAJ. *He takes a few steps forward, facing him.* I asked the operators to go to lunch early. Yes, I did. I know, I know at least one operator must always be on station. *He doesn't say anything for three seconds.* Now answer the question, Commander. *He's standing very close to him now.* What happened to my best friend, Ronald Osaida... or as he was known at VLORs... *He raises his voice.* Agent Eron!!

CO. ADDAMS. *He starts peculiarly looking at the teenager.* Hm.

AGENT CAJ. *He raises his voice even louder. He appears to be upset.* Don't give me no bullshit!!!! *He's quiet for two seconds.* I want the damn truth!!!!

AGENT Z. Caj?

AGENT CAJ. *He doesn't bother looking at Z. He keeps his eyes locked on the commander.*

CO. ADDAMS. *He sighs. He looks away from Caj, looking at the floor while touching his chin.* What did I say the last time you brought this up? *He removes his hand off his chin.*

AGENT CAJ. *He appears to have calmed down a bit.* I must know the truth.

CO. ADDAMS. I told you the whole st – *He's cut off.*

AGENT CAJ. *He raises his voice again.* That's a lie; Eron was faithful to this organization!!!!

The two teen agents stare at each other for a few seconds. They're both surprised and scared at the way Caj is mouthing off to their commanding officer. They turn to look at them again.

CO. ADDAMS. *He's eyeing the angry agent, not showing any kind of emotion.* I think you need some time off to clear your head.

AGENT CAJ. *He activates his V-Link, and his lower arm-blades materialize in the ready position. He points his right pointer finger directly at his commander and starts speaking.* I'll take time off after you tell me the truth about my best friend.

AGENT Z. *He whispers.* Don't do it, Caj.

AGENT CAJ. *He lowers his right arm and starts tightening both of his fists.* Lie to me again.

The VLORs commander is looking at the three agents. In his mind, he concludes that his cover is done. He breathes out, inhales, and exhales slowly once. He raises his head, staring at Caj, Z, and Jeifii through his peripheral vision.

Addams blitzed! The three agents jump and immediately prepare themselves. They missed what just happened because of how fast he moved. He punched Caj in the neck then kicked him, using the steel-toe part of his dress shoe. He pushes Caj in the direction of Jeifii and Z.

The door immediately opens, and the man runs out of the room and down the hall. Z becomes furious. He materializes his blade and goes after him.

AGENT Z. No!!!!!!!!! *He chases after him with his blade in hand.*

AGENT JEIFII. Get back here now!! Z!!!! *She is on one knee trying to help Caj stand.*

AGENT CAJ. *He stands up.* Damn it. *He faces the girl.* Whatever happens... *Stay* in this room! I mean it!!! *He turns his body, facing the door.* I'll get Z before he gets himself killed.

AGENT JEIFII. *Her eyes go wide as she stands up, watching him run out of the room.*

A few minutes later....

Agent Z is starting to catch up to the commanding officer. Addams decides to stop running. He turns around, looking at the approaching agent with a conniving smirk on his face. The boy stops running, standing at least twenty feet away.

The man starts smiling. His arms are at his sides. Z charges forward, but a skinny rope held by Caj immediately pulls him back.

AGENT Z. *He hits the floor, landing on his buttocks right beside the older agent.* Ow. *He lets go of his blade, and it de-materializes, going back into his V-Link.*

AGENT CAJ. *His eyes were on Addams.* I'm sorry about this, buddy. *He quickly swung his right foot, kicking Z in his chest.*

Z's body lifts off the floor a little and hits the wall to his left. He is holding his stomach.

Addams raises both of his eyebrows and starts grinning. He immediately throws up two fingers and waves them at the eldest agent. He lowered them, turned around, and took off running down the hallway. Caj chases after him.

A few minutes later...

The commander had just reached the Geared'NReady transport room when he heard muffled footsteps. He turned around and knew the agent was close to catching up to him. He continues running toward the Emergency Escape Shoot and jumps in headfirst.

He's rocketing down the shoot. Caj makes it into the room, stops running, listens to the Emergency Shoot powering down, heads over to it, and jumps into the same one.

A few seconds later...

They have been transported to the ground below. They are both kneeling on one knee. As the two stand up, neither bother to check their exact coordinates to know where they are located. Caj has materialized his lower arm-blades and has them out before him, ready to defend himself against this traitor.

AGENT CAJ. You'll pay for your actions against a former member of VLORs.

CO. ADDAMS. *He starts laughing in a way he has never shown before. He stops after five seconds.* I'll tell you one thing. *He points his right pointer finger at him.* You will be the one to learn today.

AGENT CAJ. We'll see about that. *He charges forward.*

The man leaps forward and grabs ahold of the teenager's arm-blades. He tightens his grip while staring deep into his eyes with a smirk. He can see the pain in Caj's eyes.

ADDAMS. What's the matter, Cajgie? *He's smiling.* Too much for ya'?

The angry teenager can't seem to break free. He jumps and kicks forward. Addams releases his weapons just in time and backs away from him. The agent fell to the ground but got to his feet quickly.

ADDAMS. Might I suggest you – run. *He's grinning.*

AGENT CAJ. You wish, traitor. *He raises his fists.*

ADDAMS. *He shakes his head, still cracking a smile.* I'm starting to see why VICE calls the VLORs agents so stubborn. Heh.

The man sprints to the agent. He reaches him in no time and jumps high. Caj raises his right arm to block from whatever might be coming his way. Addams swings his leg, kicking Caj in his left shoulder. The force of it was much greater than what he was expecting.

The teenager opened his mouth wide, feeling the pain surging through. He falls to the ground, holding onto his now bruised arm. Addams is standing over him. Caj quickly tries to sweep kick his legs from underneath him, but Addams does a backflip. The second he lands, he kicks the agent in his left oblique. Caj's mouth opens wider. He is feeling the pain internally.

Out of the blue, he heard the cry of the wind when something slashed the air beside his head. The commander used the upper rising block to stop it. It was the agent's leg. After blocking his opponent's sidekick, the commander pushed the agent and threw a front kick. The agent blocked it. The commander threw a front kick again; the agent ducked and threw a punch at the commander's chest with a resounding *Kiai*. The commander coughed, giving the agent enough time to throw a roundhouse kick at the commander's head. The commander was not expecting the agent to be so good. He tasted blood on his lips.

ADDAMS. Enough playing. *He thought.*

He turned around and prepared himself for the showdown. He shouted and threw a back kick, followed by a punch to the chest. The agent coughed hard. He was visibly perplexed. He expected the man to fall after receiving a roundhouse kick. The agent shouted and threw a back kick, then a front kick, followed by another back kick. The commander blocked the first two but took the last one. He did not let the effect of the kick last longer and responded by throwing a punch at the agent's chest, who blocked it. The man threw another punch at the agent's chest, which he took.

The commander took a few steps back, then threw a punch just below the sternum and ended the fight by throwing a kick aimed at the ninja's neck. The ninja agent gasped for the air and fell to the ground. The commander took a sigh of relief, wiping blood off his face.

The man turned around to leave but heard the agent's footsteps behind him. He turned around and noticed the agent with his right arm blade. Blood was dripping down the agent's face.

ADDAMS. So, you will not stop? *He muttered.*

The agent swung his weapon at the man; the commander ducked and punched the agent in the chest. The weapon fell from the agent's hand. The commander picked up the arm blade and swung it with all his capacity once and then again.

Red color spilled across the dirt. A loud shriek echoed as two arms fell with a thud.

CO. ADDAMS. Take that as a warning. You best stay out of my way, or the little ones will pay worse. *He turns around and takes off running.*

Twelve minutes have passed…

Caj's body teleports to VLORs HQ. He appears on a stretcher bearing inside the Infirmary Ward. Z and Jeifii are standing over his body. Z is still hurt when Caj kicked him but understood it was for his safety.

AGENT Z. *He's showing that he's scared, looking at how his mentor is moving around on the stretcher.* Addams did this to him? *He gulps.* What'll he do to us if we fight him?

AGENT JEIFII. *She's afraid, looking at Caj with a worried look on her face.* I don't know. *She's quiet for some time.* We'll have to take him down. *She looks at Z.* All of us… Together… Working as a team! We can't be scared. He was fooling us this entire time. Like – Who is this man?

AGENT CAJ. *Speaks faintly.* You guys…

The two agent teens stare at Caj.

AGENT CAJ. You guys don't go near him! *He starts coughing, and it sounds very, very bad.* Stay aw – *He starts coughing again while holding his sides.*

The VLORs medical service droids emerge from their corners and position themselves around him. The two agents start backing away from the stretcher and make their way to the door.

AGENT JEIFII. What'll we do without a commanding officer?

AGENT Z. No clue. We must tell the others… ASAP!

They exit the Infirmary Ward, turn around, and look one more time. Caj turns his head forcibly, ignoring the medical droids, trying to tell the two agents something important.

AGENT CAJ. *He's breathing at a steady but still not normal pace. W— Worry about that later. Ah!! He was stuck with a huge needle from a machine. He inhales and exhales slowly. You— He immediately passes out thanks to the needle that was injected into his skin.*

The doors to the Infirmary Ward close, and the two agents start walking down the hall.

AGENT Z. *He looks at Jeifii.* We should tell Angela about what just happened.

AGENT JEIFII. *She nods to Z.* Then, we'll call in the others.

The two make their way to the training room.

AGENT Z. What's this?! AH!!! Something's wrong with our V-Links. *He looks up at the girl.*

AGENT JEIFII. Z… *Her body is fading away.*

The boy soon meets the same fate. He's transported out of VLORs and on a corner of a city next to an alley.

Not even giving the boy time to process what happened at VLORs, a new threat appears.

Something shoots out of the sky and lands, materializing right in front of him in the form of … *HIM!* With darker clothing and a slightly darker skin complexion, it raises its head and looks at the sky above.

Agent Z is shocked to see a clone of himself standing before him. Did Curdur get a new change of clothing?

The clone punches him in the face, which stuns him unexpectedly. It sends a kick to his solar plexus, which sends him stumbling backward. Again, he is taken by surprise. Quickly, the clone speeds to his right and grabs him from behind, pulling him by the neck going further into the alley.

Once in the alley, the clone tightens his grip around his neck, choking him in a headlock. Frantically, the agent flips his upper body up and, in the same motion, grabs the clone by its elbows to put him off balance. As he flips back on the ground, he lifts his enemy's elbows over his head. The force sends him flying over the head, and the clone smacks on the ground. He looks unemotional and quickly gets to his feet. He moves to Z with a cold purpose in his eyes.

Agent Z moves to the clone in defense. This time he is ready. The clone glides to him.

The agent sends a punch to its face, but it quickly dodges to the other side. The clone strikes him on the right side of his face; then the left with an open hand technique- his right-hand strikes the other side of his chest and neck. He then closes both fists and sends several power punches to his stomach, all at lightning speed. He switches from his left foot to the right, pulls his arm back so that his elbow is behind his head and level with his shoulder. He summons power. His fist glows with golden fire energy, and he punches Z in the chest, opening his palm only at the last second of impact. The power blast sends him flying back.

The agent teen crashes into a wall. He grunts in pain, stunned, but he's determined to fight on.

He stumbles to the clone and sends several wild punches at him; the clone swiftly dodges to the left and right, evading his fists. He kicks the clone in his lower right leg.

A small effect on the clone who only slightly stumbles. Z kicks him in the other leg, seeing the opportunity to destabilize him and kick him in the stomach.

The clone grabs his leg and changes his footing to be on the opposite side of him. This is all in one move. He lifts his arm in the air making a claw shape with his fingers. He sends his claw hand crashing down on his leg. There's a cracking sound, and he falls to the ground.

The clone sends a kick to his face, and the boy rolls out of the way. It sends another kick to his face, but Z moves in the other direction; the clone grabs him by the ankle and drags him. Desperately, he kicks the clone wildly. The clone stumbles slightly. The boy attempts to stand up.

He barely gets up, but the clone pounces on him, grabs him by the neck, and strangles him. Z grabs the clone by his elbows and shakes him until it lets go.

Agent Z lets go of his elbows, sends a kick to his stomach, and then strikes with an open palm square in his face.

The clone takes one stumble back and looks into his eyes. He changes his stance into a more assertive stance. There is a cold expression in his stare.

The clone sends many punches to his face and body, four to each side of his head with lightning speed, and then the shoulders, chest, each side of his ribs, and finally an open palm to the stomach. This combination is fast that his body is all a blur, and it looks like he has several arms superimposed over each other as he punches faster than the speed of light.

Agent Z stumbles back.

The clone moves to him quickly. He jumps in the air effortlessly, spinning around and sending a power kick to his opponent's face. As his foot connects with his face, fire comes out of his foot. Z's face is blackened immediately, like hot ash coming out of a fire. He is sent flying back by the force of it.

The clone jumps in the air and down in the shape of a star. He sends several sweeping kicks to his lower legs, spinning his body around with incredible skill to repeatedly kick each leg. He drop-kicks his opponent in the left leg and lands on the ground with legs split and arms in the air, making the shape of a starfish.

Agent Z falls to his knees. The clone sends an open palm strike to his lower chin and upwards, which sends his face backward.

He sends several open palm strikes to his neck at incredible speeds. It bends his knees and springs up in the air. As he does this, he spins his body around, pulls his arms to his waist, and elbows behind him, fists clenched. His fists are now balls of fire.

The clone spins in the air and sends a roundhouse kick to Z's face, stunning him more.

The clone sends a barrage of fire punches to the boy's face and body. Five to each side of his head, each one is striking him with force. He sends several punches to the chest and his ribs, then one huge one to the stomach, sending his opponent back a step. He sends a punch to the center of his chest and then raises his fists and crashes down onto his skull with such force that Z falls to his knees. As it lands on the ground, his fists are now aflame with fire.

The clone stares with coldness, spins, pulls his right arm back, and sends one final fireball punch to his opponents' face. Z falls backward and hits the ground with a massive thud, his form changing to his everyday attire.

Just as the clone is about to deliver one final blow, a loud screech sounds off in its body. It screams, grabbing both sides of his head. The clone yells and shoots in the sky, leaving the scene.

Meanwhile…
HiiWell Beach…

Kiyla's staring out into the distance. She's quiet for a few seconds, still unsure about her new ability. She is standing near the water's edge to gain control over her powers.

KIYLA GERALD. *She sighs.* I guess I'm stuck with this – *She pauses for a while and starts looking at her hands as she's able to turn into a liquid state. She sighs again.* Whatever this is– I'm stuck with it. *She stops playing with her water abilities, lowers her arms at her sides, and stares out into the distance again.* Well, the moment of truth… Can I walk on water?

One step at a time, she starts walking on water. She stops walking, takes one huge breath, and takes one step like she's walking up a flight of stairs. She surprised herself.

The girl starts controlling the water, and it looks like she's surfing. She seems comfortable with her new abilities.

KIYLA GERALD. Ah-ha! Yeah! I'm – I'm surfin' without a board!! *She's riding the waves, bending her knees as she's moving gracefully through the waves.* This IS SOOOOO CRAASSSSHHHHHHHH!!

Meanwhile, inside the operations room at VICE HQ...

The VICE Commander's eyes turned a deep shade of red as he stood at the center of the room, staring at every person around him.

XAVIER. I'm disappointed. *He shook his head vigorously as he corrected.* No, disappointed is an understatement. I am furious at you all!

GRAVSIGHT. What happened was...

XAVIER. What, what? You got something to say while I'm speaking? *Staring at him directly.* What happened is that you all messed up royally. That's a simple fact; anything else is a fallacy, one I won't entertain anymore. *He scolded his subordinate.* That was no assigned task, but after Talgitx left, I made it clear... Do NOT let them leave without a direct order from myself. It was simple enough, and yet you all managed to fuck it up... They slipped out of your hands, and those little bastards are scurrying to whatever hellhole they'll find in the ground.

MACHE. We had no idea how they managed to get here. Floral's V-Link had been disabled when she got herself captured by Dunan's soldiers. *He stated, a morose look on his face.*

XAVIER. *He throws his shoulders up.* How the hell would you know when you can't focus on exact things? I didn't task anyone to go out on a suicide mission against that wizard! You all were here besides the two co-commanders I just brought on board. Just how? *He barked and paused for a few seconds. Then, he suddenly pointed at Mache.* You!!! *He exclaimed.*

MACHE. *He was staring at the ground but peeled his eyes away from the concrete and glanced up.* Yes? *He asked in a shaky voice.*

XAVIER. You are one of the most intelligent people in this room, yet that doesn't seem to show very often. The last task I had you handle, you failed. Now, with your comrades, you've failed me again. I should have you punished gravely for this. *He turns to everyone.* All of you!!!

No one dared say a word back as decorum rented the room. After a moment of silence, the commander resumed speaking.

XAVIER. Defending– Protecting should be much easier than attacking. You conserve your energy, sit back, and the only thing that needs to be done is supervision. *He smacked his forehead with his palm in quick successions as he said.* It's why I can't comprehend how a team of powerful individuals wasn't able to secure a few kids. They were captives! Captives!! Until Talgitx made them honorary fields despite his distaste for cross-humans. When I took over, I kept it. *He regained his composure and began to speak in a lower tone.* I can't seem to wrap my head around it. One might even think one of you collaborated with them to provide them an escape. Perhaps that's why ShaVenger is staying under the radar. *His eyes thinned in suspicion, his gaze fixed on the scientists Falakar, Gravsight, Mache, and Mario Vega.*

As they saw him looking at them, they quickly shook their heads to prove their innocence.

XAVIER. *He sighed audibly.* If not collaboration, then it's insubordination. Punishment should be meted out.

DARIUS HELMS. They're sorry, we... are sorry. Jayn and I will take a more serious approach.

JAYN TALGITX. Oh yeahhh. *Cracking his knuckles.* I'm nothing like my father. Heh-heh.

XAVIER. *He clicked his tongue.* What I like to hear. But– No, we're way past 'sorry.' Since you've all failed me, I have no choice but to step in full time.

As he uttered the last word, a dark purple beam began to circle around him. It grew brighter with each second, accentuating his menacing facial features.

VH UNIVERSE
APPENDIX PAGE 1

LOCATIONS, CITIES, TOWNS, AND STATES

Hidendale Springs, Illinois *Thirty minutes north of Dowers City, IL.*

- Hidendale Observatory *Home of an all new exhibit with twenty planets on display.*
- Centransdale High School
    - o *At the corner of Centransdale High School (right end of building)… you can turn left to get to Westick Blvd. There's an alley next to a convenience store.*
    - o *At the same corner of Centransdale High School… you can turn right to get to Venue Ave. If you continue walking straight, you'll reach Cuues Marketplace.*
    - o *At Centransdale High School (in between the left end and right end of the building), if you exit out of the side doors and turn right, you'll be walking away from the school (your back is now facing the school as you're walking away from it). Continue walking away from the school and you're approaching Blake Street. Continue walking straight down this street to NH Pharmacy. Continue walking, you'll pass NH Pharmacy. The next street is Valmar Street (approx. 100 steps). You're walking one hundred more steps to Florestses street. There are many shopping centers in the area.*
- Cenbaile Street *This Street cuts through Tarainound Street. It's near Remeliat Street.*
- Venue Avenue
    - o Cuues Marketplace
- Westick Boulevard
    - o Convenience Store next to an alley
    - o Centransdale High School

- Blake Street
    - o Going towards NH Pharmacy
    - o NH Pharmacy opened in the Fall of 2107.
- Valmar Street
    - o Passing NH Pharmacy
    - o Hidendale Defenders Police Headquarters. *Two floor office space, car storage garage.*
    - o Italia Ricci's Italian Guardalian Restaurant. *Two blocks from Hidendale Defenders HQ.*
- Florestses Street
    - o Many shopping centers in this area.
    - o Ion Foods *Sells nutritional snacks and your regular grocery.*
- Himswelm Street
    - o Going to Narthaniel Park District
    - o Abigail's Home for Youths Foster Care is here
    - o The corner before you reach the foster care is Qwinzale's Convenience Store
- Benjamin Weismans Boulevard *Position yourself at Kiyla Gerald's residence and from there, four blocks north from Jayla's home.*
- Remeliat Street *Intersects with Tarainound Street.*
- Tarainound Street *A main street and a really long one. This street is a one-straight shot to many restaurants, convenience stores, and many cities.*
- Drekal Park District *The closest park to Tarainound Street with many art pieces in the center of the park.*
- Narthaniel Park District *The closest park to Himswelm Street, with one walkway and a children's park.*
- Abigail's Home for Youths Foster Care *Located on Himswelm Street next to Narthaniel Park District.*
- Drenden Mountain *Located behind Hidendale Observatory.*
- Marquee Arcade *Located on Cimdal Avenue, a few blocks away from Tarainound Street. The only arcade in town, filled*

with a wide variety of video games, including virtual games, two-player games, and more

- Teen Realm Media Center 'T-Realm' *A place for teens. It's located a block away from Cimdal Avenue. There's video games, fast food buffet, information counter server, free internet access, virtual televisions to watch all your favorite movies and shows.*
- Maxie's Bar & Grill *Located down the street from arcade.*
- Crumarus Hospital *Located west of Tarainound Street. The hospital is closer to Wayworth Bridge, leading to Ococo Town, Illinois.*
- HiiWell Beach *A wide beach where couples, families, and young adults come to enjoy their free schedules. There's clean waters thanks to Kale County's Newoluir's Lake that lies behind Stratum Oil Industries and MechaWaste in Dowers City, IL. Stratum Oil and MechaWaste helps to purify the water supply. Unfortunately, there's a few problems with the Diamond and Ore Okiewa Chemical factory. Sometimes, there's chemical leaks that are detected in the water's supply. There's a bit of a huge distance between. Once chemicals make contact with the small lake in Dowers City, it travels through the underwater tunnels and eventually make contact with the waters at this beach.*
- Aions Hospital
  - o *This one huge hospital. There are many patient room spaces, several offices for all higher staff member, four recreational rooms for patient recovery, two family waiting room centers filled with many forms of entertainment and prayer pamphlets, and three information centers for the three entrance zones (Zone Alpha, Bravo, and Charlie) to the hospitals. There is no entry past the information centers unless all personnel show a form of identification. They're very strict on this policy.*
  - o Room 2118, Hall E *Mr. Maxill stayed inside this room. Wealthy members stay here.*

Kale County, Illinois *Fifteen minutes south of Hidendale Springs, IL.*

- Kris Helmsdale Recreational hall
- NH Pharmacy *A smaller pharmacy compared to the others.*
- Miss Missy's Daycare *Located on Mitchel Street.*
- Governor Stephan Gunneim's place of birth
- Ion Foods *Sells nutritional snacks and your regular grocery. Ten minutes near Mitchel Street. Located on Rodabagel Avenue.*
- Iron Row Apartment Complex
- SpeedWay Rail Lines *A smaller and miniature sized train station. There's only two train services in and out of this area.*
- Stratum Oil Industries *Third office location.*
- Newoluir's Lake *lies behind Stratum Oil Industries*
- McVanders Crafts N' Supplies, INC. *Abandoned since 2089.*
- Pyro and Dyro's mother's home, Mrs. Amelia Daggerton. *On Rouche Street*
- Derick Jackson's home. *On Nathom Street, down from Iron Row Apartment Complex.*

Dowers City, Illinois *thirty minutes south of Hidendale Springs, IL.*

- VICE Secret Warehouse *This is where unnamed VICE scientists constructed many electronic emitters and the place DiLusion destroyed.*
- MechaWaste *A garbage waste and recycling separating facility.*
- Chainberland's coffeehouse *Located on Quail Street.*
- Kelo Ritz's home and secret lab. *(Local Residence)*
  - o Gravers Street
- Dale's Shopping Center *Located on Quail Street, down from 43rd street, turn left.*
  - o VicLow *A designer shoe store.*
  - o DQ's Deluxe Grocery
  - o Kang's *A fashionable, gothic and emo style clothing store.*

- o Lu's *An expensive female clothing store. Sell dresses and stylish leggings.*
- o Pens-R *A store selling a variety of different kinds of pens.*
- o CinAEma *A two-room theatre. Shows current and old-school movies.*
- o Dac 'O Noodles *A Japanese and Swedish combo restaurant.*
- o Burger Junior *A fast food hangout spot for young adults. Sells Kids Meal's, including a burger, French fries, soda and or milkshakes.*
- o Icy Sam's *A frozen yogurt spot.*
- o R Ams GO *Sells a variety of designer shoes. No dress shoes.*
- o Men's Style-House *A variety of business suits, including dress shoes.*
- o Click-Clack Toys *Sells many different and noisy children's toys.*
- o Ani<>More *A teen chill spot. Has toys, barbies plus action figures, and video games to sell. The public can also view the televisions, displaying commercials of the newest items soon to be on sale at the store.*
- Diamond and Ore Okiewa Chemical Factory *located in the little forest of Dowers City*
  - o There's an unnamed lake right behind this factory. It's small but under the water there's underwater tunnels connecting to Newoluir's Lake in Kale County and HiiWell Beach in Hidendale Springs, IL.
- Q National Bank *Located on 44th & Pulaski Avenue.*
- NH Pharmacy+ *A store and there's a kiosk across from it.*
- Iron Steam Factory *The employees help create reinforced iron steel for building. This is on Quail Street. This building has been repaired in the beginning of the year 2098.*

Flavrare County (Town), Illinois *fifteen minutes north of Valousse City, IL.*

- One of Kelo Ritz's homes and one of his secret laboratories *Located on Gravers Street.*
- Mackie's Donuts Store
- NH Pharmacy *A smaller pharmacy store, compared to the others.*
- Gowdon's Prison *This place houses many inmates for all sorts of crimes.*
- Lexus Street *It's near a wide, open field, just down from Mackie's Donuts Store.*
- Iris's Fashion Jewelry Store
- Ion Foods *Sells nutritional snacks and your regular grocery. 30 minutes away from Gravers Street. Located on Noturor Street.*
- SpeedWay Rail Lines *SpeedWay Rail Train going in and out of the town.*
- Vickie Male's Play Park and Art Street *A children's playground and many pathways where lots of artwork are displayed.*

Valousse City, Illinois *thirty minutes south of Dowers City, IL.*

- Lincoln Oaks Mall *A huge shopping center with great but mostly expensive stores and a very few affordable ones.*
- NH Pharmacy
    o *A larger pharmacy. The largest one compared to the others in nearby cities. There is a plaque on the wall when you walk inside. It is the CEO, Neal Heartman. Mr. Heartman was involved in a tragic accident that cost him his life. This man dedicated his life to discovering a cure for cancer.*
- Anaheim Industries: Applied Sciences Division *Curtis Jemore Anaheim, owner and CEO*

- Lorisdale National Park *This park has trails lined with art sculptures, a center fountain, a children's playground, and a 3D walk-in house*
- Stratum Oil Industries *The Company's second office location.*
- Valora Docks *A docking port for fisherman with two warehouses for housing boats.*
- First National Bank
- InQuiZiehion
  - o *A local newsprint and media organization, also deals with online web content. Stan Bough is the editor-in-chief. This place is a tall building located on the west side of the city, at the corner of Seventh Street and Fifer Lane. The building's most distinguishing and famous feature is the enormous silver scroll sitting at an angle on top of the building.*
- Marwolon *A huge men's and women's department store.*
- Starwoks Coffee House
- Valousse Convention Center
- SpeedWay Rail Stations *SpeedWay Rail Trains going in and out of the city.*
- TechStrumm Industries *At the start of the New Year, a project was pushed forward. A sign is placed in front of the old building in January 2108 reading, "Coming Soon! Vale Corp-Industries"*
- R.Stop Tavern *Nowhere near the city. Three miles going southeast away from the city.*
- Ion Foods *Sells nutritional snacks and your regular grocery. 30 minutes from the Lincoln Oaks Mall. Located on Himole Street.*

Laroouse City, Illinois *An hour and thirty minutes west of Valousse City, IL.*

- Skyyas Airport

- SpeedWay Rail Stations *SpeedWay Rail Trains and GoRail Alpha Line, Bravo Line, and Charlie Line trains come in and out of this city from others faraway cities.*
- Nicolás el alimento *Spanish restaurant with many delicious foods. Located on Dekonkae Avenue.*
- Cromane Street *Walking away from Nicolás el alimento's Spanish restaurant.*
- Anqua Industries *An organization that finds new ways for living a comfortable life. There are many departments.*
  - o *Ewellon Department is the nation's leading competitive energy provider. The Anqua team and Ewellon staff participate in every stage of the energy business, from generation to competitive energy sales to transmission to delivery. Ewellon alone works in finding new ways to distribute electricity to various places, businesses, and residences. The president of this department, Tom Ewelling, is the creator of ELiPiP. A small device (no bigger than your average cell phone). This is a new unlimited power source that many businesses desire to have in their possession. It's clean, renewable energy. This device can receive and generate massive amounts of electricity within the programmed area.*
- Adlum Corporation
  - o *An organization that sponsors high-level corporate level campaigns. They work to support other growing companies, ensuring the best for the buck!*
- Starwoks Coffee House
- DOMs Arcade *This is the place where video game players, from all over the country, come to challenge each other for top prizes!*
- Emptied Meat Factory. *There's nothing here. It's abandoned*

Methphodollous Island *Located somewhere close off the East Coast of the United States*

- Primous Facility *A facility that houses psychotic individuals who have had mental breakdowns, hardened criminals, and the like; there is also talk of the facility being used to hold cross-humans*
- Security Station *VLORs personnel authorizes access to the gates of Primous.*

Naphilia Town, Illinois *Forty minutes east of Hidendale Springs, IL.*

- o A quiet suburbs. There is not much here. This is a just residential neighborhood.
- SpeedWay Rail Lines *SpeedWay Rail Train going in and out of the town.*
- Sysis June Lake *The beach where DiLuAH's ship crashed at night.*
- Clifaran Mountains *Ciemere Peak is the highest point and located on the center mountain.*
- E.X. PLODES Amusement Park *This ginormous theme park is currently being built. Projected time to be completed is sometime in the year 2108.*
- Fall Lake Retirement Home *Senior citizens over the age 70 are welcome.*
- Lake Meadows Apartments *Six floors of 3 bedroom spaces with one bathroom, one kitchen space, and a living area. Garages are in a separate building right next door to the property.*
- Ion Foods *Sells nutritional snacks and your regular grocery.*

Marina Bayou Harbor, Illinois

- o *Head south down Tarainound street. Three hours away from Hidendale Springs, Illinois.*
- Nelskex Park

- Starwoks Coffee House
- Construction Site: 'NEW! Suites Ft. Starwoks Coffee House' *Counchone Street.*
- A shipyard *Filled with tons of small fishing boats.*

Ococo Town, Illinois

o *Drive on Wayworth Bridge to enter this town. The town is west of Tarainound Street, leaving Hidendale Springs, Illinois.*
- VeVideer Forest *A huge forest twenty miles from Hidendale Springs, Illinois.*
- Dokomo Park
- Starwoks Coffee House
- Casavol Beach *These are open waters (ships are free to pass through but not stop unless they're a small boat. The two piers are small. Civilians are welcome to enjoy their free time here with their families and loved ones. There's a few beach-styled restaurants near the waters.*
- Abandoned Warehouse *fifteen minutes away from VeVideer Forest*
- Old Carsodova Mansion. *This home is in pretty good condition. There's vines covering the entire house and stretching through the front yard garden that has grown expeditiously wild in under ten years being unoccupied.*
- Courtyard Gardens. *One Street west from the Carsodova Residence, lies the deceased family's former yard where they hosted many special occasions, including Bar Mitzvah ceremonies.*
- Courtyard Guard House. *Center of the Courtyard Gardens and behind lies old sewer systems leading to Gyrasion Providence, Gradelia City, and stretching farther out to even more exclusive cities and states far away. This was used long ago by founding families, but nowadays there's plants surrounding the area and no one living today knows about it.*

316

Gyrasion Providence, Illinois *Two hours and thirty minutes west of Tarainound Street*

- A seaport allowing U.S. Navy ships to dock because a base is located in the area.
- Medayo Drive *There are ten really huge houses. The wealthy lives here. Five bedrooms, three bathrooms, two kitchens spaces, a living area, and a dining area. There are garages attached to each house.*

Winndow City, Illinois

- o *A small city located right outside of Gyrasion Providence, Illinois. Two hours and forty minutes south of Tarainound Street.*
- Winnix Airlines *A small airport. There are a few airplanes that come to this airport.*
- Kaydale Hospital
- Starwoks Coffee House
- Vonrou Street
  - o Chochi's Convenience Store
    - ▪ Blanche Avenue
  - o Mars Millennium Apartments
- Ion Foods *Sells nutritional snacks and your regular grocery. Located on the worse part of town. On the verge of being shut down due to low numbers.*

Gradelia City, Illinois

- o *This city was built in the year 2019. This city became a major tourist attraction after the year 2030. There are many different restaurants, from every culture in the world.*
- NH Pharmacy

- Balibai Street
    - Sushi Round'Omore
    - Arrow Left → Tavern
    - Ion Foods *Sells nutritional snacks and your regular grocery.*

Melaro Village, Indiana

- Juvenile Detention Center
- Starwoks Coffee House
- NH Pharmacy
- Ion Foods *Sells nutritional snacks and your regular grocery.*

Cauitry Town, Michigan *A very quiet town to live. The crime rate is down to zero percent.*

- Meliftorra Docks
- Crescent Boulevard *There are twenty townhomes, lined on both sides of the street.*
- Velneo Street
- Delrio Matte Grocery
    - *At the end of Crescent Blvd, you'll get to Velneo Street. You'll have to turn left or right because it cuts through.*
- Starwoks Coffee House
- Delmont's Bank

Lamont Town, Michigan *One hour and forty minutes north of Hidendale Springs, IL.*

- Teekee Forest *A huge forest. There is nothing but trees.*
- Starwoks Coffee House
- NH Pharmacy
- Ion Foods *Sells nutritional snacks and your regular grocery.*

Falarbor Bay, Montana *A quiet place to live. There's a lot of boats and many fisherman.*

- Bayside Park *A children's park. Many themed fish slides and swing sets.*

Floraston, Montana *A lovely little town. A very nice place to live.*

- Moravale National Park *There's a tall building in front of it.*

Lake County, Montana *A moderately-sized city. A business area.*

- Lake County
- Polson Airport
- Ion Foods *Sells nutritional snacks and your regular grocery.*

Valey Sray, Colorado

- o *A huge valley of empty unused lands. There are no cattle or animals here. The land is occupied with nothing but palm trees that are spaced twenty feet away from each other. About twenty yards out, there is nothing but grass and the mountains lie past there.*
- Boosechaimou
- MieLiMeiLi Desert *This place resembles a large desert but it's just a huge crater-sized hole in the ground. There is nothing near this place, no stores, etc.*

College Station, Texas *A city in East Central Texas in the heart of the Brazos Valley.*

- SpeedWay Rail Stations *A station where multiple trains leave and enter from different cities and states around the world and*

the station, with tracks, connecting to Melova-Metro Train Station in Melovaton City, South Carolina
- Stratum Oil Industries *Main Office Location*
- Stratum Oil Employees Parking Garage *Outside near Stratum Oil Industry's Main Office Building*
- Starwoks Coffee House
- NH Pharmacy

Port Aransas, Texas *A city in Nueces County, TX*

- Stratum Oil Industries *Fourth built location*
- Stratum Oil Conference Hall *Location across the street from the main office building on Duole Street.*
- Tektons Shipyard
    o Dozens of boats are stored.
- Marc's Warehouse *This place has been deserted for years. This place is undergoing a foreclosure (starting in the year 2042) that has yet to be settled.*

Arnesto Capital, Texas *Island on southern Texas border, points to Baton Rouge, LA*

- NH Pharmacy

Varilin Capitol, New York *A new, small island city sixty minutes from New York City*

- NH Pharmacy
- Tipalerdale Manor
    o *A wealthy mistress lived and owned this home (been in her family for generations) before she died, leaving the house to an Asian immigrant turned successful businessman, in a few short years. The businessman is a Mr. Cinah Nyani Eroiisaki. The man built many*

accessories to the home but there's some additions that are a mystery to the public.

- Starwoks Coffee House
- Jake's Donuts Shop

Chribale Isle *A newly but small, secluded island near Sandulay Island. There's only a forest here.*

- An unnamed and uninhabited forest turned into SciQui's personal prison.

Merritt Island, Florida *Twenty minutes from Vinrail County, FL. via the Merry-Jorry Ferry.*

- NalVa Space Station: Ground Unit
- Mariberea Harbor Ferry Port *Take a ride on the Merry-Jorry Ferry*

Vantlonon City, Florida

- Toxic Waste Dump
- Transportation Express Bus Center
- Starwoks Coffee House
- Ion Foods *Sells nutritional snacks and your regular grocery.*
- Ever Wanderah Flower Fields
  - o *This is the main attraction to the city. A city filled with many different kinds of beautiful and exotic looking flowers.*

Lorelaville, Florida *Forty minutes away from Lake City, Florida*

- NH Pharmacy
- Nieu Springs Central *A middle class neighborhood with many houses and apartments. This place in on Babalou Avenue.*

- Starwoks Coffee House
- Babalou Avenue connects to Calamaz Street.

Vinrail County, Florida *A small railroad town. Few civilians living here.*

- SpeedWay Rail Lines *SpeedWay Rail Train going in and out of the town.*
- NH Pharmacy

Fuuluchi Capitol, South Dakota

- o *An island city similar to New York but much smaller and more suburban. The city is media-based, everyone has some kind of talent... whether musical, art, etc. Everyone who is born and raised here has high hopes to making it big and traveling to Hollywood Vale one day to seek out their dreams. Hollywood Vale is located on Sandulay Island.*
- Melanie's Dance Theatre for Performance Arts
- NH Pharmacy
- Starwoks Coffee House
- Ion Foods *Sells nutritional snacks and your regular grocery.*
- Dwelco's Pharmaceuticals
  - o *The pharmaceutical industry develops, produces, and markets drugs or pharmaceuticals for use as medications. Pharmaceutical companies may deal in generic or brand medications and medical devices. They are subject to a variety of laws and regulations that govern the patenting, testing, safety, efficacy and marketing of drugs.*
- Fuller Street
  - o Saint Frances de Lou Public High School
    - *The school is on Fuller Street, but he has to cross railroad tracks to get to the school. The tracks lead toward a bridge going directly over water to the next town. Rithmul Street is where he actually lives.*

The streets cross each other. Fuller Street is longer. The school is a straight shot from Rhin's house, approximately about twenty minutes away and the tracks is where the separation lie.

- Rithmul Street
    - *A secondary Street Rhin's house lies on besides saying Fuller Street.*
- Nthorow Avenue
    - Leads to Aorthordocee Bridge
        - *Takes you off the island and to the mainland of South Dakota.*
- McGregor's Street
    - *Intersects Fuller Street, leading to the local school, Saint Frances de Lou High School, and the shopping center. Mr. Bhim Phantolok's place of residence is located here.*
- MiiChi's Vir-Cade
    - *A virtual arcade with more virtual reality games, including 3D augmented reality games.*
- RaisDale Plaza
    - RaisDale Cinema
    - Norisa's Hair and Makeup Salon
    - Chuck's Barbershop
    - T&N's Shoe Tailor
    - Starwoks Coffee House
    - VicLow *A designer shoe store.*
    - Chip N' Curry *Japanese cuisine.*
    - New-World Center Stage *Center Plaza, shows off new talents.*
    - Mitch & Mike's Emporium
    - Jack Burgers N' Aimee's Hotdogs
    - J&J Grocery
    - Skate O' Skate Rink Rail *A huge roller skating rink with rails used by extreme daredevils and large ramps for experienced skateboarders and bikers.*

HighTech City, Georgia

- Home to the HTQ Police Force
  - o **HighTech City HQ Police Force** --- lies in the center of HighTech City. The police force have orders, from Captain Sky Duebron, to protect the city and nearby towns. The whole operation is run by the Captain. The people under him are his officers, his operators, his detectives and his Junior Squad Division also referred to as the In-Training Division.
- GeoComm Enterprises *Second Built Location*
- Dutanburg Trail Park
- Techy Mountains
- Downtown Bus and Ship Port Station
- HighTech Central Plaza has a Memorial Fountain and a Statue of the Founder
  - o *The founder, Damone Allikust, is a war hero who gave his life to many Americans. He was a General in the U.S. Army. He moved on to serve as the first Commander at HighTech City's Police Force. He was the one who got a bill passed to start a youth training department, the JSD (Junior Squad Division), in order to train new soldiers and police officers. His focus was to help inner city children gain skills that will help make them excellent leaders. As a young man, he fought in a mystery war against the Jolt'Tweillers and the Shoc'Weillers. The President of the United States, at the time, kept this a secret from the public... that and a VLORICE agent got involved. BORN: October 20th 1987 - DIED: June 6th 2064*
- Information & Travel Building
- Editorial Office is located inside. *This is a small news and media firm. It doesn't do too well now that the Inquiziehion is growing ever so popular around the world.*

- Hii'Est Beach *Beautiful but has a few minor annoyances*
- Hii'Est Beach Café
- Hii-Est Pier *Near Tech-Trail Forest*
- Starwoks Coffee Mini-House
- Ion Foods *Sells nutritional snacks and your regular grocery.*
- Tech-Trail Forest
- HighTech Bridge *connecting to Curross Town*
- Transportation Express Bus Center
- HighTech University

Niechest Town, Georgia *The town is known as a flourishing Garden City. The town's growing every day.*

   o *Border of HighTech City, north of Techy Mountains*
- Madam Urathane Alma's cottage is in Techy Mountain area.
- Neirolo Cavern. *An inter-dimensional gateway to the multi-worlds. This place has Transporter Relics inside the cave, buried under rubble. It wasn't intentional.*
- NH Medical Clinic
- Cheesar Forest with a Melody Lake
- M'Burgers 'n Shakes
- Starwoks Coffee House
- M'Burgers 'n Shakes *Opened March 2107*
- Mec's Family Bar & Tavern
   o *There's a small garden outside.*
- *le Restaurant*
- *le Cafe et tu*

Curross Town, Georgia

   o Border of HighTech City, south of Techy Mountains
- Medical Facility for Psychiatric Help

NieCross City, North Carolina

- NiLum Facility Jail
- NH Pharmacy

Atlanta, Georgia

- Fish Market

Melovaton City, South Carolina.

- o *There are three entrances into this city. When Melova Desert ends, you'll enter the city's southern gate. When heading out of Meadowy Way, you'll be leaving out the northern gate. The last remaining entrance is in front of NickelsFront Mall. This is the east gate. The east gate is between the other two entrances, left side once entering Melovaton City. Melova Square is the center of the city where the flamboyant mayor hosts events in the city. Melova Square is in front of the east gate and behind Melova Square is NickelsFront Mall.*
- Melova Desert *The only way into the city. The South Gate is located here.*
- GeoComm Enterprises *The Main Office. There are only two in the United States.*
- Sysmosis Shopping Center *Groceries, Clothing, Everyday items & more*
- MelFlora's Talent Stage *A small, circle stage in the center of the city. Tourist Attraction.*
- Starwoks Coffee House
- Medical Facility: Psychiatric Help
- Melova-Metro Train Station *Ride anywhere in the United States.*
- Vale Industries-Corp: TRI Communications Department *Two locations in the U.S.*

- Meadowy Way *Way out of the city, located by West gate. Continue walking to Cattesulby Woods.*
- Cattesulby Woods. *Keep walking you get closer to Eximpplest Town, SC.*
- NickelsFront Mall *The East Gate.*
- Melova Square.

Eximpplest Town, South Carolina.

- Catsugue Forest *This forest is connected to Cattesulby Woods.*

Great Similiete, Nevada.

- Fort Oxnile
  o Naval Spec Ops Command Training Facility *Jayn's last duty station.*

In the year 2020, California broke into three new peninsulas, which drifted from California's original position. **Oirailie Island** is a new island that drifted north and is now the Northern California Peninsula. Oirailie Island's eastern beach points toward Washington State. **Sandulay Island** is the second newest island, which drifted west and is far off on its own. **Qudruewley Island** is the third newest island. It drifted southeast. The three new California peninsulas, all large islands, each have a Northern Beach, an Eastern Beach, a Southern Beach, and a Western Beach.

Oirailie Island

- Northern Beach *This beach is unkempt and dirty in the year 2107. It's been this way for a while. A hidden laboratory was discovered, after exploding, in the year 2082.*
- Eastern Beach
- Western Beach

- Southern Beach

Sandulay Island

- o *The city of San Francisco is here with little to no change as in the year 2007.*
- San Drean
  - o NH Pharmacy
  - o Pellious Medical Clinic
  - o Angelica's Rare Finds Shop
  - o Starwoks Coffee House
  - o T&N Convenience Mart
  - o Hollywood Vale *Quite similar to the old and a more evolved Hollywood*
  - o FropYoli Shop *This place is a local ice cream shop.*
- Northern Beach
- Eastern Beach
- Western Beach *This area is nothing but ruins of old destroyed buildings. Due to the destruction of the old Golden Gate Bridge, this island became lost to the California Peninsulas. There may or may not be humans who live here. There's a place where plants and vegetation grows, but this island is mostly uninhabited.*
  - o Cremmosis Street
    - *An abandoned convenience store boarded up with steel plates with metallic bolts.*
    - *Sillieosis Pavilion Park*
  - o Delloris Avenue
  - o Ruins of the old Golden Gate Bridge
- Southern Beach

Qudruewley Island

- o *The two cities, Los Angeles and San Diego, are still very much the same as in the year 2007.*

- Northern Beach
- Eastern Beach
- Western Beach
- Southern Beach

To get to Marina Bayou Harbor, Illinois...

Head south down Tarainound Street... Yeah! That long street. It is exactly three hours away from Hidendale Springs, Illinois. (If you are walking on foot.)

Miryova Price's Residence

She lives with her daughter, Jayla Price. The two live three blocks down the street from Zadarion's home. Miryova rents a space in the apartment building, near a suburban area.

The suburban area is a residential area existing commuting distance to the main street, Tarainound Street.

The building is painted a dark orange color, with white horizontal lines painted on building. The building is much larger than Zadarion's home. His home is a two-story house.

At Miryova's residence, there's an entrance in the front and through the left side of the building (facing from the street). There is one back entrance as well, leading to Miryova's handmade garden. She talked to the landlord about building a garden. Miryova grows distinguished and exotic flowers that are out of this world! They would make you believe you're living in Paris, France and various other locations. There is a minimum number of African Americans living on her block, Cenbaile Street.

New Waii Island is a small island located somewhere in the Atlantic Ocean. At the end of the twenty-first century (2095) an island lifted from under water in the middle of the Atlantic Ocean, right across somewhere near the south part of South America. A few people from all over the world flocked to and inhabited this new island. The island became overpopulated within a few short months. The island is believed to be the lost city of Atlantis that disappeared a long time ago. A few nonbelievers that say this is a fairy tale. The people of the new island are referred to as, Atlantis Dwellers. Within a year, a city was built. Still the only city on the island, it is called **New Waii City**.

Mount Caubvick is a mountain located near Labrador and Quebec. This is in the Selamiut Range of the Torngat Mountains. In 2015, Mount Caubvick was one of the highest points in mainland Canada east of Alberta).

Detroit-Windsor Tunnel was the fourth international border crossing between Michigan and Canada. This was not built as a bridge, but as an underground tunnel. It connects the Interstate of 75 in Detroit with Highway 401 in Windsor, the tunnel opened in 1930. In 2107, no vehicle has permission to cross this old international underwater crossing. The tunnel collapsed in the year 2040, creating a gorge.

Moose Mountain is a peak in the Sawtooth Mountains of northeastern Minnesota in the United States. The elevation dropped few feet (1689 feet (515 meters) in the year 2017 and currently 1574 feet) above sea level. This area is located close to Lake Superior and reaching 1087 feet above its waters.

Quad Cities. Around the compound of cities, at the Iowa-Illinois border, near the Mississippi River, this area includes three main towns... Rocky Pavilion (used to be known as, Rock Island), Central Moline (used to be called, Moline and East Moline but now one), Davenport, and Little Bettendorf, Iowa. These are adjacent communities.

In the year, 2045, Little Bettendorf, and the closer communities, went through many tragic earthquakes occurring in Illinois starting

May 16, 2045. The shock which knocked over many brick-made chimneys at Moline (now Central Moline) was felt over 550,000 square miles and strongly felt in Iowa, Wisconsin, and a little bit in certain parts of Michigan. Buildings swayed in Chicago, but microscopic near this city. There was fear that the walls near the city's dams would collapse, but nothing too tragic happened.

Two months later and a second intensity VII earthquake struck on July 22, 2045, knocking down brick-made chimneys in Davenport, Illinois, and in Central Moline, and Bettendorf, Iowa. Over forty windows were destroyed, bricks loosened, and plaster cracked in the Moline area. It was felt over only 32,425 square miles.

On August 03, 2045, a sharp but local shock occurred at Vicpol, a small and quiet town of about 250 people. The magnitude three shocks broke chimneys, cracked walls, knocked groceries from the shelves, and contaminated the water supply. Thunderous earth noises were heard. It was felt throughout the Quad Cities, and all towns less than ten miles away (these other cities suffered little changes). Six aftershocks were felt. It is thought-provoking to correlate this shock with the May 26, 1909, shock and the 1968 shock (all had maximum intensities of VII, but two had distinctively large feet areas more than 250 times greater than that of the Tamms earthquake).

These earthquakes changed these towns forever. Molina became a barren wasteland.

Fifty years later, the year 2095, a Spanish drug lord, Aleixo Ricardo Adoración, brought tyranny to the area.

Despite it being uninhabited, Adoración, brought all kinds of people to this area. They were underground slaves, so no one knew about them. These people were on LOST & FOUND lists posted in almost every grocery store; a few from the United States and many from Spanish countries.

Sometime after VLORICE split into two separate organizations, the former VLORs commander sent an agent to bring an end to Adoración's reign. After that, the people there were free to live in peace. Many businesses were started, and everyone lived as merchants, selling to make a living with the goods they either found or made by hand. The United States Government wanted to help these people financially, but someone deep in connections with the president and House of Representatives somehow made them forget about the people in Moline. This place, currently, resembles Mexico in the year 2015.

VICE Basement *An unknown room where Scientist Mario Vega does his secret experiments and invents new technology. Mario Vega never sees the light of day.*

VH UNIVERSE
APPENDIX PAGE 2

VLORs & VICE TECHNOLOGY, EQUIPMENT, AND GEAR

The V-Link *(see photo at the end of Book one)* is a high-tech digital watch that combines with the user's central nervous system. It transforms the civilian into his or her agent gear, is used to summon artillery and weapons, can teleport the agent, and is activated by the agent's thoughts and physical movements. Its features include:

- **Headset.** *The V-Link headset is worn on the forehead and used to communicate with people who are also wearing one*
- **V-Cuffs.** *A small, round, slick piece of metal that opens into a spiral and binds around an enemy to immobilize the person.*
- **Invisi-Dome.** *A circular barrier used to cover an area of a city or town, which cannot be seen by normal civilians and also prevents them from seeing what is happening inside the barrier. These keep civilians safe and prevent foes from escaping. Any VLORs member with a V-Link can enter a dome. Once activated, a dome affects all technology in the area, and any normal civilian inside one will have his or her memory of the experience automatically erased. Invisi-Domes also have restoring properties to fix property damage.*
- **Tiny Grenade Pellets.** *Exploding bombs that don't do heavy damage.*
- **Flame Igniter.** *Resembles a pocket lighter, but thin and long. It produces quick flame.*
- **Deflector Shield.** *A near invisible shield. Once activated, it's in the shape of a circle. Able to see through it and nothing can get through.*

- **Gasoline Capsules.** *A capsule that contains gasoline inside it.*
- **Holo-Messages.** *3D telephone calls.*
- **Q3 Explosives.** *Small devices that send sonic screeches to clear away particles such as dirt, small rocks, and the like.*
- **Q6 Explosives.** *Medium-sized devices that sends sonic screeches to clear away heavier material.*
- **Q9 Explosives.** *Small, cubed devices that expand and send sonic screeches that can destroy everything within a one-mile radius.*
- **Scope Lens.** *A tool that gives the agent the ability to see through walls.*
- **Tiny Daggers.** *Tiny swords for throwing at your opponent, used only by Agent Rahz.*
- **Tracker.** *A small disk, about the size of an American dime that, when attached to anything, allows the user to follow an individual.*
- **BIO-Beings.** *A new technology, not revealed until VLORs & VICE VOLUME II, was manufactured using Anaheim's technology. They are digital human bodies made to engage in missions as part of a project that was terminated after Curdur (an evil inside Agent Z) was born.*
- **V-Inducer.** *A small object that, when thrown, closes around an object or a physical being. Once trapped, whatever is inside the V-Inducer is destroyed by a blaze of fire. Nothing can resist the intense flames a V-Inducer can produce.*
- **V-Veil.** *A small, dime-sized coin. Once attached to a person, it turns them invisible. If the person is unconscious, they will remain that way as long as the device is in place.*
- **V-Haler.** *The V-Haler is a protective body suit, equipped to protect agents from terrible flames.*
- **V-Shield.** *An invisible shield that covers an individual, shielding them from bodily harm.*

- **V-Copier**. *This is a built-in function. It can produce multiple copies of anything, tangible or intangible. Although, the copies are like intangible objects.*
- **V-Absorber**. *This is a see-through thin blanket. Once it materializes and a person throws it, the very thin blanket unfolds and surrounds any kind of small particles such as... sleet, hail, sand, dust, etc.*
- **V-Line**. *A very thin and strong rope.*
- **TripCoin**. *Can change its weight.*
- **V-Cushioner**. *A small object, inside of a capsule. Once a person lets go of it, it can increase in weight. This causes it to weigh roughly about five hundred tons. It can later turn into a large seat cushion to soften a fall.*
- **V-PoLi**. *A function in the V-Link. A general purpose lie detector test, enabling VLORs to uncover hidden truths. This function embedded into the V-Link, once attached to a body, can read a person's mind. It uncovers what's fact and / or deceptive.*
- **V-Medical Supply Kit.** *Primary medical equipment used in the field. This kit is connected to VLORs HQ's medical center database. The VLORs medical center has many items.*
- **Silent Dyber.** *A small device capable of blocking out all forms of noises and communication, including speaking and breathing, for miles.*
- **V-MeMinifiers.** *These are small earpiece devices that materialize into an individual's ear to block out annoying noises at high frequencies. These small devices work very well.*

NEW TECHNOLOGY

Creator… Scientist Rayley Nickolson

- **Scanner Satellite.** *A main satellite in outer space. It is cloaked and not easily detected. This is now separate from VICE. VICE is in the works of attaining their own. The V-Link connects to this satellite as well as VLORs's personal satellite that is attached to their base of operations… wherever VLORs HQ is located.*
- **Vactra Boots.** *Footwear with built-in gliding and rocket devices that enables agents to go airborne or to skate two inches off the ground.*
- **Vactra Flight Board.** *A glider that materializes from Z's V-Link and Agent Z's mode of transport.*
- **Vactra Sword.** *Agent Z's first sword. He is still a novice swordsman while using.*
- **Vactra Cutters.** *Lower left and right arm blades that eject from devices on the agent's wrists and Agent Caj's main weapon.*
- **Vactra Daggers.** *Sharp twin blades and Agent Rahz's main weapon.*
- **Vactra Blasters.** *A blaster every agent is equipped with. Emits a laser blast.*
- **Vactra Armor.** *In progress of being perfected. Arm extender with blaster. A metallic band that can expand, making an arm blaster. In the near future will be able to become a suit of armor.*
- **Vactra Bubbles.** *Transparent bubble traps.*
- **Vactra Boppers.** *Boxing gloves that pack a devastating, dynamic punch.*

- **Vactra Cycle**. *Operator Agent Rev. Travels through rough seas.*
- **Taser-Blades.** *These resemble regular Taser's but they're like daggers.*

Weapons Origin from... Unknown and now disbanded clan of Japanese warriors.

- **Shibarion Blade**. *Agent Z's re-designed sword. His main weapon of choice.*
- **Shibarion Blade-Blaster**. *Agent CQua's main weapon. Able to manually change into a blaster or into a blade.*
- **Shibarion Swigger**. *Agent JeiFii's weapon of choice. Able to change into a V-Tracer and a Whip-like lash (think of a lion tamer).*

VH UNIVERSE
APPENDIX PAGE 4

MYSTERIOUS AND
MISCELLANEOUS OBJECTS

- **Repliara Crystatite.** *A rare crystal that copies a person's identity. If the imposter's appearance cracks, white lights expel out of the person who has taken another's appearance, returning that person to his or her normal self. The inventor is a mystery even to this day.*

- **The Flamethrower Unit.** *Built by Curtis Anaheim, The Fire Starter. Slightly resembles a normal MK-47 but it is much larger.*

- **SupeXoil.** *Capsules containing a viscous liquid derived from petroleum that can be used as a fuel or lubricant. The petroleum has been modified with an unknown substance. The scientist who created this technology is a mystery. This special oil was converted from crude oil to diesel fuel and then to an unknown chemical. It is used to power machines and only Stratum Oil Industries has access to it.*

- **SupeXelectric.** Capsules containing an electric substance used to power machines and created by Stratum Oil Industries.

- **Dale's QPad.** *A money transfer device used by Dale Jr. It is just an electronic keypad.*

- **ELiPiP.** *This small device (no bigger than your average cell phone) is a new unlimited power source that many businesses desire to have in their possession. It's clean, renewable energy. This device can receive and generate massive amounts of electricity within the programmed area.*

- **Silencer Stag.** *A thin needle-like twig-shaped object. If makes contact with the skin, one will pass out.*
- **T-04 Zero Memory Gas Spray.** *A spray that will wipe memories.*
- **Vex Armor Emblem.** *An item found by Agent Z and his little band of creature-friends during his time on planet Vexion.*
- **Opla Whistle.** *A normal looking whistle that can emit a silent sound capable of memory erasing.*
- **Paranormal Detection Reader, PDR.** *A device made by Louis Gravnelle. He built this unique device in order to pick up supernatural activity anywhere.*
- **The Cryo-Cap.** *A regular capsule with a coordinate codes panel embedded into the device. This can put a human in cryosleep (a state of suspended animation) and teleports individual to any location typed into its system.*

VH UNIVERSE
APPENDIX PAGE 5

VH UNIVERSE TIMELINE

1999

- Krarnaca crash lands on Earth.

2007

- This year marked the end of the Shoc'Weillers and the Jolt'Tweillers, a race of lightning warriors and a superior form of homosapiens. A secret government assault was ordered by the president of the United States on December 31, 2007. This mysterious race of people had to be extinguished because they were a danger to mankind, according to the United States Military. Guardian Gai was attacked. He was struck by the deadly attack, The Deat'Low. This powerful attack can immobilize a person and it infects them with a horrendous illness. He died on October 1, 2007. Tundarick was also killed that same day, protecting him because it was his main job.

2020

- California broke into three new peninsulas, which drifted from California's original position. The three new California peninsulas all have a Northern Beach, an Eastern Beach, a Southern Beach, and a Western Beach. All three peninsulas are huge and contain many cities.
- **Oirailie Island** is a new island that drifted north and became the Northern California Peninsula. Oirailie Island's eastern beach points toward the state of Washington.

- **Sandulay Island** is a new island that drifted west, and is far off on its own. This is the Western California Peninsula.
- **Qudruewley Island** drifted southeast and became the Southern California Peninsula.
- A new island near the island of Japan was named, **Iitchii Mils** by the Japanese locals in the area. The Supreme Family, Wasaki, lives here and rules the island with their elite troops of ninja assassin warriors. Today, the Leader of the Wasaki family has stopped all actions on creating order in Japan and Korea. He sits and relaxes in his castle. In the future, he will have a few children who will be banished across the globe for their terrible natures. In the future, one of his children, the youngest, will be the only one left at the Wasaki home.

2021

- A younger Asarios (Asari) and a younger Maleena (Malee) were sent to Valdesmon for their crimes, by the Great Wizards of planet Xeiar.

2030

- This year saw a marked rise in unemployment in the United States.
- Dale Falakar Sr. had four Stratum Oil facilities built in various places in the United States.

2068

- Madin Doro Torres was born.
- Richard Maxill was born.

2072

- Cinah was born

2076

– Xavier Marshall was born

2077

– Xanpo was born

2079

– Tundarick was reborn.

2080

– A mysterious sheet of metal crashed on planet Earth.

2082

– Samuel Marshall brought his six year old son Xavier to a secret lab on Northern Beach on Oirailie Island. The secret lab was destroyed.

2085

– DiLuAH's ship recovered from its malfunction in outer space, and his ship crashed on planet Earth near Sysis June Lake in Naphilia Town, Illinois. The ship exploded, and the passenger escaped. Miles away in Hidendale Springs, Illinois, where he had long been buried in a cave deep underneath the city, the cursed knight's tomb cracked open.

2088

– Xavier Marshall returned home with father after a long trip on their overseas adventure. Eleven-year-old, LeiSean Juhnen, appeared in the Namorant Dimension, on planet Vrec.

2089

- Thirteen-year-old, Xavier Marshall, fell in love with beautiful girl. Drey (Sirus Langford) was born. Michel Johnson was born. Cinah left Japan.

2090

- Jack McKoy was born. Ronald Osaida was born. Krarnaca, now known as Doc Krarn, was hired into VICE.
- June of this year, unemployment dropped 10 % in the United States.

2091

- Jodana Uvarla was born.

2092

- Jacque Baller was born. Joel Rodriquez was born. Lin Yiu Gustov was born. Gai Tunh Chi was reborn.

2093

- A war took place in the Namorant Dimension (Damonarian v. Quinoragoras). A few individuals, including Mayana's parents, arrived on Earth.
- Xavier Marshall collapsed and slipped into a coma. Rhin Kashioko was born. Jennifer Wayner was born.

2094

- Ryan (Zada) 'Z' Jones was born. Mhariah (Zari) 'Rahz' Johnson was born. Jayla Price was born. Kiyla Gerald was born. Alecxander 'Shocker' Jackson was born. Morgan Wiles was born.

2095

- A new island floated up somewhere in the Atlantic Ocean and was officially named New Waii Island. Rivi was born and later found on the island by elder Krojo. Valery Maxill was born.

2096

- Eraine 'Floral' Delpro've was born.

2098

- In the Namorant Dimension, the remaining Quinoragoras took refuge on planet Devina. They took over the Devion's home world. A young knight (Jaylin) was born. The mysterious cursed knight crawled out from under Drenden Mountain, located in Hidendale Springs, Illinois. The cursed knight explored this new world.

2100

- Mayana 'Maya' Johnson was born.

2102

- Young Alec was eight years old when he saw his mother's lifeless body dangling from a light pole on Sandulay Island.

2103

- Joel Rodriguez became a cross-human. He started calling himself, ShaVenger.

2105

- Dani discovered information about her uncle, Raymond Dilles, also known as, The Gallant Gamer. During the takeover of the twins' new virtual world, she uncovered the hacker's identity and what he's done in the past. A recent event mentioned why he was imprisoned at NiLum Prison and later released on good behavior in the year 2105.

2106

— Ki'liana (Kiley) Jones was born.

2107

— *Friday, June 9, 2107,* A Centransdale High School graduate, Morales Ewelling, stalks Mr. Anaheim and begs him to hire him.
— *Monday, June 12, 2107,* Donny and Sally knocks over Agent Z in Bayside Park. The park is located in Falarbor Bay, Montana.
— *Monday, June 12, 2107,* a young man, Agent Eron, is in the city of San Drean, located on Sandulay Island. He's enjoying one of his favorite treats inside FropYoli's Ice Cream Shop.
— *Tuesday, June 13, 2107,* Mitch and Rich are sentenced to do six months of community service and will begin their house arrest from June 13th 2107 to March 13th 2108.
— *Tuesday, June 13, 2107,* Unknown drunk driver who killed Brady Forbes and Michel Johnson will serve twelve years at Gowdon's Prison. The penalty is six years, but there were two deaths.
— *Thursday, June 15, 2107,* Mr. Sturgess McMillan committed suicide. He refused to be taken into custody after Agent Caj brought an end to the terrorist organization known as ZEXTERN.
— *Sunday, June 18, 2107,* Mrs. Amelia Daggerton dies in her home on Rouche Street located in Kale County, Illinois.

- *Friday, August 04th, 2107,* A medium-sized odd-shaped stone fell out of a portal after DiLusion and Commander Xavier returned to Earth via the same portal.
- *Wednesday, September 13, 2107,* Agent Z battled a new guy after defeating and destroying a mysterious new robot in Valousse City. During the confrontation, he deduced that Eron was wearing a special suit close to the ones him and Rev wear as VLORs agents. He plans on finding out the identity of this newcomer.
- *Wednesday, September 13, 2107* – Agent Z went to SciQui's personal island home and asked him a series of questions pertaining to the mysterious armband and the Vex Armor Emblem. He seems to be satisfied with SciQui's responses.
- *Tuesday, January 01, 2108* – Reesa McCulkin is hired at the InquiZiehion.

VH UNIVERSE
APPENDIX PAGE 6

THE NAMORANT DIMENSION

There are ten planets, surrounding one lone moon. One planet was moved.

Junio's Moon
- Guardian of Malithia Reign's Here
  - o The center of Namorant and Pluto's *(The moon located in the Isolated Dimension.)* connecting twin.

Sol Moon
- Main Moon in Namorant and it acts like the Sun does in the Isolated Dimension.

Devlerlue Moon
- This moon is closest to planet Devina and only helps it out – providing energy and nutrients to plant life, etc.
- The time on planet Devina is based on the setting of the red and blue internal skies. The colors on this moon shift patterns, letting the Devions know when it's day out or night out. The sky remains dark and never brightens.

Vrec Planet
- Home to the Vrecians
  - o A race of Homo Sapiens that live above the planets core.
- Home to the Damonarians, morphed Homo Sapiens that live on the surface of the planet.

- Crayos Forest is an ancient forest. Inside the forest is a device capable to transport an individual to other worlds. Located on the planet's surface.

Vexion Planet
- Home to many different breeds of creatures
  - *PLACES*
    - Maranious Forest
    - Kilanene Valley
    - Keikien City
      - King Keikaie's Castle
      - Keikien Lands
    - Volsus Caverns
    - Mooinz Valley
    - Kepler Forest
      - Forest of the Fallen
    - Vantronus Valley
    - The Dark Land, formerly an empty field of grass. This area is now corrupted by dark energy. Anything that touches this area is changed forever. There's no telling how they'll be changed… either genetically or mentally.

Coroth Planet
- Home to Homo Sapiens, very similar to Earth humans but their bodies are more sturdier.
    - i.e. Kokashi, Dreyke, DomiNix and Xhirsten's new home
  - *PLACES*
    - Council of Coro
    - Methordarion Temple
    - Rapture Forest

- Coroth Pavilion is the home where everyone lives. The houses are built right beside each other.

Vaoth Planet
- Home to Homo Sapiens with a green-colored skin tone.
  - i.e. Chloe, Prince Warzen
  o *PLACES*
    - King's Temple *(current King is King Diyas Warzen II)*
    - Rullie Lands are three areas of nothing but tall trees. These are homes for creatures living on the planet.
    - Vaoth Pavilion is the home where everyone lives. The houses are built right beside each other.

Naoth Planet *(New Coroth)*
- Homeworld to Homo Sapiens, very similar to Earth humans but their bodies are more sturdier. This planet is new. People living on Coroth founded and inhabited this planet. A female (Nical Winterl) had a few people from planet Coroth transferred to a new inhabitable planet, planet Naoth. She became the Queen. The current queen is her granddaughter. This planet is primarily ruled by females. The males that are born on this planet are sent to planet Coroth. It's like an exchange.
  - i.e. Quarah and new home for Goriah
  o *PLACES*
    - Queen's Palace *(current Queen is Veriala Winterl)*
    - Diesca Palias are two areas of nothing but tall trees. These are homes for creatures living on the planet.

- Naoth Pavilion is the home where everyone lives. The houses are built right beside each other.

Xirxion Planet
– Home to Xirxes Race.
   o This world is a waste land. A laser was fired from an unknown location via space portal and wiped out the entire species. They're all extinct. There is only one Xirxes child that lives.

Quidior Planet
– Home to Quinoragoras Creatures.
   o This world is a now a wasteland. A beginning to a Great Devastating War (Quinoragoras v. Damonarians). An uninhabitable world.

Devina Planet
– Home to the Devions
   o A very peaceful but a small race of creatures. There is a small population of them.
   o *PLACES*
      - Camp Qui (Tecquine Lands)
         • Verrosl Stream is the only place to find water.
         • There are no hills or mountains in this area.
      - Quidior Capitol
         • Built in the middle of both camps in the middle of nowhere. A Quinoragoras tower where the revived King Gorvin spends most of his time.
      - Camp Nor (Deckaquine Lands)
         • There's a small amount of water, inside the only two mountains in this area. This area is a harsh environment. Many

Devions try to avoid coming to this area. If a Devion hangs around here, they're most likely trouble.
- Somewhere deep underground, very close by, lies Dextorey's laboratory.
- Frezarden Top is a tall mountain. It's extremely very cold at the top.

Xeiar Planet
- Home to all-powerful Homo Sapiens
  - o They look like Earth humans but their bodies store endless amounts of magical energy (Xeiar Magic). i.e. Wizards, Witches, and Oracles. There are also many monstrous creatures. A few of them are similar to those from planet Vexion.
  - o This planet is now a great distance away from the other planets. A magical barrier prevents non-magical creatures from entering this world.
  - o *PLACES*
    - Gateway to Valdesmon World lies behind Grand Xesus.
    - Grand Xesus is a meeting place for the Great Xeiar Wizards.
    - Council Pavilax is a stage-like area where the guilty (for any crimes) are brought before the Great Xeiar Wizards. King Makliton granted authority for the three Great Wizards to deal with the wronged.
    - Xeitri Lands are four areas of nothing but tall trees. These trees surround Grand Xesus. There are creatures, living on the planet, who make their home beyond this area. Xeiar wizards live anywhere they like. The majority of them live in-between Xeitri Lands and Grand Xesus.

- Xai Pav is the home where everyone lives. The houses are built right beside each other.
- McKelnor's Cliff
- Valley of Blist
- Los Xeiar is an area where the old kingdom burned down. What remains is nothing but old and torn down castle ruins. This area is a great distance away from Xeitri Lands.
- MaKahMer Volcano is a long way from Xeitri Lands. It's all the way on the other side of the planet. There are trees at the bottom of this volcano.
- Xanpo's Place is a small island near MaKahMer Volcano. It's a safe house. Sally and Donny's residence.

Extiepenia Planet
- Home to homo-sapiens whose powers derive from supernatural and paranormal forces.
  - i.e. Goriah's place of birth
  - They resemble Earth humans but their eyes are monstrous. Their eyes are alien.
  - Deep underground lives powerful ghost creatures, Penialia's. Once awakened from slumber, they seek an Extiepian and makes them their host body. Penialia's are transparent creatures. Their bodies are ghostly.

THE ISOLATED DIMENSION

This dimension is believed to be the center of the universe.

Earth Planet
- Home to Homo Sapiens
  - o i.e. Humans, many different species of animals, and lots of different plant life.

Vegues Planet
  - o 2,000,000,000 Light years away from Earth
- Home to Morphenile Creatures with purple skin
  - o i.e. DiLuAH and CoLesTro

Kao 95th Planet
  - o 2,000,000,000 Light years away from Earth
- Home to Reptilian, many legged creatures
  - o i.e. Doc Krarn

Vartan Planet
  - o 2,000,000,000 Light years away from Earth
- Home to Block, stony mole-like creatures
  - o i.e. the former King Varnican

VALDESMON WORLD

The dark prison world is the ultimate prison used in the Namorant Dimension by the Great Wizards of Xeiar and other powerful entities. There were many creatures (aliens) imprisoned in this dark prison.

DARKEIL DIMENSION

A dark hell. An afterlife where the former living call home.

Everyone living entity from the Namorant Dimension believes Darkeil is an afterlife for all former living entities. The former living spirits have no possibility of a return. There is a slight possibility that a living spirit may still be alive if sent Darkeil by mistake. Everyone from the Isolated Dimension (especially on planet Earth) call this, Hell.

VIRT WORLD

A special digital world created by Dani and Rani Darivele,
using a gaming console from 1991 they found.

LOCATIONS

- Mill's Red Road. A long road (almost like Tarainound Street), connecting to many places. This is the one and only road in this digital world.

VH UNIVERSE
APPENDIX PAGE 7

XEIAR SPELLS

Ventis – *Summons a cloud of paralyzing / sleepiness / poison smoke*

Nieeth – *Summons a see-through shield*

Nieeth-Thro – *Flicks away any attack with the sweep of a hand*

Gorgantro – *Creates stone pillars around a target and traps the person*

Nozespro Cuulazostras – *A wizard's special attack in the form of a BlastBeam*

Nozespro Cuulazostras Zestras – *A BlastBeam with electricity around it*

Blitargo – *If enemy is close, they are immediately pushed away*

Lita – *Illuminates the entire area within a fifty foot radius*

Cofrea Camoses Tarar – *A mixture of colorful lights and a barrage of attacks*

Healoris – *Able to heal a person but not the user*

SwiftRun – *Able to run at incredible speeds*

Deparo – *Able to disappear for seconds. Longer, depending on the user's power*

Cloudoose – *Clouds appear to create cover for escaping*

Scolifix – *A forbidden spell used to absorb an opponent's life force*

Fluse 'sposure – *A light brightens the area and brings an opponent out of hiding*

Wharsh – *A blast of water shoots out of the user's hand*

Vlornoc – *A spell that gives strength to the user*

Fileepio – *A wisp of fire shoots out of the user's hand to burn something*

Con para fornar recta – *Easy levitating spell*

Gorgo – *An easy lifting spell*

Bargo – *Fires a blast at an enemy*

Succuption – *Vine-like ropes close around an enemy*

Metio Verte – *A melting spell*

Con'tride – *Binds the victim in invisible ropes and tightens slowly*

Felieesous – *A levitating spell with a slight boost of power. It can also shoot an energy attack.*

Meschespa Vintigara – *Give life to plants. As an alternative, it's used as an energy blast.*

Vinlux Disparia – *Capable of making everything appear to be normal (someone who wishes to remain hidden).*

Quespri – *A transport spell only used to on planet Vrec and only used on transporter relics.*

Vin Lux Cumei – *Devastating spell that attacks the insides of an individual if used successfully.*

Bargo Excamei – *Utilizing another spell word, this spell can obliterate anything in its way.*

Mumeius Vecento – *Used to levitate user.*

Quipistorah – *A high level wizarding transport spell.*

ZesCuul Prelor – *A higher level blast beam similar but deadlier to Nozespro Cuulazostras.*

Mebictos Tencrias Oarede – *Summoning an inanimate object into a weapon.*

Vuevortis – *Torrent of water crashing. Multiple water strikes.*

Levanor Zhu Restural – *Healing spell.*

Nel Zul – *Works with Levanor Zhu Restural to undo binding spells, unlocks a source power.*

Respleta Espiliost – *A temporary binding spell, may be long term depending on user's power.*

Lutrids Spponallo – *Remedy destructive spells, turning the effects to normal.*

Parulliysis Sustotalus – *Paralyzing.*

Zracnqium – *Summons chains to bind someone.*

Rieeisco Vuesperusio – *Clapping hands together for thunderous ground tremors.*

Ignitiatious – *Lifting boulders from beneath and launching them.*

Xtermieyyo Celessisius – *A wisp of air coming from the sky to form a tornado.*

Depressislestitus – *Destroys and cancels out.*

Vobiiat – *Creating fissures in the ground below.*

Reec Gargantum – *Creating parallel lines of smoke forming by wind to act like blades.*

Levitaite Eniyeeto Tyrani Immedeni – *Powerful Terrakinesis.*

KAKLISTA

Kaklista is the ancient form of magic known to certain wizards, hunters, and huntresses. Kaklista is off-brand magic. A form of Xeiar spells.

Resposha – *A magical beam of light energy.*

Resposheer – *A magical barrier that reflects any physical being.*

Ranchuse – *A spell used to create a secure area, staying hidden. Can use for training purposes.*

Resmend – *A powerful spell used to make anything freeze in time for a few seconds.*

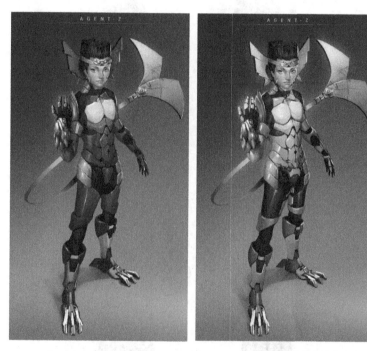

Armored Agent Z   Armored Agent Z Stealth Mode

Primous Facility Guards   CRYSTALIA

Cyphur McDonald and Krojo

Dexter McClain

Dominic Rewels

IL Mayor Stephen
Gunniem

Imposter
Grandpa Jones
Daniel Williams

Jacob Landslot
Normal

Jacob Landslot
SWOOSH

Jacob
Landslot

Jacob Landslot
Future as
Teenager

Kamalei Nakos

Katire Katie Lenore

Kiyla Gerald

Kiyla

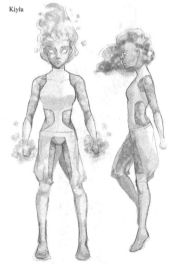

Kiyla Gerald

Kiyla Gerald Aquine Watia

KNIGHTS Gobon
Ground Knight

KNIGHTS Gobon
Ground Knight

KNIGHTS Navas
Water Knight

KNIGHTS Navas
Water Knight

KNIGHTS Mageario   Lilori Daniels
Air Knight

Reporter Riza McNeil

Cinah Nyani Eroiisaki.

NEW SHIBARIAN CLAN
Leader Cinah Nyani Eroiisaki

SHIBARIAN CLAN
Caitlyn Wasaki

SHIBARIAN CLAN
Dexter Ikeda

SHIBARIAN CLAN
Ada Kobayashi

SHIBARIAN CLAN
Njara Ikeda

Shoneil Grailer

Shoneil Grailer
Graizoid

Social Worker
Anbigala Reeds

Wayne Adler

Team KYROSX
Cloudis Monroe

TEAM KYROSX
Domos

Team KYROSX
Ron Battleton

TEAM KYROSX Ray Snake
Gardner Snake Form

TEAM KYROSX
Ray Snake Gardner

VICE ANDROID
Michel Johnson

VICE Commander
Darius Helms

VICE COMMANDER
Jayn Talgitx

VICE Commander
Talgitx - Former

VICE SCIENTIST
Doc Krarn

VICE SCIENTIST Doc Krarn

VICE SCIENTIST
Doc Krarn Servant Krarnaca

VICE SCIENTIST
Mario Vega

VLORs TRAINER
Alexander Torres

VLORs TRAINER
Tim McGraw

VLORs TRAINER
Lisa Miller

Zhariah

Agent Zhariah

Zhariah Rahz Form

Agent Caj

Dexter

⟶ AU of
Dexter
* not creepy-looking
lol *

↑
DARK LORD

⟶ Another AU
version of
Dexter

Dexter McClain Sketches

The Coree - Paisley
Biggleswurthe - AR32
Assault Rifle

The Coree - Adalynn
Weinerman - AR32
Assault Rifle

Thomas Jeffery Addams

Printed in the United States
by Baker & Taylor Publisher Services